I'D PAID THE BROTHERS ONLY FOR THE USE OF THEIR FORGE....

I completed nailing the shoe on the sorrel and put the hammer back in the box of rusting tools I'd taken it from. When I turned around they were all standing there. Floyd was aiming his double-barrel scattergun at me. The girl was next to him, then Bob.

"Sister Earl says you ain't got no sweetheart," Floyd said.

"Sister's right, son. And, I'd appreciate you aim that greener in another direction."

"Sister Earl ain't got no sweetheart neither, except for me and Bob when we take us a notion. Sometimes we're sweethearts with her."

"What's your point, boy?"

"Sister Earl says she wants to marry up with you!"

They were just standing there, at the edge of the shed where the shadows were the deepest. The cold feeling that had started to crawl through my guts turned to a kind of sick stab as I looked down the length of the double-barrels Floyd had pointed at my middle. There are a lot of ways to die in this world and none of them good. But the prospect of taking a belly full of buckshot and being torn in two, was another matter altogether.

"What'll it be, mister?" Floyd asked. I heard him click back the hammers of his shotgun.

I muttered something that sounded like yes.

"At true?" the girl said. She stepped close so she could look in my face to see if I was lying. She was standing between me and Floyd. I had maybe a second to think about it.

I brought my self-cocker up with my right hand at the same time I pulled her down out of the way of my left. Floyd squeezed both triggers of the shotgun as he fell dying, and Bob's scream was cut short as the buckshot struck him in the face and carried him halfway across the shed.

Then there was a long hard silence before the girl began screeching.

WILLIAM W. JOHNSTONE
THE PREACHER SERIES

DUST ON THE WIND

Bill Brooks

Pinnacle Books
Kensington Publishing Corp.

http://www.pinnaclebooks.com

PINNACLE BOOKS are published by

Kensington Publishing Corp.
850 Third Avenue
New York, NY 10022

First Printing: January, 1998
10 9 8 7 6 5 4 3 2 1

Printed in the United States of America

To Paul and Ruth Bailey for letting me sit at their table and other acts of kindness

1

Ben was dead.

It had been a long hard ride from Deadwood. If you've ever taken the trip, you know what I mean. If you haven't, take my word for it; it's a hard ride.

I stepped from the Deadwood to Cheyenne Stagecoach feeling like I had gone twenty rounds with John L. Sullivan—and lost!

I waited for the driver to hand me down my Dunn Brothers saddle and my Creedmore rifle. The possessions of a man like me.

I'd made up my mind that I was going to tell Ben that I was resigning—if that was the right word for it—as an employee of The Beadle Detective Agency, Cheyenne, W.T. I'd only been in the detective business a couple of months, since coming north from Texas. Ben Beadle had been kind enough to offer me a job when I had none; he needed a man, I needed to clear out of Del Rio. We both hoped it would work out. But my last assignment in Deadwood had nearly killed me in more ways than one. And even though I'd been lucky enough to survive and solve the case, I had also broken the trust of my friend and boss.

Ben and I had been friends ever since our misspent youth when we'd both worked for old Jess Chisholm punching cattle, and later driving them north to the railheads in Kansas. It was where Ben and I learned the hind-end of a cow from the front, and how to ride and rope and shoot pistols. And at the end of the cattle drives, we learned how to drink raw whiskey and gamble a bit, and the pleasures of a woman.

Just a pair of fuzz-cheeked boys learning to grow up and become men. That's what old Jess and his cattle operation did for us. In between the first time and the second time we worked for that good man, we fought in the war. Ben got shot three different times and me twice. We both came out of it all right except for the bad dreams.

After the war and our second go-round with punching cattle, Ben and I drifted our separate ways. We both ended up getting married, and we both had sons. And we both saw our wives and sons die long before they should have.

Over the intervening years, Ben and I crossed paths and stayed in touch with one another because good friends weren't something that fell out of the sky every time it rained.

So it was a hard decision for me to return to Cheyenne and tell Ben I was quitting, and the reason why.

On my ride back from Deadwood, I'd had plenty of time to think about everything that had happened to me. For one thing, I'd fallen in love with a woman—the wrong woman. And as much as I tried not to, I was still carrying a small craziness inside of me—like a bullet too close to the heart. But the real problem was, the woman I'd fallen in love with was also the woman Ben had once fallen in love with.

That was the thing that I'd come back to tell Ben and the reason I was going to quit. I felt like I'd broken his trust in me.

There were some other reasons for my decision as well. I didn't care much for getting shot at or threatened or beaten up. All of which happened to me in Deadwood. I was still sore and hurting in places I couldn't speak about in decent company. By the time I'd climbed down off the Concord stage, I felt like I'd been rode hard and put away wet. And when I looked at my reflection in the big plate glass window of the telegraph office, I saw a weary man who needed a shave, a hot bath, and a bottle of good Tennessee whiskey.

That is exactly what I planned to do before I saw Ben, but my plan was about to change in a heartbeat.

The weather was damp and gray, threatening rain, as I started toward Kung Chow's where I had a rented room in the back of the ancient celestial's laundry. I hitched my saddle over my shoulder and carried the heavy Creedmore in my right hand. Seemed old drifters were always carrying their saddles and rifles to one place or another. *Drifting, like the wind.* A good horse and a good home were hard luxuries to come by, and harder still to keep. But I had plans that as soon as I finished settling up with Ben, the first order of business was to purchase a good horse. I was tired of carrying the saddle. Beyond that— well, beyond that I had no plans.

It began to drizzle, a light cold rain pelted the brim of my Stetson; it was just one more inducement to hurry up and find that hot bath and the comfort of some Jack Daniels. I hadn't gone a block when I heard a brass band start to play the first strains of a mournful dirge. Farther up the street, I could see old man Klingbill riding high up top of his new glass-sided hearse that was being pulled by a pair of dappled grays.

Klingbill wore a stovepipe hat and a claw-hammer coat over a boiled shirt. His young Mexican assistant, Jesse, sat next to him looking cold and miserable from the drizzle. A six-piece band trooped along behind the hearse playing the funeral march.

I stopped under the eaves of the White Elephant Saloon and waited and watched as the procession passed. I made a cigarette and smoked it and wondered who the unlucky soul was inside the black crepe-draped coffin. A few of the town's citizens followed along on foot and in buggies behind the band.

The men all wore suit coats, the women black dresses and hats with veils. I watched as they headed up the street, turned the corner at the north end of town, and headed for the city cemetery, what some called boot hill.

A number of people watched the procession from door-ways—mostly saloon doorways—having taken a break from their normal activities. Funerals, fires, shootings and cuttings always drew the curious, and even gamblers and whoremongers would take time out from their activities to witness such events.

I stubbed my cigarette and hefted my saddle once more. Only this time, a familiar voice stopped me.

"Too bad about your friend, McCannon."

I didn't have to turn around to recognize who it was: Dave Beltrain, Cheyenne's chief of police.

"What was that?" I said, turning to face a man I didn't care for.

He looked at me with the flat pushed-in features of a pug fighter, the dull eyes that could read a card or leer at a woman but could not express even the remotest amount of compassion. Dave Beltrain, gambler, pistoleer, mankiller and lawman; just the sort of man a lot of town councils hired as their policeman. The thinking generally went: It took a desperado to tame a desperado.

"I said, it's too bad about Beadle," Beltrain repeated. He wasn't alone, he never was. He had two of his deputies with him; men that were better at getting him a beer or a woman then they were at understanding the law. The one, I recognized as Bill Longly, a Texas gunfighter sometimes called, Long Bill. Longly's reputation included several dubious shootings while serving as a city marshal in places like Big Springs and Tascosa and other one-horse towns trying to rid themselves of the bad element by hiring the same.

The Longlys and the Beltrains usually didn't last long before they were fired. But there was always another town looking for a gun tough to do their dirty work, so such men were never long without jobs—unless someone killed them first. It was apparent, no one had killed Longly yet. Beltrain probably enjoyed the idea of having a man like Longly working for him; like keeping a mean dog around just to see who he'd bite next.

But it wasn't Longly that troubled me, it was what Beltrain had said.

"What about Ben?" I said.

"That's him passed by in that meat wagon," Beltrain said, picking at his back teeth with the nail of his little finger.

"Somebody murdered him, McCannon!"

I dropped the saddle. My self-cocker was in easy reach, resting on my left hip in the cross-draw holster. I was prepared to pull it. More than prepared.

"Who killed him?" I said, feeling the hot anger race through my blood like a prairie fire.

Beltrain, for all his deficiencies as a man, was a stone gunfighter and he knew a man ready to fight him when he saw one. He took an instinctive step backward nearly bumping into Longly.

"Hold the hell on before you pull that piece, McCannon!"

"Tell me who killed Ben?" I repeated.

"Not me, goddamit!"

I kept my eye on all three of them. The third man, whose name I didn't know, was short, squarely built like Beltrain, same black moustaches only not as well trimmed and cared for as Beltrain's. I could tell by the way he shifted his gaze, he wasn't up to a fight unless he was forced into one.

"I'll ask you one more time, Beltrain, then I won't ask again."

"It happened two nights ago. Me and the boys were in the Blue Star when someone ran in and yelled, 'Fire.' We ran outside, saw the blaze. Whoever did it, burned him up in the fire. We found what was left after the ashes cooled. There wasn't much. Old man Klingbill said he'd bury the remains regardless—him and Beadle were friends. That's all I know about it. That's all anyone knows."

"I don't believe you!"

"Hell, go down and look see if his office ain't burnt to the ground. Burned up Etta Landrow's millinery shop next door, too. Town fire department had a hell of a time keeping half the damn town from burning down. Lucky it rained that night or it would have."

Maybe I just didn't want to believe that Ben had been murdered. Maybe I just wanted to take it out on Beltrain because he was the one that told me. Whatever it was, I knew I had to get it under control.

I stood waiting, looking into their faces, challenging them

to make something happen. And when they didn't, I picked up my saddle and walked away.

Kung Chow looked up from his bowl of soup. Some of the soup still clung to his long thin chin whiskers like yellow dew.

"Mistah Quint! You back!"

I dropped the saddle on the floor and laid the Creedmore on the counter without bothering to take them back to my room.

"How about taking care of these for me, Kung?" I asked. "I've got to go see about something."

He looked sad, sad as an old hound.

"I sorry Mistah Quint about what happened to Mistah Ben."

"Me too," I said. Hearing Kung confirm it, made it real for me, Ben's death. It put knots in my guts and something painful pressed against the sides of my temples. I thought I'd left the killing back in Deadwood, but now I was right back in the middle of it again.

Kung stared at me with those sad hound eyes of his; I wondered how much tragedy a man like him had seen in his lifetime to have given him such sad eyes. Probably a lot more than anyone suspected.

"Poor, poor Mistah Ben," Kung muttered, shaking his bony skull.

"I'll be back in a while, Kung."

The two burned-out lots between the other buildings that showed the scorch of the fire along their walls, looked like rotted black gaps between teeth. The charred remains of a few thick timber posts were all that were left. That and the burnt smell.

I headed for the cemetery.

By the time I arrived, the mourners were just leaving, heading back for town. Some raced; it was cause for celebration, a burial was. A reason to get drunk and raise a little hell because you never knew when your time was coming.

Only Claude Klingbill and his Mexican assistant, Jesse, remained behind to fill in the grave.

I asked Klingbill if I might take over the shoveling from him and he allowed me to. His face was sweaty and his hands shook. It took twenty minutes for me and the boy to fill in the grave. It had stopped raining by the time we finished. I made a cigarette and offered the boy one which he gladly took.

"What can you tell me about this?" I asked Klingbill.

He was a tall, cadaverous man with deep-set eyes and a dark beard. He could have passed for the twin brother of our late president, Lincoln.

He was checking the harnesses of his team. His tall stovepipe hat was beaded with raindrops.

"I know as little or as much as anyone," he said. "Our dear friend was . . . obviously murdered, perhaps shot, his office set afire with him still in it. Whoever did it, certainly must have had . . . some deep anger against him. That, or just plain crazy . . ." Klingbill's voice seemed to catch on the rising wind and get carried off.

"That's it, you don't know anything more?"

He shook his head.

"No. Me and Jesse did the best we could considering . . . ah . . . the situation. Ben was my friend, you know. I gave him a good coffin. It's the best I could do."

"I'll be glad to pay the expenses," I offered.

"No. It's not necessary. Do you want a ride back to town?"

I told him no. He was wise and experienced enough to understand a person's need to grieve alone. He and Jesse climbed atop the hearse and he snapped the reins over the haunches of the grays and started back down the hill keeping the hearse's wheels in the same set of muddy tracks they'd cut earlier.

The cemetery was surrounded by a black wrought-iron fence with a gate and a high arch. The gray tombstones were stained dark from the earlier rain. Some were tilted, their epitaphs worn away by time. They were cold reminders of the fragile mortality of good men and bad alike. The strong and the weak.

It seemed odd to me that it was the one way I'd never thought about Ben: In death. He'd always been such a solid, enduring man. A man who'd outlived his wife and child and many of his friends as well as enemies. He wasn't the sort of man you would attach the fragility of dying to. We weren't that much different in age, yet somehow, Ben had seemed much older and wiser.

He had been there for me when Mary Lee and my infant son, Samuel had died. He had gotten drunk with me and let me raise hell and cry about it and feel sad because of it. And when he said he understood, I knew he meant it, because he'd lost a wife and a son, too. And after I'd shot the Mexican bandit, Pancho Vega, and had to leave Texas, it had been Ben who offered me a job. I felt like I owed him a lot, and now I wasn't going to have the chance to pay him what I owed him.

Unless I could find the man that killed him.

2

I didn't know where to begin to find Ben's killer. By the time I walked back from the cemetery, afternoon had turned to evening under the sunless sky and the on and off rain, which only added to my bad mood.

I needed that bottle of mash whiskey and the bath now, to try and sweat out some of the anger I was feeling and set my thinking straight again. I went back to Kung's; the old man had left a lantern lit for me, and the door unlocked; he was no where around.

I pulled the only clean shirt I had from my saddlebags and headed to Chester Stutt's bathhouse. Persimmon Bill Edwards, Chester's assistant, if you could call him that, was curled up on the floor asleep with his hands between his knees.

The old man claimed to have been a fur trapper and Indian fighter in his youth; he didn't look like much of either lying there on the floor with his hands between his knees. He simply looked old and broken down, a man waiting for the last beaver hunt.

I looked around for Chester, didn't see him, so I rang the bell on the counter. In a few seconds, he appeared from behind a curtain, a napkin stuck down the front of his shirt, a piece of fried chicken in his right hand.

"McCannon!" he said, his voice full of surprise. "You back from Deadwood?"

"What's it look like, Chester?"

He grinned, showing some of his missing teeth. Then he saw Persimmon Bill curled up on the floor asleep and the grin fell off his face.

"Hey there you old alky!" Chester shouted. But Bill didn't so much as wiggle a toe.

"Lord! I'm going to fire that old fool someday," Chester declared, coming from behind the counter and kicking Bill on the soles of his boots until the old man started and sat up.

"I'm docking you fifteen cents for sleeping on the job!"

"I wasn't sleepin'," Bill argued. "I was just contemplatin' what work I was goin' to do next."

"Where I come from they call laying down with your eyes closed, sleeping, you crazy old coot!"

"Well you must come from the moon then—"

"I came to get a bath and a bottle," I interrupted. I wasn't in a mood to listen to the two of them bicker back and forth like washerwomen.

Bill said, "I'll get ya a bottle," as he worked his way off the floor. He rubbed his eyes and licked his sunk-in lips that no longer had any teeth behind them for support.

I gave him a dollar for the bottle and fifty cents extra for his trouble; he looked like he might weep at the blessing.

Chester finished his piece of chicken as he poured into the zinc tub several buckets of hot water he maintained on a big iron stove.

"I suppose you done heard what happened to Ben?" Chester said around a mouthful of the chicken.

"I came here for a bath and a little peace," I said.

"It's a bad thing," Chester continued. "Ben shouldn't have had to die like that."

"Nobody should," I said, taking off my clothes. Some of the wounds and bruises I'd received in Deadwood were beginning to heal.

Chester looked at me and said, "Looks like you took a beating and then some."

"You have a bar of soap I could use to scrub with?" I said, choosing to ignore Chester's curiosity.

Chester said: "What's this world coming to, that somebody would burn up a man like Ben Beadle right in his own office?"

I didn't know.

When Chester finished fixing the bath, I climbed in. It had the shock of a thousand needles piercing my flesh.

"You want to go check on that old Indian fighter?" I asked. "I could sure use that bottle." Chester didn't look any too happy about leaving the comfort of his living quarters to go out into a cold damp night, but business was business, so he agreed to do it.

"He's probably drank up that fifty cents you gave him and is working on your dollar," Chester grumbled as he pulled on his coat. "Didn't I tell you once before not to give that old man money before he finishes the job? Hell, he's liable to have run off to Nebraska with some whore now that he's got a little money."

"I don't think a man could get all the way to Nebraska on just a dollar and fifty cents," I said.

"You don't know Bill, then," Chester muttered as he went out the door.

The silence of being alone in the room was welcome. The bath water was plenty hot and I closed my eyes and welcomed its relief to my bruised and battered body.

Somehow, even knowing what I knew, Ben's death still didn't seem real to me. It was like he would come through the door any minute and ask me how I'd made out up in Deadwood and how was Alexandra Dupage, the woman we'd both fallen in love with. The woman I'd broken our trust over. But the door didn't open and Ben didn't walk through it. And, I knew he never would.

I'd lost my wife and son to the milk sickness several years previous. And along the way, I'd lost more than one or two friends to drownings and knives and gunshots. And now I'd lost another friend. The plain truth is, you never get used to losing people you love, and you never get over it. And of all the faces that flooded my memory just then, not a one deserved the fate they were given.

Persimmon Bill's grand and sudden entrance, broke the spell that had set me to visiting the ghosts. I knew an octoroon woman in New Orleans who called them *haints*.

"Sweet Jesus!" Bill announced charging into the room, slamming the door shut behind him. "Gettin' cold as well-digger's nuts outside!"

"Did you bring that bottle of Jack Daniels I sent you for?"

He grinned. It was like looking into a wound, the mouth without any teeth.

"Gotter right hear!" He pulled the bottle from his coat pocket and handed it to me, then stood there staring like a dog watching its master eat a ham.

I pulled the cork and took a long tug.

"Chester thought maybe you'd met some whore and run off to Nebraska with her," I said.

Bill clucked his tongue.

"Chester's imagination is the only thing that could run off to Nebraska on a night cold like this," Bill said, smacking his lips. It was a strange, debilitating sound.

"Grab a glass and I'll give you a taste," I said. "Then, I want my privacy."

He was gone and back before I could finish a second pull on the bottle.

I filled his glass. His eyes grew moist.

"You understand, don't you?" he said.

"Understand what?"

"About how it is for men like you and me."

"Tell me," I said.

He held the glass inches from his mouth, his eyes fixed on it like cat watching a mouse that it was getting ready to pounce on.

"Me and you," Bill said, peering over the glass. "You understand about the Big Lonely?"

I didn't say anything.

"Chester, he don't understand. Citified. Never been no

where, never done nothin'. Most men is like Chester," Bill said, bringing the glass an inch closer to his mouth.

"They got their warm beds and fat wives to rut around with. They got their workadaddy jobs and their Sunday suit clothes. They got their mean little bastard kids who run around screamin' and hollerin' if they don't get their way. They got everthin' but they don't got what me and you has got, do they, Mac?"

"What have we got, Bill?" I asked.

"We got ourselves, boy! We got our *damn* freedom. We been places, seen things, done things them talleywackers could only dream about. We knowed women of the wildest variety, and set down to poker games with some of the meanest most notorious bandits in the West. We've crossed wild rivers and seen the ocean! We drank likker outta a whore's slipper and been rich and been busted! Hell, they ain't none of them ever done some a the things we done!"

"It's not all been good times, Bill. Lest you forget."

He looked at me then, his eyes narrowing to the seriousness of a man who was near to seeing his last season.

"No, it sure by God ain't! That's the part I'm talkin' about, you an me bein' the same—we both knowed the Big Lonely, all that space in between the good times, dint we?"

"Yeah, maybe so," I said, not wanting to admit that Persimmon Bill knew a lot more about the true nature of my soul than I was comfortable with.

"Goddamn right!" he declared and tossed the glass of whiskey down his gullet in one great gulp.

"See," he said, wiping his soft, caved-in lips with the back of his hand. "Men like me an' you an'—God rest his soul— Ben, we done what we done 'cause there wasn't any other way for us *to* live! Men like us is just like a bunch of wild horses that goes where they want, does what they want!"

He held out his glass again. I pointed to my pants that were lying across the chair. "Take a dollar and buy your own bottle, Bill. I'll need the rest of this." He winked, slapped his leg, retrieved a dollar from my pants and headed for the door.

Pausing, he turned, his eyes red and rheumy, struggling to hold the light of old fires now burning out in his soul. "Thing is, Mac, a man does all that livin', what's he end up with? Can't ever get it back, can't ever find it again. Nothin' left but the Big Lonely. Sometimes it feels like its goin' to swallow me whole . . .'' Then he closed the door behind him and the room was quiet again.

Chester, and some of the other men who knew Persimmon Bill, claimed he was a fraud, that he never did hunt beaver up in the stony mountains, or that he never fought Indians, or done any of the things he claimed to have done. I thought maybe they were wrong about Bill. And, I think Bill knew more about the human condition than a roomful of physicians. I hoisted my glass in the old man's honor, then drank the rest of the whiskey just to numb my senses.

By the time I'd finished the bottle and the bath water had grown tepid, I was ready for a warm bed and a long night's sleep. Anything to keep me from thinking about what Bill had called the Big Lonely. Sleep tonight, I told myself through the heavy haze in my brain, and tomorrow will take care of itself.

I climbed out of the tub on unsteady legs and dried myself with a rough towel then dressed. I laid a dollar on the counter for the bath, tugged my Stetson down on my head and headed for my room at Kung's.

As I sprawled across the small bed in the back room of the laundry and listened to rain peck at the window, I thought of how life has a way of changing our plans without our willing it. How it sometimes takes us where we really don't want to go, but to a place where we need to go in order to find ourselves.

I closed my eyes, listening to the rain dancing against the glass and wondered what fates were at work that would bring me back from killing of innocent women in Deadwood, to the murder of my friend.

And would those same fates lead me to Ben's killer, or perhaps to my own death?

3

I got lucky. That night I didn't dream, I wasn't visited by the haunting images that are usually awaiting me: the faces of the dead, the clatter of musketry in some wilderness with men dressed in blue and gray mingled together on the ground, their wounds spilling out their life's blood, the crying sounds of my son, Samuel.

Someone was calling my name from out of the distance. I opened my eyes to the glare of sunlight coming through a sooty window opposite my bed. Kung was standing in the doorway calling my name.

"Mistah Quint, Mistah Quint. You wake?"

I rolled over, sat up, took a deep breath and let it out. The realization that I'd made it through a night without dreaming was like a small gift. Then I remembered about Ben, and the good feeling went away.

"You want some tea, Mistah Quint?" Kung asked. He was wearing a red silk jacket and red silk pants and black slippers. He stood barely five feet tall and weighed maybe ninety pounds wet. And when he moved, the silk of his clothes whispered.

"I appreciate the offer, Kung, but tea won't get the job done this morning."

I don't know if he understood my need for bone-jarring thick black coffee so bitter and vile it either wakes you up or kills you; but that is what I needed to get all my vital parts working again. I doubted Kung had ever spent time on a cow outfit; if he had, he would know that old drovers don't drink tea first thing in the morning, if they drink it at all. Maybe tea and whiskey mixed together, but never just tea by itself.

"What you do now, Mistah Quint?" Kung asked as I slowly got dressed; the hot bath and whiskey the night before had done wonders, but they hadn't cured everything; I was still a lot stiff and sore.

"You mean about Ben?" I asked.

He nodded. When I looked in Kung's aged face, I saw mysteries that would never be solved.

"I don't know exactly, Kung. I'll ask around. Somebody had to have seen something. Someone didn't just walk into Ben's office, kill him, then set fire to the place and walk away again without anybody seeing anything."

"T'rrible thing," Kung muttered. "Very t'rrible thing."

Yeah. I'd seen men killed in lots of ways in my time, but it took someone special to kill a man the way Ben had been killed.

I walked over to Little Dick's Diner and took a seat near the window. Then I remembered the last time I tried to eat breakfast sitting in front of a window: King Fisher had tried to shoot me through the glass and nearly succeeded. It'd been just one more reason why I had been glad to leave Deadwood.

Little Dick saw me, came around from behind the counter, limping from an old busted leg and hip he got when a horse fell on him. The bones never healed right, and that was his last time on a trail drive.

He brought a pot of coffee and two tin cups and sat down across from me. Smoke from a cigarette dangling from his lips curled up into his craggy face and caused his right eye to squint.

"You heard about Ben?" he asked.

"Yes."

Little Dick had one of those old cowhand faces that if you looked into it long enough, you could see deserts, the great plains, the Llano Estacado, and a thousand head of cattle being driven up by a dozen dusty riders all rolled into one. He had watery blue eyes that were permanently squinted from too much sun and wind and tobacco smoke. And when he poured the coffee, you couldn't help but notice how his hands were scarred and rough with large knuckles and crooked fingers.

When I said that I'd heard what happened to Ben, Little Dick just looked at me for a long time without saying anything.

"He was my friend," Dick finally said.

"He was my friend too."

"It ain't how a man like him should end up," Dick said, stubbing out the cigarette he was smoking, then rolling another shuck and lighting it.

"No, it's not," I said, tasting the coffee, spooning in an extra load of sugar.

"You know what's worse than anything?" Dick said.

"What?"

"Nobody even knows who done it!" He shook his head, looked through the window at nothing in particular. Just looked.

"Somebody knows," I said.

He turned his head, looked at me like I was a wide river he was going to have to cross with a herd of Mexican cattle and a crew of greenhorns.

"Who'd know that?" he asked.

"The man who killed him," I said.

"Shit! I'll bet he ain't talking!"

"He will when I find him."

Dick squinted through the blue haze of his cigarette.

"Let me go with you."

"I know you want to," I said. "But maybe it's better you stick around here and keep your ears and eyes open. Just in case whoever did it is still hanging around."

"What about you?" he asked.

"I'll go where the trail leads me."

He looked out the window again.

"Ben was in eating breakfast the day he was killed," he muttered. "He always like the same thing: burnt bacon, eggs, grits with lots of lick poured over 'em.'' Little Dick was staring through the blue smoke.

"I just couldn't bring myself to go up the hill and see him put in the ground. Seen too many of my boys put in the ground. Couldn't stand the thought of seein' another one. Not Ben, anyway.''

"Ben would have understood," I said.

"Sure. He'd a known."

I drank some more of the coffee.

"Goddamn cattle!'' Dick cursed, as though he was back there on one of those drives instead of looking out the window at nothing at all.

"We drove a lot of them north,'' I said.

He turned to look at me again.

"Yeah, we sure as hell did, didn't we?'' He had a smile that lifted the corner of his mouth where the cigarette was dangling.

The door opened and a woman with honey-colored hair came in and took a seat at one of the tables.

I watched as she removed her gray gloves and put them in the reticule she carried. She was a good-looking woman with fair skin. Tall, by most standards, with light gray eyes. She wore a tie-back dress and a wool capote. Her hair was pinned with combs. Her hair looked like it would fall to her waist if she unpinned it.

Dick hadn't seemed to notice her; his mind was still somewhere else, in a place that was no more. Then he mashed out his cigarette, stood, and said, "I hope you find him, Mac. Find him and kill him and be done with it. That's all I hope. No trial, no anything. Just like he done Ben. At's the way it ought to be.''

"Who's that woman?'' I asked.

He looked around, said, "Oh, that's Etta Landrow. It was her shop that got burned down in the fire. Sweet disposition.''

Then he looked at me with a knowing look and added, "Single, too.''

I watched as he limped back to the kitchen; an old busted cowboy the good earth was waiting to reclaim. Just like the rest of us.

I went over to Etta Landrow's table. She looked up.

"We haven't met," I said.

"No," she said.

"My name's, McCannon," I said. "Quint McCannon. I was a friend of Ben Beadle."

"Oh. Ben. Poor dear man, how awful."

"Do you mind if I ask you a few questions about the night of the fire?"

She had the rarest gray of eyes of any woman I'd ever met. Gray, but clear as glass.

"No. Please, sit down, Mr. McCannon."

I took a chair opposite her. She introduced herself. I told her I already knew who she was. She seemed surprised. Then I told her how I knew.

"I guess in a small town like Cheyenne," she said, "no one is a stranger."

"I've seen you before. Once or twice on the sidewalks."

"Funny I didn't notice you," she said, the gray eyes taking stock of me. "I would think I would have noticed you, Mr. McCannon."

"Well, I'm usually dusty and hollow-eyed," I said. "I had the good fortune to have a bath and a shave last evening."

She tilted her head slightly.

"What is it you wanted to ask me?"

"Did you notice anything unusual that day of the fire, any strangers hanging around?"

She spent a minute thinking about it. It gave me time to notice that she was even more attractive close up.

"No," she said. "I didn't see anyone around that day that I didn't know."

"I'm told the fire started sometime in the evening. How late were you in your shop?"

Again, she thought about it, then shifted her gaze back to me.

"I usually leave around five-thirty," she said. "But I had to stay over that afternoon. I was trying to get a special order ready for Mrs. Tanner. She needed it the next day. So, I'd say

I left around closer to seven." She gave a slight shrug of her shoulders. "Does that help you in any way?"

"But it would have been dark by then," I said. "Maybe not long before the fire was started."

"Yes, I suppose so," she said. "As a matter of fact, I remember hearing the fire brigade shortly after I got home. The men were running around, shouting. Then I saw the flames." The sadness showed on her face. Her lips trembled slightly.

"I'm sorry for your loss," I said.

"It was everything I owned, Mr. McCannon. I am forced to leave Cheyenne now. That's the worst of it."

"You've given up on starting over again?"

She shook her head.

"I've no money to start again."

She hadn't been the first woman I'd met lately who'd had to start over. I felt sorry for her, only this time I was in no position to help.

"Well, I won't trouble you further. Enjoy your breakfast, Miss Landrow. And I wish you well."

I started to rise from the table. Her eyes followed me as I did.

"I'm very sorry for you," she said. "It was a terrible tragedy. I wish I could have been more helpful . . ."

The gray eyes searched mine. I thought I saw something in them that went beyond sympathy, but it wasn't the time or the place to explore what might be behind that look.

I stepped outside. The sun was glancing off the tin roofs of the buildings, but the air was noticeable in its chill. Winter would arrive soon. Winter up in the high country was something you could feel coming just by taking a deep breath. I leaned against a post and made myself a shuck.

No one had seen anything.

I struck a match and touched it to the end of the cigarette. It seemed damn curious to me that a cautious man like Ben could be murdered and there were no witnesses to anything. I wasn't buying it.

I saw Bill Longly step out onto the balcony of the Blue Star Saloon. He yawned and stretched his arms. He was wearing just his drawers, his galluses undone, his hair tousled. Then I saw one of the Blue Star's employees, a working girl who went by the name of Shady Sue, join Long Bill on the balcony. She tried to wrap her arms around his neck. He said something, then pushed her away, and when she tried wrapping her arms around his neck again, he slapped her. Then a few seconds later, they both went back inside the room they'd come from.

Bill was rough trade; I felt sorry for the woman. Hell, I felt sorry for all the women who had to earn their living like Shady Sue. Then I heard laughter drifting down from an open window of the same room Longly and Sue had gone into. It made me wonder if my concern wasn't sometimes misplaced.

I let go of the thought just in time to see a lone man riding a big, chesty morgan down the center of the street. He led a pack mule, but it was plain to see he was no prospector on his way to the Black Hills.

He was a manhunter.

I watched as he reined in at the White Elephant Saloon and tied up his animals. Then I watched him jerk the brass-fitted Henry from his saddle boot and take it inside the drinking den.

Normally, I wouldn't have given it any more thought than that. I'd seen manhunters before; plenty of them. But this one was different. I knew this one.

I crossed the street, stepped into the dim confines of the bar. He was there leaning against the bar, his hands atop the long sweep of mahogany, a pair of silver dollars resting next to a bottle and a glass.

"Jake," I said. "Jake True."

I saw him stiffen. A man gets called by his name in a strange town, he gets himself ready for a fight. Only I hadn't come to fight.

"Relax, Jake. I'm not here to do you harm."

He turned slowly, and when he did, I could see the pearl handles of his revolvers showing from his waistband. He squinted through the dim light.

I told him who I was before he had a chance to recognize me.

"McCannon?"

Then he remembered, but still didn't come away from the bar, or show any signs he wouldn't pull one or both of his pistols if the mood struck him.

"Been a long time," I said. "What was it, El Paso?"

"Tombstone," he said.

"Yeah. Tombstone." I remembered then. That rough little hellhole of a town. Jake had served as its city marshal for less than three months. Right up until the time he shot a woman he had been living with. Even Tombstone wouldn't stand for such an outrage and fired him.

"How's Dora?" I asked.

Even in the poor light, I could see him smile; the large teeth flashing beneath the shaggy moustaches.

"Hell, Dora's fine," he said. "Married and got three little screamers. Lives up in Montana last I heard."

"You mind I buy you a drink?"

"No. I don't mind," he said, "Come right ahead."

That time of day, the bar was nearly empty except for the two of us, the barman, and Persimmon Bill sleeping on the billiard table.

"You know that was an accident," he said, "that thing that happened between Dora and me. I never meant to shoot her."

I half thought about asking him why, if he hadn't meant to, he had shot Dora. I remember her as having been a working girl out of the Crystal Palace and Jake and she had been some sort of married. But marriage in a place like Tombstone can mean a lot of things other than a legal ceremony.

I decided to forgo the subject of Jake's shooting Dora.

"You on the dodge?" I said. "Or, are you looking for someone."

"Looking," he said.

He was well built, not very tall, and when he spoke, he had a slight lisp that lent a feminine quality to his voice. But if you watched him long enough, watched the cautious way he carried himself, the way everything was deliberate about him, then you would know that he was a thoroughly dangerous man.

I was about to ask him who he was looking for when he

said, "I heard you killed Pancho Vega down along the border. That true?"

"It is," I said.

"Well, you did the world a favor."

"Maybe so. But none of his relatives thought so."

He leaned on the bar, lifted another glass of the busthead, stared at it for a moment, then swallowed it and set the glass down again, deliberate in his movements.

"You didn't say who it was you were looking for," I said.

"Real bad actor," he said. "A colored. A freedman from down in the Indian Territory. Name's Elijah Hook."

"What'd he do to get you after him?"

"Killed some people. Said to have killed two or three down in the Settlement, down around Eufala. Then he killed two or three more in Texas. Shot a man in Colorado as well. Killed 'em every way there is to kill a man. Shot some, knifed some, even strangled one man, they say. Hell, they say he even burned that fellow in Colorado! Shot him full of lead and burned him in his cabin."

That got my attention.

"You want to tell me more about that part?"

I waited until he poured himself another glass of whiskey. He did it with the same great care and deliberation.

"Which part?" he said.

"About his burning the man in Colorado."

He studied the whiskey before drinking it, just like the previous glass and the one before that. Then he set the empty shot glass down on the bar again.

"They believe he did it because the fellow was supposed to have a cache of gold buried on his property. That's about all of it I know."

"That the only one he burned?"

"Far as I know. There could be others. The marshals say he's killed fourteen men. But, it could be more, it could be less. Who the hell knows. He's got half a dozen rewards posted on him. Adds up to a little over eight thousand dollars. Now you know why I'm looking for him."

"What makes you think he's come this way?"

He eyed the bottle, started to pour, set it back down again, put the cork in it.

"I've been tracking him for a month. I figure he's heading north, to the border."

"Why north, why not south?" I asked.

"Why anything, McCannon? You ever see a smart criminal, one that thinks things through?"

"A friend of mine was killed the other night," I said. "Shot, then burned."

He looked at me.

"That's too bad."

"It sounds like it could be this Hook fellow."

"Could be."

"Then I want to go along."

"I don't share reward money, McCannon. It's not in my nature."

"I'm not asking you to share."

"What are you asking me, then?"

"To go along, like I said."

"This one, I have to bring in alive in order to collect on," he said. "You along, that might not happen."

"I can go after him on my own," I said. "That means I catch him first, you're out the reward money.

"I drink too damn much," True said. "Why else would I shoot off my mouth and tell my business to you?"

"You'll get your reward money, Jake. I just want to make sure my friend gets justice."

"Damn mighty noble principles," he said. "Why don't you just stay here and let me catch Mr. Elijah Hook for you. He'll get hanged, I'll get my money, and your friend will get justice. Everybody will be happy—except Mr. Hook of course."

"Then I'll go alone," I said. "Thanks for the tip."

"Ah Jezzus, McCannon!"

4

I left Jake True standing at the bar in the White Elephant while I went to get my things and find a place to buy a horse. I stopped by the cafe and asked Little Dick if he knew where a man could buy a good horse and he said there was a man named Simms west of town who had some good stock. Little Dick offered to take me out there in his wagon.

"You leaving town so soon, Mac?"

"I maybe got a line on who killed Ben," I said.

"Ben must have turned you into a better detective than I thought," Little Dick said.

"No, I just got lucky."

"How'd that happen?"

"You remember an old Colt name of Jake True?"

Little Dick looked at me.

"Yeah, I remember him. What about him?"

"I ran into him over in the White Elephant. He's been trailing a fugitive. A man wanted for murder. This man murdered and burned one of his victims."

"Son of a bitch, that *is* a lucky break!" Little Dick said.

"Yeah," I said. "It does seem to be."

We reached Simms's spread less than an hour later. A lodge-pole corral seemed to be the main attraction. There were several waddies riding the rails, and several more inside trying to stick to some rough-looking stock.

"That's Simms standing there in the beaver hat," Little Dick said as we pulled up.

Simms looked more like a whiskey peddler than a horse trader wearing that beaver hat, old army jacket and checked pants. Underneath the jacket, he wore a paper vest but no shirt. His belly bulged over his belt; it looked like the head of a balding man.

"He's a rarified individual, Simms is," Little Dick said.

"How so?"

"Hell, just look at him," Dick snorted.

"I don't care how he dresses," I said. "I just care about whether he has a decent horse I can buy."

Dick checked the reins of the bay pulling our wagon, then "hallooed" Simms who turned around and came our way.

"Little Dick," Simms said as he walked up to us. He needed a shave and a little bath water wouldn't have hurt his appearance any, either.

"This is Quint McCannon," Little Dick said. "He needs to purchase a saddle horse."

Simms extended his hand and I shook it.

"Tall man like you needs a tall horse," Simms said, appraising me as I climbed down from the wagon.

"I prefer them that way," I said.

"Got one you might be interested in," he said. "Over there." He ran his tongue across his bottom teeth, then spat.

The horse he indicated was a lineback buckskin with a nicely formed head and hindquarters.

"Have to warn you," Simms said. "I won't take less than fifty dollars for that gelding."

"I don't have fifty dollars, Mr. Simms."

"At's too bad. It'd make you a good animal." Then he looked around, leaned and spat and said, "Got another over yonder in that little corral—speckled bird, rough as a cob. Bites on occasion. But overall, she's a sound horse. Ain't for the faint of heart, you understand. I'd take thirty for her."

I walked over and looked at Mr. Simms's speckled bird. She had spotted hindquarters and the rest of her was the color of rust with flecks of white dappled in. She had some mustang in her, some thoroughbred too, it looked like. She stood there alert at our approach, her ears pricked and her eyes dark and wet. Her nostrils flared as she tested our scent.

"She ain't as big and tall as that buckskin," Simms said. "But the price is right."

I crawled between the rails and the mare pawed the ground and snorted as she watched me. I talked a little Spanish to her. One thing I learned from Pancho Vega, the bandit I'd shot down in Del Rio, was, that horses love to be talked to as much as women. And there is no better lingo than Spanish to talk to either.

The mare's ears flicked to the sounds of voice as she continued to keep a sharp eye on me. I figured if I made the wrong move on her, she would either try and kick me to death or bolt right over the rails. I asked Simms to hand me a rope, then let out a wide loop and made my approach, the whole while talking lingo to her. She did a little dance with her hind feet, but I let fly the loop and it dropped over her neck and she gave a toss of her head, but didn't try to run out from under it.

"Watch her close!" Simms called. "She's liable to think you're a carrot or an apple and take a chunk outta you!"

I got up close enough to put my hands on her.

"Look," I said in Spanish. "I've only got thirty dollars to buy a horse and you're the only thirty-dollar horse around here. One way or another, you and me have to get along. Let's just do it the way that's easiest for us both, eh amiga?"

Then I walked her over to the rail, took one of the saddle blankets and laid it gently across her back. Then dropped the saddle on and cinched it. I asked Little Dick to hand my the hackamore hanging on a post and I slipped that over the mare's nose.

"What ya sayin' to that beast?" Simms asked.

"Just love talk. Sometimes it works."

"Oh," he said, as if that was all he needed to know about speaking Spanish sweet talk to a horse.

I climbed aboard and she threw me in three jumps, then stood there staring at me, challenging me to try again.

"I guess that love talk didn't work," Simms grinned, seeming to enjoy the show more than I thought was necessary.

I climbed aboard again, and again she threw me, only this time it took five jumps.

Simms was trying hard not to bust the belly band on his paper vest. Little Dick just rolled his eyes. It had been a long time since I'd tried my hand at busting broncs. And every time I hit the ground, I remembered why I'd quit the profession. It wasn't bad pay if you didn't mind getting your brains kicked in and your bones busted and landing on your head in the dirt. After a couple of seasons of trying my hand at it, I decided it was undignified—getting half killed by hammerheads.

The third time I took the saddle proved to be a charm, if you can call it that. I got her settled down to a trot around the ring and she only tried to scrape me off twice. But she finally understood I only had thirty dollars and she only cost thirty dollars and I wasn't getting off—that was the just the way it was going to be.

"Damn fine lookin' animal, Mr. McCannon!" Simms declared. "Lookit her trot. Maybe I set the price too low."

"Here's your thirty dollars, Mr. Simms," I said after I was satisfied the speckled bird would do. I just had to be careful not to turn my back on her and let her take a bite out of me. Other than that, I figured we'd get along fine.

Simms took the money and stuffed it in his pocket while I unsaddled her and tied the speckled bird to the back of Little Dick's wagon.

"Anything else I can do you for today, Mr. McCannon?" Simms asked.

"No sir. I don't believe there is." Little Dick grinned all the way back to Cheyenne.

"I think he was a sorry son of a gun to have let that ugly horse go so easily," Dick said.

I looked back at the bird trotting along behind the wagon.

"She's not all that ugly, do you think?"

Dick grinned harder and said, "She is."

I led the speckled bird down to the local livery and told the liveryman to put a new set of shoes on her and throw an extra ration of grain in her feedbag. Then I walked over to the White Elephant where Jake was still standing at the bar drinking in a deliberate way.

"Well," he said. "I hope you have come to tell me that you have changed your mind about going with me." When I said I hadn't, he simply turned the shot glass between his fingers and said he was leaving first light and asked me if I knew of any good whores in town. I told him I wasn't familiar with the local trade but that he might try a prostitute named Shady Sue, over at the Blue Star. I figured if nothing else, it would cut into Long Bill's time and that in itself would be doing Sue a favor.

After I left the White Elephant, I headed back to my room behind Kung's laundry. I didn't have a lot to pack, but I put an extra shirt and a pair of socks into my saddle bags along with a bar of soap, a razor, and extra loads for the self cocker and the Creedmore. The last thing I put in, was a leather-bound book Alexandra Dupage had given me the day I'd left Deadwood. It was by a fellow named Cervantes, and the book was entitled *Don Quixote*.

"You should read this," she said. "He reminds me a little of you." I hadn't gotten around to reading it yet, but thought someday soon I might.

There was a knock at my door. I thought it was probably Kung asking if he should hold my room until I got back. But it wasn't Kung, it was Etta Landrow.

"I remembered something about that day," she said.

"Do you want to come in?"

"Is it proper for a woman to come into the room of a gentleman stranger?" she asked.

"Well, we're not exactly strangers," I said, "And I've never been accused of being a gentleman, Miss Landrow, but if you'd rather not.''

She stepped into the room, looked around without being obvious about it.

"So this is where you live," she said.

"It's a temporary home."

She smiled.

"Don't you feel a little closed in?"

"I mostly just sleep here when I'm in Cheyenne," I said. "Only lately I haven't been in Cheyenne all that much. It's not much, but then I don't require much."

"Bachelors," she said, the amusement evident in her voice.

I looked around too. She was right. A bed, a chair, a single small dresser with pitcher and pan, and a mirror. Hardly what most folks would consider home.

"Yeah, we're a poor lot as human beings go," I said. "Bachelors are."

"I didn't mean it that way," she said. "I just find it funny how single men live such temporary lives, while we women seem to be in constant search of permanency.

"It wasn't always like this for me."

She studied my face for a moment.

"How was it for you, Mr. McCannon?"

"You wanted to tell me what it was you remembered about the day Ben was killed?" I said, wanting to change the subject.

Etta Landrow was a wise enough woman to have seen it in my expression, my unwillingness to share the intimacy of what I once was.

She walked over to the small window that looked out on a alley lined with barrels and busted wagon wheels. All the refuse didn't stop the sun from shining, however. It shone brightly through the window, and became trapped in her honey-colored hair. She turned and looked at me once more. She could have been a painting hanging on some rich man's wall.

"Yes," she said. "I'm sorry I didn't remember it earlier when you first asked me, but there was something that occurred just before I left my shop that evening Ben was . . .''

I waited for her to tell me.

"I remember that just before I left my shop, I heard what sounded like an argument coming from Ben's office." She shrugged her shoulders. "It was hard to tell for certain. Even though our buildings shared an adjoining wall, the sounds were very muted."

"So you can't say whose voice it might have been that was in the room with Ben that afternoon?"

"No."

"You didn't see who it might have been? You didn't see someone coming out of his office after that?"

Again, she shrugged.

"I left my shop shortly afterward. I had to deliver the special order hat I'd been working on that day to Mrs. Tanner. I'd promised to have the hat ready for her by no later than eight o'clock that day. She wanted to wear it at the opera house that evening. That's all I know." She looked at me apologetically.

"It isn't much, I know. But, you seemed so determined, I thought I would just tell you what I remembered after I'd had some time to think about it."

"Well, it probably was nothing," I said. "Ben had lots of clients from what I knew. Maybe one of them was unhappy with the bill for his services."

She nodded.

"I see you're packing. Are you leaving?"

"Yes. First thing in the morning. I might have a lead on who killed Ben."

She blinked.

"You already know something?"

"Possibly," I said.

She looked relieved.

"So you will be gone for a time?"

I sensed I was about to say or do something that I shouldn't. It wasn't just that she was an attractive woman physically. It had to do with the way she talked, the way she looked me directly in the eyes as she spoke. She had a way of tilting her head slightly when she listened. Maybe it was just the way the sun was coming through the window and catching in her hair.

I didn't know exactly what it was about her, but I was getting a feeling.

I barely knew Etta Landrow, and I hadn't yet put out all the flames that once burned so hotly for Alex Dupage. I chalked my idiot urge up to the fact I had once more lost someone I cared about and was feeling a little lonely and alone.

I opened the door for her. That's what a sane man would do.

"Yes, Miss Landrow, I'll be gone for a time," I said. "Thank you for coming by."

"Well, I wish you well in finding this person, whoever he is," she said. Then she started for the door and I moved aside to let her exit.

She started to, then stopped.

"If this man is as . . . as cruel as he seems," she said. "Then I fear for you if you *do* catch up with him."

"I appreciate your concern, Miss Landrow. And believe me, I'll keep in mind his talents."

She started to say something else, changed her mind, then paused and said, "Maybe when you return, you can come and see me and tell me if you were successful in your search, Mr. McCannon."

"Maybe," I said. Our eyes met and held for a full few seconds longer than they should have. And then she turned and left.

I waited a minute or two, then left the room. The sunlight was banking off the metal rooftops, casting long shadows of horses and men down the wide dusty street. I watched Etta Landrow as she walked north. I drew up a chair and rolled myself a cigarette and smoked it and watched the shadows of late afternoon grow longer.

Maybe if I got lucky, Jake and I would catch Elijah Hook and that would put an end to it. Then maybe I could find whatever in the hell it was I had been looking for such a long time.

Seemed to me, there had to be someplace out there in those mountains and meadows where an old drifter could go and put himself up a regular house and sit on the front porch and watch the sun rise and set while he had his coffee and tobacco. There just *had* to be, and I was intent on finding it as soon as I caught Ben's killer.

I was still thinking of those things when Long Bill Longly shot the Mexican kid, Jesse, over a ten cent glass of beer.

5

The pistol shots were like whip cracks. They came from the direction of the Blue Star Saloon, three doors down and across the street from where I was sitting.

I saw the kid stagger through the doors of the Blue Star holding his side. The same youth who had earlier helped me bury Ben. He was just a boy, really—young, straight black hair, skin as brown as the desert. He had a wide-eyed look, like he'd been surprised, or maybe had seen something that didn't exist for the rest of us.

Long Bill followed him into the street, a pistol in his left hand trailed blue smoke. The kid seemed lost, staggering this way and that, blood soaking the bottom half of his shirt, spilling through his hands.

Several more people came out of the Blue Star behind Long Bill; they were holding their whiskey glasses and beer mugs. One of them was Dave Beltrain, the city marshal, Long Bill's boss.

Bill followed the kid outside as he staggered into the street trying to find some direction of escape. A teamster driving his freight down the center of the street had to jerk hard the reins of his team to avoid running over the boy.

Jesse took two more stumbling steps, then fell to his knees. He was muttering in Spanish, asking for his mother, asking for God to save him, praying for his life.

It wasn't any of my business, not really it wasn't. But that didn't stop me from wanting to put a few rounds into Bill Longly.

He was standing over the kid, watching him die. So was Dave Beltrain and the others, like it was some sort of stage play or a circus they'd paid money to see.

Maybe Bill was surprised that I was interfering with his entertainment, maybe he wasn't.

"Why'd you shoot this boy?" I asked.

Longly snorted, looked at me much the same way he'd looked at Shady Sue on the balcony of the Blue Star that morning just before he'd slapped her.

"Mind your own business, McCannon!"

I looked at the crowd.

"Somebody take this boy to Doc Price's," I said. Everyone seemed nearly as disappointed that I had interfered as Long Bill did. Then to his credit, Dave Beltrain ordered a couple of the bummers to carry Jesse over to Doc's office. Jesse moaned when they picked him up. Moaned and leaked blood all over their boots.

"I'll ask you again," I said, having never taken my attention from Long Bill. "Why'd you shoot that boy?"

"Go to hell, McCannon!"

"One of us is about to."

Dave Beltrain grew an amused look on his fry-pan face.

"Better watch it, McCannon, Long Bill's a fast man with a gun, or didn't you know that?"

"First him, then you, Beltrain."

He lost the smile.

"That a threat? You threatening to take on the entire Cheyenne police department? 'Cause that's what it'll be if that's the way you want it!"

"What the hell kind of law is it that would shoot an unarmed boy?"

"He was stealing a glass of beer—Long Bill's beer!" Beltrain said, as if that justified anything.

"A ten cent beer and you shot him for that?"

"Yeah, and I'd shoot the little greaser again if he was to try it again! I hate goddamn greasers! I had my fill of 'em in Texas!" Bill swore.

Beltrain had moved out to the side of Long Bill, the other deputy had taken a similar position to their right. The rest of the crowd figured they might get their money's worth after all. Hell, I didn't much care. There were just some things I couldn't walk away from. This was one of them.

"We'll bury you next to your pard, Ben Beadle," Beltrain said. "How'll that be, McCannon?"

Long Bill was a gun hand, and so was Dave Beltrain. The deputy I couldn't be sure of. I'd concentrate on Longly and Beltrain and worry about the remainder of Cheyenne's police force if I was still standing at the end.

Longly already had his gun in his hand, but I could see it in his eyes: He wasn't entirely sure that I wasn't fast enough to kill him.

That was the thing about a pistol fight, few were willing to be the first one to take a bullet. You had to be willing in a gunfight. I could see it in Longly's face that he was hoping Dave Beltrain would make the first play, and Beltrain was waiting on Longly to be the one. I guess the deputy was waiting for both of them, hoping they'd kill me in the process so he wouldn't have to be tested.

Time seems to stand still when you're in a situation like that. That's what it seemed like—that time was standing still.

Then a loud voice from back of the crowd caused it to separate down the center and allow a new player to enter the act.

Jake True was carrying a shotgun with sawed off barrels. He had it aimed directly at the guts of Longly, but if he pulled the triggers, some of the buckshot would hit Beltrain and the deputy and maybe one or two others standing near them.

"I use dimes in my loads," Jake said. "You boys ever seen what a load of dimes will do to a body?"

The three didn't seem to know exactly how much damage a shotgun loaded with dimes could do. If they did, they weren't saying. Suddenly, it was as quiet as a boneyard.

"Something like this will tear a man up real bad," Jake said. "I know, I seen it done."

Beltrain studied him for a long hard second.

"Who the hell are you?"

"Does it really matter?"

Longly started to speak, but Jake cut him off with a short wave of the twin barrels.

"Naw, don't waste your breath, mister. Either get to it, or get the hell on down the street!"

"These men are deputized officers of the law," Beltrain managed to say, though his heart wasn't any longer in the argument. "And I'm the city marshal."

"Well, I guess they can put that in tomorrow's newspaper and on your gravestones so everyone will know," Jake said. "Go on, make your play, my beer's getting warm!"

I could see it in his eyes, Jake True was thoroughly drunk, but his hands didn't shake, and I don't think he much cared if there was more blood to be shed or not, even if it ended up being his own. He was set for a fight.

The others could see it too, that Jake didn't care. And seeing it, cost them their will.

"Come on, Bill," Beltrain mumbled. "We got a poker game to finish. Fred, you go on over to Klingbill's and tell him his gravedigger's been in a accident and is over to Doc's getting taken care of."

Jake waited until they dispersed before cradling the shotgun in the crook of his arm.

"Thanks for the help," I said.

"You change your mind about going with me yet?"

"No."

"Well, I'm through drinking now," he said. "I reckon I'll go see that whore you told me about—what was her name again?"

"Shady Sue," I said. "But I'd keep that shotgun handy next to the bed if I were you."

"Why's that?"

"That tall gentleman you just threatened to deposit that double load of dimes in is Sue's common-law husband."

"Well now, I'll just see if I can't talk her into getting a divorce," Jake grinned. Even drunk, he could be scary.

I walked over to Doc Price's to see how Jesse was. Klingbill was there when I arrived.

"I'm told you stopped Bill Longly from finishing him," Klingbill said. "For that, I am grateful. I think of Jess as my own son."

"How bad is he?" I asked Doc Price.

"How bad would you be if you got shot twice in the body?" Doc said, without interrupting his treatment.

"I wish I could have stopped it sooner," I told Klingbill.

Jesse moaned even though Doc had put him under with a sponge soaked in ether.

"Why did this happen?" Klingbill's cadaverous features were stricken with the grief he felt for the boy. His head full of questions no one could answer, or if they did, none of them would have made any sense.

I couldn't bring myself to tell Klingbill the boy had been shot over the theft of a ten cent glass of beer. I didn't need to remind him of how cheap life had become on the frontier. He'd buried enough men to know that already.

"I wish the boy good luck," I said. Klingbill looked up from where he'd been staring at his hands. There wasn't anymore words we could tell each other that would change anything, so we didn't try.

I walked over to Little Dick's Cafe intending to have supper before checking on the speckled bird then going back to my room. But halfway there, I decided that's not what I really wanted to do.

Little Dick was standing at the counter with a cup of coffee in one hand and a cigarette dangling from the corner of his mouth. His left eye squinted against the smoke.

"Mac," he said. "I heard you, Beltrain and Long Bill almost rubbed each other out!"

"If it hadn't been for Jake True," I said, "we probably would have."

"Longly," Dick said. "He shot that kid who was Mr. Klingbill's helper? Jesse Torrez?"

"Yes."

"For what?"

"For a glass of beer."

Without changing expressions, Little Dick said, "Why ain't I surprised?"

He poured me a cup of coffee.

"Let me ask you," I said. "Do you know where Etta Landrow lives?"

He squinted through the smoke.

"North end of town. A little clapboard house with flower boxes under the winders. Hard to miss. The only place that end of town with flowers under the winders."

"Thanks."

"None of my business," he said.

"Then don't ask."

"I won't."

Then as I got ready to leave he said, "She's a nice lady from what I know."

"Thanks for the coffee," I said. "Next time, leave out the arsenic."

"Next time leave a nickel on the counter."

I figured the speckled bird might like a chance to throw me in the dirt again, or show me how fast she could run if I gave her her head. I stopped by the livery and put my Dunn Brothers saddle on her, then spurred her into a dog trot before putting her into an easy lope. When we both got comfortable with that, I gave her her head. The wind almost took my hat. She was quick and she was fast and I if I had let her, she might have run clear to the mountains.

"You sure don't act like any thirty dollar horse," I told her as I slowed her to a walk on the way back to the town. Of course, she hadn't taken a bite out of me yet to prove she actually *was* just a thirty dollar horse.

But it wasn't the speckled bird I was thinking about as the

little clapboard house with the flower boxes under the windows came into view.

I reined in, dismounted, and tied the bird to the picket fence out front. "Don't eat the lady's flowers," I instructed. The bird simply eyed me like it was me she'd rather try eating.

I knocked on the door and when it opened, Miss Landrow didn't seem all that surprised to see me.

She didn't say anything, but stepped back to allow me to come in.

I remembered to take off my hat.

She just looked at me.

"I didn't really want to spend the evening alone," I said.

"I'll hang your hat up," she said.

I viewed three-dimensional photographs through a stereoscope in the parlor while she fixed dinner. We ate at a small table sitting across from each other. I couldn't really say what it was she'd fixed; my mind was not on the meal.

Later, we went into the parlor and drank sherry and I asked her to tell me about herself and she did. And then she asked me to tell her about myself and I did, or at least as much as I was able to without revisiting the old places of the heart that still brought too much pain.

The hours went by and she had to light a lamp, but I asked if we could go into the other room, where the fireplace was and we did and I built a fire and that was all the light the room needed as far as I was concerned.

We sat on the floor in front of the fireplace and I told her how, the first time I saw her, I thought she was attractive and she blushed slightly, but I could tell that she knew already, before I'd even said it, what I thought of her.

We talked until the fire burned nearly down and I offered to go outside and bring in some more wood and she said that it wasn't necessary then I offered that maybe I should leave.

"I thought you didn't want to be alone tonight?" she said.

"I don't."

"Then why do you want to leave?"

"I just thought . . ."

She placed the tips of her fingers on my mouth.

"I don't want to be alone tonight, either," she said.

The kiss was like something we'd both been waiting for all our lives. Her mouth was sweet, flavored by the sherry. Her hair smelled of soap and when I unpinned it, it fell over my hands like strands of silk.

And when I pulled my hands away to unbutton her blouse, she kissed them first. I took her face and held it and kissed her mouth again. She made a sound that made me want to kiss her harder.

I felt the coolness of her fingers trace over my chest, and I felt her smooth bare skin under the tips of my fingers, velvety and warm in a way that made me weak and hungry for her all at once.

And there, in the muted light of a dying fire, I lifted her to me, her hair cascading over my face, her breasts brushing my chest, her bare legs entwining mine, and no words were needed to explain or confess our desires.

Only the burning coals, only the long sweet night, only the lonely wind outside our door, were to witness our truth.

6

Old habit woke me early, the light outside the windows was shaded somewhere between darkness and dawn. I felt her there beside me, Etta Landrow, her hair soft and silky on my shoulder and chest, her face close to mine. I didn't want to disturb her, but Jake True said he was leaving at first light and I wanted to be leaving with him.

"Etta," I whispered.

She stirred.

"Etta, I have to be going."

She opened her eyes, looked at me in the dim gray twilight. Sometime during the night, she had gone into the bedroom and brought back a blanket and we had wrapped up in it. It felt good to have her there next to me under that blanket. That kind of good that made you never want to leave.

Her fingers traced the curve of my jaw.

"I have to leave," I said again.

She was a woman who spoke openly with her eyes.

"Kiss me before you go," she said.

I did, a long lingering kiss that sent heat through my veins.

I got dressed while she watched me from the warmth of the blanket. The room was cold, the fire long gone out. I could hear the wind scratching along the outer walls of the house. Outside looked cold and dark and uninviting. It seemed I was always leaving what I wanted for what I didn't want, always moving away from the warm places of the heart to the cold places of the unknown.

"How long do you think you will be gone?" Etta asked.

"Hard to say. Jake True has been chasing this man for more than a month and he's still chasing him. Jake's the best manhunter I know of, that means the man he's chasing is going to be hard to catch." I saw the look in her eyes. "Maybe with two of us, we'll catch him sooner rather than later."

"I may be gone by the time you get back," she said. "That is if you were intending to come back." I was reminded of what she had said yesterday about having to leave Cheyenne because of losing everything she owned in the fire.

"Where will you go?" This time it was my turn to feel disappointment.

"I have an aunt who lives in Nebraska," she said. "Perhaps I'll go there first."

"I have a friend in Nebraska," I said. "His name is Billy Cody. He lives near North Platte." I went on to explain that Billy often ran a touring company of actors and did stage plays throughout the country and in between engagements, he led hunting parties for the rich and famous. I also explained that Billy had a jealous wife and plenty admirers, many of whom were young actresses.

"He sounds like a very interesting man," she said.

"A lot of people think he is. There's even been some dime novels written about him."

"North Platte is not that far from Ogallala," she said. "My aunt lives in Ogallala."

"In case you get around North Platte," I said. "You might stop in and see Billy and tell him you're a friend of mine. I'm sure if you still need work, Bill would give you a job."

"As an actress in one of his stage plays?" she smiled.

"Why not, Etta, you're attractive enough. More than attractive enough."

"You don't think that Mrs. Cody would be jealous," she teased.

"Probably so."

"Why do I get the feeling you have lived quite an untamed life?" she said. "You and your friends."

"You wouldn't be that far wrong."

"Do you suppose you could tell me more about it someday? Your untamed life?"

"Maybe someday," I said.

I rubbed frost from the glass and looked out the window after I pulled my boots on. A blood red sun was peeking over a slate gray horizon.

"What are you looking at?" she said.

"I just hope that thirty-dollar horse of mine hasn't eaten up all your flowers."

She laughed.

"It wouldn't matter," she said. "The frost will have killed them anyway."

I walked over to where she was, reached beneath the blankets and took her in my arms again. I could feel the heat of her, the warm sweet scent of her being causing me not to want to let go.

"You're an uncommon woman, Etta. I just wanted to tell you that."

I looked into those clear as glass gray eyes and knew I'd miss her before I got as far as the town's limits. But it couldn't be helped. Jake wouldn't wait for Jesus.

"I have this feeling," she said, "that I will never see you again. Why do I have this feeling?"

"I think you're wrong about that."

She smiled.

"I hope that I am."

I kissed her and walked out into air so cold and brittle you could almost hear it cracking as you passed through it. The speckled bird stood there asleep, oblivious it seemed to the cold night. But as I came up to her, her ears pricked up and she rolled those big dark eyes in my direction.

"Don't ruin the last few good hours of my life by trying to

bite a chunk out of me,'' I warned. I swung up in the saddle making sure I kept the bird's head in check, just in case she was hungry after having spent the night eyeing Etta's flowers.

Jake True was adjusting his gear on the pack mule in front of the Inter-Ocean Hotel when I rode up. He looked first at me, then at the speckled bird.

''Never seen a horse with quite that coloration,'' he muttered. ''Exactly what color would you call that?''

''Don't know that there's a name for it,'' I said.

He tightened a knot on his pack.

''I seen a dog once in a Comanche camp that was about that color,'' he said, moving around to the opposite side of the mule in order to tighten another knot. ''It had a real sweet taste to it, that dog did when me and those Comanches ate it. Course that was before the Comanches started fighting the white man and you could go into their camps and eat dog with them. You can't do that anymore.''

When he was satisfied the pack was well set he walked over to have a better look at the speckled bird.

''I wouldn't get too close to her, Jake.''

''Why not?''

''I'm told this mare bites.''

He stopped his advance and simply looked at her.

''Look at her eyes,'' he said. ''I wouldn't be surprised if that horse won't someday fall over on you first chance she gets, or kick out your brains! She looks like she hates white people as much as the Comanches do. If you paid more'n ten dollars for her, you paid too much.''

''I paid thirty,'' I said.

He simply shook his head and said, ''Let's get going.''

We followed the road northwest toward the blue mountains. Even from a long way off, you could see the blue mountains had fresh snow in their peaks. Etta was right, the cold weather would kill her flowers.

Clouds the color of cannon smoke drifted against a light blue sky. Even though it was that late in the year, we could feel the heat from the sun on our backs. A broad plain of silvery sage spread before us clear to the mountains and you could smell the sweet scent of the sage whenever the wind came from the right direction.

We rode most of the morning without conversation, then stopped around noon by a small tributary whose waters flowed from high up in the mountains clear and cold as metal. We built a small smokeless fire and Jake set a pot of coffee on to boil and a pan of bacon to fry.

"I was wondering if we were going to take time to eat lunch," I said.

"I take it you worked up quite an appetite last night," he said, looking at me across the fire like some little devil was whispering in his ear.

"What would you know about where I was last night?" I said.

"Ran into Little Dick over to the White Elephant around ten or eleven. He was drinking peach schnapps. He told me you went to see some woman."

I rolled myself a cigarette waiting for the chuck to be done. I figured I wasn't interested in holding a conversation about Etta, or what we had done last night.

Wind swept down from the mountains and we ate our lunch in the great silence of that country before mounting up again.

We rode the rest of the afternoon in the same general silence, our gazes fixed on the distant range ahead of us and the blue mountains that never seemed to get any closer. I figured Jake was still recovering from his bout of drinking and maybe his honeymoon with Long Bill's woman. I meant to ask him about that when we stopped for the evening. Sort of as a payback for him asking Dick about where I'd spent my night.

We found a spot along the same meandering stream we'd been following as it cut through a stand of cottonwoods where the banks had washed away exposing the roots of some of the trees. I tended to the horses while Jake prepared our meal. Then after we finished eating, I made myself a cigarette and offered my makings to Jake.

He took out a pipe instead and smoked that while we sat

around the fire watching the night crawl over us and our little camp. The sky turned from a silvery blue to a soft rose then to black velvet that began to fill up with stars.

"How far behind Elijah Hook do you reckon we are?" I asked.

"Three, maybe four days," Jake said, sucking on the stem of his clay pipe. "Been three, four days behind him for the better part of two weeks. He's like those blue mountains, it don't seem I ever get any closer no matter how much traveling I do."

"He must be a hard man to catch if you haven't caught him yet," I said.

"We'll catch him, just a matter of when."

"It takes a lot of patience to trail a man," I said. He nodded.

"Takes the patience of an Apache," he said. "Ain't nobody at's got the patience of an Apache. But I do my best."

"There's got to be easier ways to make a living, Jake." I said. "A man your age."

"I suppose there is. I've even tried some of 'em. I tried selling Bibles door to door once in St. Louis. I didn't sell many Bibles, but you'd be surprised how many lonely wives just sit around the house all day wishing they had someone to talk to and maybe a few other things as well."

"Well I wouldn't think even a good salesman could get rich selling Bibles," I said.

"No. But after meeting all those lonely women, I can see why some of those drummers do what they do. It may not be good money but there sure is a lot of potential for having fun."

He grinned like a coyote.

"But it won't for me, selling Bibles—or most of that other stuff you have to do in the cities to make a go of it. I guess a hard bark like me can't change much. Hunting men is what I'm best at. 'Sides, it gives me a real good chance to see some real pleasant country."

"Sleeping on a hard ground and eating fried pork would seem to me to get old at some point, Jake."

"Anything can get old," he said.

"What happens when you run out of desperados to chase?"

He looked at me like I had just fallen out of a tree.

"You think that day's ever going to come—that there ain't going to be any desperados to chase?"

"No, but the day may come when you're not able to chase them anymore," I said.

"Then I'll chase whores instead," he laughed. "They're slower than desperados and a only half as dangerous."

"Speaking of which . . ."

"Long Bill's woman," he said, tapping the ashes out of his pipe against the heel of his boot. "I was wondering when you were going to ask me about that. Let me tell you, Mac, she was worth every red cent. Damned voluptuous woman. Lusty, you might say!"

"Did you keep that shotgun handy the whole time?"

"That and other things," he grinned.

A wolf howled somewhere far off in the great black emptiness, then was answered by another. Pretty soon a chorus of howls raised from the valley floor, and then just that quick they stopped, and the sudden silence almost hurt your ears to listen to it.

It snowed sometime during the night and we woke under white blankets.

Jake jumped up and ran to a tree and relieved himself, then ran back and set up a pot of coffee and began frying bacon.

"Can't wait until I can get back to Texas," he said, rubbing his hands. "It ain't nearly this cold in Texas, 'cept up around Dallas where they get ice storms. Sometimes the ice storms get so bad a horse can't stand up and will slide right out from under you. Seen ice so heavy on trees, it'd break 'em. I don't care much for Dallas when there's ice there. I prefer a little farther south."

We got started on the trail as soon as we finished our meager breakfast. For the first hour of the ride the air was still cold enough that the breath from me and Jake and our horses came out like train steam. But by midmorning, the sun had climbed high enough in sky that we could feel its warmth on the backs of our hands and necks and we ended up having a pleasant ride all the way to a small town named Broken Wheel.

It was just a collection of log huts. Whiskey dens mostly.

"How about stopping for a drink?" Jake suggested.

"A little something to oil the bones," I replied. He nodded, we reined in, tied the horses to the rail, and went inside a low-slung log affair you had to duck down to keep from bumping your head.

The light was so dim inside I couldn't see the other customers, but I could smell a good many of them. Jake and I stepped up to the bar, which was a raw plank resting atop two whiskey barrels.

A bulldog wobbled from behind the bar on short thick legs and sniffed at our boots.

"Don't mind Petey," the man behind the bar said. "He's just checkin' to see if either of you is a bitch."

"Your dog can't tell a human from another dog?" Jake asked.

"Naw, he's blind. Happened when he was a pup and I was carrying him around in my knapsack in the war."

"What war?" Jake said.

"How many wars has been fought in the last twelve years?" the barman said.

"You talking the War between the States?"

"At's right. Pea Ridge," the man said. "That's where Petey got blinded. A Yankee cannon shell blew up half the troop and blinded my dog."

"That's a hard story to believe," Jake said.

"Petey's going to be eighty-four years old come Christmas day," the man said. "In dog years, that is."

"Mister, give us a drink and quit fooling around, huh?" Jake demanded.

The man rolled his eyes, and Jake shook his head.

"A eighty-four-year-old blind bulldog," he said. "I've heard everything."

We drank the whiskey without spilling any of it—the true sign of men who appreciate the scarcity of drinking liquor on the frontier. Then Jake asked the barman if he'd seen a black man any time recently.

"The Double X out east of here's got two or three negro cowboys," the man said.

"I don't mean cowboys," Jake replied. "I mean a lone black man who you ain't ever seen before, someone like that."

The man rubbed his knuckles in one eye.

"I don't know, mister. Them colored people all look pretty much the same to me."

"Like Indians all look the same," I said.

"Yeah, like Indians," he said.

"Mister, maybe that Yankee shell screwed up more than just your dog's eyes," Jake replied, sarcastically.

"Did you see a black stranger or not?" I said, beginning to lose my own patience with the man.

"Might have been a colored man through here a few days ago," he confessed seeing that neither Jake or me appreciated his stalling or his blind dog sniffing at our heels.

"Anyone would know would be Miss Maple. She runs a cat house down the street. Got a colored whore works for her. Girl named Sugar Brown. Guess they named her right, cause she's brown as brown sugar and just as sweet."

"I guess they don't all look the same to you then, do they?" I said, but the man didn't get it. Jake took hold of my elbow and steered me to the door.

"That man's dumber than a knob," he said.

We found the brothel easily enough; it was between two whiskey dens and had a red painted front door.

Miss Maple was a heavy-set woman with powdered cheeks and a gap between her two front teeth when she smiled. Jake asked her about Elijah Hook and described him. She confirmed that a man fitting Hook's description had visited her house three nights back.

"Could we talk to the girl he was with that night?" I asked.

"She's busy right this minute," Miss Maple said. "You boys can wait for her to finish her present business, or you could have your pick of another gal, though I only got one other, not counting me who is undisposed at the present. Monthlies, you know."

"No, I had me a good whore two nights ago and am still

recovering from it," Jake said. "I think I'll just wait here in the parlor if you don't mind."

"How about you, lanky?" she asked turning to me.

"No thanks. I'll wait in the parlor with Jake."

"Well, you two are the first men that's ever come in here just wanting conversation," Miss Maple said. "You boys ain't clever are you?"

"What do you mean, clever?" Jake said.

"You know, the type of men that don't like girls? The type that likes other men instead?"

"I like girls plenty!" Jake growled. "Didn't I just say I was with a whore two nights ago?"

"Well, I don't mean nothing by it," she said. "Just that I know there are some men is clever is all."

"Well *we* ain't like that!" Jake declared. "Now if you'll inform your girl we're waiting to talk to her, it'll be much appreciated."

After Miss Maple left us sitting alone in the parlor, Jake said, "You imagine that? "Her thinking you and me are *clever?*"

"Takes all kinds," I said.

"I don't much care for this burg," Jake said. "Blind bulldogs and a big jolly whores that think any man who don't want to buy a whore is clever. I'll be damned!"

We sat with our hats resting on our knees until the negro girl, Sugar Brown, came into the room. She was waif thin, wearing a cotton shift, pretty, with dark freckles across her nose.

"Miss Maple said you gents wants to see me?"

Jake told her the reason.

She sighed, languished on the horsehair settee across from us and said, "Yes, I remember Mister Elijah Hooks. How could a gal forget? He was like a wild stallion." She sighed again and rolled her eyes.

Jake said, "So you got a good look at him?"

Sugar Brown stopped her swooning long enough to say, "Why *yas,* I surely did. I seen more of that man than his mama did the day he was born."

"Well then, I guess you got a *real* good look at him," Jake said.

"Why you be wantin' to know 'bout Elijah for anyhow?" Sugar asked, one bare leg crossed over the other, her small brown foot swinging back and forth.

"Because he has killed several men and is wanted by the law," Jake said. "And you're lucky he took a liking to you, or who is to say you might not have ended up being his next victim."

Sugar Brown's eyes grew large and white, then she giggled. "Oh no suh, the only thing that man'd be killin' is a poor gal's heart."

"I don't suppose he said anything to you about his future plans?" Jake asked.

"I don't suppose this heartbreaker told you which direction he was headed?"

"No, but I sure enough wished he had." Sugar Brown said.

"Why is that?"

" 'Cause if I knew which way he went, I'd go catch up wit him and become his reg'lar gal."

"Then you must have mush for brains young lady," Jake said.

Sugar Brown rolled her eyes and said, "Jus' ain't no way I can explain his powers over a female."

"Powers!" Jake grumped as he headed for the door. "I've seen and heard enough in this town to last me two lifetimes."

He was still grumbling as we walked back down the street, ". . . blind dogs and lovesick whores. I guess I've seen and heard everything! Let's get riding before a pink elephant comes trotting down the street."

7

Jake was all for quitting the town then and there, but I persuaded him that we ought to stay long enough to buy a hot meal. We found a place that advertised itself as MA'S RESTAURANT and grabbed up a couple of chairs at a table near the kitchen.

Jake sniffed the air.

"Smell's like that Comanche camp where I ate the dog," he said.

"It beats trail grub," I reasoned.

"I ain't so sure," he said, squinting at the chalkboard where the menu was scrawled.

It proved out that the restaurant was run by a German couple. The man cooked and the wife washed dishes and served the meals. The man was short and as thin as a stick. The wife was stout as a dray horse and taller than her husband and wore a dark dress that showed sweat stains. There was something else about her that didn't fail to get Jake's attention.

"You ever see bosoms that large on a woman before?" Jake said as soon as the woman had taken our order and walked back to the kitchen.

"Once, in San Francisco," I said. Jake was easily fascinated by the unusual and could be downright single-minded about any subject that caught his interest.

"Well I ain't never seen any that large," he said. "Those big bosoms were to fall on a man's head, they'd likely break his skull."

"Well, there is probably not much chance they'll fall on your head and break it," I said, "So I guess you are safe."

He grinned.

"Biggest ones I ever seen was on a gal in Ulvade," he continued, not content to let the subject drop as a matter of conversation. "Tits so big you couldn't hold a whole one in your hand. But nothing like that German lady's."

"Jake, you have a way of wearing a subject plum out," I said, which made him laugh and stomp his feet.

"Is dere some*ting* wrong?" the woman's husband asked, coming out from the kitchen upon hearing Jake stomp his feet.

"No, we was just killing the roaches," Jake laughed.

The man looked at the floor but didn't see any dead roaches. Then he looked at Jake and me as though we had escaped from the loony bin.

"Oh, I see," the man said, then went back to his kitchen shaking his head and muttering.

In a few minutes, the woman brought us out two plates of beef and beans and set them down in front of us, almost hitting Jake in the head with her bosoms as she set the plates down. Jake ducked out of the way, waited until she'd left again, then smiled so broadly it caused his ears to lift.

The beef was as tough and stringy and the beans were overly sweet.

"This is poor grub," Jake said. "These beans got sugar in them. I ain't never liked sweet beans. We should have gone someplace else to eat our supper."

"It's the way German people cook their food," I said. "They like to use lots of sugar. Besides, this is the only restaurant we've seen in this town. And if even if there *was* another restaurant, you would have missed seeing those big bosoms."

"That's probably true," Jake replied. "But right now, I'd

rather be eating beans that weren't so sugary and beef that wasn't so stringy rather than look at big bosoms."

I ate my own sugary beans in silence, but the beef was beyond redemption.

"How about we stop off and get us a bottle to take with us on the trail?" Jake said. "I got a feeling, it's going to get mighty damn cold tonight."

"I've no objections, Jake."

He set his knife and fork down beside his unfinished meal.

"I'm done," he said. "Maybe the next cowboy that comes in can finish this ol' steer. I hope he has got sound teeth and a good stomach whoever he is!"

We paid the bill and walked next door to a whiskey tent and bought a bottle of whiskey.

"This ain't snakehead whiskey is it?" Jake asked the barman. "This ain't something you brewed up yourself out back and dumped snake heads into, is it?"

The man said he had sent all the way to St. Louis for his liquor, and that Jake could read the label if he didn't believe him.

"Well don't get insulted," Jake said to the man. "But I've drank snakehead whiskey before and don't ever want to drink it again. Just 'cause it's got a St. Louis label on it don't mean jackshit to me."

It was already dark by the time we mounted our horses and rode out of the town. We topped a ridge and looked back at the distant yellow lights.

"Maybe we should have found us a hotel room back there," Jake said as a blast of icy wind rattled through our clothes.

"In the mood you were in, you would have probably ended up shooting the desk clerk if we had," I said. "It's better we make camp out here where you can't shoot anybody."

"Aw hell, Mac," Jake said, already working on the bottle. "My nerves are up, that's all."

"Well maybe that St. Louis whiskey will help to calm them down."

He laughed, offered me the bottle, which I took for no other real reason than to ward off the cold. I no longer had the need to drink the way I once had. With the night so clear and full of stars, the air was freezing.

We found a sheltering stand of pines and made camp. I built a fire while Jake took care of the animals. I had just settled in front of the fire with my palms held out to relieve the numbness when I heard Jake howl.

"Goldang!" he yelped and walked over to the fire holding his shoulder. "That damn crow bait of yours just took a bite of me!"

I made Jake sit down where the light was good and looked at his shoulder. The skin was barely broken beneath the heavy coat and shirt he was wearing. The clothing had prevented the speckled bird from doing too much damage.

"You are lucky, Jake. That mare hardly clipped you," I said. "I tried to warn you not to turn your back on her."

Jake rubbed his shoulder and looked glum.

"Bit by an ugly horse . . ." he muttered as he worked on the bottle of whiskey. "Ugly horses, blind bulldogs, lovesick whores and women with giant bosoms. I believe I have not had such an eventful day since I camped on the Nueces River with ol' Mr. Pester's twin daughters."

Jake hooked the neck of the bottle, took another swallow, then grinned at the thought of Mr. Pester's twin daughters and the day he had camped on the Nueces River with them.

We sat around the fire watching the flames dance against the black air and passed the bottle back and forth until it made its own sort of fire in our bellies and in our veins.

As I sat there in the mute stillness surrounded by deep shadows and a sky that was awash with stars, I began to get that bone deep feeling of what Persimmon Bill called the Big Lonely. I'd felt it plenty of times before. It always had a habit of sneaking up on you at night when whatever home you may have had sometime in your life seemed like a thousand miles away.

I looked across the fire at Jake, a man much like me in certain respects: Drifter, a man who got by on his wits and pistols and instinct. A man who, like myself, had no one waiting for him to come home to, no one worried he wouldn't.

Something swooped through the air just above our fire—

perhaps an owl—and the cold solitary flight of the creature seemed to flap its wings against my soul.

Jake sat wrapped in his blanket staring vacantly into the flames, remembering, I suppose, the precious moments of his life: A pair of pretty girls camped with him on a Texas river; a good horse he once owned; his first whore and his first taste of whiskey. That's what the Big Lonely did: it made you remember the sweet places in your life and realize the cold places you'd come to.

For Persimmon Bill it was the beaver he'd hunted and the Indians he'd fought and loved and maybe even a woman he'd come close to marrying.

"Tell me about the time you were camped on the Neuces River with Mr. Pester's daughters," I said to Jake.

He didn't seem to hear me. I didn't ask him again to tell me the story, I knew he was too busy enjoying it for himself.

I pulled my blanket up and put my feet closer to the fire and settled in for another night on the prairie. One more night on a trail to nowhere. That's the way it seemed.

The wind blew cold down from the blue mountains.

"How can it be so damn cold when there ain't even any snow on the ground?" Jake said suddenly. I guess the cold wind had caused him to come back from the Big Lonely.

"Not much of a life, is it?" I said.

"Ain't we had this discussion once before?" he muttered.

I rolled a cigarette and tried my best to keep the wind from blowing all my tobacco out of the paper. I thought of Etta Landrow there in that spare moment. I wondered if she'd packed her belongings and was on her way to Nebraska. Then that thought led me to a second: Billy Cody.

He was probably this very night sitting in that big house he'd built on the North Platte with a bunch of his cronies and several adoring young actresses nestled at his feet while he recounted stories of his stage-acting or his buffalo hunts with dignitaries and royalty.

Maybe after Jake and I caught Elijah Hook, I would ride over to Nebraska and stop in and see Billy. In spite of his bloated fame, Billy was still a good man at heart—once you got him out of the company of actresses and Ned Buntline.

In the old days, Billy and I liked to drink—a lot. Billy would get drunk and maudlin and relive the old days of his youth, before anyone but his closest friends knew who he was.

I asked him once why he just didn't take his wife, Louisa, and settle down and live a quiet life. When I asked him that, he had simply looked at me and said: "Mac, once you've become famous, you can't never be anything else but that."

"Well what is so terrible about being famous?" I'd asked.

"Nothing," he said. "And everything." Then he looked at me with his clear blue eyes, handsome as a racehorse in all his fine buckskins and polished riding boots and silver spurs and said:

"Fame is the worst kind of disease a man can get, Quint. It's worse then ten cases of the clap or the yellow fever. It's worse than dope or whiskey or sexual urge. It's worse than any kind of sin because there ain't no redemption. Once you've experienced it, you can't ever get enough of it. Goddamn if you can!"

Then his sweet blue eyes narrowed and he said: "But do you want to know the worst part about all of it? It scares hell out of me is what it does."

I tossed my cigarette into the fire and looked over at Jake. He was asleep, sitting up, hugging the nearly empty bottle of whiskey that had come all the way from St. Louis. I laid back and tugged my hat brim down over my eyes and listened to the rhythm of the horses cropping grass.

I hoped Etta would find Nebraska to her liking, and I hoped Billy was swapping lies with some sweet young actress, and I hoped Ben was resting in peace and that I would soon catch his killer.

8

Jake woke with a hoot.

"Hey damn!"

I came up with the self-cocker in my hand thinking there was trouble, that maybe we were under attack by road agents or renegade Indians. It was nothing as dramatic as that. Jake was bucking out of his blankets along with the young prostitute, Sugar Brown.

"What the devil you doing here?" Jake cawed.

She stood there shivering in the cold dawn.

"I want to go with you to find Elijah," she said through chattering teeth. She wore an old army campaign coat and a flop-brimmed hat and loose trousers that fluttered about her ankles. She looked for all the world like some poor sodbuster standing there in a pair of run-down brogans.

"Find Elijah!" Jake swallowed several times in exasperation over the surprise package.

"Yes suh," Sugar Brown said, chattering like a squirrel.

"Do you intend on arresting him and collecting the reward money too?" Jake asked, not at all happy with the unexpected turn of events.

"No suh," Sugar Brown said. "I want to find him 'cause I

in love with him. There ain't never been no man make me feel
like Elijah do.''

"What does this look like!" Jake declared, flinging his arms
out. "An expedition for the lovelorn?"

Sugar Brown just stood there shivering, the whites of her
eyes showing little fear from under the soft brim of her hat.

"And what were you doing in my bedroll?" Jake demanded.

"Trying to get warm—it mighty cold out here, or ain't you
noticed?"

The wind was whistling through the holey parts of Jake's
drawers. Boots and hat and underdrawers, and a big Colt pistol
in his hand, the wind whipping up his backside. Jake True
ought to have been a man embarrassed, but he wasn't.

"Well who told you you could climb in my bedroll with me
anyhow?" Jake demanded. "Why didn't you climb in Mac's
bedroll with him instead?"

The girl looked at me.

"I would have if I'd known you was goin' to be such an
ol' grump about it. Most mens wouldn't mind if I's to climb
in their bedrolls wid 'em. I remember now, Miss Maple sayin'
how she thought maybe you was a clever man—"

"Don't say that!" Jake warned. "I ain't clever!"

"Jake, maybe you ought to get some clothes on," I suggested. "The girl's right, it is mighty cold. You're liable to
freeze off some of your vital parts."

Jake looked down at his condition and said "Oh", then
quickly started putting his clothes on. Sugar Brown giggled
when Jake tried to get his pants on without removing his boots
first, which only caused him to stumble and fall over his saddle.
He gave her a fearsome look because of the giggle.

Jake finally got his clothes on and said, "You go on back
to town now, child and leave us alone."

"No suh, I ain't goin' back to town," Sugar Brown said.
"I come to find Elijah."

"Well, do you see him anywhere around here?" Jake
scowled.

"No," Sugar Brown said. "But I know you is lookin' for
him and I aim to follow you until you find him."

"Follow me?"

"Yas suh."

"You can't follow me," Jake argued, getting his galluses untangled.

"Why not?" Sugar Brown said. "It's a free country ain't it?"

Jake walked around in tight little circles, tugging and pulling on his hat, taking it off and putting it back on again.

"I won't allow it!" Jake said, "And that's that!"

"Can't stop it nohow," Sugar replied. "I ride where I wants, goes where I wants, same as you."

Jake walked a little way from camp, then walked back again.

"Jezzus, Mac, can't you do something here? Can't you try talking to her?"

"I don't know what I can say that you haven't already," I told him. "I guess if she wants to ride all the way to the blue mountains, she can. But, I figure she'll go just a little way, then turn back. What else can be done?"

He rolled his eyes, shook his head and walked over to his gear and started packing it on the mule, muttering the whole while.

"He say he goin' try to stop me?" Sugar Brown asked.

"No. But I don't think you are going to be welcomed with open arms in his camp. You sure you don't want to ride back to town?"

"No," she said watching Jake pack his mule. "I'll just tag along back yonder a ways. Don't want to be in his ol' camp anyhow. Grumpy ol' man."

"You probably just gave him a start, waking up and finding you there in his blankets, is all," I said.

"Humph!" Sugar said. And with that, she marched to a little sorrel staked out on a long rope and climbed aboard, prepared to go wherever Jake and I went.

I looked at Jake who was tying knots in his ropes, but he was paying no attention to me, or Sugar Brown. I went over to her.

"You know it's not safe out here for a woman alone," I said. "Hell, there's a every kind of sorrow and danger."

"I won't exactly be alone," she said.

"I don't think Jake is going to slow down just so you can keep up, Miss Brown. In fact, he'll probably travel a little faster just because of you."

"He won't have to do no slowin' down for me," she said. "Me and little Cheater here can keep right up wid anywhere that big ol' sassy man wants to go."

I gave up and walked back over to Jake.

"I guess we don't have much choice," I said.

"Lovesick whores . . ." Jake muttered. "What next?"

Finally, he finished his packing then turned to me and said irritably, "Do you know how to make coffee? Because I sure could use some coffee on a cold dreadful morning such as this."

Jake refused to budge from camp until after he had drank three cups of black coffee and eaten several strips of burnt bacon. I fixed Sugar Brown some of the coffee and bacon and carried over to her. Jake stared off at the blue mountains refusing to acknowledge her presence in camp.

"This sure is some good grub," Sugar Brown said. "Good coffee, too."

It just seemed to irritate Jake all the more to hear Sugar Brown compliment me on my coffee and bacon.

Finally, Jake was prepared to leave. Sugar Brown mounted her little sorrel. Jake acted like she wasn't there. I gave the girl my blanket to wrap over her shoulders.

"Thank you kindly," she said and took the blanket.

"There's a lot of empty country out there," I said, "and all of it's cold. Least back in town, you'd be warm."

"I don't reckon I would, seein' as how I told Miss Maple I quit last night," she announced stubbornly. "Miss Maple don't like her girls quittin' on her. Ever' girl that quits, means Miss Maple got to take up the slack for her. Miss Maple said she gettin' old and her back be hurtin' her from all them cowboys ridin' her. I thinks maybe it's jus' 'cause she's fat and can't get her wind and move around like them young rascals want. Either way, Miss Maple don't take kindly to her girls leavin' her. Reckon I won't be goin' back there, even if I wanted to."

Jake, paying no attention to the girl or me, set out toward the blue mountains at a quick pace. Sugar Brown put her little sorrel into a choppy trot.

I spurred the speckled bird ahead until I caught up with Jake.

"She still back there?" he growled after several miles without bothering to turn around to look for himself.

"She is, Jake."

He rode along glumly for several more miles. Occasionally, he would ask me for a report on the girl's location and when I would tell him she was still on our heels, he would grunt and knee his mount to a little faster pace.

"You're going to wear out your horse," I said at one point.

"It wouldn't be no great loss to the world if that fleabag you are riding was to wear out," Jake declared. But the speckled bird was doing just fine. In fact, she seemed to enjoy the quick pace and the clear cold air of the high country.

I couldn't say the same for Jake.

The sun followed us and the air turned pleasantly warm and we stopped by a small creek for our noon meal. Sugar Brown halted her little sorrel a hundred yards from our resting spot. She dismounted and sat on the ground watching us.

"We can't just ignore her, Jake," I said as he unwrapped some beef jerky and hardtack.

"Why can't we?" he said. "Feed her and it'd be just like feeding a stray cat. I don't want to encourage her, I want to *discourage* her."

"Well, she can have my portion," I said.

"That's up to you," Jake said. "You keep feeding that gal your food and pretty soon you'll end up looking as flea-bitten as that ugly horse of yours."

"Careful Jake, I think the speckled bird understands human talk." He tossed me a look then settled into making himself a sandwich of jerky and hardtack, what I once heard a captured young Rebel call "possum cake."

I walked out to where Sugar Brown sat on the ground and gave her my portion of the beef jerky along with the hardtack.

She took it without a word and chewed it.

"He still bein' mean about my comin' along?" she said after a few minutes of chewing her possum cake.

"He's still not happy that you are following us," I said.

"Why's he so mean an' contrary, and you so nice?" she asked.

"He's not so mean," I said. "He's just got his ways."

"He really goin' to take Elijah back to Ft. Smif to get hung?"

"Yes."

"Why?"

"Because Hook is wanted for murder," I explained. "In fact, the reason I'm riding with Jake is that one of the people Elijah Hook murdered is a friend of mine."

She shook her head. Jake was sitting with his back to us, facing the blue mountains.

"Elijah ain't never killed no men except maybe one that was trying to kill him furst," Sugar Brown said.

"How would you know that?"

"Man got such tender hands an' a tender heart. Couldn't be no way a man wid such tender hands and heart be killin' nobody."

"Well, I'm afraid you're wrong, Miss Brown."

She quick turned her attention to me, her large dark brown eyes snapping with determination.

"No suh. I ain't. I's a woman, and womens knows about they mens. An' me, I seen all kinds of mens. Been wid all kinds—good an' bad. Womens know. *I know.*"

"Well, that may be. But I know Jake well enough to know he wouldn't be wasting his time chasing after an innocent man."

"Jus' cause that mean ol' boot say Elijah guilty, don't mean he is," Sugar said.

"It's not just him that says Hook is guilty," I reminded her.

"Who else say he is?"

"The law."

"Huuuh! Law don't know more'n I know. Law ain't never felt those tender hands a Elijah's. The law ain't never looked into his sweet brown eyes or heard the tender way he talks."

Sugar Brown had stopped chewing on her jerky and was just sitting there, her eyes big and round, remembering.

"Well, I'm sure the law doesn't care much about those things, Miss Brown. I know Jake doesn't, and to be honest with you, I don't either."

"Elijah ain't what you think he is," she said, staring up at me like an awe-struck child.

I walked back to where Jake was sitting cross-legged, staring at the blue mountains.

"You talk her into going back to Broken Wheel yet?" he asked.

"No."

"Damn fool girl," he muttered. "Well, let's get going."

"It'd make sense to allow her into camp," I suggested as we mounted our horses. "She could cook and clean the plates as payment for her meals."

"Next thing you'll want me to do is stop at the nearest town and buy a fiddle so we can have dances every night," Jake growled.

"It might not be a bad way to pass the evenings," I said, only this time Jake wasn't in the mood to be humored.

We arrived in Laramie, a rugged frontier town seated on a high plateau near the Snowy Range, just at dusk. We could see the lights twinkling against the rosy glow of distant sky.

"We'll check around here," Jake said, reining his horse and mule in front of a saloon. "I'll ask around and see if anyone's seen Hook."

"What about her?" I asked.

Jake looked around; Sugar Brown was sitting astride her tired little sorrel half a block distant.

"Aw hell, McCannon, go and see if you can get a couple of rooms for the evening. Meet me back here."

I said to Sugar Brown as I went back to where she was sitting, "I think you're starting to grow on him."

"I hope I ain't," she said.

I asked a man standing out front of a billiard parlor, where I could find a hotel. He looked at me, but mostly he looked at Sugar Brown.

"Up at way," he pointed with his nose after he'd gotten a good enough look at the girl.

We tied up out front and went inside.

"Need to rent a couple of rooms," I said to a pocked-face kid sitting behind the desk. He was reading the latest issue of the *Police Gazette*. His feet were propped up on a crate and he hadn't noticed our arrival. He had carrot red hair that was wild and uncombed. All that wild red hair and a sharp bony beak made him look like a rooster.

When I told him I wanted to rent the rooms, he looked up, but right away, his attention went to Sugar.

"Huh?"

"I said we'll need a couple of rooms for the night." I couldn't be certain he heard me the second time; his attention was all over Sugar Brown.

Sugar leaned over the desk and smiled brightly at him.

"You see somethin' you like, child?" I thought the boy might swallow his tongue.

"Rooms," I said a third time, only this time with a little more force. "Two of them."

He fumbled getting a set of keys from a box, while I scratched the name *Billy Cody* on the register with a nib pen.

"You wait here in the room," I said to Sugar when we got inside one of the rooms. Then I tossed her one of the keys.

"I'm going to go scout up Jake, then we'll all go get some supper together."

She said, "You want rest there on the bed for a little bit first?"

"Why?"

Then she laid her hand on my forearm and said, "Jus' wonderin' if maybe you wasn't lonely for a gal. You was awful nice to talk ol' grumpy into not runnin' me off and bringin' me food and gettin' me this room . . ."

"No Sugar. I'm not lonely for a gal." She looked half disappointed, half relieved.

"You sure?"

"I'm sure."

"Well, if you change your mind later, jus' give a little knock, okay?"

Another time, another place, I thought as I went back down the stairs and out into the streets of Laramie. Another time, another place, and I might have taken Sugar up on her offer. But fortunately, I was no longer a man that lonely, or that young.

I headed down toward the saloon where I'd last seen Jake. The town seemed quiet enough. Wasn't a one of us to know that within the hour, Jake would push the wrong buttons on a gunfighter named John Wesley Hardin, the randy young desk clerk would end up with a face full of lead, and Elijah Hook would kidnap Sugar Brown right out from under us.

9

I walked back to the saloon where Sugar and I had left Jake tying up his animals. The horse and mule were still outside. The windows were yellow smudges of light. The place seemed to have a life of its own, its belly full of laughter—carousing men and shrill women. Someone was pounding the keys of a piano—a woman was singing in high falsetto voice.

I stepped through the double doors. The air was close, smoke-filled, like every saloon I'd ever been in. Some things you can count on, like the smell of a whiskey parlor. Blue haze from cigars and hand-rolled shucks hung in the air like mist over a bayou. Sweat and cheap perfume and stale beer, smell so thick you could almost cut it with a knife. The clink of glass and poker chips falling in-between the laughter. Each voice sounded a little louder than the next. It could have been Saturday night, maybe Friday. I'd lost track of the exact day, but then it didn't matter. Whatever night it was, it was hell-raising time. The good folks, if there were any, were all at home, sitting around a supper table. The rest of us were in this place.

The name of the place didn't matter. The Silver Dollar, The Longbranch, Delmonico's. They were just names for the same thing. I undone the bottom two buttons of my sheephide coat as I pushed my way through the crowd. Close in as it was, it didn't hurt for a man to be prepared for whatever trouble might break out. With the bottom two buttons undone, I could reach the self-cocker riding on my left hip.

I worked my way through the crowd till I reached the bar. I kept an eye out for Jake but failed to catch sight of him.

A barman wearing a towel and carrying a pair of empty mugs with flecks of beer foam still clinging to them asked me what I'd have to drink. I ordered a whiskey and waited for him to return with it.

While I waited for the whiskey to come, I got a closer look at the woman standing next to the professor at the piano. She was tall and her hair was platinum and she wore a blue velveteen dress. She couldn't sing very well, but she was giving it her best. Most of the rowdies who were paying attention didn't seem much interested in her singing. They were mostly fuzz-faced cowboys, and a few old bachelors.

She finished her song just as my whiskey arrived and some of the men up front clapped and hooted and stomped their feet.

"Sing us another, Lily!" someone shouted. She smiled without conviction and nodded to the professor, a tubercular man with garters on his sleeves who immediately began clinking the keys.

"Fifty cents," the barman said as he slid my drink across to me. I laid the money on the bar and took the drink in hand. My funds were low, so I took my time enjoying the simple luxury of manufactured whiskey.

The woman began singing, "Old Folks at Home," a sentimental song that was guaranteed to bring tears to the eyes of maudlin men made even more maudlin by heavy drink and lonely places. Already, some of the men up front were bowing their heads and shaking them sadly.

"At Lily," the barman said, wiping up a wet spot from the bar with the towel. "She knows how to make those gents cry in their beers, even if she can't sing a lick."

I held off finishing the rest of the whiskey in my glass a few moments longer, until the woman finished her song to a great outburst of emotional applause as several of the cowboys and old bachelors pushed forward and dropped money into a mason atop the piano. I lifted my glass in salute, not so much for her rendition, but for her instincts of knowing how to survive in an otherwise difficult world. She deserved what she got, the silver out of those thirsty men's pockets.

I swallowed the last of the whiskey and it barely seemed to touch the weariness of an all day ride, so I ordered one more. While I was waiting, the blonde diva pushed in beside me and said, "That was very nice of you."

I looked at her and said, "What was very nice?"

"To raise your glass to me."

"I didn't think you'd be watching."

"My eyes are used to the poor light," she said. "And used to the normal crowd of faces. Yours is new. Would you care to buy a lady a drink?"

"Sure, why not," I said. How could I refuse, even though my pockets were nearly empty? "What exactly do you drink?"

She told the barman to bring her a peach brandy.

"My name's Lily," she said. "I was named after Lily Langtry, the actress. Have you heard of her?"

"No," I said. "But then, I don't go to very many plays."

She smiled and tasted her brandy.

"Neither do I," she said. "Laramie doesn't even have an opera house."

"Well, it must be a great loss for all who live here," I said. It took her a moment, then she laughed.

"You didn't say what your name was," she said.

"Quint McCannon."

Her face brightened.

"I have a brother named Quint," she said. "He lives in New York."

"Here's to names," I said, touching my shot glass to hers.

"So Quint," she said, some of the peach brandy still glistening on her upper lip. "Are you a cowboy?"

"No. I was once, but not anymore."

She had a small mole just to the right of her mouth. Somehow it seemed to fit her smile. I caught the look she gave me as I drained my glass. In spite of my instincts, I didn't mind it so much, the way Lily was looking at me. Maybe I should have, considering a lot of thoughts were still back with Etta Landrow. I tried to push the look out of my mind and concentrate on locating Jake.

Several men tried to buy her drinks while we were standing there having small talk. She graciously turned them down. Most of them took it well, but a few looked glum.

"I'm all for some place quieter," she said. "How about you?"

"I'm here looking for a friend," I said. Her look turned to mild disappointment. It was something I could feel as well as see.

"That's too bad," she sighed tipping up the brandy glass.

"I need to see him."

"Then what, after you see him?" she said.

"I guess it depends on what he has to tell me, if anything."

"How long do you think all that will take?" she asked.

"Not long."

"I have a room not far from here," she said. "A girl gets lonely for the company of a gentleman."

I looked around. "There doesn't seem to be any shortage," I said.

"Not if a girl's not choosy," she said. "I'm choosy."

"Give me a minute," I said. Then I asked myself what the hell was I doing as I looked around for Jake.

I left Lily standing at the bar as I made my way through the crowd until I spotted Jake. He was at a table with three other men playing stud poker. From the winnings in front of him, he wasn't doing too badly. I figured whatever "scouting" he had done so far in the way of finding Elijah Hook had been put on hold. Hell, I should have gone back to the hotel and waited for Jake to show up. But I didn't.

"Did you find your friend?" Lily asked when I returned to where she had been standing at the bar. A cowboy wearing angora chaps was trying to buy her a drink.

"Yes, I found him," I said. "But right now, it looks like he's busy."

"Good," she replied. She hooked her arm through mine.

"I don't know this is such a good idea," I said.

"Walk me to my place, give yourself time to decide. You don't want to come in when we get there, I won't force you."

We went out into the chill air. Lily had wrapped a heavy wool capote over her shoulders. "It's not far, my room," she said.

It was a small dwelling at the end of the street, behind a butcher shop. We went in. There was a bed along one wall, a small travel trunk at the foot of it. There were curtains hanging in the window and a small wood burner in the corner. Several tintypes rested atop an armoire; images of family I guessed; she pointed them out as she removed her cloak.

"That one's my brother, Quint," she said. "The one who has your name. He's a typesetter's apprentice for one of the newspapers in New York." She identified a mother and father and two younger sisters from among the other portraits; all still living in the East, New York and New Jersey.

She built a fire in the woodstove and the room quickly grew warm. She produced a bottle of peach brandy and a set of glasses and poured us each a drink. We sat on the side of the bed, the only place to sit, and I listened while she told me more about her family and how she had joined an acting troupe touring the west.

"By the time we arrived in Laramie, we were broke," she said, pouring herself a second brandy and unlacing her shoes.

"Some of us took what work we could. Others booked passage back to New York. That was last summer," she said, sipping her brandy. "As you can see, I'm still here."

"Why didn't you go back to New York with the others?"

She tilted her head just enough to show me a smile that didn't come from happiness.

"The director of the troupe convinced me to stay here with him. He had a weakness for cards and the obscure, and I had a weakness for him. He ended up leaving in the middle of the night with an eighteen-year-old chippie named Frances, and I've not seen or heard from him since." She stared at the wallpaper for a time, her teeth biting the edge of her lower lip.

"I thought I was old enough and wise enough not to be fooled by a man. I was wrong."

"That still doesn't explain why you stayed on instead of going back home," I said, thinking there were no words adequate when a woman tells you a story like that.

"Maybe I'm still waiting for him to come back," she sighed. "Maybe I've not learned just how much a fool I am."

Sitting there close together like we were on the side of the bed, I could see she was not as young as she had first appeared back in the tavern. I could see too, that she had watery brown eyes that were looking into some pretty faraway and awful places of her past.

"I was married once," she added after a long pause, "to a banker. We lived in a large white house with shutters and rolling lawns. For a time, I thought it was all I would ever want or need, that big house and a rich husband."

"But it wasn't."

She looked at me.

"It was until a handsome, sweet-talking, young dentist who was better at poker than pulling teeth came along and convinced me it wasn't."

"So he divorced you," I said, "the banker?"

"No. He shot the dentist and went to jail."

"Love makes some men desperate," I said.

"It wasn't love," she said. "Not on George's part. For him, it was more like stealing to have this other man come into his life and try and take something that belonged to him. A matter of embarrassment, not of love."

"A lot of men might have done the same thing," I suggested.

"Of that, Quint, I have no doubt," she said. Then, without bothering to set her glass down, she gave me a long and full kiss.

I wasn't sure it was something I wanted to happen, but I didn't do anything to stop it either.

"There's just some nights I don't want to be alone," she said. "This is one of them."

"Why me, Lily? You could have had your choice of men?"

"I told you, I'm choosy. You don't look like the kind of

man who will hurt me, lie to me, or ask me to marry him. You know how long it's been since I had a man like that?''

I didn't know.

"I don't want your life," she said. "I just want some of your time."

I touched her hair, she kissed me again. Her mouth tasted like the peach brandy, her breath was warm against my neck. Maybe I wasn't being as honest with myself as I could have been. Maybe I didn't give Etta Landrow as much consideration as I should have there in that wanting moment. But I told myself that Etta was an uncertainty, like all the other uncertainties in my life, and Lily was here and now and professing her need for me. There is something powerful about a woman needing you. So, I didn't try any harder than that to stop it.

Without bothering to turn down the flame in the oil lamp, she undressed.

"I'm not as young or pretty as I once was," she said.

I reached for her, pulled her down to me.

Her hands unbuttoned my shirt, her lips fluttered over my chest, the tips of her fingers trailed down my ribs.

She paused, drew away, looked at the scars her fingers had found welted from my flesh.

"What are these?"

"Nothing," I said, "just the marks of living an eventful life."

"Do they still hurt?"

"Not in ways I can explain."

She kissed the scars and whatever doubts I had about being here with her began to abandon me.

Her breasts were small and soft in my hands and she shuddered when I touched them. "Like that . . ." she whispered.

"Like this . . . ?"

She moaned.

She reached for me and held me in ways that caused my breath to come up short. I closed my eyes and drifted through the pleasures of her hands and kisses, through the soft warmth of her flesh and womanly scent until I felt myself being drawn into her, felt her strong hips moving against me, and felt myself becoming one with her. And her loneliness and mine found each other as we suffered the heat of each other's passion.

Sometime later, I awoke in the cold stillness of the room. The fire in the small stove had gone out and the lamp had extinguished itself. Lily lay there beside me asleep and unmoving. It took several seconds for me to regain my bearings. And when I finally did, I left the bed as quietly as I could and found my clothes and dressed.

"You don't have to leave at this hour . . ." she said, mumbling, still half asleep.

"I was hoping I wouldn't wake you."

"I was dreaming," she said, "of a beautiful white horse. I was riding through a meadow of pretty wildflowers on a beautiful white horse."

"I have to go and meet up with my friend," I explained, pulling on my boots.

"I was young again, just a girl," Lily said, her voice as soft as a girl's. "I've had the same dream before. It always makes me feel good when I dream it."

"Will you be all right?"

She lifted herself to one elbow. "Yes, I'll be okay."

"I'm sorry about this, having to leave like this," I said.

"Don't be," she said.

I finished pulling my boots on and then slipped into my coat and took my hat from the back of a chair.

"Do you think you'll ever go back home to see your people, Lily?"

"Someday," she said. "When I get tired of waiting for Eddy to return."

I kissed her cheek and she said, "Thank you." I had no words to give her back, but I knew she probably didn't expect any either.

I stepped out into a night as black and cold as a cheater's heart. The sky glittered with stars that were beyond a man's reach, but not beyond his dreams. Most of the whiskey dens and gambling houses still operated and their lights glowed like the eyes of allycats.

I walked back to the log saloon where I'd last seen Jake

playing stud poker. I wanted a cigarette but waited until after I got there and stepped inside.

The whiskey parlor wasn't as lively as it had been earlier; I suppose a lot of the cowboys had drifted back to the scattered outlying ranches, to their lonely bunks where they thought about women like Lily, or a lost sweetheart.

The poker game was still in progress, and Jake True was still having a good turn of luck, judging by the chips stacked in front of him. The man behind the bar asked me what I wanted to drink and I told him coffee if he had any. He grumbled, but said he'd fix some. I waited and watched the game and tried hard not to think about Lily or Etta Landrow.

I made myself a cigarette and smoked it while waiting for the coffee to be made. I turned my attention away from the table only long enough to strike a match, but in that fleet second, something happened, and when I turned back, Jake and another man were facing each other—the other two players having scrambled out of the way.

The room became so quiet I could hear the cigarette paper of my shuck burning.

"What'll it be, mister?" I heard Jake ask the other man.

"Don't know, but you've been winning hands all night."

"Luck and skill," Jake said. "That's what poker is, or ain't you heard that?"

"I heard," the man said.

The man was not large or unusual in appearance in any way. He wore a straw sombrero but otherwise dressed plainly. There was nothing about him to attract attention unless you knew a pistolero when you saw one. A man who makes pistols his business will have a way of standing with his good side turned slightly to you. He makes a small target.

"You accusing me of cheating?" Jake said.

"Ain't accusing you of anything," the man said. "But it is awful damn strange you winning most every hand."

I circled to get a better look at the man, to see him under the light from the twin lights hanging over the table.

And when I got around to where the light was better, I saw just who it was Jake had offered himself up to.

"Jake," I said.

Jake didn't turn his attention away from the man, but said, "What, Mac?"

"Time we got going."

"Can't you see I'm in a situation here?" he said.

"It doesn't have to be a situation, Jake. Fact is, it's damn late and we've got an early start ahead of us in the morning."

The man standing across from Jake, the one I moved around to get a better look at, moved his head enough to see who I was.

"You this man's friend?" he said.

"Jake's a partner," I said.

"Then you better get him home before he gets himself killed. All those winnings aren't going to do him any good where I'm about to send him."

Jake stiffened at the challenge, but I couldn't allow it to happen. Not with this man, I couldn't. Jake was a pistolfighter in his own right, but no match for the man across the table from him.

"Jake, I need to talk to you about something," I said.

"We'll talk later, Mac!"

"No, we need to talk now!"

For an instant, I thought Jake would pull his Colt, but my warning must have pierced his mule mind, for he slowly turned his attention to me.

"Can't this wait?"

"No, Jake. It can't."

Still, Jake was in a precarious situation. He naturally did not want to turn his back on the man, and yet, he knew there had to be a damn good reason why I was interfering. There was.

"Let me take my friend home, Hardin," I said. "He's not a card cheat—he's just lucky."

I saw the recognition come into Jake's face at my mention of the man's name. But it wasn't fear or anything akin to it; Jake wasn't the type to be afraid, not even of the devil or John Wesley Hardin.

"He's awful damn lucky," Hardin declared.

"Let me put it to you this way, Wes," I said. "If you draw

on him, you'll need to be fast enough to shoot us both, and I don't think you are. Maybe you can see some reason for some of us to die here tonight, but you'd be the only one who would."

Anyone who knew anything, knew of the reputation of John Wesley Hardin. He was not known as a generous man when it came to a gunfight. But, he wasn't stupid, either. Two against one, spread out as we were, there just wasn't any way he was going to get us both. Either Jake would kill him, or I would.

Hardin let another few seconds pass—just long enough to maintain his sense of honor, then said, "I'm going to walk over to the bar and have a drink. After that, if you boys are still present, there just ain't no telling what might happen next. I'm damned nerved up."

Jake started to say something, but I said something first.

"It's not worth dying over, Jake."

Jake was mad as hell when we hit the street.

"What was that all about, Mac!"

"He would have killed you," I said. "Or, me."

"What makes you think it wouldn't have been him that would have gotten killed?"

"It would have been him, too. But he would still have killed one of us, Jake. And to tell you the truth, I wasn't planning on dying in some damn dirty saloon over a hand of cards."

"You didn't have to butt in, you know!"

"Yeah Jake, I did have to butt in goddamn it!"

"No, you're wrong," he said.

"Look at you, Jake. You're drunk and in the wind! Killing you would have been as easy as killing a blind mule. Hardin wouldn't have thought twice about!"

Jake swallowed then, because I had spoken the truth. He was drunk even though he walked a straight line. And while the whiskey made him braver than he ought to have been, it also made him slower too. And Wesley Hardin didn't need any extra advantage.

"I got us rooms at the hotel," I said to Jake's sullen silence. Maybe he was thinking how close he came to dying. If he was, all the better. Maybe next time he decided to get in a poker game with someone as quick and ill-tempered as John Wesley Hardin, he would refrain from the whiskey.

We arrived at the hotel only to find several guests standing outside in their nightclothes.

"What is it, a fire?" I asked one of them—a balding man in a long night shirt.

He rolled his eyes and said, "A man's been killed up there!"

"Up where?" Jake said.

"In one of them dern rooms!"

It was more a feeling than anything else, the sense that Sugar Brown was somehow involved. I looked around but didn't see her among any of the shivering guests. "Let's go!" I said to Jake as I rushed inside.

I found the door to her room wide open. I also found the pock-faced desk clerk with his drawers down around his ankles squatting beside the bed. It looked like he had washed in blood. He was dead as a man can get.

"What the hell!" Jake said.

The kid was the only one in the room. Sugar Brown was gone. I went down the hall, saw the back door had been kicked in, saw the stairway that led to an alleyway.

"Who would have done this?" Jake said when I got back to the room.

"Guess," I said.

"Hook?"

"Who else would come steal that girl in the middle of the night?"

"Goddamn!" Jake declared. "Here we been chasing him, and he's been following us!" Then Jake noticed the boy and said, "Who's he?"

"Just a randy kid who knocked on the wrong door."

Jake swallowed hard.

"You think Hook did him because of the girl?"

"I don't know why else," I said.

"You want to leave tonight, or first light?" Jake asked.

"There's no point in trying to trail them tonight, Jake. You know that as well as I do. Besides, you're drunk enough you might fall off your horse and break your neck."

"I rode two hundred miles once across the Llano Estacado drunk as a coon and never one time fell off my horse," Jake argued.

"How would you know if you had?"

Jake looked at me and said, "I'm going to bed before something else up and bites me in the ass."

I considered the abilities of a man who could cut the trail of Jake True without Jake's knowledge as I slipped the big Remington self-cocker under my pillow that night. It was cold comfort, that big three-pound pistol under my head.

If Elijah Hook could murder a man like Ben Beadle and steal the colored whore right out from under our noses, then there was no telling just what else he could do, if and when he was ready.

Well damn his soul if he decided to come visit again.

10

The next morning, as soon as it was light enough to cut sign, Jake and I followed a double set of tracks leading from the alleyway in back of the hotel to the south road.

"You see that?" Jake declared, through bleary eyes. "He's turned around and is now heading south."

"I see."

"But why south? Why ain't he still heading north?"

"Maybe he's changed his mind as to which border he wants to cross," I suggested.

"Damn sonofabitch!" Jake moaned. "Gonna make me chase him all the way to the Mexican border if he can!"

"Warmer that direction," I offered.

"Farther, too!"

As we followed the tracks through the back alley, I saw Lily standing in the doorway of her little cabin, a tin cup of coffee in her hand. Our eyes met, but we didn't speak. Jake noticed her as well.

"Fine-looking woman," he said. "You know that gal?"

"We've met," I said.

He twisted his neck in order to keep looking at her as we rode past.

"Pretty hair," he said.

I allowed myself a few moments of the previous night's memory, then let Lily slip away from my thoughts. It wasn't something I wanted to carry with me the rest of the trip, Lily's memory.

"We push hard," I said to Jake, "we might catch Hook in three, four days."

Jake was still nursing a sore head from all the hard liquor from the night before. His eyes were rimmed red and he kept swiping at his moustaches.

"That is if he ain't behind us somewheres," he groaned. It was something I'd considered as well—that Elijah Hook was tracking us instead of the other way around.

"You think he maybe killed the girl?" Jake asked.

"No. It wouldn't make sense to kidnap her if he was just going to kill her."

"A man would have to be damn sweet on a gal to take such risks as he took last night," Jake said.

"Maybe there was more to it than that."

"How so?"

"Maybe he wanted to prove to us he could do it, steal the girl out from under us."

"Crazy son a bitch then," Jake said, swiping his moustaches again.

"Maybe not so crazy as we might think."

Jake rode on for the next few hours without further comment; I knew his head must have felt like an anvil from all that busthead whiskey he soaked up. I learned one thing in my drinking days, it was not to put cheap liquor in you. Good Tennessee mash, now that's another thing.

The day was cloudy and looked as though it would either rain or snow before it all was said and done. We crossed several tributaries, and in every one, the waters looked like black under the dull gray sky. A stiff wind blew out of the northwest and pushed tumbleweeds across our path. Once, a jackrabbit broke from the cover of a greasewood bush and Jake tried to shoot it with his Colt but missed. The damn thing was as big as dog and when Jake's big pistol went off, the jack bolted behind a clump of sagebrush and was out of sight before Jake could pull the trigger a second time.

"I could almost taste that rabbit roasted on a stick," Jake said in a forlorn voice.

"Did you really think you'd hit it with that big iron?" I said.

We stopped at noon for a lunch of hardtack and beef jerky and canteen water and gave the horses a blow. Off to our west, we could still see the blue mountains, only now, their peaks were obscured by a bank of clouds so gray and heavy you could almost smell the snow in them.

"It's damn well gonna come a storm," Jake declared. "I can feel it in my feet."

"How does a man know from his feet whether it's going to snow or not?" I asked, enjoying a cigarette.

"You remember Gettysburg, don't you?"

"It would be hard to forget," I said.

"Got both my feet broke when a caisson rolled over 'em trying to get to the top Little Round Top," Jake said. "Hurt like hell. Hadn't been for my feet gettin' broken though, I might have been killed—most everybody I knew got killed that day. My feet got broke by that caisson and I lay in the grass a long time. Never did make it up Little Round Top. So I guess in a way, it was lucky my feet got broken—except now, whenever it's going to come a storm, they ache like blue blazes!"

"We all got hurt in that war, one way or another," I said.

"Don't I know it," Jake moaned as he pull his boots off and began rubbing his feet. "I sure wish I'd been far-sighted enough to have bought an extra bottle of mash in Laramie. I could use a little taste of medicine on account a these feet of mine."

"I would think maybe you had put enough medicine in you last night that your feet wouldn't be troubling you for at least a week or two," I said. "I doubt if Wes Hardin *had* shot you last night, that you would have even felt the bullet."

Jake stopped rubbing his feet long enough to give me the eye.

"Well, getting shot by Wes Hardin couldn't have hurt much more than these feet of mine are hurting me now," he said, grimacing as he rubbed his feet. "Unless you've had your feet run over by something as heavy as a caisson, you can't begin to know what it feels like."

"I wish I had a drink to give you, Jake. Hell I almost wish I had one for myself."

"Everything was going along smooth for me until I ran into you back at Cheyenne," he grumbled. "Ever since that unlucky day, it's been one setback after another. And now my feet are aching."

"Well, I am sorry about your sore feet, Jake. But running into me doesn't have anything to do with you suffering."

Jake pulled his boots back on with much agony then hobbled to his horse and rode off at a quick pace like he was trying to outrun the pain in his feet. Or, maybe it was just my company.

We followed the double set of tracks the rest of the afternoon, Jake complaining every so often about how bad the pain in his feet was and saying how it was going to snow sometime soon. The gray sky seemed to lower itself just over our heads and the wind tried to push its way up under our coats and steal our hats.

Every passing hour, the sky grew darker and settled in all around us so that by late afternoon, we not only could reach up and touch it, we were riding in it. It was damn cold traveling and damn uneventful until we saw a man sitting on the carcass of a dead mule that was still harnessed to a bright blue and yellow wagon.

The man looked up as we approached.

"How do," he said. His clothes were dusty, especially the knees of his pants. He wore a claw-hammer coat with satin trim and a battered plug hat that was tied on by a long wool scarf.

"What are you doing sitting on a dead mule out here in the middle of nowhere?" Jake asked.

"Waiting for someone to come along, sir," the man replied.

"Well, that's plain enough a blind man could see," Jake said. "But that wasn't quite my point."

The man brushed the dirt off the knees of his pants, then stood.

"I'm Jonas Fly," the man said, then touched the brim of his hat in a formal and gentlemanly way.

"I sell patent medicines, as you can plainly see by my wagon."

Written on the side of the wagon in large black letters were the words:

FLY'S PATENT MEDICINES & BITTERS,
JONAS FLY, PROP.

CERTIFIED PHRENOLOGIST—DENVER

"What's that last part mean?" Jake asked. "That freeno-gist?"

"In quite simple terms it means, sir, that I am practiced in the science of reading the bumps on a person's head in order to determine his character."

"Reading the bumps on a person's head?" Jake said.

"That is correct sir."

Jake turned and looked at me. "Well, I guess I ain't seen everything like I thought I had."

"I guess not," I said.

"That still don't explain you sitting out here in the middle of nowhere on a dead mule," Jake said. "Even if you can read a person's head bumps."

"I had the misfortune of buying a colicky mule in Laramie yesterday," the man said. "My previous beast came up lame and I traded him, along with ten gold dollars, for this colicky mule. I also had to throw in two bottles of my patent medicine which will cure everything known to man—but alas, not to mules—at least not to mules that are colicky."

"Well maybe you should invent a patent medicine that would help a colicky mule," Jake suggested. "Then you wouldn't be in such a poor situation as you are now."

"Believe me," said the man, "I couldn't agree with you more."

"Say, you didn't see a big black cuss riding by with a little bitty colored girl with him, did you?" Jake asked.

"No sir, I did not see such a man."

"Oh," Jake said, the disappointment plain in his voice.

"But," Fly added. "There were one or two riders that went by here late last night. Unfortunately, they did not bother to stop. They seemed in quite a hurry judging by the sounds of how fast their horses were running. It might have been the party you are looking for."

"Well maybe so," Jake said. "But if it was them, it is lucky for you that they didn't stop, or you might be just as dead as your mule."

Fly swallowed hard and his eyes got a little buggy.

"Surely you can't be serious."

"I'm as serious as a tax collector," Jake said, then added: "Say, does that patent medicine of yours cure feet pain?"

It took the man a few seconds to find his voice.

"I . . . believe I should have something in my wagon that will relieve the discomfort of painful limbs."

Jake pulled out his watch and looked at it.

"It is just about suppertime," he said to me. "Maybe we ought to just make camp here and get an early start."

I didn't quarrel with the decision. If Jake was right about a storm coming and we pushed on past dark and got caught out in it, we would probably end up lost.

I took care of the horses this time while Jake and Jonas Fly scouted around in Fly's wagon for the right pain remedy.

"This ought to do," Fly said, handing Jake an amber bottle with a cork stopper. Jake held it out at arm's length and read the label before taking a taste.

Jake smacked his lips and said, "It's a bit bitey, but it warms you."

Jonas Fly said, "Give it a chance to work, I think you'll see that taste isn't everything."

Jake plopped himself down on his saddle and pulled off his boots and wrapped his feet in one of his blankets while I built a fire.

"How did you come by your affliction, sir?" Fly asked him.

Jake explained how his feet had been ran over during the battle of Gettysburg and how they'd troubled him on and off ever since. "Whenever there's going to come a big storm, or any change in the weather," Jake said, "that's when they start barking. Like now. If my feet ain't failed me, it's one hell of a storm on the way. Ought to hit us anytime."

Jonas Fly looked all around him, in every direction. It was cold and dark and getting more so by the minute.

"I would admit," Jonas Fly said, "that the conditions do seem ripe for some sort of change in the weather. A little snow perhaps, but I see nothing to indicate a storm."

"You will," Jake said. "A big one, too."

Jake continued to work on the bottle of bitters that Fly had given him while I unpacked the mule and brought to the fire enough supplies for supper.

"May I contribute something to the repast?" Fly asked when he saw me slice bacon into the black frying pan.

Jake looked at him from across the fire.

"Repast?"

"I've a fruit cake in the wagon—a gift from a woman I know back in Duluth."

"Fruit cake!" Jake tipped the bottle up then brought it down again. "Well hell, I ain't et a fruit cake in twenty years—bring her out! And I'll make us a pan of biscuits if someone will fetch my dutch oven outta my pack."

"What do you think?" Jake asked when Fly went into the wagon to get his fruit cake.

"About what?"

"Him!"

"What about him?" I said.

"You really think he can read a person's head bumps?"

"I've heard tell there are people who can," I said.

I didn't know what was in the medicine bottle Jake was sampling, but it seemed to be doing the job on him judging by the unsteady look in his eyes and the happy look on his face.

"That helping your feet?" I asked.

He looked down at the lumps of his feet beneath the blanket.

"Don't hardly feel them," he said. "Come to think of it, I

don't hardly feel my legs either." Then he snorted a laugh and held up the bottle. "Damn stuff makes you feel good, Mac; you ought to try a little."

"Not tonight, Jake. One of us should probably stay on the alert."

"You think Hook will double back and try to kill us in our sleep?" Jake asked without the least bit of concern.

"Anything's possible," I said not feeling quite as confident as Jake about the matter. But then I wasn't tossing down whatever blue balm was in that bottle of his.

"To tell the truth Jake, it's a possibility that Hook could double back on us."

"Who might kill us in our sleep?" Jonas Fly said, walking into the light of the fire carrying a gaily decorated cake tin and a can of peaches.

"You don't have to worry there, Mr. Fly," Jake said. "I ain't gonna allow nothing to happen to you and these wonderful patent medicines of yours. You got another bottle of this? It's working miracles on my sore feet!"

Fly looked at me with owl-like eyes. He had an unusually large head for such a small man.

"Not to worry," I said. "There's not much chance anyone's going to come and kill us in our sleep; especially if there's a big storm brewing out there."

Fly looked uncertain.

"And after you get me another bottle of medicine, Mr. Fly," Jake said, "maybe you could read my head bumps."

By the time we had finished eating, we could almost feel the storm without actually seeing it, like it was waiting just at the edge of our camp, just beyond the firelight. The night sky had a blood red quality to it.

Jake forwent eating very much supper, choosing instead to concentrate on the small amber bottle Fly had given him.

"It makes me feel sorta like I'm floating," Jake said.

"What'd you put in that medicine bottle?" I asked Fly.

He offered me a weak smile. "I always mash in one or two opium pills," he said. "The rest of the formula is a secret." The opium pills explained Jake's happy mood.

"You reckon you are ready to read the bumps on my head?" Jake asked. "My feet are feeling much better and I feel like having my head bumps read."

"Certainly, sir," Jonas Fly said.

"What'll I have to do?" Jake asked.

"Simply remove your hat, close your eyes, and be very relaxed."

"Oh, I'm real relaxed," Jake said. "Thanks to this wonderful curative of yours."

Jake closed his eyes while Jonas Fly felt around his head. Fly's bony fingers searched and felt their way through the dark tangles of Jake's long uncombed hair.

I rolled myself a cigarette and watched the show while I kept an ear toward the night.

"Ah . . . here at the occipital area, I can feel a ridge that indicates you are a man of truthful character," Fly said after a few minutes of probing around in Jake's hair.

"And this bump here at the parietal region speaks of a man who is highly determined." Jake looked pleased with the interpretation while Fly continued his search for more bumps.

". . . and these, here in the frontal portions," Fly continued, his eyes closed, his chin lifted. "These show a man who . . . who . . ." Fly lost his voice again.

"Who what?" Jake asked, opening his eyes, wanting to know exactly what it was Fly had discovered in the nest of his hair.

"These bumps . . . show a man much given to a violent nature . . . I'm afraid . . ."

"Oh," Jake said, settling down once more. "I thought you were going to tell me my bumps said I was clever, or something like that."

"Clever?" Jonas Fly said.

"It's not what you think it means, Mr. Fly," I said, enjoying my cigarette and the bump-reading display.

"It's something a dang jolly whore called me," Jake said, sipping from the patent medicine bottle. "Of course, what does a jolly whore know about anything?"

"Indeed," Fly said.

Then, it started to snow, just as Jake had predicted.

"Look at the size of those flakes!" Fly cried. "They are nearly as big as fancy belt buckles!"

"I told you it was going to snow big," Jake said, closing his eyes and letting the snowflakes collect on his face.

"Well, what if we are snowed in come the morning?" Jonas Fly asked. "What will we do then?"

"Seeing as how your mule is dead," Jake said. "I don't know why you are so worried about being snowed in. That dead mule of yours sure ain't going to take you anywhere whether it snows or not."

Fly swallowed like he had an apple stuck in his throat.

"Don't worry about it, Mr. Fly," I offered. "Tomorrow, we'll hitch up one of the horses to your wagon and escort you into the next town so that you can buy yourself another mule."

"Only this time," Jake said, his face nearly covered under the big snowflakes, "don't buy a mule that's colicky."

11

Sometime during the night I dreamt of bayous and Spanish moss hanging from cypress trees and the blackened smoke of burning plantations. I dreamt of dead horses still in their traces lying bloated along the road, their legs stiff, their bodies black with rot. And marching along the road were long columns of men in dusty blue tunics heading straight into the blaze of a setting sun like they were marching to their final fiery death.

But something troubled me awake. Something that seemed to go right through my flesh and gnaw on my bones. I opened my eyes and saw I was surrounded by a world of white. In spite of my blankets, my teeth were chattering. The snow that had begun the evening before, had continued throughout the night and by morning, Fly's dead mule was buried except for one ear sticking up. The air felt so cold, I thought if someone fired a pistol it would shatter.

Jake and I had been smart enough to move our bedrolls under the medicine wagon before going to sleep the previous night; it was lucky for us we had or we might have been as buried as Fly's mule.

Jake stirred from his sleep about the same time I did. He sat up and nearly hit his head on the bottom of the wagon as he did. Instead, he caved in the crown of his hat. He removed it and looked at it before punching it up again and settling it back on his head. He blew breath into his hands as he surveyed the wintery scene.

"Well, it is a good thing we stayed here last night and didn't keep going—else, we'd be out there somewhere under all this snow, maybe fallen down in some arroyo with our legs broke."

"We'll play hell picking up Hook's trail now," I said, feeling like my bones *were* broken as I tried to climb out from under the wagon.

"Maybe that murdering devil is himself laying at the bottom of some arroyo," Jake said. "Who's to say he could find his way any better in a snow storm than we could?"

"Well maybe the storm will have at least slowed him down," I said.

We could hear Jonas Fly moving around in his wagon just above our heads.

"I wonder if Fly has any more of that foot medicine," Jake said. "Only it ain't my feet that hurt as much now as it is my head. Them bitters's got a kick to them."

I was trying hard to get my parts in working order when I noticed what was wrong.

"Jake, our horses are gone."

"What!"

We swept out the snow drifts surrounding the wagon and climbed out into the sharp glare of sun coming off the snow.

"Maybe they laid down to go to sleep and got covered up," Jake suggested; but we both knew that wasn't the case.

We saw a line of shallow depressions leading toward the blue mountains.

"Well, at least we know they didn't run off of their own accord," I said, after a quick study of the tracks. The tracks had nearly been covered up with snow, but there were still the slight cupping of footprints alongside those of the horses leading off in single file.

"Indians must have come and stole them!" Jake said.

"Possibly."

"I don't know who else but an Indian would come out in a

snow blizzard and steal horses," Jake stated. "Indians love to steal horses more than they love to hunt or screw their women."

"Does it really matter whether it was Indians or not?" I asked.

"No, I guess it don't," Jake replied glumly.

Jonas Fly appeared from inside his wagon; he had a long woolen scarf wrapped around his neck and was wearing heavy mittens on his hands.

"My, oh my!" he declared, looking at all the snow. "You were right, Mr. True, about the storm being a big one."

"Our horses have been stolen!" Jake announced.

"Stolen!" Fly yelped. "But how can that be?"

"They just come in the middle of the night and stole 'em, is how!" Jake declared.

"Who would come during a snow storm and steal our horses?" Jonas asked.

"Indians, most likely," Jake said. "They went off toward those blue mountains." Jake pointed toward the jagged line of peaks in the far distance with his grizzled chin.

"Well, what will we do now without any horses?" Fly said, stamping his feet and slapping warmth into his hands.

"We'll have to go after 'em," Jake said.

Jonas Fly stared hard at the white emptiness but did not see either the horses or whoever had taken them.

"But how will you go after them with your sore feet, Mr. True?" Jonas asked, his voice filling with distress as he stood with his gaze fixed on the vast open horizon.

"My feet are only half sore," Jake replied. "It's my dang head that hurts!"

"You stay, I'll go," I said.

"I'll go too," Jake said.

"With your bad feet, you'd only slow me down, Jake. Stay here in camp with Mr. Fly."

Jake looked unpleasant about it, but he and I both knew that if he went along, we would never stand a chance of catching up with whoever had taken our horses."

"You don't catch up with them by tomorrow noon," Jake

advised, "it means they got too good a jump on us—you might just as well turn around and come back."

At least the thieves hadn't stolen our supplies along with the horses and mule. I made myself a small pack of food and took both canteens of water. Then I took one of the coals from last night's fire and smudged my cheeks under my eyes to cut down the glare of the snow. Finally, I made sure I had enough loads for my self-cocker.

"Ain't you taking that big Creedmore?" Jake asked.

"Too heavy to carry if I'm going to travel fast," I said.

"Well what if you get a chance to shoot them thieving sonsabitches?"

"I'll just have to shoot them with my Remington, Jake. I don't suppose it will matter all that much to them what they get shot with if I have to shoot them."

"Well shoot 'em even if you *don't* have to for putting us through all this inconvenience!" Jake growled.

I was already walking away from camp, following the shallow depressions in the snow.

Once I got out of sight of the camp, the land seemed as lonely as any I'd ever been in. It struck me that a man could die out in this great emptiness and no one might ever know it; a man could die and his bones could turn to dust and be carried away by the wind and that would simply be the end of his existence. The sad truth of the matter was, plenty of men had died just that way. *Dust on the wind.*

I walked all that day with the great silence broken only by the crunching of my boots upon the snow and the sound of my labored breath.

My moustaches turned to ice, but the rest of me stayed warm because of the pace I set. My one advantage over whoever had stolen our horses might be that they might not consider the possibility that anyone would follow them on foot through the deep snow, and therefore might not be in any great hurry. It was about all the hope I had. That, and the fact that most criminals I ever dealt with were not very smart to begin with.

I rested for only a few minutes at a time, long enough to

catch my breath, sip some water, and have a smoke. I was counting on the horse thieves taking a lot of long rests.

Once or twice, I had to force myself back to my feet again. Trudging through the deep snow took a lot more energy than I was used to. There hadn't been much of my life I could recall not doing my work from the back of a horse.

I pushed on.

All day, I forced myself to keep going, following that single line of tracks toward the blue mountains. Gradually the tracks started to become a little fresher. *I was gaining on them.*

By late in the day I decided to take a prolonged rest. The sun was beginning to set just over the mountains, casting long shadows of distant pines across the snow.

I'd rested near a meandering tributary that cut through the snow like a wet black snake; I refilled my canteens and boiled a little water for coffee.

At least the wind wasn't blowing like it normally did in that country and that made my rest a little easier. I rolled a cigarette and smoked it while having my coffee. It made me wish I was back in Little Dick's Diner in Cheyenne having a slice of pie to go along with my coffee before setting out to go visit Etta Landrow. I'd been thinking about Etta Landrow a lot more than I'd planned on.

Maybe it was squatting there all alone in a valley of snow with the blue mountains off in the distance and the unending silence pressing in on me that caused me to think of Etta again. One thing Persimmon Bill had said about knowing the Big Lonely was, it made a man think about women—the ones he'd known, and the ones he wished he'd known. Maybe that was why I was thinking so much about Etta.

I closed my eyes against the ache of tired burning muscles. I felt as exhausted as I'd ever been and it was tempting to shallow myself a place in the snow and just let sleep take over. I closed my eyes against the sting of sun glare and when I did, white flashes of light burst inside my skull and my arms and legs throbbed with the pain of a thousand needles.

I snorted at the thought, but it felt like I had been carrying a *damn* horse across my back all day, tired as I felt.

With one great effort, I managed to get back to my feet, the sun had now gone behind the mountains and a moon as round as a fancy silver buckle had risen in the deepening blue of sky. In another hour there was enough moonlight reflecting off the snow that following the tacks wasn't a problem. If I was right, and the horse thieves didn't believe they were being followed, they would be in camp somewhere not far ahead of me. If I was wrong—well, I didn't want to think about if I was wrong.

I stopped only when I had to, and only long enough to catch my breath, maybe have a quick smoke, then move on again. The thought of catching the horse thieves was all I needed to keep putting one foot in front of the other every time I thought about quitting. That and the thought of maybe someday riding to Nebraska to see Etta Landrow again.

After what seemed forever, dawn finally broke behind me over the eastern horizon—a red ball of shimmering sun balanced atop the shimmering glaze of icy earth. I stopped long enough just to watch it. It gave me a good feeling seeing the sun come up again.

I moved on.

Finally, I reached a point where my legs felt too heavy to take another step. I rested against the base of a bluff and leaned my back against the incline. The fiery pain shot through my legs and into my groin. I caught my breath and tried rubbing life back into my legs and thought of Jake and the way he'd tried to rub the pain out of his feet. With the sunrise came a wind that began to blow stiffly kicking up snow dust. I was somewhat protected by the bluff as I rested trying to feel the sun's warmth on my face and hands. It wasn't much comfort, but it was some.

I remembered Jake warning that if I didn't catch the thieves by noon this day, I should give up and turn back. The question that nagged me now was whether or not I had enough left to make it back to the camp. I didn't know how far I'd traveled the last twenty-four hours, but considering the pace I'd set or myself, it was a greater disance than what I wanted to think about doing again on foot.

I rolled myself a shuck with the last of my makings and took my time smoking it, enjoying the moment. I didn't know if I'd have that many more moments in this life to enjoy. Being afoot on the frontier, I was at the mercy of just about anyone on a horse, including renegades and road agents. It was damn foolish of me not to have carried more fire power. The thought of carrying that big Creedmore rifle of mine didn't seem like such a burden to me now.

I finished the cigarette and forced myself up the slick rise to the top of the bluff. That's when I saw it: Down below, sat a small weathered cabin with a tin roof that shone dully under the morning light. A crooked stovepipe spewed black smoke. But the thing that really drew my attention was the six horses and one mule bunched together in the corral twenty feet from the cabin. You'd have to be blind not to spot the speckled bird among the bunch.

I dropped to the ground hoping no one inside the cabin had spotted me. There was no way of knowing who, or how many were inside the cabin. Between the bluff and the cabin, there was just a lot of open ground. I thought for a moment about taking my chances trying to cross that coverless patch of ground, but if someone was sitting in the window of the cabin, I'd be a dead man before I made it halfway. I eased myself back below the brow of the bluff and settled in. I thought about what Jake said regarding the patience of Apaches. I wanted to steal back our horses, I'd have to wait until dark to do it.

There is nothing so slow as time when you're just waiting for it to pass. Every few minutes, I'd make my way back to the top of the bluff and check for signs of activity down in the cabin. I remembered the book that Alex Dupage had given me the day I'd left Deadwood. I had carried it in an inside pocket of my coat thinking that someday I'd find time to read it. Now, it looked like that day had come.

It had a soft leather cover and the paper was of good stock, the print on the fly leaf fancy. It felt good just to hold it in my hands, feel its weight, know that I didn't have to spend the day just staring at the sky or over the top of the wind-swept bluff. *Don Quixote.*

I wondered if Señor Quixote was anything like Pancho Vega,

the Mexican bandit I'd shot down in Del Rio. I'd been friends with Pancho Vega up until the evening he became insanely jealous over the affections of a sloe-eyed Mexican whore we both had taken an interest in.

It wasn't one of the proudest things I'd ever done in my life—shooting Pancho Vega. But, Pancho was a man with a wild lust and impatient heart, and sooner or later someone was going to kill him. It just happened to be me. Jealousy has killed a lot of men over the years—Pancho Vega wasn't the first. Still, I'd just as soon it had not happened the way it did. The man was a friend and I've often missed sharing a bottle of mescal and a few good jokes with him under the warm border winds of south Texas.

But it's long been too late for that.

"At a certain Village in La Mancha . . ." The pages were thin, the print small. *". . . there liv'd not long ago one of those old-fashion'd Gentlemen who are never without a Lance upon a Rack, an old Target, a lean Horse, and a Greyhound."*

How many old boys had I known over the years that put all their faith in a good horse and kept a hound for a companion.

Every now and then, I stopped reading long enough to take a peek over the top of the bluff. The sun rose higher in the sky and started to bring with it some real warmth. Along toward noon, the only thing that kept it from being a pleasant day was a cup of coffee and a shuck to go with it. That and nailing those horse thieves down in the cabin.

". . . he very calmly rode on, leaving it to his Horse's Discretion to go which Way he pleas'd . . ."

Well damn, if that hasn't spoken the truth of half my life: drifting wherever my horse wanted to lead me.

Suddenly, I heard a door open and close on a set of rusty hinges. I put the book away and looked over the top of the bluff. I couldn't tell if it was a man or a woman bundled up in heavy clothes carrying a water bucket. I watched as the figure went to a rain barrel at the side of the cabin, shattered the plate of ice formed atop the barrel, and filled the bucket.

Then I watched as the person carried the bucket of rainwater back inside the cabin. A few minutes later, a man came out and raced for the nearby privy. Seconds after that, another man and a boy came out of the cabin and walked to the corral.

From where I was kneeling, they didn't look so much like horse thieves as they did a family of poor squatters.

A few minutes passed while the man and the boy pitched some apples from a bucket over the fence to the horses. The speckled bird was the first one to get in line for the eats, pushing and biting her way to the front.

"Lookit that ugly mare, pa!" the boy shouted. "She the one tried to bite Fester on his arse?" the man laughed. "Yeah son, she nearly did, too. Your uncle Fester jumped three feet high off the ground!"

The man came out of the privy pulling up his galluses and casually strolled over to the corral.

"Teeter asked me if that scratchy mare was the one nearly bit your arse clean off!" the man with the boy said. He wore a floppy-brim hat that fell halfway over his eyes.

"Damn near put a bullet in her ugly hammer head," the man with the galluses said. "I wonder does she like eatin' them winter apples as much as she does humans?" the man with the big hat said with a broad grin. The boy laughed and scratched his haunches. The man with the galluses didn't seem to share in their humor.

A woman came to the door of the cabin and shouted "Biscuits are ready—come eat!"

"You think that mare'd eat a biscuit was we to give her one?" the man with the big hat said to the boy. "I don't know pa, I never heard of no horse that would eat a biscuit." The man pushed back the brim of his floppy hat as he looked at the man with the galluses. "I never heard of no horse at would eat an arse, neither, Teeter!" The man with the galluses said, "Shit! I'm goin' to eat my breakfast!"

Two men a boy and a woman. It made my decision easier.

When I kicked open the door and pointed the self-cocker at the men, the woman said, "Henry, we got company."

12

"Mister, you come to rob us, you rode a long way for nothin'," said the man the woman called Henry. He was still wearing his flop-brimmed hat and I could only see some of his eyes as he tilted his head back.

"Please don't shoot my pa, mister!" the boy cried. His face was peppered with freckles and his front teeth were crooked.

The other man sat there with his palms atop the table, his head half turned as though he was afraid to look at me directly but was still curious to see who had come to rob him.

The woman was moon-faced; her hair was pulled straight back and tied in a bun so tight it looked like it had to hurt. She had small nervous eyes that looked at me like I was just one more problem that had come into her life like the bad weather.

"Henry's serious as the plague," she said. "We ain't got a chamber pot or hardly a window to throw it out of. Can't you see that?"

"I didn't come here to rob anybody," I said. "I came for that speckled horse out in your corral, and the others you stole."

The other man, the one wearing his galluses down, shifted his gaze fully in my direction. His left eye turned inward toward his nose. He was holding his fork wrapped in his fist, a piece of ham speared on the tines.

"Fraid not, mister. Didn't steal them animals, bought 'em."

I looked at the woman, then at the two men.

"Like she said, don't look like you have a pot. I'd be curious as to how you bought a pair of good horses and a sound pack mule."

"Bought 'em for a jug of likker, a sack full of corn dodgers, and a pair of blankets. At's how," the man with the bad eye said. The piece of ham on the end of his fork dripped grease onto the table.

"I walked a long way to get those animals back," I said. "Lies are the last thing I want to hear right now."

"He's tellin' you the truth," the woman said. "Christ if he ain't."

"Stealing horses is a hanging offense," I said. "I was to hang you boys, wouldn't anyone blame me." I was mad enough to hang them, but I'd settle for them owning up to it and being men about giving me the courtesy of the truth.

"Well, you can hang Fester there," the woman said. "He ain't much good fer nothin', 'cept eatin' and layin' round sippin' likker. So him, I don't mind so much you hangin'—though he didn't steal them horses or that mule, neither."

"Shut yer' trap, Sis!" the man with the galluses and bad eye cawed.

"Henry," she continued, ignoring the man, "me and him's wed. You was to hang him, you'd be leavin' me a widow, and this young'n and orphan. I won't sit here an' swear to you he ain't never done nothin' wrong in his day, but he's tellin' the truth about tradin' dodgers and blankets fer them animals."

My gaze switched the boy. He nodded, swallowed hard.

"Swear to God, mister."

"Renegades," I said. "Is that what they were—the ones who traded horses for a meal of corn dodgers and whiskey and a pair of blankets?"

The man wearing the hat shook his head causing the brim to flap up and down.

"Wan't no Injins. It was a big black cuss and a little scrawny colored gel. Come through late last evenin' leadin' them horses and that mule. Said he'd trade 'em fer somethin' to drink and somethin' to eat and somethin' to keep warm with. I looked at those horses and said to myself, This ol' boy's either crazy or desperate. Hell, I seen me a deal and took it. Wouldn't you?''

"If I hang you from that tree out yonder," I said, "I guess it might not be as good a deal as you figured on."

"I guess not," the man said, then swallowed.

The woman said, "Ain't I always said little comes of little, Henry?''

"Yes you have, Minnie. But I thought this was one of those times when some good fortune had fell my way." She crossed her arms and stared at him.

I looked at the man with the bad eye.

"You want to go out and tie a rope around those horses and that mule and bring them around?''

He shifted his weight in the chair.

"I'm still thinking about hanging you," I said. "Hanging you wouldn't leave this woman a widow nor that boy an orphan, but it might just make me feel better for the long walk I've had."

He pushed himself away from the table, gave the woman a hard look. Then he stood and pulled up his galluses with a hard snap over each shoulder and went outside.

"You want somethin' to eat, mister?" the woman asked. "You look gant."

I shoved the self-cocker back into the cross-draw holster I wore on my left hip and sat down.

"Some of those corn dodgers and that ham and maybe a little of that coffee," I said. She gave her man a look and he gave her one back that told her to go ahead and fix a plate. I kept my eyes on the man and the boy until she brought me the food.

"Got no sugar fer yer coffee," she said. "Sugar costs money."

"I can do without sugar in my coffee," I said, trying hard not to cram the food into my mouth all at once. The ham was salty and the dodgers hard and the coffee hot and tasteless, but it was one of the best meals I'd eaten in a while and it kept my spirit from departing to the hereafter, and for that I was ever grateful.

By the time I finished the coffee, Bad-eye stepped back into the cabin. His face was red from the raw wind, and no doubt the effort of trying to put a rope around the speckled bird while at the same time trying to keep her from taking a bite out of him.

"Your hosses is ready," he said unhappily as he walked over and stood in front of the cookstove and rubbed the palms of his hands together.

"Did that mare try and bite you on the arse again, Fester?" the man wearing the hat said trying hard to keep any sign of a smile off his face.

The man, Fester, never took his bad eye from me.

"Don't know why anybody'd want to steal that ill-tempered ol' cayuse anyhow," he grumbled. "An' don't know why a man'd walk all the way out here in the toolies to get her back, neither!"

"There's just some things that can't be explained," I said. "Which way did the colored man and the girl go when they left here?"

"Couldn't say," the man wearing the hat said.

"Why not?"

"It was dark."

"It wasn't that dark, besides, there was a moon out. Moon on snow," I said. "Easy for a man to see which way the man and girl were headed."

"They went south, mister," the woman said, chewing a piece of ham. "Henry and Fester feels like its a wrong thing to do, give up a man at's on the dodge. But not me. I don't want no horse thieves or cutthroats hangin' around here nohow. They went south!"

I started to leave.

"That buck," the man Henry said. "He wan't no common thief. Treated that gel special, took good care of her. Christ, his hands was bleeding from the cold! I guess if he wanted to, he could've raised all sorts of hell round here. But he didn't. He just took them corn dodgers and that jug and blankets and thanked us for 'em and went on his way.''

"Well, that makes me feel a whole lot better," I said, with no effort at hiding my sarcasm. "The fact that he stole my horse and traded it for some damn corn dodgers!''

The boy rolled his eyes and giggled and the woman tossed him a hard look.

"What's south of here?" I asked.

The woman's husband, spat and said, "Canyons, rocks, and one little ol' town called, Buffalo Tongue. It ain't much, but it's got a whore stands over six feet tall and a one-eyed lawman named Billy Dogget. The thing they say about going to Buffalo Tongue is, if one don't get you, the other will.''

"Have a good day," I said. "And next time you think fortune has smiled on you, ask for sale papers. It might save you from getting hanged.''

"I'll do it," the woman said, "even if Henry and Fester is too lazy to ask.''

Fester kept his bad eye on me while I put a foot in the stirrup and swung aboard the speckled bird.

"At's one bad-blooded hoss, mister. Someday you might regret having walked all this way just to get her back.''

I turned the bird's head without bothering to look back. I figured with the way she could eat up ground, I'd be back in camp before midnight. It felt good not to have to walk, not to have to face the prospect of it.

The thing that bothered me though, was just how easy Elijah Hook had come into camp and stolen our animals. He could just as easily slit our throats or fired a bullet into our brains.

The question was: Why hadn't he?

13

"Well, I see you found my horse and mule," Jake said as I rode into camp. "But why'd you have to bring that snapping turtle you call a horse back with you? Couldn't you've swapped her for something that was better natured?"

I ignored Jake's comments and went directly to the fire and poured myself some coffee. "You have any tobacco?" I asked.

When he lent me his makings, I rolled a cigarette and said, "You'll never guess who stole our horses."

"Who?"

"Hook."

Jake looked like I'd hit him between the eyes.

"That's one bodacious sonofabitch, then!" he declared.

"I don't know if we're chasing him, or he's chasing us—but I do know I'm getting tired of playing these games with him." The coffee tasted dark and bitter like it had been brewing over the fire for a long time.

Jonas Fly walked into the light of the campfire.

"Here," he said, handing me a plate of beans and a large roasted turkey leg. "Mr. True shot a wild turkey this afternoon. I'm not much of a cook, but I did the best I could."

"Hook's got at least a two day jump on us," Jake said.

Then shifting his gaze to the surrounding darkness, "Unless he happens to be sitting out there right now watching us, that is. You think maybe he could be out there somewheres, Quint?"

"Well if he's not, I know where he might be headed," I said. "This is wonderful turkey, Mr. Fly."

"Thank you sir, I did the best I could under these crude conditions."

"Where's he headed?" Jake asked.

"South, and the nearest town that direction is a place called Buffalo Tongue. I figure from the condition he and the girl are reported to be in, they'll have to stop there and get resupplied."

"We'll be slowed down if we have to hitch up the horses to Fly's wagon," Jake said.

"Jake." The look on Jonas Fly's face said it all.

"I know, we can't just leave him here," Jake said.

Fly looked relieved.

"We can start tonight," I said.

The speckled bird was not too happy about being hitched to the wagon and she tried to bite Jake and me several times in the process of putting the harness on her. But she had to learn that if she was to remain my horse, she'd do what I asked of her. And once hitched, she got along just fine.

We rode throughout the night. I snatched a few hours rest in the back of the wagon, while Jake and Fly rode up front. It was the first real sleep I'd had in the last thirty-six hours, and even at that, it was a fitful sleep, full of dreams that made little sense. In one dream, I dreamt of Pancho Vega. In the dream, he and Etta Landrow were riding a white horse across a shallow river while I stood on shore and watched. The water splashed up around them like handfuls of diamonds tossed against the sun while Pancho grinned through his dark moustaches and Etta clung to him tightly. It gave me a sad feeling, like I was losing both of them and would never see them again. I awoke feeling sad lying in the back of the wagon alone like that.

We reached Buffalo Tongue late in the afternoon of the following day.

It was a squalid collection of log huts and whiskey tents grown up either side of a wide muddy street. Judging by the size, there were maybe three or four hundred souls living in Buffalo Tongue. How they got there and why they stayed was another question.

It didn't take us long to see or smell how the town had come by its name. Just as we rode up to the first set of buildings, there was a twenty foot high mound of buffalo bones: skulls, ribs, and leg bones large enough to cover an entire a city lot.

"My word!" Jonas Fly said. "It looks as though every one of the great beasts that ever roamed the plains has ended up here."

"What in the hell would they want to collect buffalo bones for?" Jake asked.

I'd noticed a railroad spur line running just north of the pile of bones.

"No doubt a shipping point," I said.

Fly was looking hopeful as we pulled into the heart of the town itself.

"I see a great opportunity here for my patent medicines," he said. "I have been in outposts such as this before. There hardly ever is a physician or an infirmary to be had. The poor residents are at the suffering of just about every sort of illness and malady. Dropsy, female problems, memory loss, stuttering, melancholy, unwanted hair and digestive interference, just to name the more common ills. Yes indeed! I should be able to sell enough medicines and bitters here to buy myself a new mule and perhaps even a suit of clothes."

The little man was alive with excitement over his prospects.

"I wish you well, Doc," Jake said. "This place looks like it could use all the patent medicines you got and then some. Your medicines might be the only thing that could save a place like this. That, or be burnt plum to the ground."

"Let's look up the local law," I suggested. "If Hook and Sugar Brown did pass through here, maybe the law would know about it."

We stopped a fat woman with a fat youngster in tow and asked her if she knew where the city marshal's office was.

"Try looking in the beds of harlots or in the bottom of the nearest whiskey bottle!" she said, her voice full of scorn. "That is where you will most likely find Marshal Dogget!'' Then she stamped away, pulling the youngster behind her as she went.

"Well, that is sure some clue," Jake grumbled. "I'm ready for a drink of liquor myself."

"Why don't you see if you can find a livery, Mr. Fly," I suggested to Jonas, "and see if they have a healthy mule to sell you. I'll swing by later and unhitch the speckled bird."

"Thank you gentlemen for your kindness in bringing me out of the wilderness. Who knows what may have become of me if the two of you had not come along."

"Just make sure before you buy another mule," Jake said, "that he ain't colicky, or you might end up stranded again and not be so lucky that two fine gents like me and Mac will come along and save you."

"I will, sir. Indeed I will."

We went inside the nearest saloon and went straight to the bar. Jake ordered whiskey, I settled for a glass of beer.

"Where's your city marshal?" Jake asked the barman.

"Dog?" the man said.

"That what you call him, Dog?" Jake asked.

"His name's Dogget," the man said. "But everyone calls him Dog."

"Well then where's, Dog?"

"Don't know, not right this minute I don't," the man said.

"Where's he usually?" I asked.

"Usually, he's either gambling or spending his time with Miss Valdalia Rose."

"Miss Valdalia Rose?" Jake said, pricking up his ears; women and whiskey always made Jake's ears prick up at the mention of them.

The man nodded; he had a large nose, fat on the end, full of black pores.

"Yessir, gents! Valdalia Rose, tallest whore west of the Mississippi!" the man declared.

"How would you know she's the tallest whore?" Jake asked. "You met all the whores west of the Mississippi?"

"No, but I've met Miss Valdalia Rose and she's taller than

any whore I ever seen," the man argued. "She's taller than most men I ever seen. Except for Bigfoot Blanchard."

"Who's Bigfoot Blanchard?"

"Man I knew back in Blue Lick, Kentucky."

"Oh," Jake said, as though that were enough to satisfy his curiosity. Then tapping his glass atop the bar, he said. "Give us another." And when the man poured him out two more fingers worth of whiskey, Jake looked him straight in the eyes and said, "I'll bet there's at least one whore west of the Mississippi that is taller than the one you got here in this town."

"I'd like to see her if there was," the man said.

"Look," I said, before Jake and the man could get into a full-blown argument about who was the tallest whore in the West. "We want to find this Marshal Dogget and talk to him. And if he is with this Valdalia Rose, we want to find her. Can you tell us where she does her business from?"

The man said, "Sure. Back on Revelation Alley. Go out the door, turn down Laredo Street, cross the spur line, and you're there—Revelation Alley. Can't miss it because the air smells like perfume."

"Which place is hers?"

"First red light you come to," the man said.

"Let's go, Jake."

"What's that awful stink?" Jake said, once we stepped back outside.

"Hides," I said. "Buffalo hides. I saw them right after I saw the pile of bones. This must be a northern terminus to ship the hides from. Did you notice that rail spur?"

"That's what I thought it was," Jake said, wrinkling his nose. "Nothing stinks worse than a pile of buffalo hides, unless it would be a roomful of buffalo hunters."

We followed the barman's directions, turned down Laredo Street and crossed the tracks and came to a row of crib houses with red lights in the windows. Jake sniffed the air and declared that he didn't smell anything but the stink of buffalo hides.

"I reckon that barman don't know the difference between perfume and rotting hides!" Jake said, irritably.

I knocked on the first door we came to then waited and

knocked a second time. Finally the door opened and a tall, big-boned woman stood in the frame.

"You gents come right in," she said. She wore a faded silk rose in her hair.

"You the one they call Miss Valdalia Rose?" Jake asked.

"I'm her, honey—the one and only! You all want to go at it together, or just one at a time? Two at a time costs more but twice the fun, don't you know!"

"We didn't come here for that," Jake said.

"Well, then what did you come for?" Vadalia Rose said. " 'Cause *that's* what I do, I don't do nothing else but *that!*"

"We're looking for the city marshal," I said.

"Dog?"

"Yeah, Dog."

"Dog ain't here," she said. "I ain't seen Dog since early this morning when he was trying to pull his pants on over his poor sore little pecker." She laughed until you could see her back teeth.

"Do you know where he might be now?" I asked.

"Well, if he ain't with me, he's usually over to the Red Beaver playing with the pasteboards, honey. You all sure you don't want to come in? I can give you a group discount, even if you do just want to go one at a time. Sunday mornings is slow around here."

"Group discount?" Jake said.

"Don't even think about it, Jake. We've got business to attend to," I warned him.

"Maybe some other time," Jake said making sure he got an eyeful before leaving.

"No time like the present," she said with a wink.

As Jake and I walked back to the center of town, Jake said, "You know, if you weren't so damn impatient, I could have screwed the tallest whore west of the Mississippi."

"How do you know she's the tallest?" I said.

"I don't, but who's to say she's not?"

"You are sometimes too easily distracted," I said.

"Well a tall gal like that is something that don't come along every day," Jake muttered. "Or every other day for that matter."

We found the Red Beaver.

"That must be him," I said to Jake pointing toward a table of men, one of which was wearing a patch over his left eye.

"How do you know that?"

"Because I was told by the man I got our horses back from that the lawman here was a one-eyed man. I don't see any other one-eyed men in here, do you?"

"Let's go ask him."

"You Marshal Dogget?" Jake said as soon as the last hand was finished being played and before the next one could be dealt.

The man looked up. He had a broad, deeply lined face and one glassy blue eye shining forth, with a heavy black patch over the other.

"Who's askin'?" His voice sounded like ground glass.

"We are," Jake said.

"Who is we?"

Jake looked at me and said, "Nobody gives an answer to a question in this town. Everybody always asks a question to a question."

Dogget had a cud in his cheek; now he took the opportunity to lean and spit into a coffee can near his feet. Then he straightened and stared some more with his one blue eye.

"We're looking for a man," I said. "A black man. He's got a young colored girl with him."

"And I'm looking for an inside straight," Dogget growled. "Everybody's looking for something."

"Why does this have to be hard, marshal?"

"You in or out, Dog?" the dealer asked, holding a worn deck of cards in his left hand and staring at the kitty.

"Deal!" Dogget said. "I didn't come here to chat about darkies."

"This man were looking for," Jake said. "He's killed some folks, and he might kill some more. If he's come this way, he might just kill some folks right here in your town. That any concern to you?"

Dogget's one blue eye moved from the cards dealt in front of him to Jake.

"You're interrupting my game!"

Before I could stop him, Jake pulled one of his ivory-handled Colts at the same instant he stepped next to Marshal Dogget and placed the muzzle against his ear.

"I don't know what makes a man like you hard to get along with," Jake said. "Maybe it's 'cause you lost an eye. Or maybe it's 'cause your girlfriend is so tall. Or maybe, it's just because you are a no-good sonofabitch! But one way or the other, you're going to say whether or not you've seen a black man with a young gal come through here!"

I saw one of the players slip his hand below the table.

"Don't!" I ordered. "This doesn't have to get bloody unless you want it to!" His hand came back up and rested atop the table.

Dogget had lost some of his color.

"Ain't seen no darkies through here . . . lately!" Dogget managed to say.

"You sure about that?" Jake said. "Because the word I got is, that this fellow we're looking for was headed this way. Now how could he be headed this way, and not come through here?"

"Don't you think if I'd seen him, I would have noticed?" Dogget uttered, his voice rising as Jake wormed the barrel of his revolver a little farther into Dogget's ear.

"Let him go, Jake. I don't think he has seen Hook."

Jake reached inside the man's coat and brought out a policeman's model Colt pistol and held it in his left hand before letting the hammer down on his ivory-handle Colt Peacemaker.

"This is a nasty little piece of iron," Jake said as he bucked open the cylinder of the smaller gun and let the shells spill to the floor. "Good for shooting men in their spleens, I suppose!"

Dogget looked mad enough to chew nails, his blue eye was fixed and glaring.

Jake and I backed out of the room.

"What the hell was that all about?" I asked as soon as we were outside. Jake dropped Dogget's pistol in a water trough.

"My patience is running low," Jake said. "I was hoping

this would be the place we'd catch Hook. Hell, it don't sound like he's even passed through here. What with the snow covering his tracks, he could be anywhere. Behind us, in front of us, who knows? On top of which, my head hurts and my feet ache. How come that black rascal can find us whenever he wants, but we can't find him?''

"He's smart, for one thing," I said. "That's the worst of it, that he's smart.''

Jake shook his head and muttered, "Smart killers and tall whores. I thought I'd seen and heard everything. I guess I ain't.''

"I'm going down to the livery and unhitch my horse," I said.

"You'd be best off to let Mr. Fly keep that ornery beast," Jake said, "and go buy yourself another.''

"I spent the last good money I had on that horse. I guess she'll have to do.''

"A fool and his money are soon parted," Jake said, sourly. "I'm going to see about buying a few extra supplies.''

I told Jake I'd meet with him in twenty minutes in front of the livery. "Yeah, yeah," he said and went off down the street.

I found Jonas dickering with the stable man over a jack mule. The man wanted forty dollars.

"But how do I know your mule is not colicky?" Jonas was asking him.

"You can see he ain't," the man insisted. "Look at how clear his eyes are. A colicky mule don't have clear eyes. They're like children—when they get sick, their eyes get cloudy. Look at his eyes, mister!''

I checked out the mule and found it to be sound. I told Jonas to offer the man thirty dollars for the mule. The man had black chin whiskers which he pulled on as he walked around in small circles contemplating the offered price.

"Thirty dollars is less than I wanted," the man said.

"I'll throw in a bottle of my Joint Fever Medicine," Jonas said.

"But I don't have no joint fever," the man declared.

"You might some day," Jonas said, "living up here in this cold climate. And if you do, you'll wish you had the medicine."

The man seemed to consider the possibility that someday he might come down with joint fever and need a bottle of the medicine.

"It's awful painful," Jonas added, "joint fever is."

"Okay," the man said. "But I want two bottles of that fever medicine, not just one."

"Why two bottles?" Jonas asked.

"Case my wife was to come down with joint fever too."

They agreed and shook hands. I unhitched the speckled bird from the wagon; she looked grateful and snorted.

"Well, I guess that's it," I said to Jonas, offering my hand. He seemed as grateful as the bird.

"I think I can earn enough money here to get me to Texas," Jonas said.

"Why Texas?" I asked.

He smiled and said, "I hear there is a lot of dropsy in Texas."

"Well, I wish you well, Mr. Fly. I think you have bought yourself a good mule this time." He looked very pleased with the mule.

"Wait," he said, as I took my saddle from the back of the wagon and put it on the speckled bird. Jonas walked over and handed me a small brown bottle. "Give this to Mr. True," he said. "It'll help relieve the pain in his feet."

"I'm sure he'll appreciate it," I said, and slipped it into my pocket.

"Maybe we'll run into each other again sometime," Jonas said with a wave as I mounted the bird and brought her head around.

"You never know what the future might hold, Mr. Fly," I said, and headed down the street to find Jake rather than hang around waiting for him to find me.

"That's right," I heard Jonas say as I rode away. "You never know what the future *does* hold."

I rode past the dry goods store, saw a *Closed* sign in the window. Jake's horse and mule weren't out front, either. I thought of where he could have gone. I figured maybe to one of the saloons. I rode up the main street looking for his animals without luck.

Then I thought of the one other place he might have gone: Miss Valdalia Rose's.

It was just before I heard the gunshots from over across the tracks where the red lights hung in the doorways and windows.

14

There were three shots, then two more. The bird was skittish about stepping across the tracks; the sudden gunfire made her even more skittish, but I spurred her across.

Miss Valdalia Rose came running out the front door clutching her side just as I reached Revelation Alley.

"I've been shot! I've been shot!" she cried, a red stain flowering her yellow dress just below the arm.

"Who?" I shouted, dismounting the bird and drawing the self cocker at the same time.

"Dog! Dog and that other man!" She sat straight down on the sidewalk, her lower lip quivering. "Oh lordy, I've been shot!"

I took a quick look; the bullet had scored a red path through the ample flesh but had done no real damage other than ruining her dress. She was lucky.

"It's not as bad as you think," I said.

"Will I die?" she squealed, her face crumpled under tears and black eye shadow.

"Someday you will," I said. "But not from that scratch." She blew a hot breath of relief and touched the back of her wrist to her forehead as she examined the flesh wound.

Then Jake came through the front door. His shirttail was out and his hat was missing, and he was limping.

Before I could say anything, he said, "Dog came in and started shooting up the place. I killed him!"

"Ten minutes alone and this is what happens?" I said.

"It wasn't the reason I came here," he said. "Not to get shot. I can't help it that Johnny Law was a jealous man."

"I don't know why that would surprise you," I said.

Jake looked at Valdalia Rose and said, "You all right, sweets?"

She squinted through tear-stained eyes and said, "No thanks to you!"

"He shot me in the hip," Jake said, calmly looking down at a bloody patch near his front pocket. "I think the bullet's still in there smashed flat against the bone. Least it feels that way."

I went inside Valdalia's crib and followed a narrow hallway to a back bedroom. There was city marshal Dogget lying across the bed, face up, his one blue eye staring at the ceiling. He had a neat dark hole directly in the middle of his forehead. A halo of bright red blood soaked the sheets beneath him. A Smith & Wesson .44–40 hung from the forefinger of his right hand. It wasn't the same pocket pistol Jake had taken off him earlier and dropped in the water trough. I guess, like most men his type, he owned more than one pistol.

I went back outside.

"He's dead," I confirmed.

"I'm not surprised, Jake said. "Never knew anyone that could survive a bullet through the brain."

"You should have known a thing like this might happen, Jake."

"It all sort of went off at once," Jake said, taking his bandanna from around his neck and plugging the hole in his hip with it.

"Me and Miss Valdalia Rose was just getting around to negotiating a fair price for her services when Dogget showed up waving a big six-shooter. She tried to calm him down, but he wasn't having any of it. He went into a rage, cussing and swearing oaths. I was trying to get my guns when he shot me. He would most likely have killed me except some of his loads were bad and didn't fire off. I got my iron and put a round in him. But not before he jumped out of the way of the first one. I got Dogget with the second round. Wonder we weren't both killed."

Jake paused long enough to look at Valdalia Rose.

"You know I didn't mean to shoot you," he said.

She tried hard to smile, but her heart wasn't fully in it.

"I've been done every way a man can do a woman," she muttered, "but you are the first man to shoot a hole through me."

"Accident, hon." Jake looked sheepish.

"She'll live," I said to Jake. "But you might not if Dogget's friends get a lynch party together and hang you."

"We better git," Jake said. "Though I don't think I can sit a horse with my shot hip."

"Grip onto the horn of my saddle," I said, taking the reins and leading Jake and the speckled bird down a back street.

"You expect me to walk to the next town?" Jake said. "If so, just leave me here where I am and I'll take my chances. This damn hip of mine hurts too much!"

"Not to the next town," I said. "Just till we clear the main section. And stop your complaining!"

Jake limped alongside the bird, holding onto the saddle horn, as I led them through the back streets and alleys of Buffalo Tongue. I finally got us to the place I wanted to be: Jonas fly's medicine wagon. It was parked out front of a saloon called THE GOODNIGHT CATTLEMAN'S CLUB.

I opened the rear door of the wagon and told Jake to crawl inside. And when he didn't move fast enough, I shoved him the rest of the way in.

"Stay there and be quiet until I come for you," I told him.

"What about my hip?"

"Drink some of that Jonas's bitters," I said. "Hell, drink all of it if it will keep you from complaining."

I closed the door before Jake could drag me into a long

conversation that would end up going nowhere. A tendency the man had.

Jonas was inside the saloon passing out flyers advertising his patent medicines and his gift for reading heads.

"Big medicine show tomorrow ladies and gents!" he was announcing as he handed out the flyers. "Come and learn about the miraculous benefits of Dr. Fly's Patent Medicines. You gentlemen who are experiencing waning desire for your wives. You women who wish to rid yourselves of unwanted hair! Hear handwritten testimony from former suffers of such troublesome and disturbing ailments as the rickets, dyspepsia, constipation and catarrh—all cured with just a few doses of FLY'S MIRA-CLE CURE!

Jonas was laying it on thick and the crowd was eager to have their internal organs invigorated and their sex lives rejuvenated judging by the way they were snapping up the flyers.

"What time tomorrow you having this medicine show, Doc?" a toothless man with a bent back asked. "Couldn't I just buy one bottle tonight? My back hurts like the dickens!"

"Noon, my dear sir—be there! No early sales! I only have a limited supply of these fine patent medicines ladies and gentlemen, and they will be sold on a first-come-first-served basis. Do not miss out on this golden opportunity! And for those who would like to see into the future, I will be doing readings of the head as well."

Jonas had them champing at the bit to buy his patent medicines and get their skulls read. Hell, after listening to him, I was ready to buy a bottle of the stuff myself. It was hard to believe that this was the same frightened little man Jake and I had found sitting on a dead mule in the middle of nowhere looking so forlorn. But, he was in his element now.

"Jonas!" I said as soon as he had passed out his last flyer.

"Mr. McCannon! What a surprise to see you! I thought you and Mr. True would have left town by now."

"We would have, Jonas, but there's been some trouble."

"Oh dear!"

"I need your help—Jake and me both do."

"Yes, yes, anything. What can I do?"

I walked him outside where we had some privacy to talk.

"Jake's inside your wagon, Jonas. He's been shot."

Jonas's eyes jerked at hearing the news.

"Shouldn't we find him a doctor?"

"If this was any other place or time, we would. But in this case, not wise. Jake has shot and killed the city marshal."

Jonas pursed his lips, but instead of saying anything, he simply whistled.

I saw a group of armed men crossing the far end of the street, heading for the red light district. They were carrying torches that bobbed like lanterns on a black sea.

"I think those may be some of Dogget's pals," I said, lowering my voice as I led Jonas over closer to the wagon. "Once Valdalia Rose tells them what happened, they'll be looking to invite Jake to a necktie party."

"Fact?" Jonas said.

"Fact. Even a hardcase like Dogget has his friends. It doesn't help any that he was the town's lawman. That alone will get you hanged in nine places out of ten."

"What shall we do?" Jonas said.

"We need to clear country, Jonas. Now."

Jonas was eager to help, but I had to be honest with him about the price he might have to pay for his loyalty.

"If they do find Jake in the back of your wagon, Jonas, they'll be in the mood to hang you as well."

He looked at me with mournful eyes.

"He saved my life, as did you, sir. What sort of man would I be if I did not try and repay the debt?"

"Just wanted you to be aware of the consequences, Jonas."

"Well aware, I am," he said.

"I'm going to lead that lynch party on a little bit of a chase, Jonas. I want you to take the south road and keep going. I'll catch up with you later."

I climbed aboard the speckled bird and put her into a dog trot down toward the tracks and the red light district.

I came close enough to see the torches had stopped in front of Valdalia Rose's crib. I heard the sputtering details of how she and her lover had been shot by Jake; how it was she who had tried to defend Marshal Dogget. Then she cut loose a wail like a scalded cat and every last man in that drunken crowd was ready to take up the cause and defend her honor and avenge the death of their amigo.

She gave a performance that would have caused Billy Cody to sign her to a stage contract.

I fired my self-cocker into the air and shouted: "I'm here for any son of a bitch that wants to hang me!" and made a big show of it by firing one or two more rounds as I jumped the bird across the tracks all the while praying a wild round from one of the rifles wouldn't find me in the darkness and split my skull open. But by the time the lynch party did open fire, I was already gone.

I knew any of them that was determined would first have to hoof it back to their horses before they could give chase. I was more worried the bird would step into a gopher hole than I was of anyone catching me.

I knew a kid on the Bandera Trail who broke his neck when he was pitched from his cow pony during a midnight stampede. I remember at the time thinking it wasn't a way I'd care to die. I was still thinking that as I rode out a mile from town and slowed the bird to and easy lope.

I got far enough away that the lights of the town looked no bigger than stars lying on the ground and I reined up long enough to listen for voices or the thunder of hooves behind me. There wasn't any, so I rolled a shuck and lit it and kept moving.

The bird seemed to know she had the game beat and just set herself into an easy rhythm, like sitting on a rocking chair is what it felt like.

She was the best thirty-dollar horse I ever knew.

I figured to ride a wide loop around the town and catch up with Jonas and the medicine wagon in a few hours. A fresh snow began falling sometime shortly after the lights of the town faded out of sight. I stayed to my plan and rode until nearly dawn before realizing something wasn't right; I still hadn't cut sign of Jonas's wagon. I considered it a possibility that I'd ridden a smaller loop around the town then I'd intended and they were still ahead of me. The snow would have covered whatever tracks they might have left.

Still, it didn't feel right. I traveled several more miles without coming on them. Then another thought came to mind; one not as acceptable as the first: I wondered if it was possible that a second lynch party had followed them from town and caught up with them. It didn't seem likely, but I couldn't take the chance. If Jonas and his wagon were not ahead of me, then they had to be somewhere behind me. I turned the bird back toward town.

I didn't make it back to Buffalo Tongue before I found the wagon. Jonas's new mule was gone, and so was he. I found Jake tied to one of the wheels. He looked half frozen with the snow clinging to his beard and eyelashes. His flesh was as pale as moonlight.

I considered the strong possibility he was dead. I dismounted and knelt in front of him and tapped him on the cheeks.

"Jake!"

He didn't move at first and when I tried to untie his wrists, he moaned.

"Easy! My limbs is froze. You move 'em . . . too fast . . . they're liable to just break clean off!" His face knotted up in pain and he said, "I'm about to piss my britches from being so cold!"

"Where's Jonas?" I asked.

Jake groaned when I tried to lift him.

"My hip! Is it still there?"

"Jonas!" I said again. "What happened to him?"

"You ain't . . . gonna believe . . . Mac! You ain't . . . gonna believe!" Jake was chattering so hard I thought his teeth would chip off.

"Believe what, Jake? What is it I'm not going to believe?"

15

I helped Jake back inside the wagon and warmed him with
blankets until the color came back into his face and he could
stop his teeth from knocking together long enough to tell me
what had happened.

"We were going along just fine," Jake said. "Then all of
a sudden, I feel the wagon stop and I hear some voices outside.
I figured it to be a lynch party. But before I could look out and
see who it was, the back door throws open and standing there
big as you please is, Elijah Hook! His face looked like a black
moon and he was pointing the biggest damn Sharps buffalo
gun at me I ever seen."

Jake motioned toward one of the bottles Jonas kept in a
wooden crate.

"You mind?"

I pulled the cork on one and gave it to him. He took a good
swallow then leaned back again.

"Damn if this ain't the coldest I ever been." Then he took
another drink and licked the dew from his lips.

"I looked him straight in his goddamn eye and said, You
are just the man I'm looking for. You might just as well put
that big fifty down and give yourself up."

"Well, that must have made him sweat like hell, Jake."

"It was worth a try, Mac."

"I take it he didn't abide by your order," I said.

"He laughed is what he did and said, mister, why you trying to catch me anyway? I told him why. Then he laughed some more and said, 'First off, ain't nobody can catch Elijah Hook if'n he don't want to be caught. Second, I ain't never kilt no innocent men, so I ain't guilty of nothing.' And third, if I was ever planning on killing a man, you just might be the first, the way you been houndin' me around.'"

Jake shook his head.

"I came close, Mac, I could see it in his eyes. All he had to do was pull the trigger and I'd have been dog scraps."

"Why didn't he?"

"That's a hell of a good question, why didn't he," Jake said. "Instead, he just made me get out of the wagon so he could tie me to the wheel. Maybe he thought it would be more painful for me to freeze to death than to eat a bullet!"

"What about Jonas?" I asked. "What happened to Jonas?"

"They took him, Mac. Hook and that young whore, Sugar Brown. They unhitched the mule and set him on it and took him."

"Hostage?" I said.

"Most likely."

"Doesn't make sense, Jake."

"It might not," Jake said. "But what does anymore?"

Jake sipped some more from the bottle.

"What now?" he asked.

"Well, I can't go after them and just leave you here," I said. "The nearest town that's safe for me to take you to is back to Cheyenne. I figure it to be about a hundred miles from here."

"Ain't that where we started from in the first place?" Jake asked. "Or am I confused?"

"You have a better idea, Jake?"

"This has been a long haul for nothing," he grumbled.

"Is it just the pain in your hip," I asked, "or have you gone back to complaining just for complaining's sake?"

"We've been defeated," Jake said, sourly. "Been beat by a damn killer and a lovesick whore!"

"You want me to take you back to Cheyenne, or leave you here?"

He was still muttering when I went around to the front of the wagon. I walked over to the bird and said, "You're not going to like this very much," then took her saddle off and hitched her to the wagon. She rolled back her eyes as I hitched her in the traces.

Jake was right, I thought, as I tied my saddle to the top of the wagon and took up the reins. We had been defeated by the killer and it wasn't setting with me any better than it was with him. I climbed down from the wagon seat and went around to back again and opened the door.

"What now?" Jake said.

"Toss me a bottle of that cure-all," I said. "I think I'm going to need it.

It took us three days to arrive back in Cheyenne. To our good fortune the weather had cleared and Jake had not bled to death. Although, he wasn't in the best shape by the time we reached the town's limits.

Dave Beltrain and Long Bill Longly and the other deputy were walking past Little Dick's Cafe when I drove the wagon up.

"You take up a new profession?" Beltrain called. "Peddling snake oil?" Longly and the other man seemed to enjoy Beltrain's humor the way dull men will enjoy something stupid. I continued on down the street without bothering to acknowledge the jibes of the Cheyenne's police force.

I pulled up in front of Doc Price's house and climbed down from the wagon. I helped Jake out of the back; he was thoroughly intoxicated, lying among several empty bottles of Fly's Patent Medicines and unhappy about having to move.

"Well, at least you didn't suffer," I said, as I helped him out of the wagon.

"I suffered aplenty," Jake muttered. "In ways you wouldn't understand. Did you miss any damn big rocks on the way here that we ought to go back and run over again?"

"I can see that Fly's medicines are good for everything but good temperament," I said, as I helped him up the steps to Doc's front door.

Doc answered my knock. He was wiping his hands on a towel.

He looked first at Jake, then at me.

"Is it your mission in life to bring me every shot-up son of a bitch in the territory?" he asked.

"Just the one's who can't defend themselves, Doc. Where do you want me to put him?"

Doc directed me to the same back room and table where he had taken the young Mexican gravedigger that Long Bill had shot over a ten cent beer.

"How did that kid make out?" I asked Doc as we put Jake up on the table and began stripping off his boots and pants.

"He's alive, but he'll be a cripple the rest of his life," Doc said. "Did you shoot yourself in the hip, or did someone do it for you?" he asked Jake.

Jake looked at him through unsteady eyes.

"What does it look like?"

"A man in your condition, I wouldn't be surprised you shot yourself. It happens all the time. Only most of you drunkards shoot yourself in the foot, or shoot your peckers off trying to show what a fast-draw artist you are with a gun. It takes a special talent to be able to shoot yourself squarely in the hip."

"I didn't shoot myself in the hip or the foot, or no where else for that matter!" Jake declared. "Someone else did it for me!"

"Why doesn't that surprise me?" Doc said. "A man with your disposition. Now just shut up for a minute and let me see what we have here."

Jake looked at me and said, "All the places in the territory, you had to bring me here?" Doc did something with his metal probe that made Jake yelp.

"If you cannot be quiet and remain still," Doc warned—"then this is going to end up hurting a lot more than it has to."

"I'll be back later," I said.

"Don't bring me anymore patients," Doc called as I headed for the front door. "Especially grumpy ones!"

I walked down the street to Klingbill's Funeral Parlor. Claude Klingbill was sitting at an expansive oak desk with a pile of papers in front of him. He wore gold-rim spectacles that were perched on the bridge his bony nose. He looked up when I entered.

"McCannon," he said. "Your's was a short trip. Were you able to find Ben's killer?"

"Not yet," I said. "We ran into some bad luck."

He looked disappointed, removed the spectacles and pinched the place on his nose where they had been resting.

"That's too bad. I was hoping for justice to be done."

"It will be," I said. "It's just going to take a little longer than planned."

"Can I get you something, a drink perhaps?"

"Coffee if you have it," I said.

"I keep some going," he said. "Back here."

We went to a rear apartment that had a bed and a potbelly stove throwing off heat. Klingbill took a tin cup from a hook and poured me a cup of hot black coffee. I wished I had a cigarette to go with it, but I'd run out of tobacco several days back.

"How's the boy?" I asked.

Klingbill had small grayish eyes, and when I asked him about the Mexican kid, the eyes watered.

"An invalid . . . Poor Jesse."

I'd seen kids maimed during the war. Kids without arms and legs. Kids missing an eye, or both eyes or a foot. Flesh and bone were no match for lead and steel.

"Where's he at, Claude?"

"In the back. I fixed up the summer kitchen into a room to better accommodate him, and I pay a local woman to come in twice a day to care for him. The rest I do myself."

"He's lucky then," I said.

"Not so lucky," Klingbill said.

"He's got you to take care of him," I said. "That's more than a lot of kids like him would have."

"But what happens when I'm not around anymore?" Klingbill said. "Who's going to take care of him then?"

"Doesn't he have family?"

"He has an uncle in Sonora, but he doesn't know where in Sonora. That's it. I'm his family. But I'm not a young man anymore. I've got a few years left, if I'm lucky. I was counting on Jess to dig my grave and put me in it and him taking over the business."

"You do what you can," I said. "Let tomorrow worry about tomorrow."

"I guess so."

"It's a good thing you're doing here, Claude."

For a long time he didn't reply.

"The really sad irony of it is," Klingbill finally said, "if Longly had killed Jesse, perhaps some charges could be brought against him for murder. But with Jesse alive, there is not even a legal recourse for what he has committed."

"I know," I said. "But, I'm a real firm believer in what goes around comes around, Claude. And I think Bill Longly will pay the for his sins someday. Men like him always do."

"It's little consolation to that boy in there," Klingbill said, "the fact his shooter is up walking around every day enjoying himself, and Jess needs help just to go to the toilet."

"Bill Longly won't always be walking around enjoying himself," I said. "Someday he'll know what it's like to be on the other end of a bullet."

Klingbill tried rubbing the weariness from his face with his bony fingers.

"I'd like to believe that, Mac, I truly would. Fact is, every time I see Longly out on the streets, I want to kill him myself." His words were as tired as his eyes. "You really think there's any justice left in this world?"

"I have to believe so, Claude. Why else would any of us keep going if we didn't believe there was still some justice to be had?"

"Maybe the only true justice is what each of us takes into our own hands," he said.

"Sometimes that's true, Claude. But let the thing with Longly go."

He looked at me and sniffed.

"It's not your way to kill a man, Claude—that's one thing. The other is, he'd most likely kill you in the trying. That kid in there needs you, like you said. Let it go with Longly, he'll get his some other way."

We shook hands and I left.

I walked to the house Etta Landrow had rented. I knocked on the door and waited, then knocked again. A man wearing a paper-collar shirt answered the door. He had heavy dark moustaches and was holding a newspaper in his hand.

"Ya," he said.

"I'm looking for Etta."

"No Etta here," he said. He had a German accent.

"Etta Landrow."

He shook his head. Then his eyes showed he recognized who it was I was asking for.

"Oh dat *voman!*" he said. "No, she's gone away, mister! Me and my *vife* live here now! Since last *veek!*"

"Did she say where she was going?"

He shook his head.

"Sorry, she didn't say nothing."

I thanked him for his trouble then headed for Little Dick's cafe.

Little Dick was wearing an apron and waiting on tables when I walked in.

He nodded his head and told me to take a seat and he would be with me as soon as he finished waiting tables.

I sat by the window so I could watch the street.

In a few minutes Dick came over and said, "Did you catch Ben's killer?"

"No. Not yet."

He seemed as disappointed as the rest of us, Klingbill and myself.

"Trail gone cold?" he asked.

"Worse than that," I said. "Jake was shot in the hip and I had to bring him back here to get patched by Doc."

"That colored do it?"

"No, but the difference is slim." Then I told him about Hook stealing Jonas from us.

"You want some coffee?"

"That and tobacco if you've got any."

"My waitress, Mary, she didn't show up for work today. That's why I'm wearing this apron."

"It looks good on you."

"Please," he said and went off to get my coffee.

I saw Bill Longly going into the Blue Star Saloon across the street. No one was with him. The sudden thought came over me that if I got up now, walked over there and shot him, what was the worst that could happen to me? I thought of the kid, Jesse, lying in his bed all day not able to move, thought of how many years he would be like that before he just gave up and died. Maybe the only true justice *was* what we took into our own hands sometimes. The thought that Long Bill was walking around free, going into the saloon to take a little pleasure from the bottle and from the woman he enjoyed slapping around just made the urge in me all that much stronger. Somehow, life seemed as twisted as it could get.

Dick returned with my coffee and some tobacco and papers and sat down across from me.

"You want to tell me how the colored stole a friend of yours?" he said, "Or do I have to guess?"

I explained what had happened, Dick sat there drinking his coffee listening like he'd heard it all before, the smoke from his cigarette curling up into his squinting eyes.

"So the thing is," Dick said, after I finished telling him. "This Hook fellow can find you anytime he wants, but you ain't able to find him. That what you're telling me?"

"Pretty much," I said.

Dick shook his head in disbelief. "And he's traveling with a young gal to boot?"

I didn't try to explain it anymore than that.

"Well, if you and Jake True can't find him," Little Dick said. "I doubt anyone can. What now?"

"Soon as Jake's able, we'll go looking for him again."

"Maybe he's just too smart to be caught, Mac."

"I don't believe that," I said.

"Well, if you're going out again, so am I."

"No Dick, that's not necessary."

"I know it ain't necessary," Dick protested. "But look at me! I'm wearing a *damn* apron!"

"You've also got a bum leg, Dick."

"Well, from what you tell me, Jake's going to have one, too. So being a little crippled up ain't no excuse for you not to let me go along. 'Sides, I used to be a damn good tracker. And the way it sounds, the two of you could stand to have a damn good tracker along next time."

"What about your business, Dick? You just going to up and close your business?"

"What the hell kind a business is it for a man to be wearing an apron, anyhow?"

"Beats starving, ending up in an old soldier's home back east somewhere."

"Hell, I can always get a job burning eggs and cowboy hash if I have to."

"I know," I said. "Let tomorrow worry about tomorrow, right?"

"Right!"

"I'll have to run it past Jake," I said.

"You do that, Mac."

Another customer came in and I watched as Dick hobbled off to wait the table. Little Dick was a good man in a world where there weren't many good men to be found.

I saw Bill Longly exit the Blue Star and knew in spite of what I'd just been thinking about doing, that I wasn't going to walk up to him and put a bullet in him just because I knew he deserved it. A little part of me still wanted to believe that I fell into that category of good men. Men like Little Dick and Ben Beadle and Claude Klingbill.

What I *was* going to do, now that I had a couple of weeks to wait around until Jake could recover enough to travel again was, take that trip over to Nebraska and see an old friend. And maybe in the process, see if I could find Etta Landrow.

16

I caught the stage east to North Platte, then rented a horse and rode to Bill Cody's ranch. Through the stands of leafless trees lining its banks, I could see the waters of the Platte slipping along like a fat gray snake under the sunless sky. Patches of snow lay in the dead brown grass making a patchwork quilt of the land. Several times, pheasants exploded from the winter grass and startled the rented sorrel I was riding. And twice, I saw small herds of whitetail deer foraging through the brittle cover.

Nebraska was like a lot of places I'd been: it had its own kind of beauty and its own kind of loneliness. When I thought of Billy Cody living out here, I thought it was a long way from New York or Denver, and farther still, from London, England. In those places he was a celebrity. A man recognized. Out here, he was as common as the deer and pheasant and wild turkey. I wondered how long at a time he could stay so far removed from his audience and not begin to miss it.

I wondered too, as I rode along, if I would find Etta Landrow. I wasn't exactly sure what I truly felt toward her. The thought of her had been buzzing around in my mind since that first and last night we spent together. I'd been with my share of women since Mary Lee's death. Most, it was simply a matter of need, a matter of being with someone when the Big Lonely got too big to carry around inside me. There were one or two that stayed with me long after I'd left their beds. Alexandra Dupage back in Deadwood was one. Etta Landrow was the other.

But with Alexandra, once the flames of passion had burned themselves out and my business in Deadwood had come to an end, she and I both knew there was no place for us to go from there. With Etta, it felt different. For one thing, we hadn't met or been introduced under the same circumstances. But still, if it hadn't been for a case of murder—Ben's—she and I might not have met at all, nor any of the rest of what happened afterwards.

But if I was an admitting man, I'd have to say, too, that a lot of my uncertainty about how I felt toward Etta had to do with how I felt toward me. My wife Mary Lee had been my one true love in life (and they say, you only get one) and when I buried her, I buried a lot of myself with her. For a long time after the funeral, I wasn't much good for anything but drifting, getting in and out of trouble, the bottle, and the beds of widows and whores.

And for a lot longer than was practicable, it was enough. But in the last few years, I'd begun to need more than just hang my hat on some woman's chair and leave my boots by her front door and my horse tied up at her gate. I began to tell myself it was just that I was growing older and tired of drifting. And I was beginning to believe it half the time. Hell, sometimes you drift so long you start to stand still and don't even know it.

Now Etta Landrow's honey hair and the way she raised herself up on that last cold morning I saw her was riding around with me everywhere I went. I guess I needed to see her one more time just to make sure of what I was feeling, one way or the other.

You could see Billy Cody's big house from a long way off. It stood out in that open country, large and square and white as a wedding cake with a porch running all the way around it. I imagined Billy could stand on his porch and shoot quail and have his hounds go fetch them and not even put his boots on. He could just bang away there in his stocking feet and whistle and the hounds would bring him the quail so Louisa could fry them up for breakfast along with his eggs.

The pack of dogs Billy always kept about started barking as I approached the house. Several long-legged hounds came trotting out to greet me, their barks crackling through the cold clear air.

I was about a hundred yards from the house when I saw him step out onto the porch. You would have to be blind not to recognize Billy Cody. He was dressed in a bright red shirt and black trousers and knee-high leather boots. He had that same long hair that Custer had, only darker than Custer's, and he sported a fine black Vandyke beard. The only thing I could see that was unusual about him was, that he was standing there alone without a crowd around him.

His dogs gathered around the sorrel I was riding then fell in behind, barking and baying as I rode up to the porch.

Billy stood there watching me, trying to recognize who I was. It had been a long time since we'd last crossed paths. I supposed he'd met a lot of people in between; any one of which might come visiting him on a crisp winter day.

Damn if he didn't look famous just standing there.

"You hounds git!" Billy called to the pack of dogs. And as though God himself commanded it, they scattered.

"Bill," I said. "It's been a time."

He looked intently for a moment then smiled broadly. He had fine teeth.

"Damn, Quint McCannon, I didn't recognize you with all that brush on your face. You've aged some."

"A lot," I said. "You mind if I get down?"

"No, of course not son," he said, coming down the steps to shake my hand. He had put on a small amount of weight around his middle, but it hadn't hurt his appearance any. His grip was firm; the handshake of a man well schooled in the art of giving firm handshakes.

"You know," he said, clapping me on the shoulder as he led the way back up the steps to the porch. "You are not going to believe this, but I was just this morning thinking about the past, about some of the friends I hadn't seen in years and you and Ben came to mind. And *damn,* here you are! Amazing about the powers of the mind, ain't it!"

"I've been thinking about you some lately too, Bill. Fact is, I sent a lady friend of mine to see you. She has an aunt that lives near Ogallala."

Bill blinked, then offered me a wink.

"Pretty gal, is she?"

"Yes."

"You know me and pretty gals," Bill said; he smiled like a prince.

"They are always welcome here." Then looking over his shoulder. "Of course it ain't exactly always tea and roses when they're about, you understand. Louisa still hasn't gotten over her jealousy—especially of actresses. She thinks they're all *tawdry* by nature. Whatever in the hell that means!" he laughed.

"I warned my lady friend about you, Bill. How you had an eye for the ladies. I warned her to watch out for Louisa too."

Bill guided me to a set of chairs a little farther down the porch and away from the front door.

"You know I'm just like a papa to the young ladies," Bill said with a look of sincerity on his face. "They all like to kiss me and call me papa. It's just their way of showing affection for me. It doesn't mean a thing."

"Sure Bill, I understand."

Then he grinned slyly.

"The God's truth!" he declared, raising his left hand and placing his right over his heart.

Bill took a pair of cheroots from his pockets and handed me one.

"Smoke?"

We sat there smoking and reminiscing about old times and about friends, the one's we'd lost and the one's that were still alive. I told Bill about Ben and he seemed genuinely saddened by the news.

"I guess this has been the worst for me, this last year," Bill said. "First Georgie went down on the Little Big Horn, then Billy Hickok got killed up in Deadwood a couple of months after that. Now Ben. They were good pards—though Georgie was a bit of a vain and foolish son of a buck at times. I am not at all surprised that he came to the end he did. You chase an Indian long enough, he's going to sneak around behind you and lift your hair!"

"Hazards of the profession," I said.

"True enough," Bill replied.

I was no fan of Custer's. We'd met once and he struck me as the sort of man whose sole interest was himself. And, like Billy, he was quite aware of his own fame. I never met Hickok, so I didn't hold any opinions on him, except that no man deserved a bullet in the back of the head. Whatever that's worth.

"I truly am sorry to hear about Ben," Billy said with a sigh. Then after several minutes of quiet reflection he added: "We're dying fast as roses in winter, ain't we Mac?"

I said I knew we were and he blew rings of smoke from his cigar and studied them as they lifted toward the overhang.

"The year hasn't been entirely bad," Bill said. "We've performed a number of stage plays in the east; Buffalo and New York City. Fact of the matter is, Wild Bill was with us for last spring. Him and Texas Jack—you remember Texas Jack?"

I said I did.

"Now there is a natural stage actor, that Texas Jack," Billy said, his eyes twinkling. "Handsome son of a buck, too. All the ladies love Texas Jack. Me, I'm not as natural an actor as Texas Jack. But Billy Hickok—whew! That man could not act worth a hill of beans. *Terrible!* Never seen such stage fright in a man—had to get good and drunk before every performance. Least, that's the reason he gave for getting good and drunk. A condition Ned Buntline himself is an advocate of—except Ned has no compunction about exhibiting himself on stage. Shameless ham! I believe the man would walk naked through Central Park and not think a thing of it."

Bill sat there smoking his cigar and smiling broadly as he

told me about various plays and actors and actresses, and about the big cities they performed in that past season and all the hell they raised and how different that life was compared to the one he led here at the ranch.

"You know," Bill said, suddenly. "If Hickok hadn't been so frightful of the stage, he'd probably still be alive today. He got scared and ran back to the frontier and straight into the arms of death! Of all the dangers he faced, the war and Indians and being a lawman in those rough cow towns, it was his fear of standing in front of strangers who admired him that ended up getting him killed . . ." Bill's voice trailed off as he stared out toward the quiet land.

"If he'd stayed with me and Jack and Ned, he'd be a rich man today. Rich and famous and alive . . ."

"He didn't know," I said. "None of us do."

Bill flicked the ashes from his cigar, looked at it, then said, "My friends are growing few in number."

"You've still got plenty of friends, Bill. I can't ever imagine you without a lot of friends."

He smiled warmly.

"Sometimes its hard to tell exactly who your friends are, Mac. If I was broke and busting sod for a living, do you think I'd have all these people coming out to the house, or wanting me to have my photograph taken with them?"

"I think you know the answer to that more than I do, Bill."

"Well," he said, stubbing out his cigar butt, "I think not— unless it was Ned Buntline and he knew I had a bottle of sour mash in the cupboard." Bill's laughter caused several of the hounds to lift their heads.

"Now, what was this about a lady friend of yours coming to see me?"

I explained about Etta Landrow, the reason I'd suggested she come to see him.

"Well, I wish she had," he said. "I would give her a job as an actress. Can she shoot a gun?"

"That's a skill I never got around to asking her about, Bill, whether or not she could shoot a gun."

"I'm thinking about putting together a traveling show," he

said. "One with Indians and buffalo and trick shooters. I've not worked out every last detail yet, but I am considering it. Maybe if your lady friend could shoot glass balls out of the air, I could hire her to be in my traveling show."

"Well, that is something you would have to ask her if she comes around," I said.

"I will. Let's go inside and say hello to Louisa. We'll see if Texas Jack has climbed out of bed yet. No use to bother with Ned, that man don't get up before noon, even on a good day."

Bill's wife was cordial, but not overly friendly toward me. She probably thought I was just another old pal, down on my luck, coming to ask Bill for a handout. She wasn't far from wrong. Bill kept almost as many old pals around as he did animals. I'm sure it had to be hard on their marriage—Bill's never being alone with her, or her house never being completely her own.

The real delights of the household were Bill's young daughters. Dark and curly-haired and with more rambunction than his entire pack of hounds. Their laughter brightened everything in the house and it was plain to see Billy loved them dearly.

After greeting Louisa and the girls, Bill and I walked into the large formal dining room. There, sitting at the far end of the table was Texas Jack Omohundro, his dark curly hair hanging down over his forehead and partway into his eyes.

"Look who's come for a visit!" Billy announced.

Jack smiled and said, "Excuse me for not getting right up, my head feels like broken glass from all the hard liquor last night."

Bill looked sheepish.

"I guess we did sort of overdo things."

We sat and had coffee with Texas Jack and soon several young women came down to the dining room and joined us. Bill introduced each by name, then stated they were all actresses in the play company. I could see why Billy was in dutch with Louisa a lot of the time.

Bill kept everyone entertained as he told stories of the old days, including me into any number of his tall tales. I felt foolish listening to it, but remained seated out of respect for my old friend. It went like that for better than an hour and I realized that maybe I had made a mistake by coming.

I excused myself and went outside. I rolled myself a cigarette and listened to the wind moan along the eaves.

Louisa came out and stood next to me.

"You don't enjoy his stories so much?" she asked. "Like the others in there?"

"They're okay," I said. "Bill enjoys telling them."

"I know," she said. "He tells them all the time."

"I think he feels he has to be entertaining," I said, feeling I was having to apologize for my friend to his own wife.

"They come and stay and don't leave," she said. "Sometimes for weeks. New ones all the time. Then in the spring, he goes away for months and me and the girls don't see him. And when he comes back, they all show up again. It's like that all the time."

"He's a very well-known man. I imagine they like his company."

"Those young women," she said. "I don't like it that he likes them so well. They like him too."

I didn't know why she was telling me the things she was except that maybe she had no one else she felt she could say them to. Maybe because I wasn't sitting inside with the others, listening to Billy entertain us with his stories, she thought I might be like her somehow, might understand her in a way the others could not or would not.

"You come to stay too?" she asked.

"No, I just stopped to say hello. I'll be leaving today."

"Those women," she said. "They call him *papa.*"

I didn't say anything. It wasn't my job to defend him. She seemed very sad, very lonely.

"It won't make that much a difference if you stay," she said, pulling the heavy shawl she was wearing tighter around her shoulders. "There's always people here. What's one more?" Then she turned and went back inside.

I figured it was time I said good-bye to my old friend. He had his world and I had mine. Things weren't ever going to

be what they once were between us—too much had changed
in both our lives.

I thought maybe I'd ride over to Ogallala and see if I could
locate Etta, or her aunt. It would be at least another week or
two before Jake was ready to travel again; there was no point
in sitting around wasting it.

If I was lucky, finding Etta would turn out better than finding
Billy Cody. At least I hoped it would.

I waited around long enough for him to take leave of his
audience. He found me adjusting the cinch strap on the sorrel,
came up and ran his hand along the flank.

"What are you doing out here all alone, Mac?" he asked.
"I don't even recall you leaving the table."

"Just needed some air, Billy."

He looked at me with a knowing gaze.

"Got to be too much for you inside, didn't it? With all them
folks, all those tall stories. I understand. Gets to be too much
for me too at times."

"Not your fault they like you, Bill."

He placed his hand on the mane of the sorrel, twined it
through his fingers.

"It's hard for me to say no to them, Quint. They expect me
to entertain them, to be papa to them."

"I know, Bill. You don't have to apologize to me for who
you are. We'll always be friends."

"I know we will," he said. "I don't want to lose anymore
of the few good friends I have left. You take care of yourself."

We shook hands.

"Where to now?" he asked as I swung up into the saddle.

"I think I'll go and see if I can find that lady friend of
mine," I answered. "Spend a little time with her. Maybe ask
her can she shoot glass balls out of the air with a pistol."

He smiled.

"You still miss your wife, don't you?"

"Yeah Billy, I do."

Then, he ran his hand along the muscled neck of the horse
and patted its shoulder.

"You take care, Quint."

"I will, Billy."

"Your lady friend still needs work, you send her along to see me. I'll make sure she gets work."

"Thanks Bill."

I rode away knowing, without looking back, he was still standing there in front of that big house filled with people who wanted his company. And I knew too, there was a part of him wishing *he* was the one who was riding away.

17

Ten miles out of Ogallala, the sorrel threw a shoe. So much for a pleasant journey. After my long foot chase to recover our stolen horses, I wasn't looking forward to another walk. The road ahead of me lay open and unused. It looked like a walk was exactly what I was facing.

I dismounted, took the sorrel's reins in hand, and started off toward Ogallala. I'd walked maybe mile down the road when I saw a farmhouse just off to the north. A wagon trace led up to the farmhouse. It was a whole lot closer than Ogallala, that farmhouse. I started up the trace and got about halfway to the farm when two youths wearing cheap felt hats stepped from behind a stand of gum trees; one was carrying a double-barrel scattergun; the other had an old Navy cap-and-ball pistol sticking from his waistband.

"What you want here, mister?" the kid with the shotgun asked.

"My horse tossed a shoe," I said. "I wonder if you might have a forge, maybe an extra shoe and some nails?"

From the shadow of his brim, he looked me over, then he looked the sorrel over. "At's a nice looking horse," he said.

"Nice but not much good without a shoe," I said.

The one holding the shotgun and asking the questions, traded looks with the other boy. You didn't have to be their mamma to see that they were bred of the same flesh and bone; both had pink fat faces and slack mouths that exposed squirrel-like teeth. What little I could see of their eyes under the brims of their hats expressed childish curiosity and a lot of hard mischief.

They wore rough leather shoes with the tongues sticking out.

"How we know you ain't come to rob us?" the kid wearing the pistol stuck in his pants said. "How we know you ain't no desperado come to rob me and Floyd and Sister Earl and burn our house down?"

They were jug-eared with minds less bright than a candle flame. Just big boys. But the shotgun the one carried made them dangerous; all I wanted was to reshoe my horse.

"Look, I'll gladly pay you for the use of your forge," I offered.

I could see them thinking it over.

"Whatcha think, Floyd?"

Floyd shrugged his thick shoulders.

"How much you willin' to pay?"

"Dollar, maybe two."

Floyd sucked his lower lip contemplating the price.

"Two sounds fair. Don't two sound fair, Floyd?"

"Hesh up, Bob, can't you see I'm tryin' to weigh it!"

I waited while Floyd *weighed* it.

Finally Floyd seemed to acknowledge that two dollars was enough to shoe my horse. He nodded his head.

"Come'n to the house."

I followed them, but every few steps one or the other looked back over his shoulder at me.

The farm was run-down: Gaps in the cross fencing, a rusting plow lying on its side next to the barn. A windmill with most of its blades missing clattered slowly in a wind that seemed as tired and worn out as the farm. As we neared the house, I smelled the hogs before I saw them. Several fat sows rooted around in a pen, snuffling at an empty slop trough.

They led me to a lean-to where a bellows and a forge stood

in poor repair. "There's the fixin' shed, mister. That'll be two dollars if you please!"

I gave Floyd two dollars. Bob snatched one of the dollars from Floyd's hand. "One each!" Bob declared. Floyd snorted, then yelped and started chasing Bob around the yard slapping him across the head with his hat. I told myself, just fix the damn shoe and get moving on to Ogallala.

I searched around until I found a shoe that might be forged and a hammer to shape it. Light filtered into the shed like cold blades of steel. Outside I could hear the brothers wrestling and grunting.

I got a fire built and pumped the bellows and with a pair of steel tongs held the shoe to the blazing heat until it grew as red and hot as the sun. Then I took it out and laid it across an anvil and began to shape it with the hammer. Metal rang off metal and sparks flew under the hammer's blows and I could feel the heat against my skin. Then something caused me to stop; I sensed a presence in the shed. I thought maybe the dullards had come to stand around and watch me bend the shoe, that maybe I was the entertainment for the day. But when I looked up, I saw a young woman in a sack dress. In the close shadowy confines of the shed and with the light coming in behind her, I couldn't get a good look at her other than to see that she was thin and had hair that looked like corn silk against the light.

"Who you be?" she said when I looked up.

"Name's McCannon, Miss."

"You friends of Floyd and Robert?" she asked. "I know most ever body Floyd and Robert knows. But I don't know you."

"No, I'm not a friend," I said. "I just need to shoe my horse."

Unlike her brothers, she wasn't wearing shoes. She had small feet.

"I paid your brothers two dollars for the use of this hammer and some nails," I said, thinking she had as much right to the money as either of them. Maybe if she knew.

"You ain't from around here," she said.

"No."

"Where you from then, you ain't from around here?"

"Wyoming," I said.

"What you doing in Nebraska if you're from Wyoming?"

"That's a good question," I said. And when she didn't seem to see the poor humor in it, I added: "I'm looking for a lady friend."

"Who'd that be?"

"Her name's, Etta Landrow. You know of any Landrows living around these parts?"

She thought about it for a few moments, then shook her head.

"Unuh."

"Well, that's what I'm doing in Nebraska, looking for a woman named Etta Landrow." I bent to the shoeing again.

"She your sweetheart?" the girl asked.

I paused. This conversation was leading nowhere. The girl was either curious as a cat, or a child lacking good sense.

"No," I said, without straightening up again. "She's not my sweetheart, just a friend."

"Well if she ain't, who is?" the girl said.

"Who is what?"

"Who is your sweetheart?"

"You know, maybe if you go ask your brothers about that money I gave them, they'd share it with you," I said, hoping to divert the girl's attention. I was wanting to make Ogallala before nightfall. It was already late in the day.

"You ain't got a sweetheart?" the girl asked, undeterred.

"No ma'am, I don't," I said. "And I'd just as soon finish shoeing my horse and be on my way. So, if you don't mind, I'd like to give this conversation a rest."

"Oh," she said, and slipped out of the shed as quietly as she had arrived.

It left me feeling unpleasant to have been so stern with her, but I didn't see any other way of getting around an endless string of foolish questions.

I completed nailing the shoe on the sorrel and put the hammer back in the same box of rusting tools I'd taken it from. When I turned around, they were all standing there.

Floyd was aiming his double barrel at me. The girl was next to him, then Bob.

"Sister Earl says you ain't got no sweetheart," Floyd said.

"Sister's right, son. And, I'd appreciate you aim that greener in another direction."

"Sister Earl ain't got no sweetheart neither, except for me and Bob when we take us a notion. Sometimes we're sweethearts with her."

"What's your point, boy?"

They were standing there, just at the edge of the shed where the shadows were the deepest, silhouettes against the pewter light; three figures looked like they'd sprouted out of the fallow ground on which they stood. I got a cold feeling crawling through my guts.

"Sister Earl says she wants to marry up with you!"

The cold feeling turned to a kind of sick stab as I looked down the length of the double barrels Floyd had pointed at my middle saying how his sister wanted to marry up with me. There are lots of ways to die in this world and none of them good. But the prospect of taking a belly full of buckshot and being torn in two, was another matter altogether. Whether I was fast enough to pull and fire the self-cocker before Floyd painted the shed with me was a question I only had to ask myself once.

"What would Sister Earl want with a man my age?" I said, trying to keep an already bad situation from going to hell in a hurry.

I couldn't see any of their faces well enough to know for certain, but I could almost hear Floyd and Bob grinning. I wasn't sure if Sister Earl was grinning too.

"Sister Earl don't mind you bein' an old man," Floyd said. "Old men can have babies can't they? That's what Sister Earl says she wants—is babies and to be married."

I knew a man in Carthage, Missouri once who had a boy with a soft brain. For years, the old man cared for the boy, fed him, clothed him, and provided for his general welfare. Then one morning the boy walked in on the man while he was eating his breakfast and struck him across the head with an axe and killed him.

When the sheriff asked the boy why he did it, the boy said: "I ain't positive."

I figured Floyd and Bob weren't too far different than that boy in Missouri with the soft brain.

"What'll it be mister?" Floyd asked. "You goin' to marry Sister Earl or ain't you?" I heard him click back the hammers of his shotgun.

I muttered something that sounded like yes.

"At true?" the girl said. "You'll marry up with me?"

"Well, like Floyd said," I told her, "you don't have a sweetheart, and I don't have one either. Might just as well you and me be sweethearts."

She stepped forward, moved a little closer so she could look into my face. She wanted to see if I was lying to her.

"Honest?" she said.

She had a small fox face with brown fox eyes.

"Honest," I said.

"Well, let's git to it!" Bob cried. "Raise your right hand mister and swear the truth."

She was standing between me and Floyd. I had maybe a second to think about it.

I brought the self-cocker up with my right hand at the same time I pulled her down out of the way with my left. The flashes of pistol fire were like twin bolts of lightning inside the shed. Floyd squeezed both triggers of the shotgun as he fell dying, and Bob's scream was cut short as the buckshot struck him in the face and carried him halfway across the shed.

Then there was a long hard silence before the girl began screeching. She clawed at me and tore free from my grip. Leaping over Floyd like a startled deer, she ran toward the house.

I stepped past the dead brothers and went after her. I found her inside the kitchen trying to cock an old rimfire five-shot. She had poked the barrel of it in her mouth. I pulled it from her hands. She fought, clawed, kicked. I held her until she stopped.

She had the look of a frightened animal, something caught in a leg trap. Her fox eyes darted back and forth; her rib cage bellowed against my arms.

"They didn't give me a choice," I said. "I didn't plan to shoot them."

She had small teeth that looked like tiny pearls behind her pale thin lips.

"You said . . . !" she cried over and over. "You said . . . !"

I kept a hold on her, letting her cry and shake in my arms.

"I'm sorry that I lied to you and said I would marry you," I told her. "I wouldn't have said it if Floyd hadn't pointed the shotgun at me."

It was like trying to reason with a disappointed child who could accept no amount of reasoning or apology for the hurt they felt.

By the time she stopped fussing, the room lay in darkness.

"I'm going to let you go now," I said. "I don't want you to try anything. I don't want you to run. I'm going to light a lamp." Slowly, I released my hold on her expecting any second for her to dart from the room. But she didn't. She stood there, stock still like her small feet were frozen to the earthen floor. I found a lamp and lit it. The room was squalid. The table was laden with dirty dishes; scraps of food were lying on the floor, the curtains in the windows were torn.

The wind had picked up and banged hard against the door. I walked over and closed it. I found a coat hanging on a hook and put it over the girl's shoulders.

"I have to go outside and bury your brothers," I said. She looked at me, murmured a sound I couldn't understand. I thought what the hell, if she was going to run, she was going to run. I had done all I could for her, all I was going to do. It was up to her whether she ran or not.

I went outside and lit a bulls-eye lantern I found hanging from a nail. I searched around in the shed and found a shovel, the only unbroken tool in the shed, aside from the hammer I'd used to forge the horseshoe. You boys are lucky, I thought as

I picked up the shovel. Hammers ain't worth a damn for digging a grave.

I walked a fair amount of distance from the house and dug a single grave. It took me several hours and several cigarettes, but sometime late that evening, I finished the job. Then, I put Floyd and Bob in the grave together and filled it in. They had lived together and died together, they might as well be buried together.

By the time I finished burying Bob and Floyd, my shirt was soaked with sweat and my belly was crawling with hunger. It didn't seem at all unusual to me that I could bury two men and be hungry. I hadn't had a meal all day.

I went back inside the house. The girl was still standing there just as I'd left her.

I found a basin, and pumped some water into it and washed my face and hands. Then I looked through the cupboards and found some grub: a can of beans, some flour, a tin of peaches. I made fry bread out of the flour and heated the beans.

I sat the girl down across from me and pushed a plate in her direction. She sat looking at it for a time, then slowly began to eat.

I didn't have anything to say to her, so I mostly just concentrated on the beans and fry bread.

"They thought you was a rich man," she said midway through the meal. "Bob and Floyd thought you was a rich man and that you should marry me."

"They were wrong," I said, "about me being a rich man."

"Floyd said you was to marry me, him and Bob would be rich men too."

"What made them think I was a rich man?" I asked.

" 'Cause of that pretty horse you was riding."

"I rented it."

"I wanted to marry up with you," she said. "Not 'cause you was rich, though. I just wanted to marry someone wouldn't hurt me every time."

"Hurt you every time?"

"Like Bob and Floyd did when they'd be sweethearts with me."

I looked into those fox eyes, the way they shifted and darted, and wondered why such sweet sorrowful eyes had to be subjected to the cruelty of pitiless men.

"They won't hurt you anymore," I said.

She looked suddenly very sad.

"What is it?"

"Got nobody now," she said. "Now that Floyd and Bob is dead."

I wanted to say she was better off, but given her circumstances, I wasn't so sure I'd done her much of a favor.

"They called you Sister Earl," I said. "How is it you have a boy's name?"

She looked up, a piece of the fry bread held between her dirty fingers, and offered me a weak smile.

"Earline. That's my name."

"It's a pretty name."

She looked back down at her plate.

"My mama run off with a Bible seller," she said. "Daddy killed himself 'cause of it. Out there in the barn. Put a rope around his neck and jumped off a nail keg." Her fox eyes darted toward the window, as though she was trying to see beyond the house clear to the same barn where her daddy had killed himself.

What good would it do to tell her that life for some, had a way of being hard and unforgiving? She already knew those things.

"After mama run off and daddy hanged himself, Floyd and Bob started being sweethearts with me . . ."

"Do you have any kin around these parts?" I asked.

She shook her head.

"We came here from Ohio. I had a baby sister, but she died before we got here. Died a long ways from here," she said. "By a big tall rock is where daddy buried her at . . ."

"Finish eating your food, Earline. It'll help make you feel better," I suggested, having lost most of my own appetite. I rolled myself a cigarette there at the table and she watched me as she ate.

"I think I'll go outside and smoke this," I said. Her eyes trailed after me as I moved from the table to the door.

"You gonna leave me here alone, mister?"

"Don't worry Earline, I won't leave you," I said.

"What about tomorrow?" she asked. "You going to leave me tomorrow?"

"Finish your meal."

I stepped out onto the porch. The night was clear and the air was cold. The sky held a million stars, each one lonely and far away.

All because the damn horse had to throw a shoe, I had ended up in this place. A star shot across the heavens like a silver bullet and dropped somewhere to earth.

Two soft-brain boys lay dead in a fresh grave while their sister ate beans and fry bread and peaches and worried about being left alone.

I'd stay the night, and tomorrow . . . well, I'd let tomorrow take care of itself.

18

Sister Earl climbed up behind me on the sorrel.

"Where we going, mister?" she asked.

"Ogallala," I told her. "You ever been to Ogallala, Earline?"

She shook her head. "Floyd and Robert never let me go with them when they went," she said. "I always wanted to go, see what it was like, that Ogallala."

"Well, you'll get to see it now."

I'd decided that the girl needed the attention of someone who would look after her interest. Leaving her there on that little hardscrabble hog farm would have been just as cruel as if I had put a bullet in her—eventually, she would have perished.

She put her arms around my waist and held on as I spurred the sorrel into a trot. It was turning into a mild pleasant day—unusual for that time of year. A warm wind blew out of the south and the sun shone against a light blue sky. A flock of Canada geese passed overhead in a dark V of flight, and twice we saw cranes standing on sand bars out in the middle of the Platte river.

"Look there!" Sister Earl said, when we came in sight of

the cranes. There must have been several thousand of them. "Never seen no birds that big in my life! Why they look like big ol' chickens on tall legs!"

We rode along, Sister Earl taking in the sights as we went, her bare legs bouncing against the ribs of the sorrel. She had the wide-eyed wonderment of a child seeing the world for the very first time.

We arrived in Ogallala by midmorning. I wondered why the town seemed so quiet until I heard a church bell ringing and realized it was Sunday morning. Sister Earl started at the sound of the ringing church bell.

"What's at?" she said.

"It's a church bell," I said. "Ringing in the sheep."

She didn't seem to understand.

"Sheep?"

"What some call folks who go to church," I explained.

"Oh," Earline said, as though that was all she needed to know about the matter.

I figured on finding the local sheriff. Maybe he would know someone who might take the girl in. An old man crossed the street in front of me; he was wearing a black coat and a boiled shirt and was bent half way over at the waist; it looked like he was carrying an invisible load on his back.

"Mister, can you tell me where to find John Law?" I asked him.

He paused, shaded his eyes with one hand, tilted his head as far back as he could and looked first at me, then the girl.

"That'd be Freddie Buck," the old man said. Then pointing with his nose, he added: "Down the street."

I thanked the old timer and touched my spurs to the sorrel's flanks. The old man watched us until we rode past.

I found the city marshal's office easily enough. I told Earline to wait there on the sorrel for me while I went inside. I didn't bother to knock before opening the door.

Freddie Buck was standing in front of an oval mirror waxing his moustaches. He turned around when I came in.

"Yes sir, can I help you?"

He was maybe forty. Heavy, with a belly that hung over his

belt. He had small round eyes and florid cheeks and a drinker's nose that was wormy with busted veins. He wore a six-point star pinned to his vest.

"My name's Quint McCannon," I said, "and I had to kill two men yesterday that lived east of here. I have their sister sitting outside on the back of my horse. She'll need to have someone take charge of her."

Maybe it was too much news for him all at once. He blinked, said, "Huh?"

He listened intently as I told him the full details.

"That'd be them Strawgrass boys you buried," he said after I finished. "Dense as stumps. Mean little peckerwoods."

"What about the girl, Earline?" I said. "Is there someone in town that would take her in?"

He looked past me toward the window.

"At her?"

"That's her."

He walked over to the window and took a closer look. Earline was watching everybody that walked past, and they were returning the favor.

"First time I ever laid eyes on that child," Buck said. "I'd ride out that way sometimes, but I never got past them boys. Seems like they spent all their time guarding that lane leading up to the house. Tried to go up it once, they said it was private property. I believe them boys would've shot me in the back had I tried."

Buck scratched the back of his neck as he stared at Earline. "I heard things about what went on out there since that girl's mama run off and her daddy killed himself. Town like this, you're bound to hear things even if you don't see 'em with your own eyes. She looks alright, though. Little skinny, perhaps."

"I imagine you could sell that place of theirs as payment for her keep to whoever would take her in," I suggested.

"Sure, sure," Buck said, finally seeing enough of the girl to satisfy his curiosity. "Listen, I'll take her over to Elmira Walden's boarding house. Elmira's in need of a housekeeper. Maybe she'll take the girl in in exchange for work."

"Mrs. Walden a good woman is she?"

"Hell, Mr. McCannon, I don't suppose it's up to you and me to be choosy as to who takes the girl in," Buck said. "It don't look as though that gal's got all her wits to start with."

"All the more reason she gets a good home," I said.

"Elmira will do all right by her," Buck said. "She's a Christian woman. Let me take her over, see what I can do."

"Before you go," I said, "do you know of any Landrows that live in the area?"

"Sure, the widow Landrow lives about four miles out. North. Big white house, can't miss it."

I walked outside with Buck and explained the situation to Sister Earl.

"You leaving me, mister?" was the only thing she said.

"I'll check back and see how you're doing," I told her.

She looked at Buck, then slipped off the sorrel and followed him down the street as easy as a puppy.

I rode north until I came to the white house. A woman was in the side yard hanging bed sheets on a clothesline strung between two large cottonwood trees. The wind caught in the sheets and billowed them out like sails.

I stood by the gate of the wrought-iron fence that ran along the front of the house. I didn't have to see her face to know who the woman was.

I didn't say anything at first; I just wanted to take a minute to look at her. She must have sensed it, for in a few seconds, she stopped what she was doing and turned to look at me.

"You ride all this way just to watch me hang sheets?" she said.

The wind had done something nice to her skin; her cheeks had a nice apple glow to them and her hair had come loose in places from where she'd pinned it up.

"There wasn't much to do in Cheyenne," I said. "So I thought I would ride up this way and watch you hang laundry."

"Well, don't just stand there, come and lend a hand if you've nothing better to do with your time, Mr. Quint McCannon."

I looped the sorrel's reins through the fence, pushed through the gate and took one end of a damp bed sheet.

"Like this?" I said.

"You look like you've had experience." Her smile was prettier than I remembered it.

We finished hanging the sheets and she said, "Well, are you going to get on your horse and ride back to Wyoming, or did you plan on staying for supper?"

"Depends on what's for supper," I said.

She put her arm through mine and said, "Come and meet my Aunt Laura."

It was a big warm house with several large and bright rooms downstairs and what looked to be several more like them on the second level. Etta's aunt was in the kitchen baking. Etta introduced us and I could smell the sweetness of bread coming off her.

"Saw you ride up on your horse," her aunt said. "Saw you from way out." Her kitchen window looked toward the road. It was the kind of country you could see someone coming from a long way out.

"You must be fond of this girl to come all the way from Wyoming to see her."

"Wyoming's not so far," I said, feeling a bit foolish about the situation.

"Far enough a man would have a special reason for coming," Aunt Laura said.

I looked at Etta; this time it was her turn to look a little embarrassed.

"Aunty," she said.

"Do you drink coffee, Quinten?" Etta's aunt asked.

"I do when I can get it," I said.

"Good, I have some brewing. If you want to wash up, you can—out in the summer kitchen." It was kind of her not to mention the trail dust I'd collected. I excused myself and went to wash up.

A minute later, Etta came out to the summer kitchen with a cup of coffee on a tray and several small cookies.

"Do you take it black, or would you like some sugar?" she asked.

There was just something about the moment: Etta standing there, the way strands of her honey hair had come free from the combs, the greyness of her eyes.

I set the coffee aside and kissed her. She smelled fresh as windblown sheets, her hair scented and soft, her mouth sweet as apples.

I held her for a long time after the kiss. It felt good to hold her, to feel the firmness of her body against mine, the way it curved into me.

"I think now I *know* why you rode all the way here from Wyoming," she whispered.

"That's not the only reason," I said.

"But it is one of the reasons."

"Yes, it's one of the reasons."

"Tell me," she said. "What's the other."

"This," I said. "I missed holding you like this, seeing your smile, hearing your voice."

She put the tips of her fingers to my lips.

"Careful cowboy, you could make a girl's heart go weak. Aunty Laura hears all your sweet talk, she's liable to call a preacher man."

"Maybe that's not such a bad thought," I said.

Etta pushed up on her toes and kissed me, long and sweetly. Then, lowering herself again, she said, "Maybe it's not such a bad thought. But I know a drifting man when I see one. You're not up for preachers just yet."

"Maybe we should spend some time finding out how much drifting I've got left in me," I said.

"Maybe." Then, in a more serious manner, she asked: "Quint, did you find the man who killed your friend?"

"No, not yet we haven't."

"I'm sorry," she said; the light coming through the summer kitchen window seemed to dance in her hair. Then pulling back, she looked at me with all the seriousness in the world.

"You say you came here to see me, to spend a little time

getting to know each other. But, that's not what I think is going to happen.''

''What do you think is going to happen?''

''I think you will be gone come morning, back to looking for your friend's killer. And, I think I will start to miss you all over again.''

I couldn't lie to her; I still had to find Ben's killer. And if I wasn't gone in the morning, it would be the next one, or the one after that.

''I think it is something I would like to do,'' I said. ''Get to know you better, spend some time with you—afterward.''

''I'd like it too,'' she said. ''Come, let's sit out on the porch while you have your coffee.''

We sat there and talked. I told her all of what had happened since leaving Cheyenne with Jake that last morning we'd been together. I told her how Elijah Hook had outsmarted us, and how he had stolen the girl and our horses. I told her about Jake getting shot in the hip, but skipped the particulars as to why.

''I always thought of criminals as not being too smart,'' I said. ''But this Hook is about as smart as they come. He's led Jake and me on a merry chase.''

Etta listened quietly. Sometimes she closed her eyes and I wondered what it was she was thinking.

''The one good thing about what happened,'' she said, ''is it's given you time to come see me. I wasn't sure that you would take the trouble to look me up again.'' She gave a soft laugh, then bit the lower part of her lip and trained her grey eyes on me.

''I thought for a time right after you left me that morning, that I'd given myself too easily to you. That you might not have respected me. Funny what a girl will allow herself to believe about a man she's fond of.''

I touched her hand, felt its smoothness against my own rough and calloused fingers.

''I always knew I would come find you just to see you again,'' I said. ''That ought to tell you something.''

She blinked, looked off toward the river you couldn't see

because it lay beyond a rise and beyond the bare black trees of winter.

"It tells me something," she said. Then she touched the corner of her eyes as though the raw wind had caused them to tear.

"I wanted to see you again, Etta. That's why I've come."

"We could have just kept the memory," she said.

"We could have, but to tell you the truth, I have enough memories already. All the memories I carry around inside me have just about worn me out from the carrying."

She was about to say something when we both noticed a buggy coming toward the house.

"Oh my word!" she declared. "I can't believe it!"

"Someone you know?" I asked.

"Tom Feathers!"

"Who is Tom Feathers?" I asked.

"A cattleman and a neighbor. He and his father own all that land you see to the west. Aunty says he's the most eligible bachelor in all of Keith county."

"Maybe Aunty invited him for supper," I said. "Why do you suppose?"

Etta tossed me a quick glance.

I couldn't say exactly how it made me feel, that a bachelor cattleman was coming to call on Etta. She didn't act like she cared for it much; but then, maybe she was just trying to be kind to me for having come all the way from Wyoming to visit her unannounced like I had.

"Maybe I should go," I suggested.

Etta looked at me sternly.

"No. You should not go," she said.

She could see I was uncomfortable with the situation; she tried to assure me.

"Tom Feathers is a nice enough man," she said. "He's wealthy and handsome. He has charm and is well traveled and well read. What else can I tell you? He would make the perfect husband for the right woman. I'm just not the right woman."

"Do you think your aunt has enough plates to set out for all of us?" I said.

"If not, you can share mine," Etta said with a sly smile as Tom Feathers pulled up in his horse-drawn cab.

Hell, it hadn't turned out like I had planned it, my trip to Nebraska. First Billy Cody, now this.

19

Tom Feathers was driving a nice bay with a white blaze face and four white stockings. You didn't have to be a horse trader to see it was an expensive horse. So was the buggy.

He wore a greatcoat over a good suit of dark clothes with a white shirt and paper collar and a necktie. Perched on his head was a little sugar-loaf hat and he wore kidskin gloves that looked as soft as butter.

"Etta," he said as he checked the bay's reins then tipped his hat without really tipping it at all. He made all the right formal gestures of a man that had come calling on a lady friend, but the whole time his gaze stayed on me.

"Tom," Etta said. "I'd like you to meet my friend, Quinten McCannon."

Tom Feathers stepped from the buggy and came up the steps, his right hand extended. I took it and said howdy and felt him put a little extra into the grip. He was as tall as me, a little lighter built and had keen blue eyes. He was freshly shaven and smelled of bay rum.

"Don't believe I've seen you around Ogallala," he said; meaning, no doubt, that he wanted to know just exactly where I was from, and what I was doing in Ogallala.

"I came up from Cheyenne," I said not wanting to pussyfoot around for the next ten minutes in useless conversation with a man I already knew I didn't care much for.

"Cheyenne . . ." He said the name as though trying to think exactly how many miles away it was from the front porch.

"That's quite some distance," he concluded.

"Yes it is," I assured him. "But, I figured it was worth the trip to see Etta again."

That caused his left eye to twitch.

"Well," he said, turning his attention to Etta. "It must have been quite a surprise to have your friend suddenly show up all the way from Cheyenne?"

"Oh, in a way, I suppose it was," she said. "But I honestly expected him before now." She gave me a smile like she knew something I didn't. I gave her one back.

Without so much as missing a beat, Tom Feathers said, "Your aunt was kind enough to invite me to Sunday dinner, Etta. How could I refuse an opportunity to share the company of two beautiful women and fried chicken?"

Etta smiled like the cat that ate the canary as she put her hand through the crook of his arm and said, "Let's go tell Aunt Laura that you're here then, Tom."

Tom Feathers removed his sugar-loaf hat before stepping through the door. I thought it was damn gentlemanly of him to do so.

I cooled my heels by taking the saddle off the sorrel and letting him graze at the end of a picket rope. I checked the shoe to make sure it was in good order. Then I walked off a little distance from the house and made myself a cigarette and smoked it.

Sunday and chicken dinner, I thought. Company and conversation. Sitting around a big table. Civil folks, talking about civil matters: the weather, crops, politics. I thought of Billy Cody, the life he was leading and Ben Beadle, the life he'd been trying to lead before he was killed. I thought of old Persimmon Bill talking about the Big Lonely and Jake True, a man more likely to die from a bullet than old age. Like Wild Bill had ended up: dead before he reached forty. Men who didn't care to sit around on a Sunday afternoon and talk politics and the weather and wipe chicken grease from the fingers onto a cloth napkin.

I wondered what sort of life awaited a man between an early grave and talking politics and eating chicken around a big table on a Sunday afternoon.

Etta came out of the house and walked to where I was standing with the last of the shuck burning down between my fingers.

"Quint, don't you want to come inside? Dinner will be ready soon."

"I feel out of place, Etta."

"Don't," she said. "You are as welcome here as anyone."

"I wasn't invited."

"You don't require an invitation. I meant what I said earlier to Tom Feathers—I *was* expecting you to come before now. In fact, I waited every day for you to show up. And every day you didn't come riding up to the house, I found myself disappointed in a way I didn't fully understand. So now that you have finally arrived, don't feel out of place. I want you here."

We ate our dinner, with Etta's Aunt Laura and Tom Feathers doing most of the talking. Tom told about the shorthorn cattle he and his father were raising.

"Not like those tick-fevered longhorn cows they used to drive up here from Texas," he said pointedly as he looked in my direction. He held a drumstick in one hand and orchestrated his conversation with it.

"What bad times those used to be, when the wild and woolly cowboys would ride north with their sick cattle, raising all sorts of hell, if you'll pardon my expression, ladies. How we ever survived either those men or their diseased animals, I'll never know."

"No one seemed to mind we spent our money as I recall," I said. He looked amused that I had joined the conversation.

"We? Were you a drover, Mr. McCannon? One of those Texean cowboys?"

"We got called a lot of things, Mr. Feathers. Cowboys was one of them. Working men was another."

"I see," he said, satisfied that I had admitted to whatever sins he believed I was guilty of for having been a Texas drover.

"Well, point of fact is, Mr. McCannon, that all the money spent by the Texean cow hands hardly made up for the troubles brought on by their wild behavior. Most of the money spent by the wild Texas gentlemen was spent in the gambling dens and on cyprians and cheap liquor. Hardly of any benefit to the decent citizens, wouldn't you say?"

Etta placed her hand on my knee beneath the table. She knew without me telling her what I thought of Tom Feathers.

"You are right in one respect, Feathers—the liquor was mostly of a cheap variety. Watered down."

He studied me for a long moment, his drumstick held aloft, the grease shiny on his finger tips. It was burning him up he couldn't drop the gentlemanly crap and say what he really felt about my presence in the same room with him.

Out of respect for Etta, I changed the subject.

"I noticed you wear a Deane-Adams, Mr. Feathers."

His smile was slow in coming, and it looked like it hurt him to have to do so.

"Yes. I prefer it over the Colt."

"If you wouldn't mind, I'd like to take a closer look at it after dinner."

"Indeed," he said. "Perhaps we could even have a little shooting match. How would that be?"

I wasn't up for pistol shooting demonstrations; in my way of thinking, that wasn't what a sidearm was for. Practice and self-defense were the only two reasons I knew of to draw and fire your pistol. Normally, I would have turned the invitation down. But there was just something about Feathers's smugness that wouldn't allow me to decline his invitation.

"Why not?"

"Good," he said, without ever once losing that smugness.

After the chicken, Etta's aunt brought out a peach cobbler that she served in small blue bowls. The cobbler was still warm and I poured a little milk over mine. I kept thinking that such a damn fine meal had to have the taint of a man like Tom Feathers sitting at the table. I didn't like him the instant I'd laid eyes on him, and I liked him even less by the time we finished our dinner.

After a few extra minutes of complimenting Laura on her cooking skills, Tom Feathers and I excused ourselves and went outside.

We walked a short distance from the house.

"What shall it be, fast draw and fire, or simply target?" he asked with all the confidence of a pistoleer. I wondered how many men he'd shot and killed from a cold draw. If any.

"How about that fence post sticking up there," I said, pointing toward the rotting stump of an old post protruding from the dead brown grass. The distance was about twenty paces. He drew and fired five times fanning the hammer back with the edge of his left hand. Three times, I saw the wood splinter from the post.

I drew the self-cocker, took my time, thumbed the hammer back and fired. I did that four more times, each time my round chewed up bark.

"That is very good marksmanship," he acknowledged. "But as slow as you were, had that post been an adversary, you would well have been killed I believe."

"Maybe," I said, "but I didn't miss." He looked doubtful.

"I would submit that it is the man who gets off the first shot who wins the day," he said.

"Only if he hits his target, Mr. Feathers. "You can kill all the air you want to, but it's not the air that's going to kill you back. Two of your rounds missed the mark."

"I have to disagree with you, McCannon," he said, pointing toward the post with his chin. "My first round did find it's mark even if two missed. Had that been a man standing out there, he would have well been dead if he drew and fired his weapon as slowly as you just did."

"I guess there's no way of proving it unless you want to put it to the real test," I said. "Do you want to put it to the real test, Mr. Feathers—or is this just a game you're enjoying playing—shooting at targets that don't shoot back?"

It was out there in front of us now, our common dislike of one another. I could see the truth knotting up in his face.

"Because my family has wealth and holdings, you don't believe that I know what it is to pistol fight a man, isn't that it?"

"It doesn't matter what I think, Mr. Feathers. All I know is, that shooting at a fence post don't count for much in this world. Staying alive, does."

"Why'd you come here?" he asked, knocking the empty shells from his Deane-Adams.

"It's personal, Feathers, keep out of it."

"She won't have you," he said. "Not in the end, she won't." He was deliberate in reloading, the sun glinted off the brass cartridges.

"Etta's a fine woman," he continued. "Any man can see that. She's too fine a woman to be taken in by a man without means. What could you offer her?"

He waited to see if I would rise to the bait. I wouldn't.

"Look out there, Mr. McCannon. As far as you can see— that is land my family holds. A woman needs a nest, McCannon, and that is the biggest damn nest you will ever see."

"What's your point, Feathers?"

"My point is, McCannon, you should ride out. Say your sentimental good-byes and ride away. Why make it hard on everybody by hanging around here? Etta's too damn polite to ask you to go, but I'm not. Do you really think you stand a chance with her?"

"I don't think you have," I said.

"Have what?"

"Ever been in a gunfight. I don't think you know what it's like to stand in front of another man's pistol," I said as I turned to walk away.

"McCannon!" he called when I'd gone about fifteen feet. I turned, he was aiming his Deane-Adams at me.

"You forgot to reload your weapon," he said. "I didn't."

"You think so?" I said. He looked uncertain.

"Everyone knows a man only keeps five shells in his piece," he said. "Everyone knows a man doesn't keep his hammer on a loaded chamber. I counted. You shot five times at that post. That means you're carrying an empty gun.''

''Put your piece away, Feathers, before something really bad takes place here.''

He blinked. He was wondering if I really *did* have one more shell left in the self-cocker or if I was riding on empty like he counted I was. He was wondering something else, too. He was wondering even if I did have a round left in my piece whether or not I was fast enough to pull it and shoot him before he could pull the trigger on me. A man with true nerve didn't have such thoughts.

Any other man, any other time or place, I wouldn't have warned him first. Too much talk in a fight just gets you killed. But, I was thinking of the woman inside the house, how I'd come all this way just to see her. I didn't want to be part of a senseless killing on a pleasant Sunday afternoon. I didn't want her to see me like that. But I damn certain wasn't going to just stand there and take a bullet from a man wearing expensive kidskin gloves.

''You've got one chance, Feathers. Put it away and walk back to the house.''

He blinked like the wind stung his eyes, then his arm sagged to his side, the Deane-Adams dangled against his right leg.

''Next time,'' I said, ''there'll be no talk.''

The color was gone from his face, his right hand shook causing the sunlight to dance off the nickel-plated barrel of the Deane-Adams.

''I think you bluffed me,'' he said as I started back toward the house. It was something he was never going to know unless he was man enough to try me—but I knew. I hadn't bluffed him. Usually I did keep my hammer resting on an empty chamber—but not when I knew beforehand I was being challenged.

Etta greeted us as we reached the porch. She could see it on our faces, the discord.

''Aunty says the gunfire hurts her ears.''

''I must be leaving now, Etta,'' Tom Feathers said. ''Please tell your aunt I had to leave and thank her again for me for the wonderful meal.''

After Tom Feathers climbed into his buggy and drove away, Etta turned to me and said, "What was that all about?"

"I think you already know," I said.

"Men," she said.

"Yeah," I said. "It usually has to do with a woman."

"It wasn't necessary in this case, Quint. You must know that already. I have little interest in Tom Feathers as a suitor, or anything else for that matter."

"I know it, but I don't think Tom Feathers knows it."

"So you quarreled over me?"

"No, not exactly quarreled, Etta."

For a long moment she stood there looking at me.

"Let's go for a walk," she said.

The wind had picked up and the air had cooled and I waited while Etta went inside the house and put on a mackinaw.

"Was your aunt disappointed that Tom Feathers left?" I asked.

"Yes, I think she was, a little."

"Which means she's probably disappointed that I was the one that stayed."

"You know," Etta said, "sometimes you don't give yourself enough credit."

"You're probably right," I said.

We walked down a hedgerow, our steps soft upon the brown carpet of dead grass. The wind swept at Etta's skirts and I had to pull my hat down a little tighter to keep it from blowing away.

"This place," Etta said. "This Nebraska; it is so plain and uneventful in appearance and yet it has a way of causing you to want to stick to it. It would be a wonderful place to raise a family I would think." She looked straight ahead when she said it.

All the openness and space did seem far removed from the rough frontier towns of Dodge and Cheyenne, and from the crowded cities of Denver and St. Louis. Walking along the hedgerow with Etta, the wind at our backs, gave me a feeling of contentment I'd not had in a long time. I had things in me that I wanted to say to her; things I had to fight back to keep from saying.

We topped a rise and there below us stood an old stone house, its sod roof partially gone.

"That place was Aunty's father's first homestead," Etta said, taking my hand and pulling me toward it. "His name was Emmett. Aunty says he gathered the rocks for the walls from the Platte river and that he laid the sod himself for the roof and that it wasn't uncommon for there to be dirt in their beds, or scorpions after a hard rain or a good blow of wind."

It was a small house consisting of two rooms. Etta said that seven people lived in the house at one time, and that four of them were buried in a little cemetery near a single cottonwood that had since been struck by lightning and now stood bone white and barren except for the top that was charred black. The tree looked like it had been there a hundred years. It would take four large men holding hands to encircle it.

The windows of the house were missing, as was the door. Sunlight streamed through the holes in the sod roof overhead. We entered at Etta's urging and stood within the walls, the sunlight warming us as she pressed herself to me.

"It seems like it has been forever," she said.

"Yes, I know."

She touched the buttons of my coat, paused, looked up at me. "Do you think I'm being too bold?" she asked.

"No."

Then she kissed me before undoing the buttons.

A lowing of wind danced along the stone walls and dust danced in the shaft of sunlight that angled like gold blades down through the broken soddy roof.

But the walls protected us from the blowing wind and the sun warmed the river stones as Etta and I sank to the grassy floor of the abandoned house.

"I could barely keep from touching you at dinner," she whispered as I drew open the mackinaw she was wearing and touched my hands to her warm blouse. "I wanted to so badly."

Her skin prickled from the coolness of my fingers until I covered her with my own body. Then the warmth came through her and into me. We touched each other, our hands careful to not hurry in their desire. I pulled the combs from her hair and felt it cascading over my hands as it fell to her bare shoulders and I laced my fingers through it.

"I have never made love outdoors," she said.

"Well, it's not exactly outdoors," I said. "But it's pretty darn close."

She laughed and threw her head back and exposed her long white neck to me and I kissed it as she drew me in closer to her, teasingly, playfully.

She whispered my name as she hovered above me. Then slowly, with her eyes closed, she lowered herself down onto me and something long and aching shuddered through my center and I called her name. Whatever contact we had with the world outside the river-stone walls of the old home were lost in our desire for each other.

Later, we lay in the slanting shadows, holding each other, unable to quite let go.

"It was like the first time," she said. "Only better."

"You are an amazing woman, Etta."

She smiled, pressed her face against my cheek.

"I can see now why they had so many children," Etta said with a smile, in reference to the family that had once lived here. "It is all so very cozy."

I raised enough on one elbow to look at her; I liked what I saw. She seemed not to mind my looking; I almost felt as though she enjoyed it as much as I did.

"Do you think me shameless?" she asked after a few moments, as I ran my right hand along her hip.

"No, not at all."

"I don't feel shameless in front of you, Quint. I feel perfectly natural, as though I have always known you and you have always known me. I know of women who won't even look at themselves naked, much less allow a man to look at them."

"It feels natural for me too, Etta. Maybe you and I are different from the rest."

Her fingers rubbed along my jaw.

"I know I can't keep you here with me forever, in this place, just as we are right now, naked and natural—but, I would surely like to," she said.

I kissed her because I couldn't help from kissing her. I felt her cling to me in that long sweet act and when our lips separated she said, "If you don't have to get back to Wyoming right away . . ."

When we finally did dress and start back to her aunt's house, the sun had set and a harvest moon was already on the rise.

"Do you think Aunty Laura will notice?" Etta said.

"Notice what?"

"How happy I am?"

"If she is any kind of observer of human nature," I said. "She'll probably notice it on both of us."

20

I stayed on four more days at the house where Etta and her aunt lived. I was provided a spare room, but most nights, Etta and I managed to find our way into each other's bed. And on the last day, Etta and I spent the morning lying in each other's arms and watched the rain fall just outside her bedroom window.

"We've become decadent, Quint, you and I have?"

"I don't mind if you don't."

The rain danced on the metal slope of the overhang just outside the window and sounded like the drumming of a thousand heartbeats with ours thrown in.

"This has been such a wonderful time for me," Etta said, turning her face toward the window, the light the color of pearl against the glass.

"And for me," I said, fully meaning it. The last four days had been some of the most pleasant of my life: The long languorous hours we'd spent together, the walks across the fields, seeing the flight of geese on their southward trek, the dark V of their flight cut against molten skies. The sound of a dry wind stirring through the brittle winter grass beneath our footsteps. And Etta, her honey-colored hair long and falling past her shoulders as she walked alongside me, holding my hand. It all seemed so damn right.

"Why not stay," she said, suddenly, turning to look directly into my eyes.

"You know why not," I said.

"I know Ben was your friend. I know you feel you need to avenge his death, Quinten. But, will that bring him back? Will it change anything in the long run?" Before I could say anything, she turned once more to stare out the window as though already knowing what my answer would be and not wanting to face it.

"What about us?" she asked softly. "How many chances will we have to find happiness? And if we don't take what is left to us now, when it's right here, will what we have still be there later on—after you've done what is *necessary* to avenge Ben's murder?"

"I don't know the answer to that, Etta."

In the time we'd spent together, I'd told her about my late wife and son. I'd told her about the war and what it had done to me, to the very marrow of me. I told her about friends of mine who had died before their time. And I even ended up telling her about Alexandra Dupage. I'd told her everything. I didn't feel I had to tell her why I couldn't stay with her. Not this time.

"Then you will go and take the risks involved in finding Ben's killer," she said, the pearl light falling over her bare shoulders.

"It's not a matter of choice with me, Etta. If you've learned anything about me in these last few days, you at least know that much."

"He means more to you than I do . . ." Her voice was barely audible against the drumming song of rain.

"Ben was my friend, Etta."

"Then you'll go, even if it means the end of us?" she said.

"That's a separate issue."

"No, it isn't. Not really it isn't."

"I think it is."

"Then we disagree."

"If that's how you see it."

A bad feeling was crawling over me. The conversation was going down a road I didn't want it to, but there didn't seem any way to stop it.

She sighed, turned toward me again, looked into my face, her eyes seeking something I wasn't offering right then. The disappointment in her gaze was as sodden as the weather.

"Why did you come and find me," she asked, "if it was only to get me to love you and then leave me again?"

"I didn't mean for it to end up this way, Etta."

Her hand reached out and touched my cheek.

"You are a dear sweet man, Quint McCannon, and one I will always love. But I can't wait for a man who will only ride in long enough to break my heart and then ride away again. This time it is because of Ben, but next time it will be because of someone or something else. I know that much about you as surely as I know anything in this life. I need more."

I kissed her lightly on the mouth and she didn't protest and she didn't kiss me back.

"I will be leaving when the rain stops."

"Yes," she said. "When the rain stops."

The rain stopped that very afternoon and a patch of blue sky broke through the slate sky sending a long shaft of sunlight crawling over the wet grass.

I'd saddled the sorrel and was preparing to ride back to North Platte when Etta came from the house and stood on the porch. It was one of the hardest damn things I ever had to do, not to go over and tell her I'd changed my mind and that I was staying.

I put a foot in the stirrup, gave it one more second of thought, then swung up in the saddle and rode the sorrel up to the porch.

"I'm sorry it has to be this way, Etta."

Her smile was lacking, her eyes brimmed with tears; but she would not let herself cry.

"I hope you find the man you are looking for, Quinten. I truly do."

"And after I do?"

She brushed the heel of her hand against the corner of one eye; a single teardrop was threatening to spill down her cheek.

''And afterward,'' she said, ''I hope you find whatever else you are looking for.'' I knew we had reached the end of the line, there was nothing more to offer.

''Good-bye, Etta.''

She may have spoke my name as I rode away, but the only thing I heard was the wind.

I avoided Billy Cody's place on the return trip and rode straight to North Platte and turned in the rented horse. I checked on the next stage to Cheyenne; it wasn't due to leave until the following morning. I checked into a hotel, then found a place to buy a drink; it felt like I could use a drink, maybe several.

I was prepared to get drunk if I had to, but I wasn't prepared for what happened next.

It was an ordinary saloon, like most: A bar along one wall, tables and chairs against the opposite wall, a glass display case for the selling of cigars and tobacco, a roulette wheel and a dice table. Nothing you would think twice about.

I ordered a whiskey and found an empty table—that time of day, it wasn't hard to find an empty table. A few others, like me, with time on their hands, stood or sat around waiting for something to happen. None of us had to wait long.

I was still working on the whiskey and my private thoughts of Etta when an old familiar face showed up—Calamity Jane. She was alone and drunk, judging by the way she was weaving her way through the place. I watched her walk straight to the bar and slap a palm down so hard on the oak it sounded like someone had fired off a derringer.

''Barkeep! Bring at bottle down thisaway, huh!''

I didn't know whether to run out the back door, hold my seat, or go up and say hello. Jane was someone I'd first met back in Deadwood. The last time we spoke, she'd promised to clean herself up and get off the drinking. It didn't look like she'd been successful at it. Jane had a lot of disagreeable traits and damn few endearing qualities, especially when she was drinking. For one thing, she was liable to say or do anything.

But in spite of everything, it was her heart that won you over. She had a good heart. So I called out to her.

"Martha Jane Canary!"

She had her back to me, standing at the bar as she was. She was dressed in her usual buckskin blouse and britches and not wearing a hat—her hair was short and choppy. The other thing was the sidearm she was wearing in her belt: A Navy Colt, the same one she claimed Wild Bill had given her just before he went off to play his last hand of cards.

She turned around in a start when I called out her name, her hand reaching for the pistol.

"Hold off, Janey! Don't pull that hog leg or I'll be forced to shoot you!"

Her eyes grew wide and she said, "Step outta the shadows ya low down sonbitch and we will see who does the shootin'!"

I couldn't help but laugh, which only managed to befuddle her all the more.

"What the hell ya laughin' at, mister!"

"Jesus, Jane. You haven't changed a nickel's worth since Deadwood," I managed to say. She cocked her head trying to recognize my voice.

"Hey there! It ain't who I think it is, is it?" she cried.

"It's me, Jane—McCannon."

She practically knocked me over saying her hellos.

"Easy Jane, folks will think we're sweethearts."

"What's wrong with that, Mac!" she shouted. "We almost was once!"

"Never!" I amended.

"Almost!"

"Not even close."

She brayed like a mule; the smell of old liquor almost buckled my knees. She eyed my empty glass. "Barkeep! Bring at bottle over here!"

The bardog set the bottle down on the table.

"Who's going to pay for this?" he asked.

"Mac here," Jane said, before I could protest her liberty with my funds.

I scratched up two dollars for the bottle and right away Jane set to work on it.

"*Key-rist!* Mac! How ya been?"

"I've been fine, Jane. What about you?"

"Gawdawful! I been bustin' a freight wagon since I left Deadwood. Here to Lincoln and back. Hard as hell work, I'm here to tell ya! Ain't no kinda work for a lady, but it's all I could get in these hard times!"

"What happened to going back East and seeing your daughter?" I asked.

She shook her head; her eyes expressing great sorrow.

"Never did get around to it, Mac. Had to raise some capital. Ya ever think how many ways there is for a gal to make a livin' out here on this frontier? Not very goddamn many! Least none they'd write home and tell their mammas about!"

"I wish I could help you out with the fare, Martha, but I'm nearly busted flat myself."

"Aw hell," she said, with a wave of her hand. "Not to worry. I'll come up with the funds somehow or other. And when I go back East to see my darlin' baby girl—by God, I'll go in style!"

"I bet you will," I said. She gave me a sloppy grin.

"Now ya know that offer between ya an' me still stands, don't ya, Mac?"

"What offer is that, Jane?"

She leaned across the table and patted my hand.

"Ya *know.*" She said it almost shyly, like a secretive child.

"Yes, I think I remember now, Jane. But to tell you the truth, a woman is the last thing I need right now."

She looked keenly disappointed. "'At's too bad, Mac. 'Cause Janey's got tricks most men ain't never heard of, much less experienced! Har! Har!"

"Well, I'll keep it in mind in case I ever do get lonely."

She looked even more emaciated than the last time I saw her.

"You been eating regular?" I asked.

"Regular whenever I can," she replied.

"If I give you a dollar will you promise to buy yourself a meal?"

Her eyes narrowed.

"I ain't in need of no charity, Mac! Hell, I got some money!"

"Let me see."

She scrunched up her face.

"Let me see if you've got money," I said.

"Well I don't carry it around on me. Gezzus *Key-rist!* Mac! Ya want somebody to come along and knock me over the head for my poke?"

"If I give you the dollar," I repeated, "will you go over and buy yourself a meal?"

She looked sullen.

"I guess maybe so."

"Promise you will, Jane."

She shook her head slowly.

"Okay, I'll take yer damn ol' dollar and buy myself some grub. But soon's I do and get back up to my crib, I'll pay ya back—that's a damn bet!"

"Alright."

"Gezzus, but I could fall in love with ya so damn easy, Mac!"

"Don't go getting sentimental on me, Jane. You know how much I hate to cry."

She cocked her head, looked at me for a serious moment, then grinned.

"I'm sure glad ya cleared outta Deadwood, Mac. Sure glad they didn't kill ya up there like they did my poor Bill."

"I was luckier than Bill."

I could see the whiskey vapors and the memory of Bill Hickok had suddenly turned her maudlin.

"Here's the dollar, Jane. Go buy yourself a meal."

She reached a hand for it, but her mind was still elsewhere.

"What about ya, Mac?"

"I just need a little privacy, Jane. Maybe I'll run into you later."

She looked hopeful as she slid her chair back from the table. Hopeful and wretched in her condition.

"I'll see ya around, huh, Mac?"

I nodded.

"See you around, Martha."

I watched as she weaved her way to the door, then saw her surrounded by the pearl light and for a second, she appeared to glow like an angel standing there in the doorway. I finished my drink and thought about what Jane had said about how hard it was for a woman to earn a living on the frontier. Then I thought about Etta, and the offer I knew Tom Feathers would make her, and the thought tore at my being that a man like him was able to offer her what I couldn't.

I returned to my hotel room in a blue funk. Stretched out across the bed in my room, I could only think of what might have been between Etta and me; the depth of my disappointment surprised me. I closed my eyes and allowed sleep to take over my thoughts, only to be awakened by the sudden clawing and hammering at my door accompanied by the screams of Calamity Jane yelling bloody murder at the top of her lungs.

"Let me in, Mac! The sonbitches are tryin' to kill me!"

21

I yanked open the door and she pushed past me.

"Hurry up and close it!" she yelled.

"What the hell's going on, Jane?"

"A little disturbance, Mac!"

I could hear footsteps down the hall, the sound of men's voices.

"What sort of disturbance?" I asked her.

"Nothin', Mac. Just a misunderstanding' is all!"

I could hear fists pounding on doors, voices shouting: "Anybody seen a thievin' little bitch?"

I looked at Jane; she looked guilty as hell, whatever it was.

Then the fists hammered at my door. I pulled the self-cocker from the holster and motioned Jane to move over into the far corner of the room where she couldn't be seen once I opened the door. It was one of the damn few times she ever did what anyone told her to do without having to be asked twice.

When I opened the door, a man with a face red as raw beef—along with several others crowded behind him—said, "We're looking for a cussed little yellow-haired whore! You seen her?"

"What she do?" I asked.

He smelled like the bottom of a whiskey barrel. His tongue

seemed too big for his mouth when he spoke and webs of
spittle clung to the corners of his lips. He was dressed well
enough; like a banker. White shirt and cravat, checked vest,
claw-hammer coat. He had a mole on the side of his nose that
sprouted small hairs.

"What?" he said.

"I asked why you were looking for this woman?"

His eyes jerked around in his head, like I'd asked him a
difficult question, one he hadn't expected to be asked.

"What the hell's it to you why I'm looking for her for?"

"You pounded on my door," I said. "Woke me out of a
nice dream. I want to know why you're so interested in finding
this woman that you would wake a peaceful man up out of his
dreams?"

He didn't appear the type who was used to having questions
asked of him. He didn't react like it, either.

"Say mister, who the hell you think you are?"

"That's not the question," I said.

His hand shot up to grab me, I brought the self-cocker around
at the same time and thumbed the hammer back. He looked
down the barrel like he was staring at a snake.

"I wouldn't do that," I warned him, "make any sudden
moves like that."

It had a wilting effect on his bravado. He took a full step
back bumping into a man standing behind him. Some of his
companions scattered back down the hall at the sight of the
Remington in my hand.

"It's late," I said. "Maybe you and your friends ought to
go on home."

The man swallowed hard, worked up enough of his nerve
to say: "You don't . . . know what you're dealing with here."

"I know you're disturbing my rest."

"Come'n Lon," one of the men behind him said. "Let's let
the city marshal handle this. At's what he gets paid to do."
His friends tugged on his coat sleeve all the way down the hall.

I closed the door and turned to Jane.

"What'd you do to that man?"

She shrugged, looked at me, then away.

"Gezzus Mac—it's not anything like yar thinkin' it is."

"Tell me why those men are after you."

She was still a little drunk; she was always a little drunk.

"He gave me his gold watch, then later on asked for it back—that's all. He's a dang ol' Indun giver!"

"You stole the man's watch."

"Naw. He gave it to me to hold for him on a bet."

"What kind of bet?"

She looked a little too sheepish.

"I'm waiting," I said. My patience was running thin.

She paced the room.

"He wanted to show me his willy worm."

I lowered the hammer on the pistol, slipped it back inside the holster hanging from the back of a chair.

"His willy worm?"

"Ya know, his wiggle bean." She snorted. "Men got all sorts of names for it, but it's all the same thing no matter how ya call it. Men jus' got a natural tendency to want to show it to a gal."

"Why would a well-heeled man like him want to show you his wiggle bean?" I asked, doubtful as to the story the way Jane was giving it to me.

"He claimed his was the biggest one in Nebraska! I bet him it wan't. He said he'd bet his gold watch on it. I said only if I got to hold the watch. That's how he ended up giving it to me."

"That's a damn thin story, Jane."

Her sallow features drew into a pout that wasn't any more real than half the stories she'd told me in the Deadwood jail the first time I ever laid eyes on her.

"Reason I kept his ol' watch was 'cause his wiggle bean wan't even close to bein' the biggest one in Nebraska. Hell, he just wanted to wave it around in front of me, embarrass me in front of all his friends is all. He called me a tramp. I spit in his face and said he lost the bet. He got mad as hell, said he'd beat me like a rug. That's when I took off!"

"Sounds to me like you just flat out stole the man's watch, Jane."

"Man's a sonbitch, Mac. Treated me like a tramp!"

I couldn't say if the tears she began to shed were real or crocodile. Jane had a way of turning her worst side to you and still manage to make you feel sorry for her.

"It was a damn foolish thing to do no matter how you look at it, Jane. And I don't much appreciate you knocking on my door in the middle of the night."

"You did the right thing, Mac, defendin' an honest woman from an abuser."

She wiped at her eyes with the heels of her hands and snuffled like a galled horse.

"Go give him back his watch, Jane."

"Why should I?"

"So the city marshal doesn't arrest you and throw you in jail. How's that for a reason?"

She sat heavily on the side of the bed, pulled the watch from her pocket and stared at it.

"I could get maybe five dollars for this watch, Mac. Enough to start a savin's so's I could go see little Janey. Now you want me to just go give that woman abuser back his watch?"

"That's what I want you to do, give it back. You're never going to get to see your daughter if you keep getting arrested and thrown in jail."

She looked forlorn over the prospect of giving back the watch.

"Can't do it," she said.

"Why not?"

"It'd go against my grain. 'Sides, I have a reputation to maintain."

"Reputation?"

"You know, like Wild Bill's. Folks expect ol' Calamity to be a colorful character. How'd it look, they think of me as nothin' but a petty thief that went around stealin' then givin' back to them what she stole from them in the first place?"

"Repentant?" I suggested.

"At ain't the point, Mac. Folks'd just think of me like some common ol' trash instead of Calamity Jane. I just can't give it back. You do it!"

I started to protest, but then she began her sobbing; a display that included several terrible sounds coughed up from her frail frame. Great tears the size of silver dollars rolled down her cheeks as she snorted and sputtered, calling out the name of her late love, Wild Bill Hickok.

"I'm comin' to join ya, Bill—*Gawd,* if I ain't!"

I had no means to stop the dramatization other than to throw her out of the room; I would just have to let her melodrama play itself out, like an unexpected rainstorm on the prairie.

"Ya just don't know what it's like to be all alone and blue in this cruel ol' world, Mac! Ya just don't know . . ."

I rolled a shuck and smoked it and waited for her to finish the dramatics. Finally she quit and blew her nose in a blue rag she pulled from her back pocket. Still, she maintained a blubbering, rambling recitation of all that had ever gone wrong with her life, beginning the day she'd been born clear up to the present.

"Don't ya see, Mac, why I can't bring myself to the humiliation of takin' that big ol' fool's watch back and givin' it to him? I'd just seem common and cheap to everyone. I'd lose my celebrity! Them yellow journalists and pulp writers wouldn't spill a drop of ink on me!" Then, she gave another horse snuffle and looked up at me like her daddy had just died.

"Give me the damn watch, Jane!"

My head had begun to hurt. It was simply easier for me to return the watch on her behalf than it was to listen to another minute's worth of her caterwauling.

In one final dramatic gesture, she placed the watch in my hand with a great sigh.

"Ya'll receive yar reward in heaven for this, Mac. I know ya will."

"When I finish returning the watch, Jane, I expect to come back here to a nice empty room. That clear?"

"Sure, sure, Mac. I ain't one to be a pest."

Halfway down the street I ran into the same group of men who had pounded on my door minutes earlier. They were knotted around a man wearing a handlebar moustache and a five-point star pinned to his coat.

"That's him, Marshal!" the man Jane had taken the watch from declared. "He's the one waved his pistol in my face—threatened me with it!"

I recognized the lawman: Eli Frost. Last time Eli and I had been in each other's company, we were shooting a game of billiards down in El Paso. I remember Eli won the game and five dollars off me then paid for my meal afterward.

"Mr. Feathers here says you threatened to shoot him," Eli said as we stopped a few feet apart on the sidewalk. He gave no recognition in front of the others that he knew me.

"I did, Marshal."

"You care to explain why?"

"He disturbed my sleep."

"That true, Mr. Feathers, you disturb this man's sleep?" Eli said, turning his attention to the rich man.

The man's name didn't escape my attention. I could see some resemblance around the eyes.

He sputtered like a faulty steam engine trying to explain himself.

"We were lookin' for this thieving little bitch!" Feathers said in loud blustery voice. "We just knocked on this fellow's door to see if he'd seen her and he starts waving his gun in my face!"

"Here's your watch back," I said, handing it to him. He looked damn surprised.

"How'd you?"

"What difference does it make?" I said, cutting him off from a conversation I didn't want to have. "That's what you were looking for, now you've found it. Go on back to your drinking."

"I want this man arrested for assault!" Feathers insisted, turning his anger on Eli.

I'd seen Eli Frost fight the Stoneman brothers in San Antone and whip both men without losing his hat. He wasn't the sort of man to flap easily, or to take abuse.

"You should let this matter drop, Feathers," Eli said. And when Feathers started to crank it up again, Eli gave him a cold stare that didn't require any more conversation.

"What about that little slut who stole my watch?" Feathers muttered.

"You got your watch back," Eli said. "And another thing maybe you ought to think about, Mr. Feathers. We got decency laws in this town. Next time you bet your watch on something, make sure it don't involve pulling your pecker out in public. Next time you do, I'll have you arrested."

Feathers folded his position like a cheap tent in a hard wind and skulked off with his cronies in tow.

"Goddam rich men," Eli said, watching the lot of them traipse off down the street. "They leave their wives at home, ride into my town, get drunk and make damn fools of themselves then expect to leave their mess for me to clean up!"

"How have you been, Eli?"

He was a man not given to humor.

"How does it look I've been?" he said.

"Doesn't look like you've done too bad—put on a few pounds maybe."

He patted his girth, the bottom part of his vest couldn't quite be buttoned all the way.

"It's my wife's cooking," he said. "Woman can cook like forty Frenchmen." Then sheepishly added. "I got married since I seen you last, Mac. A woman named Emma."

"How'd you end up here?"

He grunted.

"Got drunk one day and fell off my horse and when I woke up, I was here, in the middle of Nebraska. I decided since I was already here, I might as well stay. I guess there are a lot worse places to get drunk and fall off your horse than in Nebraska. How about you?"

I told him why I was in the territory and then I asked him if the man who'd lost his watch was the same Feathers that owned a lot of land over by Ogallala.

"That's him, you know him?"

"I know his boy."

"Oh yeah," Eli said. "Same damn cut as the old man—rich and arrogant."

"Can I buy you a drink, Eli?"

He shook his head.

"No. I gave liquor up along with most of my cussing and wild ways. I attend the Free Baptist Church and sing in the choir. Things like that happen when you get married. The wife's home waiting for me. Best I get on back. You know how that can be, a wife waiting home for you."

"Glad to see you're doing well for yourself, Eli. Glad to see some of us have not been planted."

He gave a half smile that on him, looked out of place.

"Not all of us yet, anyways," he said.

I shook his hand, thanked him for his courtesy in handling Feathers, then told him I'd be catching the stage out in the morning.

"Oh," he said. "Do me a favor, huh?"

"What's that?"

"If you see Martha Jane before you go, tell her to find another town. Tell her its a request, not an order. But tell her if she decides to stay, I'll arrest her and throw away the key."

Then Eli walked into the shadows and was gone.

I never got the chance to tell Calamity what Eli had said about leaving town. She was already gone by the time I returned to my room. I found a handwritten note lying on the bed.

Dere Mc. Thanks for yr. assistance once again. I hope that old fool is happy he got his pocketwatch returned him in good order. Maybe next time he'll learn not to bet it on his wiggle bean. Ha Ha. Me, I'm clearin out. I seen enough of this burg to last me a lifetime. I'm thinking about goin to Santa Fe. They say the wether there is good for what ails you. Take care. Yrs. Truly, Martha Jane Canary.

Well, at least it saved me the trouble of asking her to leave. On the other hand, it was folks like Jane that kept life on the interesting side. I hoped she would find Santa Fe to her liking.

In a few more hours, I would be on the stage headed back to Cheyenne and with any luck it would be a long time before I'd run into Jane again—even if I did feel half sorry for her.

I flopped on the bed and rolled myself a shuck while I tried hard not to think about another woman—Etta Landrow. Hard as I tried, however, thoughts of her kept creeping into my mind as I tapped tobacco into my paper and curled up the ends.

I didn't want to think that maybe this very night, Tom Feathers was sitting with her in the parlor sharing spiced wine and intimate conversation. But I did and it gave me a tight feeling in my gut.

Instead, I tried to concentrate on getting back to Cheyenne and seeing the job done that Jake True and I had started: catching Elijah Hook and taking him to trial if he gave us that chance. If he didn't, well, it didn't much matter to me if he wanted to put up a fight and maybe save us the trouble of escorting him to jail. I was feeling in a foul mood.

The damndest thing was, I couldn't figure the man out. He had outsmarted Jake and me, and he had led us on a merry chase. He'd stolen Sugar Brown, our horses, and finally Jonas Fly right out from under us. He could have saved himself the trouble and ran, but he hadn't. That was the most puzzling part, why he didn't run and keep running.

The man had to know if Jake and I caught him, he would end up at the end of a rope, or we'd kill him if he tried putting up a fight.

I sat there in the dark watching the glow of the tip of my cigarette and tried to fit it all together and all I kept coming up with was a bad feeling.

22

Doc Price looked disappointed to see me standing at his door again. He looked beyond my shoulder.

"You bring anymore shooting victims for me to patch up?"

"Not a single one this time, Doc."

"Then you can come in." He stepped aside, the room smelled of mineral spirits.

"How's the last patient I brought you?" I asked.

"Limping. But then, I ain't surprised. The bullet chipped off a piece of his hip bone. Thing like that will cause a man to limp permanent."

"The big question is, will it interfere with his dancing?" I said.

"Only if he's dancing with a big fat woman and she falls on him. You want a shot of bourbon?"

"Is it recommended?"

He looked into my eyes without a glint of humor.

"From what I can observe," he said, "it is."

"What's your diagnosis, Doc?"

"Death, son. You and Jake and the others like you. I look into the eyes of you boys and I see nothing but death. You're surrounded by it, have been all your lives. Guns, knives, horses falling on you, whatever it takes. A hundred ways for a man to die and you boys know them all. Men like you and Jake . . .'' he shook his head, walked to a medicine cabinet and pulled out a bottle and two shot glasses and poured us each a drink.

"Is Jake up to riding yet?" I asked.

"If he don't mind a little pain," Doc said, testing the bourbon with tentative lips before tossing it down.

"How's the Mexican kid, Jesse?"

"Same as he was the last time you asked me," Doc said, sourly. "He'll always be the same clear up till he takes his last breath. And that may not be for awhile, poor little bastard."

Doc closed his eyes, tossed down his bourbon, then licked his lips and blinked.

"Same thing could happen to you or Jake the next time you catch a slug," he said. "You ever imagine what that'd be like, paralyzed like that, lying in a bed all day, staring at the ceiling counting fly specks waiting for somebody to come in and turn you so the bed sores didn't eat through to your bones?"

"No Doc, I don't ever think of it in that way."

"Why not?" He said it almost angrily, his gray watery eyes challenging me for an answer. "It happens! Bullets can do a lot worse than kill you!"

"I know it happens, Doc—we both do."

He poured himself a second glass of the whiskey, said, "Cheers" and tossed his down. He sat there for a time staring at his empty glass before putting the bottle back in the cabinet.

"Forget what I said," he muttered. "Just sometimes it gets to me—the destruction of the human flesh. I should have taken my old mother's advice and become a lawyer; relieving men of their money and holdings is a lot easier than relieving them of their pain and misery."

"It's good work you do, Doc."

"Yes, I suppose some days it is. Other days, I am not so certain."

"I've been reading this book," I said, "about an old man who rides out to fight windmills. He believes they are giants and that flocks of sheep are invading armies."

"Don Quixote," Doc said with a half smile that showed his big horsey front teeth. "I'm familiar with the work."

"I just wonder if sometimes we're not like that," I said, "believing we're doing the right and good thing when all it is is just windmills and flocks of sheep in front of us."

"Everyone is as God made him," Doc quoted from memory, "and much worse."

"All we can do is try, Doc."

He nodded.

"Go collect your friend and get him the hell out of here," Doc said. "He's sitting out back, restless as a pimp in church. He just can't wait to go out and get himself shot again."

"Thanks for everything, Doc."

"Do me a favor, will you?"

"What's that?"

"Watch your backs."

Jake was sitting in a wheelchair trying to roll a cigarette.

"Doc said you're up to riding," I said.

"About time you got back."

"I was only gone five days."

"Six. And I've been ready to ride since day before yesterday."

"It doesn't look it."

"Aw hell, I don't need this," he said, standing up. "I was just sitting in it waiting for you to come back. I planned on leaving tomorrow whether you came back or not."

"Well, I'm here now."

He had a little hitch to his step as he crossed the porch and asked me for a match to light his shuck with. "Shot a piece of my hip bone off, now my damn leg's about an inch or two shorter than the other one," he growled around the blue smoke of cigarette.

"Tennessee Bob had one leg shorter than the other," I said. "You remember Tennessee Bob, don't you?"

He tugged the brim of his hat a little lower over his eyes and started off toward the livery. I fell in alongside him.

"I figured you got married, or something," Jake said.

"Why'd you figure that?"

''The way you looked all moon-eyed when you left here.''

''Went up to see Billy Cody,'' I said.

''Bullshit, you went to see that woman, what's her name.''

''Etta, you mean?''

''Yeah, Etta. Hell, I was you, I'd have married her and not come back. I'd be laying up in a nice feather bed right now with her in there with me. Wouldn't get up till Christmas, and maybe not even then, I had a looker like her. Why'd you come back?''

''You know why? And besides, I doubt you'd just lay around in a bed all day even if there was a good-looking woman in it with you.''

''You don't know.''

''Let's stop a minute and see Little Dick,'' I said.

Little Dick was waiting on a man and woman and three children who were all sitting around a table in the middle of the dining room. They were eating fried chicken and butter-beans. Dick saw us and hobbled over.

''You walk like I do,'' he said when he saw Jake.

''I'd have to have both hips shot up to walk like you,'' Jake said. ''Both hips shot and a horse fall on me.''

''You boys want some coffee?''

''No,'' Jake said. ''We don't have time for coffee.''

''Don't mind him, Little Dick, he's just irritable,'' I said.

''From what?''

''From not lying in a feather bed with a pretty woman.''

''Hell, who wouldn't like to be lying in a feather bed with a pretty woman?'' Little Dick said with a crooked grin.

''We got riding to do,'' Jake grumbled, acting as though he was ignoring both of us.

Little Dick said, ''Did you ask him?''

''Ask me what?'' Jake said.

''Little Dick wants to ride with us to go after Hook,'' I said. Jake gave me a look.

''Ain't we lost enough time already?''

''That's the whole point,'' Little Dick interjected. ''The trail's gone colder than a well-digger's nuts.by now. Anybody around here knows about tracking a man, it's me.''

"Tracker!" Jake declared. "What the hell we need another tracker for? Any ol' time Hook decides we ain't been doing a good enough job, *he* tracks us! He's done stole our horses, a whore, and a medicine drummer right out from under our noses!"

"That's true," I said, "but if anyone can find him it would be Little Dick. He hunted half the Apaches in Arizona before becoming a cowhand on the Chisholm."

"Aw hell, do what you want!" Jake growled. "But I ain't sharing the reward money, tracker or no tracker!"

"That's fine with me," Little Dick said, yanking off his apron. "I'd almost pay to go with you."

"Say!" the man sitting at the table with his family called out. "Can we have some more chicken and some extra butterbeans?"

"You can if you'll go in the kitchen and get 'em," Dick said. "And when you and them young'ns are finished stuffing your beaks, lock the door when you leave and put the closed sign in the winda."

Jake said, "If you're giving away fried chicken, I wouldn't mind having a little myself."

"I'll bring a sack of it along," Little Dick said.

We told Little Dick we'd meet him at the stables.

"I should have brought it up sooner about Little Dick wanting to go with us," I said to Jake as we left the diner.

"I guess it could be worse," Jake said.

"How so?"

"Little Dick could have offered just to bring along a sack of butterbeans instead of his fried chicken. I never was big on butterbeans."

We rode out of Cheyenne within an hour.

The next day, we arrived at the place where Elijah Hook had stolen Jonas Fly and his mule. The wagon was still there, but all the patent medicines inside were missing.

"Lookit that," Jake said, peering into the back of the wagon. "Damn thieves come along and stole all Jonas's patent medicines! What the hell is this country coming to?"

"Well, they didn't steal the wagon," Little Dick said. "That ought to give the rest of us decent citizens some hope."

"Wonder they didn't," Jake muttered. "A wicked place like this, folks steal everything—including whores!"

While Jake was philosophizing about the state of the union, Little Dick was searching the ground for sign of tracks.

"How's he going to find any good sign? Why its been more'n a week since that black devil stole Jonas!"

"I don't know, Jake. But if anybody can cut sign, it'd be Little Dick. He's got a knack for tracking."

Jake offered me a doubtful roll of his eyes.

Little Dick hobbled over to where we were sitting our horses and said, "They went that way." He pointed toward the blue mountains with a finger as gnarled as an old twig.

"That's west from here," Jake said.

"I know which direction it is," Dick said. "I've got eyes."

"That means he's changed direction again," Jake said. "First north, then south, now west. You sure its the ones we're after that's made them tracks, Little Dick?"

"You said they had a mule with them," Little Dick said. "That set a tracks shows up as two horses and a mule. The mule is unshod and the tracks are shallow. You said that this Jonas fella wasn't too big a man. That means he was sitting that mule. The big man, was riding a horse of about sixteen hands judging by the length of the stride. The girl was on a shorter horse. They're heading west."

"I'll be goddamn," Jake said. "Can I please have a piece of your chicken now, Mr. Johnson?"

"You may."

23

Once more we found ourselves riding toward the blue mountains. Jake rode along contentedly eating several pieces of Little Dick's fried chicken.

"This is mighty good chicken, Mr. Johnson," he commented more than once. "I think I'll save the leg bones and make whistles out of them."

"Whistles?"

"That's right. A little music wouldn't hurt this expedition any."

"I never heard of making a musical instrument out of a chicken bone," Little Dick said.

"Well you can," Jake said, "I learned how from a Sioux woman."

"That's interesting."

Jake produced a bottle of mash whiskey from his saddlebags and passed it to Little Dick. Little Dick took a long pull and said, "Goddamn but that tastes pretty good."

"How'd you end up with your leg all bent?" Jake asked Little Dick. Jake was never one to stand on manners.

"Horse fell on me. I was riding along pretty as you please and the son of a buck just went over on me. Rode for years, all up and down the trails, the Bozeman, the Goodnight Loving, the Bandera, the Chisholm—never once had a horse fall over on me. Had horses shot out from under me and drop dead of the staggers when being chased by Apaches and Comanches, but never had one fall on me until that day.''

"That is a stroke of bad luck,'' Jake said.

"Worst part of it was,'' Little Dick said, taking liberty with Jake's bottle. "I was on my way to see my sweetheart that very day. I was going to ask her to marry me. It was a Sunday. I remember it was a nice pleasant day like this one. I was just riding along going to see my sweetheart when it happened. Her name was, Josephine Dart. Tall gal, pretty as you please.''

"You never made it then?'' Jake asked, his curiosity now up as he gnawed on a drumstick. "You never got to ask your sweetheart to marry you?''

Little Dick shook his head sadly, took another pull on the bottle of mash.

"No, that horse fell on me and crushed my leg and pelvis and squashed my insides. They thought they was going to have to bury me that very evening. The pain was so bad, I was wishing they'd just get their shovels and bury me without waiting for me to die. Then I begged them to shoot me in the head, but no one would. Then a doctor rode all the way from Tascosa and gave me a bottle of laudanum and asked was I a Christian man and said he would pray with me till my time came. The laudanum helped more than the praying.''

"Well wasn't that doctor able to set your leg straight once he seen you were going to live?'' Jake asked, tossing the drumstick bone over his shoulder.

"I thought you was going to make a whistle out of that bone?'' Little Dick said.

Jake reached into the sack and pulled out another drumstick and said, "I forgot. I'll just have to eat another chicken leg and save the next bone for my whistle.''

"I don't believe you can make a whistle out of a chicken's leg bone,'' Little Dick said skeptically.

Jake went on chewing the drumstick while ignoring the comment. "You never did say why that medico wasn't able to set your leg straight after that horse fell on you, Mr. Johnson."

"He wasn't much of a doctor for one thing," Little Dick said. "He mostly treated sick animals and took care of burying the dead. I think that's why he rode all the way out from Tascosa in the first place: He figured the boys would take up a nice collection to have me buried. I found out later that when he wasn't treating sick animals or burying folks, he gave haircuts and only charged twenty-five cents and was considered to be the best barber in the panhandle."

"Well I hope he was better at cutting hair then setting people's bones," Jake said. "Your leg is as crooked as a cottonwood branch."

"I don't know," Little Dick replied, "I never went to him for a haircut."

"I'd say you saved yourself a good two bits, then."

"It was my poor luck to have my horse fall on me in a country where the only doctor was a man whose best talent was hair-cutting."

"That is poor luck," Jake said. "All the way around."

"The great sadness was, I never did make it out to Josephine's that day. And by the time I *was* able to get around well enough to ride a horse again, Jo had run off and got married to a goat rancher."

"A goat rancher!" Jake seemed incredulous. "Who in their right mind would ranch goats?"

"This man that Josephine married," Little Dick said, "that's who."

"That *would* be a hard one to swallow, Mr. Johnson," Jake commented dryly, "to have your leg busted and set by a quack then find out your best gal run off and married a man that ranched goats."

"It wasn't the best year I ever had," Little Dick said, "I can tell you that."

They passed the bottle between them as we rode along, all the while commenting on the deficiencies of doctors and women in general, and goat ranching in particular.

My own thoughts were of Etta Landrow; I didn't have a lot to contribute to the conversation of my companions.

Our journey remained uneventful for the remainder of the day, and that night we made camp near a clump of cottonwoods along a sweet spring that trickled cold and clear. Little Dick said he would cook our supper if we would gather firewood.

"My leg is aching something terrible," Jake said. "Gathering firewood ain't in my book." I offered to gather the wood while Jake made himself a comfortable place to sit and nurse a fresh bottle of mash.

Little Dick made biscuits for our supper that night along with some extra for our breakfast the next morning. We ate the remainder of the fried chicken and washed it down with coffee; except for Jake who preferred to wash his supper down with the mash whiskey.

It was a good meal and afterward we sat around and smoked and shared some of Jake's whiskey and talked about the old days, the places we'd been, the times we'd had—both the good and the bad. And gradually, the conversation wound down and we were all left to our private thoughts as we lay looking up at the stars.

That was the best and the worst time of night—when the conversation ended and the sleep hadn't yet begun. I pulled my blankets up tight and kept my feet pointed toward the fire. It was a cold night and getting colder. Lying there thinking about it, some nagging doubts came into my mind. Doubts about the man we were chasing; Elijah Hook had outsmarted us so far; that in itself was troubling. Jake was a professional manhunter, yet he'd been outfoxed and I'd been outfoxed with him. That combined with the fact of how easily he had murdered a man like Ben Beadle, didn't exactly cause me to want to close both eyes at night knowing the man was still out there in the dark somewhere.

So far, Hook had cost me a good friend and probably the love of a good woman. I wanted to get it over with, to end our business. Maybe when it was ended, I would ride back to Nebraska and see if Etta was still a free woman. I heard the call of a gray wolf, felt the heat of the fire against the soles of my boots. That and the mash whiskey finally forced me into a fitful sleep.

The next morning we were awakened by a hard icy rain; it fell out of the sky like a bucket of cold nickels and seemed to freeze as it hit the ground.

"Look's like breakfast is out," Jake grumbled.

"Unless you want me to sit around in this frozen rain and cook," Little Dick said, his own mood sour because of the nasty weather.

"There's bound to be a town somewhere along this road," I suggested. "Maybe if we leave off with the griping and get a move on, we'll come to it." No one argued.

"How come it ain't snow, I wonder?" Little Dick said after we had ridden for a time in the ice storm. "It's cold enough to be snow. Why's it have to be ice. All the damn luck!"

"It's just one more thing," Jake grumbled, his moustaches heavy with ice particles. "It's been my poor luck ever since I stopped in Cheyenne that first time and ran into McCannon." Jake looked at me from under the brim of his wet hat.

"Nothing against you," he said. "Just that if I'd never stopped to wet my beak that day, I probably already would have captured Hook and had him halfway back to Ft. Smith by now."

I didn't bother to throw in my two cents on the subject. I saw no point in discussing what might have been. Then I saw them coming through glittering ice storm—the band of Indians.

"We've got company," I said.

Jake and Little Dick jerked up their drooping heads, the ice seemed to crackle off their slickers when they did.

"What the hell you think they're up to?" Little Dick said.

Before anyone could offer a reason, the forelegs of Jake's horse buckled and sent him sprawling. Then, I heard the crack of the rifle.

I swung the bird around and offered my hand to Jake at the same time I kicked my right foot free from the stirrup.

"Get on!"

He was still half stunned from the tumble he'd taken but he grabbed my hand and with a struggle pulled himself onto the back of the bird. She didn't care for it much, having to haul two big men, but she responded to my command as I drove my heels into her flanks.

"Where?" shouted Dick.

"Anywhere but here!"

Little Dick tried to grab the lead rope of the pack mule.

"Leave it!" I yelled, and he did.

We raced our horses across a sage-covered valley coated with a thin layer of ice that shattered like glass under the hooves of our mounts. I looked back in time to see that one of the renegades had caught the pack mule, but the others were still on our heels. With the bird having to carry both me and Jake, the race would not be a long one. Several times bullets went whistling past our heads. I think we were all holding our breaths, waiting for one of the bullets to find its mark.

After a mile, the bird started to labor under the load. Little Dick's roan passed her and with every second, opened a wider distance between us.

I looked back again and saw the renegades were gaining on us with their swift mustangs. Little Dick and his roan were several hundred yards ahead of us, then I saw him top a rise and disappear over the other side. The bird was doing her best, but her best wasn't going to be good enough, not with two riders on her back.

The renegades were less than a hundred yards to our rear and as we started up the rise, I figured we would have to stop near the top and make our stand.

The icy rain stung like bees attacking our faces and hands.

Then Little Dick appeared at the top of the rise again and waved us on.

"What the hell's he doing?" Jake shouted.

I urged the bird on and she gave all she had and took us to the top where we saw the walls of an old cabin at the bottom of the slope.

"It ain't exactly Ft. Abraham Lincoln," Little Dick shouted through snapping ice rain, "but it'll do!" Then jerking his Winchester free from his saddle scabbard, he began firing at our pursuers while I raced the bird down the slope.

We made the walls of the cabin just as the band of renegades reached the top of the rise, Little Dick coming in behind us. Several rounds slammed into the cabin's walls as we took cover.

"Thank the son of a bitch who built this cabin!" Jake said, taking up a position alongside near a window.

"Yes, but he could have left a roof on it," Little Dick said with a relieved half grin.

"Who do you reckon those peckerwoods are?" Jake asked, peering around the sill long enough to have two more rounds slam into the walls.

"From what I could see," I said, "they looked like Sioux. But then, I'm not an expert on Indians."

"Maybe once we whip them, we can ask them," Little Dick said, ducking around an opening long enough to rapid-fire his Winchester. The renegades had slipped back beyond the rise, no doubt holding a powwow as to how they were going to smoke us out.

"Do we try and make another run for it?" Dick asked after the better part of an hour had passed with no further sign of the renegades.

"Two horses, three men," I said, "you figure out what our chances are."

"Maybe they got tired and left," Jake said. "You know how damn funny Indans can be about waiting around for something to happen."

"You want to take a walk up that hill and find out?" I asked.

He looked sheepish at the suggestion.

"I wish it would at least quit this damn freezing drizzle on us," Little Dick said. "I could stand a smoke."

"I wonder what did happen to the roof," Jake said, looking up as he shielded his face with one hand. "Somebody steal it?"

The walls were still in good order, though they sagged at the northwest corner. All the glass was gone from the windows.

"Maybe a big wind came and blew the roof off," Little Dick suggested. "Sometimes they get cyclones out in this country and they blow roofs off places."

"That's probably what happened all right," Jake said. "A cyclone came along and blowed off the roof and blowed out all the windows and whoever was living here had to leave."

Jake pulled out his bottle and said: "Least this didn't get broke in all the commotion," and took a pull before passing it to Little Dick and me.

"What about those Indans, Mac, you seen any more of them up there?" Jake asked.

I looked but didn't see anyone.

Then came a roar that sounded like rolling thunder and we all looked at one another. Then twice more the sound came.

"That's a Big Fifty," Jake said. "Sharps buffalo gun!"

"What the hell!" Little Dick said, taking a peek through one of the missing windows.

"I used to hunt buffalo on the plains. I know a Sharps when I hear one," Jake assured us.

"You reckon one of those peckerwoods has a Sharps with him?" Little Dick asked.

"If he does," I said, "what's he shooting at?"

"As long as it's not us," Jake said, "I don't care. Any gun that can kill a buffalo from five hundred yards ain't something I want aimed at me."

Several more shots from the big gun crashed through the air, then forty minutes passed without a sound.

"I'm getting damn tired of sitting here freezing my backside off," Jake said.

"Well, I don't see how that's going to change any," Little Dick said. "Unless this ice rain stops or you go and build a new roof and put it on over us."

"Screw this!" Jake said and stepped outside the walls of the cabin. "Let me borrow your horse."

Little Dick said, "Go right ahead, just don't get him shot, okay?"

"I'll go with you," I said. "I'm tired of the damn ice too."

"I'll wait here, and cover you boys," Little Dick said. "I'm a damn sight better hitting what I aim at if I ain't on the back of a horse."

I rode with my self-cocker in my right hand, Jake rode with

his Winchester resting across the horn in front of him. We took it slow up that hill just in case the renegades were still there waiting for us. It was hold your breath time.

What we found when we reached the top caused us both to pull up short.

Four of the Indians were dead, their faces gray under the formed ice; each had holes blown through them the size you could put your fist through. The rest were nowhere in sight.

Jake and I looked at each other.

"What the hell went on here, Mac?"

"I don't know."

The realization was slow in coming, then we looked at each other.

"Elijah Hook," I said.

Jake nodded.

"Must have been."

24

"What's going on here, Mac?"

"Damned if I know," I told Jake.

He sat down on a large rock and stared at the dead renegades; I had been right: they had the markings of Sioux braves. The thing was, they were ragged, thin, the soles of their moccasins torn. The ice glazed their faces causing them to look ghostly in death.

"Did you notice?" Jake said.

"Yeah," I said. The dead were all young men, not one looked older than nineteen.

"Kids," I said.

He nodded.

"Still," he said, "they would have killed us given the chance."

"I know."

"Why'd he do it, Mac? Why'd Hook hang around and kill these bucks? It don't make no damn sense."

"Nothing makes any sense," I said.

Jake looked around, his gaze scouting the mist.

"Jezzus, he had to have shot these boys from over yonder

in that little stand of trees. Must be better'n five, six hundred yards and through a hard rain.''

It seemed impossible for anyone to make a shot like that. To make it four times, seemed damn right unreal. I could barely make out the ghostly stand of distant trees.

"I still can't cipher it, Mac. Why Hook did it?''

"He wants us to know he's out there,'' I said. "He wants us to know he's not going anywhere—that he's not running from us.''

Jake kept shaking his head in disbelief.

"Gives me the chills worse than this ice rain, Mac.''

"I caught the feeling, too.''

"Why don't he just come out and fight us if he ain't going to run anymore?''

"He wants to do it his way, and in his time. He's not worried about us catching him, Jake. He knows we can't.''

Jake wiped the wet out of his eyes and busted off bits of ice from his long moustaches.

"The hell we can't!'' he exploded. "I'll not only catch him, I cut his damn head off and take it back to Ft. Smith in a gunny sack if I have to!''

"You know something,'' I said.

"What's that?''

"He could be sitting in those trees right now, sighting in on us with that Sharps. All he'd have to do is squeeze the trigger and we'd be dead men, just like these poor ragged boys.''

Jake looked out toward the soft outline of the ghost trees, staring hard through the silver sleet. His face knotted up.

We both felt it, the death waiting for us.

"Let's get the hell back down to the cabin!'' Jake said.

"What's up?'' Little Dick asked as we rode up to the shack.

"We got company,'' Jake said, handing the reins of Little Dick's horse back to him.

"Who?''

"Elijah Hook, that's who.''

Little Dick squinted from under the caved-in brim of his hat.

"How you know that?"

"He killed several of those Indans that was chasing us," Jake said. "They're laid out just the other side of that ridge with holes in 'em big enough to see the ground through."

"The buff gun we heard," Little Dick said. Jake nodded.

"Shot 'em from a good five hundred yards, maybe more and through the dang ice rain," Jake added. "Those Indan boys never knew what hit 'em!"

"It don't make no sense," Little Dick snorted.

"You got that right!" Jake reached for his bottle, saw it was almost empty, took a hit, passed it to Little Dick.

"You want a try at this first?" Little Dick said, holding the bottle out to me.

"No, you go ahead." Dick asked me was I sure, I told him I was and he swallowed the last of mash and set the empty bottle on a windowsill. "Here's to the old boy who put up this cabin and saved our sorry hides."

Jake stared at the empty like it was a sweetheart leaving town.

"So it ain't so much we're chasing him as he's chasing us, that it?" Little Dick said, licking his half frozen lips.

"It seems to be the case," I said.

"Then why not just sit right here and wait for him to come to us?" Little Dick said.

"I ain't sitting out in this damn ice rain any longer'n I have to waiting for some crazy sonbitch to show up so's he can put a hole through my guts!" Jake declared. "You want to sit around and wait, go right ahead!"

"Damn if I wish it wouldn't stop raining ice on us so I could make myself a cigarette, my nerves are up," Little Dick said, pacing the cabin.

"Yeah, well you better figure out a way to smoke it wet," Jake said, "because you might not get the chance later on."

Little Dick shifted his gaze from me to Jake then back to me.

"What's he saying?"

"Nothing. Let's get going."

"Where?"

"Anywhere but here."

We took turns riding double with Jake. The ice storm didn't let up until later that afternoon when it turned to snow.

Jake glanced up at the sky then tucked his chin into the top of his slicker and said, "I didn't think it could get any more cold or miserable, but I was wrong."

"I think there is a place ahead of us called, Whiskey Hill," Little Dick said as soon as the rain turned into snow.

"That sounds like a good bet to me," Jake said, then muttered: *Whiskey Hill.*

"At least I recall there being a town with that name," Dick added. "It could have a different name by now, or a cyclone could have come along and blown the town away like it did the roof on that cabin."

Jake tossed Little Dick a hard look.

"Well, I hope it's still there," he growled, "cause I could stand a drink and some dry clothes and a plate of grub to go with it."

Little Dick's memory proved to be accurate, because an hour later we hit the town of Whiskey Hill, only the signpost had the name crossed out and a new name painted below it:

PAINT TOWN

What we saw were a few low-slung log huts, several large tents and a few old Conestoga wagons that had been converted into living quarters. A kid with a good arm could have thrown a rock from one end of the town to the other.

"Look there!" Jake said, pointing toward one of the buildings. There were at least a half dozen hand-painted signs like the one on the edge of town. They had been nailed to the front of the largest of the log structures.

Roy Bean, ATTY AT LAW
COLD BEER   HORSES BOUGHT & SOLD   NO CREDIT
LAND FOR SALE   JUSTICE OF THE PEACE

"Whoever that Roy Bean is," Jake said, "he's got the market cornered on enterprise in this town."

"I wonder does he fix hobbled legs, too?" Little Dick said with a sly grin.

"Let's hobble inside and find out," Jake said. "Even if he can't fix a hobbled leg, least we'd be out of this miserable climate."

We ducked inside under a low doorway. Two men were playing dominoes in a corner with an upturned pork barrel for a table. Another man was asleep in a chair, a black and white dog was sleeping near the man's feet; the dog had its paws pointed toward a potbelly stove and his head resting between them. A woman with tired features leaned against the plank bar and stared at us like we were goats.

Sitting in the center of the room was a man paring his toenails with a pocket knife. He wore a plug hat and a shirt missing the collar. He needed a shave and maybe a bath judging by the looks of his condition. He had the stub of an unlit cigar clenched between his teeth. He seemed genuinely pleased at our presence.

"You gents look half froze and fully miserable. Won't you step up to the stove and warm yourselves?"

"Your sign outside says you sell cold beer," Jake said. "That mean you sell whiskey too? I sure don't want to drink anything cold, like cold beer on a day such as this."

"Sorry," the man shrugged. "My whiskey man ain't come by this week. It must be the weather at's holding him up. You want anything to drink, it'll have to be beer."

"I was hoping for whiskey," Jake said, plainly disappointed. "Beer's best on a hot day, not a cold one."

The man closed up his pocket knife and examined the yellow horn of toenail he'd been trimming before pulling on a long gray sock over his foot.

"Whiskey's hard to come by this far out from civilization," the man said. "Even on the best of days. What was it, Lum, last July when that one whiskey peddler was found shot full of arrows? I believe it was July, wan't it?"

One of the men playing dominoes looked up and said, "Uhhuh."

"Okay, make it a beer then," Jake said. "I guess a beer is better'n nothing."

"How 'bout you boys?" the man asked. "You want a beer, too?"

"Not me," Little Dick said. "I'd as soon run naked and jump in a rain barrel on a day like this as drink a cold beer. You sell tobacco and papers?"

"Sure, cigars too."

"No, I just want some makings so's I can roll myself a shuck."

The man pulled the beer tap and filled a glass for Jake, then he reached under the counter and laid some makings on the counter for Little Dick.

"How about you lanky," he said to me. "You want a beer, some tobacco, maybe?"

I had taken a position by the potbelly, trying to warm myself and dry out my duds. I took notice that the two men playing dominoes were well armed with Hopkins and Allen revolvers; so was the sleeping man. It didn't mean much sometimes in that country for a man to go about armed. But, you never knew whether it meant anything or not until the time came.

"No, I'll just catch a little of this heat, you don't mind," I said.

"Sure, help yourself, heat's free. Maybe when you warm up a little, you'll be in the mood to purchase something."

Little Dick rolled himself a cigarette while Jake drank his beer. The click of the dominoes was about all that could be heard for the next few minutes.

"I'm Roy Bean," the man behind the counter finally said. "Who might you boys be?"

"We're not from around here," Jake said, ignoring the question. "You want to pour me another beer?"

Roy Bean pulled the beer tap again filling Jake's glass then used a paddle to scrape off the head before sliding it across to Jake.

"Like I said, my name's Roy Bean; I'm sorta the big dog here in Paint Town. Not that that means a hell of a lot."

"That give you permission to ask a man his business?" Jake said sourly over his beer.

Roy Bean blinked.

"Just that I ain't never seen none of you boys around here.
I like to know who comes into my town," Roy Bean said.

"You own the whole town?" Little Dick said, the smoke
of his cigarette curling up into his eyes, "or just this here?"

"What's worth owning, I own," Roy Bean said. "The rest
is up for grabs."

"We're just passing through," I said, knowing that as cold
and wet and miserable as Jake was feeling, it wouldn't take
much to goad him into a fight. And the one thing we didn't
need right at the moment was another fight.

"Passing through," Roy Bean said, as though he had to
think about what that meant. "I also mention I'm the mayor
and chief of police?"

"Mayor?" Jake said, looking up from his beer. "What sort
of mayor pares his toenails in front of a lady?" Jake glanced
over at the woman leaning against the end of the bar. So far,
she had not said a single word. But when Jake said the word
lady, she laughed.

"Mister, you must have me confused with someone else.
Hell, a lady is the last thing you'll find in Paint Town."

"Pardon me all the hell for the mistake," Jake said.

"You want to go to the back room with me?" she asked
Jake. "It'll cost you two dollars but it'll be the best damn two
dollars you ever spent."

"I guess I didn't stop here to buy a woman."

She looked at Little Dick.

"How about you shorty?"

Dick looked around the room, saw that she was talking to
him. He straightened up from the way he'd been slouching
with the smoke of his cigarette curling up into his right eye.

"Two dollars, huh?"

She smiled in a tired way. She looked like she hadn't gotten
much sun in her life. Pale.

"I reckon I could go that," Little Dick said, then he looked
at me. "We got time?"

"I guess until we can buy another horse and get dry clothes,
we're not going anywhere."

He dug into his pockets and came out with the money.

"Two dollars," he said, handing her the money. "Lead the way."

He followed the woman to the back and beyond a curtain.

"How about another beer while you're waiting for your friend to get his business done back there with Cleopatra?" Roy Bean said.

"Cleopatra?" Jake said. "That her name?"

"Her real name is Dot, but she prefers to be called Cleopatra; say's Dot ain't a very exotic name for a whore."

Jake slid his empty glass back across the bar and waited for Roy Bean to fill it.

"I knew a whore in Durango called herself the Queen of Sheba," Jake said. "Cleopatra, huh?" Roy Bean grinned.

"Heard you say you're in need of a horse," Roy Bean said as he filled the glass then swiped off the head with his paddle before pushing it across to Jake. "What happened, did you boys lose one?"

"Some renegade Sioux jumped us half a day's ride from here," Jake said. "They shot my horse out from under me." That seemed to get everyone's attention, including the man who'd been sleeping in the chair.

"Sioux!"

"I don't think you have to worry much about them," Jake said. "Four of the bunch that jumped us has gone to the happy hunting ground. The other two are probably halfway to Canada by now."

"You certain about that," Roy Bean said. "That those Indians run off?"

"Certain as anyone can be about an Indan," Jake said.

The domino players went back to their game and the man sitting in the chair closed his eyes once more.

"Oh, well that's good news that you boys put a little hurting on those heathen reds."

"I suppose it is," Jake said. "Have you seen any strangers around here besides us?"

Roy Bean licked his lips.

"There was a big black cuss through here the other day.

Had a sweet little brown gal with him and a man riding a mule.''

Jake and I traded glances.

"What he do while here in town?'' I asked.

"He was looking for a game of poker. Said he was needing to kill a little time while he waited for some friends of his to show up. He won forty dollars in a card game.''

Jake rolled his eyes.

"That sonbitch!''

"You the friends he was waiting for?'' Roy Bean said.

25

Jake settled into getting as good and drunk as he could on beer while I stood by the potbelly letting my clothes dry. The two men playing dominoes concentrated on their game, and the man sleeping in the chair remained that way, and so did his dog.

Roy Bean played several tunes on a mouth harp while Little Dick and Cleopatra were making themselves scarce in the back room.

"Play 'A Cowboy's Lament,' " Jake said to Roy Bean. "You know that one?"

"I believe I do," Roy Bean said. "And after that, I'll play, 'The Roses Bloom In Spring.' How will that be?"

"If it's sad, I'd like to hear you play it," Jake said. "Right now I'm feeling blue and would like to stay that way for a time."

Roy Bean began to play the ballad. A mouth harp can be a mournful instrument to begin with if played the right way; hearing "A Cowboy's Lament" only made it sound all the more mournful.

By the time Roy Bean finished playing that sweet sad ballad, and the one about roses blooming in spring, Jake looked like

he might bawl in his beer. "Play those two again, would you?"
he requested. Roy Bean happily obliged.

Nearly two hours passed before Little Dick and Cleopatra
emerged from behind the curtain that led to the back rooms;
they had their arms around each other and Little Dick's eyes
looked dreamy. When Jake asked what had taken so long, Little
Dick acted as sheepish as a schoolboy that had gotten caught
playing hookey.

As soon as Roy Bean finished playing his sad ballads on his
mouth harp, Little Dick ordered beers for everyone in the room,
then he and Cleopatra found themselves a private table.

"I'm as happy as I've ever been," Dick announced.

Jake looked at him.

"About what?"

"Lord Jake, ain't you got eyes?" Little Dick said. "Cleo's
an outstanding woman."

Jake blinked several times.

"Maybe it's because this beer is warm that I feel so terrible
in my skull," he said.

"Maybe so," Little Dick said.

The lateness of the hour forced Roy Bean to go around the
room lighting lamps.

"You boys plan on spending the night. I could rent you a
room for three dollars."

Jake continued to stare at Little Dick and Cleopatra.

The wind outside rattled the windows.

"Snow's gotten awful deep out there boys," Roy Bean said,
checking the weather conditions as he passed by one of the
windows. "A man on a small horse was to run in one of them
snow drifts, wouldn't nobody find him till spring. You boys
ought to consider staying out this storm."

Jake looked at me and said, "How you reckon that black
devil is gonna make it out there in this storm? Sitting out there
with no shelter of any kind. Him and that skinny little gal and
poor ol' Jonas?"

"I don't know, Jake."

"It may just be that he won't make it," Jake said. "Maybe

he'll freeze to death. Maybe this storm will do what we ain't been able to—end the bloody trail of Elijah Hook!''

''That's a possibility,'' I said.

Jake did not seemed convinced.

''He'll figure out something; I'd damn well bet on that.''

The man sleeping in the chair finally opened his eyes, looked around then nudged the dog awake.

''Come'n Jeff Davis, time we went home and had our supper.''

When the man pushed opened the door and nudged his dog out ahead of him, a blast of cold air and snow rushed into the room like an unwanted guest.

The two men playing dominoes looked irritated.

''Damn fool!'' one of them said.

''How 'bout that room, boys?'' Roy Bean said. His eyes seemed to glitter with the prospect of doing business.

Jake walked over to the window, looked out for a long hard moment, then walked back to the bar.

''I don't reckon there is a real hotel nearby?''

''Not for a hundred miles there ain't,'' Roy Bean said.

Jake reached into his pocket. Little Dick said, ''Don't pay extra for me. Me and Cleo have made our own arrangements for the night.''

''Is that why you're so damn happy?'' Jake said.

''Wouldn't you be?''

''Which way is the room, mister?'' Jake grunted, slapping two dollars on the bar.

''Room's normally three,'' Roy Bean said, eyeing the money before putting it in his vest pocket. ''But, looks like there ain't nobody else will be wantin' it, so I guess you can have it for two.''

Roy Bean grabbed a lantern, then struggled into a bear coat and led us out the back door to a small shack. ''In here,'' he said. ''I'll get a fire going.''

There were four cots along the walls and a wood burner in the center. It wasn't the Inter-Ocean, but it beat hell out of a cold ground and a blanket of snow. I volunteered to take care of our horses; Roy Bean said I could put them up with his next door at his livery. He said that come a break in the weather, he'd be happy to sell us a good horse for Jake to ride on. Jake said, "I'll bet you would. Is there anything you don't have the market cornered on?"

"Not in this neck of the woods," Roy Bean said with a wide grin. "See you boys in the morning. Breakfast is a dollar—all the hoecakes you can get down your gullet if you get to the table before they run out."

I fought my way through the windy snow and gathered in our horses—Little Dick's roan and the bird, and led them over to the livery and grained and put them up. Then I went back to the shack and crawled in the cot and drew the blankets over me.

Jake had been sitting there in his underdrawers and socks staring at the little wood burner; it glowed like a cherry. Then, he reached out and doused the lamp's wick. The room grew dark except for the cherry glow of the wood burner.

"I got a bad feeling about this business," Jake said. "I almost wish now, I'd gone down to New Mexico and hunted me a killer rather than this devil, Hook."

"He's no different than anyone else," I said. "He can get caught the same as any other man." I said it, but I wasn't so convinced as I made it sound.

"I've chased lots of men in my life," Jake said. "But I never chased one like this one. Most men will run, those that don't will stand and fight. I never had one do both."

"He hasn't really fought us, Jake," I said. "He's just played a cat and mouse game with us so far."

"You know how you reckoned he shot and burned Ben up?" Jake said. "I think he'll probably do that to us if he gets the chance. That, or worse."

"He's just one man, Jake. There's three of us."

"One man!" he snorted.

I could tell by the way he slurred his words that he had managed to get drunk on the beer.

"We'll get him, Jake."

"That was a sad thing," Jake said, "the way Roy Bean

played that mouth harp. Made me feel bad down to my bones. Made me think of when I shot Dora.''

''You said it was an accident, Jake.''

''It was, but I still feel bad it happened. That and other things I've done in my life. A man does certain things he can't ever get over.''

''You said she came out of it okay, that she went off and got married and had kids.''

''Oh, it ain't so much I shot her,'' he said. ''It's we didn't end up together. I think I loved her about as much as I can love a woman.'' I heard him stretch out on the bed, heard the way the dry shucks in his mattress shifted when he lay down.

''Hard for me to think of Dora with my bullet in her and her with another man right this very minute—lying in bed next to him . . . him maybe . . . well, you know.''

''I would think getting shot by your sweetheart would have a bad effect on a romance,'' I offered. ''Maybe if you hadn't shot her Jake, it might have worked out between the two of you.''

''I guess you're right about that,'' he said. ''But I don't think that was what made her go off and marry another fellow. I think there was something more to it than that. Something about me she couldn't abide the thought of for the long haul.''

I thought of what Etta had said about needing a man full-time in her life.

''We've all made mistakes,'' I said.

''Some of us more'n others.''

I wondered if maybe Etta was spending the evening sitting in her parlor with Tom Feathers right this moment. I could almost hear the sound of her laughter, feel the touch of her hand on the back of my wrist, smell the sweetness of her perfume along the curve of her neck.

''Cleopatra,'' Jake said.

''What about her?''

''I should have taken her up on her offer before Little Dick did. If I had, it'd be me lying in a cozy bed with her right now instead of him.''

"Like I said, Jake, we all make mistakes. Time to get some shut-eye."

"It's the damndest feeling," Jake said.

"What's that?"

"Knowing Hook could squeeze the trigger on us anytime he takes a notion, knowing he's out there somewhere keeping an eye on us. What sort of killer hunts the men who's chasing him? We could step out the door in the morning to make water and he could do it then. With that damn buffalo gun, he could take us off at the neck and we'd never know it until it was too late."

"Think of it this way, Jake," I said. "If that's what his intentions were, he probably would have shot us by now. I think he's got something else in mind for us."

"I don't know why I let Little Dick beat my time with that whore, Cleopatra . . ." His voice sounded distant, then I heard him snoring and I was left to think my own thoughts. Thoughts about a sweetheart left behind, and a quick killer on my trail and neither thought brought me any comfort.

26

It didn't stop snowing for three days, and when it finally did, snow was piled up to the roof tops.

"We'd need horses with wings to get through the drifts," Jake said, morosely.

Little Dick said, "I don't mind the snow so much."

"Of course you don't!" Jake declared. "You got somebody to keep you warm at night!"

Little Dick smiled as Cleopatra brought him a cup of coffee for his breakfast then sat on his lap while he sipped it.

"Well, I can't help it I was smart enough to know a good thing when I saw one," Little Dick said. "She asked you first, but you turned her down. Don't blame me for having good horse sense."

"Horse sense!" Jake grumped.

"Well at least the sun's finally out," Roy Bean said, peering through one of the frosted windows he had wiped with the palm of his hand. "That's one thing in you boys' favor."

I had just come back in from checking the horses; it was cold enough to make all the old wounds and injuries I'd ever suffered come alive. Bits of ice clung to my moustaches.

"How is it out there?" Jake asked.

"How does it look?"

"That's what I thought."

I helped myself to some of Roy Bean's coffee and smoked a cigarette along with it. We were all getting restless, except for Little Dick—he was acting more like a lovesick man every day. Jake said it would take a stick of dynamite to get the smile off his face.

"So you own a business over in Cheyenne?" I heard Cleopatra ask Little Dick as he sipped his coffee. "What sorta business?"

"A restaurant," Little Dick said.

"You must do alright for yourself then," Cleo said. "Being a business owner, I mean."

"I make a living," Dick told her. "Got a little four-room house, friends, it's a good life."

"How about some more sugar in your coffee, hon?"

"Thing is," Little Dick was saying to Cleo, "I can use me some permanent help. It's hard to find a good waitress these days—one that'll stick with you. They're always running off with the first cowboy that asks them. I guess they think ranch life is a whole lot easier than waiting tables."

"Waitress, huh?" Cleo said.

"Well, it wouldn't have to be a waitress exactly," Little Dick said. "It could be more'n that if I could find the right person. I was to find the right gal to throw in with me and help me out, she could even be like a partner to me—you know, someone to tote the books, handle the business side of things."

"What you figure you'd pay for someone like that?" Cleo asked.

"Depends on who it was," Little Dick said. Then with a wink, he added: "What sorta qualifications she might have."

"What kinda benefits might a job like that have, besides the pay, I mean?" Cleo said.

I could hear Little Dick swallow some of his coffee.

"I reckon the benefits would be worthwhile the right person came along," Little Dick said.

"Hmmm . . ." Cleo said.

"Well I'll be damned!" Roy Bean declared as he stood looking through the window.

"Damned about what?" Jake asked.

"There's someone coming, trudging through the snow drifts! Must be a damn crazy man to be out walking through the snow as deep as it is!"

"He's walking?" Jake said. "Not riding a horse?"

"He's walking," Roy Bean said. "If that's what you want to call it."

Jake got up and went over to the window and looked out. I took up a position at the other window. There, far out on the sea of snow a small dark figure floundered in the drifts.

"You know that man?" Jake asked. "He from around here?"

"Can't tell," Roy Bean said. "He's too far away."

We watched the man fall several times, only to rise again, take two or three steps before falling. He was the only thing moving out on the frozen wasteland and his efforts seemed pathetic.

"I don't believe he's going to make it," Roy Bean said. "Look there, every time he falls down, it takes him a little longer to get up again. He'll probably just fall one of these times and not get up. It's not uncommon for a man to freeze to death in a blizzard and not be found until spring. One of the damn cruel aspects of this northern country. Weather'll kill you as quick as anything."

Little Dick and Cleopatra came over and stood next to me at the window. "Poor man," Cleo said. "He looks like a wounded bird that has fell from the sky."

"He might *have* fallen out of the sky," Little Dick said. "Where *else* would he have come from?"

"Well, he sure didn't fall out of the sky," Jake said. "Who ever heard of a man falling out of the sky?"

We watched the lone figure continue to struggle and it was evident that he wasn't going to make it without help.

"You have snowshoes?" I asked Roy Bean.

"In that pile over there behind the counter," he said.

I went over and strapped them on. They weren't the easiest contraptions to maneuver in. I pushed out through the door with my hat pulled down tight over my ears and the collar of my coat turned up against the wind. I struggled to get purchase atop the deep snow, and found to my amazement that the snowshoes kept me from sinking.

I looked back once at the four faces watching me through the frosted glass, then started in the direction of the man; he'd fallen and hadn't gotten up.

It took me a good twenty minutes to reach him. And when I did and rolled him over, I was surprised to see the frozen face of Jonas Fly. His eyes were frosted shut and his lips were blue. I slapped his cheeks until his eyelids fluttered.

It took him a few seconds to recognize me, and when he did, he offered me a weak smile.

"Mr. . . . McCannon."

"How the hell did you get out here?" I asked.

He muttered something, pointed off in the distance, then fell silent. He was nearly frozen to stiff and completely exhausted. We were both lucky he was a small man, easy to carry. I got him over my shoulders and started back toward the distant buildings of Paint Town with him. It was like carrying a bull calf, and twice I had to stop to rest.

Jake and Little Dick scrambled out to help me as I got near Roy Bean's place. When they saw who it was, they said, "Jezzus!" in the same breath.

We got Jonas inside and stripped him of his cold wet clothes and wrapped him in blankets and put him next to the stove. Jake thought we should pour beer down him.

"What for?" Little Dick said.

"So's we could warm him up from the inside," Jake said.

"Beer don't warm you from the inside the same way whiskey does!" Little Dick said. "Less you was to heat it first."

I suggested hot coffee instead.

"His lips are as blue as a Montana sky," Cleo said. "And feel how cold his skin is." Cleo said she would fix Jonas some beef soup and Little Dick offered to help her.

"I sure wish I had some whiskey to give him," Roy Bean said. "But it looks like now that the real snow has come, I won't have any whiskey until spring. Unless we get an unexpected thaw."

"How do you reckon he escaped from Hook?" Jake asked.

"That's a good question," I said.

Jonas fluttered his eyes and saw Jake leaning over him.

"Why . . . Mis . . . ter True," Jonas stuttered.

"That's something," Jake said, "you escaping from that black devil and making your way through this blizzard!"

Jonas waggled his head back and forth.

"Not . . . es . . . caped," he uttered. "Let . . . me go."

"What?" Jake said.

"I think he's saying Hook let him go," I said.

Jake gave me a confused look.

"I know," I said. "It doesn't make any sense."

Jonas's teeth began to chatter, then Little Dick and Cleo returned with a bowl of beef soup and Cleo fed the soup to Jonas a spoonful at a time saying, "Careful hon, the soup will burn your tongue you don't blow on it first."

"How'd he get here?" Little Dick said.

"Says Hook let him go," Jake said.

"Let him go?" Little Dick said. "Well, if he let him go, why'd he steal him in the first place?"

"If I knew that, the sonbitch would be in irons already?" Jake said, pacing the room.

"Lookit my Cleo," Little Dick said proudly. "She's nursing him back to life."

Cleo had Jonas's head propped on her lap while she spooned him soup; he was staring up at her like she was an angel.

In a short time, Jonas was nearly back to normal.

"Tell us about Hook letting you go," Jake said.

Jonas rolled his eyes, reluctant to take them from Cleo.

"He just turned me loose is all," Jonas said, then returned his gaze to Cleo again. She smiled and said, "You want some more soup?" Little Dick noticed how Jonas was watching her and acted a little put out by all the attention.

"Just like that," Jake said, "he turned you loose?"

Jonas nodded.

"It was cold and getting colder and we had very little shelter except for an old army tent that the three of us could barely fit into,'' Jonas said. ''It was quite intimate, the three of us huddled inside that tent together. I guess that may have been the reason Mr. Hook pointed me to the direction of this place and told me I was free to go, because of how small and intimate it had become there in the tent for the three of us.''

''Did he hurt you in any way, torture you?'' Jake asked.

''No. In fact, he proved very agreeable in every respect. He enjoyed sitting around a fire at night and telling tall tales and ghost stories. He enjoyed singing, too. He has quite a nice baritone voice.''

''Ghost stories! Singing!'' Jake said.

''It was all very entertaining,'' Jonas said.

''What about your mule?'' Jake said. ''That black devil was so agreeable, why'd he steal your mule and leave you afoot in weather such as this?''

''He didn't exactly steal my mule,'' Jonas said. ''We ended up having to eat it.''

''You ate your mule?''

''We had to—we didn't have anything else to eat,'' Jonas said, looking for the moment a bit shaken by the memory.

''Did he mention the reason why he kidnapped you in the first place, Jonas?'' I asked.

Jonas finally took his gaze from Cleo and looked my direction.

''He said the reason he took me that night was to insure that you and Mr. True would not kill him if you caught up to him. That he would trade me for his freedom if it came to that.''

''Well, there you go,'' Jake said. ''I guess *Elijah Hook* ain't such a saintly fellow after all is he? A man that would trade your life for his?''

''Oh, he said he wouldn't kill me unless it was absolutely necessary,'' Jonas countered. ''He seemed quite clear on that point. And, I believe he would have kept his word.''

''You could have died out there in that snow, frozen to death!'' Little Dick chimed in. ''I think Jake's right, this Hook ain't quite the patron saint he'd have you believe.''

''No, I'm afraid I disagree. He said that he would watch me

through his gun scope until I reached the safety of this town. He said if it looked like I would fall and not get up again, he would do what was necessary so that I wouldn't suffer. He said freezing to death wasn't as bad as some might think.''

''Well, that was mighty damn generous of him, don't you think?'' Jake said, sourly.

''What about Sugar Brown?'' I asked. ''Is she alright?''

Jonas sighed, tilted his head and said, ''She and Mr. Hook are much enamored with each other. They are like happy children, with the exception of course, that they know you are after them and will try and capture him.''

''Well, he's right about that, Little Dick said. ''That's why we've come all this distance and put up with this miserable weather, so we can capture him.''

''This damn snow!'' Jake declared. ''Soon's it's melted down to a tolerable level, we're going after him!''

''Oh, I almost forgot,'' Jonas said, reaching inside his coat and bringing forth a letter. ''He asked me to give you this.''

I took the piece of paper and unfolded it. Written in pencil were the words: *''I ain't guilty!''*

''What's it say?'' Jake asked, stopping his pacing long enough to look over my shoulder.

I handed the note to him and watched the strain in his face as he read it.

''The hell he ain't!'' Jake said, wadding up the piece of paper and throwing it into the stove.

''You spent some time with him Jonas,'' I said. ''Why didn't he just keep running when he had the chance?''

Jonas shrugged his shoulders.

''He said that he was tired of running from white men.''

''Then why doesn't he stand and fight!'' Jake interjected.

Jonas looked up at him, licked his lips.

''He said he doesn't have any quarrel with you. I think he is hoping that you will get tired of chasing him and give up.''

''Well, he's wrong!''

''He is very crafty,'' Jonas said. ''I think you should know that.''

Jake leveled his gaze at Jonas.

"Sounds like you and him became bosom pals, Fly."

"He treated me kindly when he could have just as easily slit my throat if such was his intent," Jonas said. "I find it hard to wish bad things for a man who shared his meals and stories and tent with me, given the hardships."

"Yeah well . . ."

"I think he's trying to prove that he's better at this game than we are," I said to Jake.

"So far he has been," Jake acknowledged grudgingly. "But that don't mean the game's gonna continue to beat us like a drum."

"What do you have in mind, Jake?"

"Lead a man to believe in one thing, then spring the truth on him from another angle," Jake said. Then turning to Roy Bean, he asked: "What's the nearest place other'n this a man could get himself supplied?"

"Bender's Fork," Roy Bean said. "More'n a hundred miles from here."

"So a man sitting out there in the cold with his belly crawling against his backbone might just as soon come riding into here as to travel another hundred miles, wouldn't you guess?" Jake said. Roy Bean nodded.

"But Hook won't come here as long as he knows we're here," Jake said. "So the trick is to make him think we left."

"Short of leaving," I said, "how are we going to accomplish that?"

"Simple," Jake said. "We will leave—or at least most of us anyway."

Jake laid out his plan to stay behind while Little Dick, Jonas, and myself rode out.

"Hook can spot that speckled horse of your's from a mile off," Jake concluded. "He'll figure we've either given up on him, or quit the town, then he'll come in. And when he does, I'll be here waiting for him."

"It's a weak plan at best," I said.

"You have another?"

The truth was, I didn't.

"We'll make a big show of it," Jake said. "Leaving."

Cleopatra said to Little Dick, "That mean you ain't coming back?"

"I hope that's not what it means," Little Dick said.

"Well it could mean that if your plan don't work out, couldn't it?" Cleopatra said.

"It's not my plan," Little Dick said. "It's Jake's plan."

Cleopatra seemed genuinely disappointed that Little Dick would be leaving as soon as the weather permitted. Little Dick's face looked as sad as a hound's.

"I was hoping you and me would get around to discussing more about that waitressing job in Cheyenne," Cleopatra said. "I'm mighty tired of the whore business—especially way out here in the middle of nowhere where there ain't that many men who come by in the first place. It's one thing for a girl to whore, it's quite another to sit around a week at a time waiting on trade. How am I ever going to save enough money to become independent at that rate?"

Now it was Roy Bean's turn to look disappointed.

"Cleo, you're the only whore I got. If you leave and go to Cheyenne, I'll be forced out of business. Cowboys don't want to ride all the way out here just to drink a beer and play dominoes and stare at Homer's dog."

"Those cowboys have all but worn me out with their cheap and unschooled ways, Roy," Cleo said. "They can make mooneyes with each other for all I care. Or, with Homer's dog if they want."

"Aw, Cleo." Roy Bean acted thoroughly disgusted with Cleo's remarks about cowboys making moon eyes with each other.

"Why don't we go on in the back room and discuss the future?" Cleo suggested to Little Dick. "You still got plenty of time before the snow melts, don't ya?"

"Well sure," Little Dick said. "Why not."

Jake watched Little Dick and Cleopatra head for the back room.

"I should have been the one she'd be discussing her future with," Jake said.

"Well maybe the next time a whore asks you to go into the

back room with her you won't be so picky,'' Roy Bean said. ''Maybe if you had taken Cleo up on her offer, she wouldn't want to leave me and go wait tables in Cheyenne with that cafe owner. Now you, on the other hand, don't even own a horse. I doubt Cleo would leave me for a man who don't even own a horse.''

Both men looked equally glum.

My own thoughts centered around Jake's plan to lure Hook into a trap. If the outlaw was half as smart as he'd proved to be so far, he wouldn't allow himself to be taken so easily. I had a lot of faith in Jake True's abilities as a manhunter, but even he had admitted he had never run up against anyone like Elijah Hook before now.

I didn't like the plan, but Jake was his own man; I couldn't force him to change his mind. We were as close to Hook as we had gotten so far—too close to not take every opportunity to nail him.

Jake had been right in one thing: with his Sharps Big Fifty, Hook could take us off at the neck from half mile and we'd never even know it until it was too late. And in that open country, we were like sitting ducks.

As plans went, Jake's wasn't much. But it was something.

27

Roy Bean called the warm winds that blew over the country the next two days, "the chinook."

"Happens," he said about the unusually warm weather.

Water dripped from the roof, trickled into wood rain barrels Roy Bean had set out. The warm winds melted a lot of snow over the next two days—enough snow that we could make a show of leaving.

Cleopatra had talked Little Dick into taking her with him in spite of Roy Bean's protests. At first, Jake was against Cleo's going as well, but when Little Dick argued that the more of us there were, the more of a show we could make of it, Jake relented and said, "I hope you two will be real happy serving burnt eggs and cleaning up spilt milk." Cleo said it beat getting rode like a quarter horse at the races once a month and paying all her earnings out to Roy Bean in bed and board.

Roy Bean said his business enterprize would be ruined and that he would probably be forced to pack up and move to Texas where he heard there was a great need for Justices of the Peace and cold beer. I told Roy Bean that Texas already had plenty of both but that there was probably still room for him if he decided to go and become a Justice of the Peace.

Ab and Lum, the two domino players put in their first appearance since the snow storm began; they didn't say much; they just sat down near the stove and began playing dominoes.

"Where you goin', Cleopatra?" Ab asked when he saw her carrying a hat box and Little Dick carrying out one of her trunks.

"To Cheyenne," Cleo said.

"What's in Cheyenne they ain't got here?" Lum said.

"Honest work for one thing," Cleo said.

"Oh." Then both men went back to their checkers game as if there was nothing unusual about the town's only whore leaving for a far-off place like Cheyenne.

"They don't seem too upset about your departure," Jake said, watching Little Dick tie Cleo's hatbox to his saddle horn.

Cleo said, "If I had to depend on either one of those two to earn a living, I would have starved to death years ago. They're just a pair of cheap old ranchers who wouldn't know a woman from a sheep. Lord knows, they probably prefer the sheep."

Little Dick grinned at that and said, "Are you about ready, hon?"

"Soon's I get my other dress trunk," Cleo said. "Can you give me a hand with it?" Little Dick followed her back inside Roy Bean's.

Jake was watching the distance.

"He's out there somewhere," I said.

"Let's hope he's watching," Jake said.

"I'll ride for a day, then circle back," I said.

"No need, Mac. I can handle him."

"As insurance," I said. "Just in case."

"What about Little Dick and Cleo and Jonas?"

"I'll send them on to Cheyenne. Little Dick's in love and wouldn't be much good to us anyhow now that Cleo's running his show."

Jake half smiled.

"For the rest of his natural life, the way it looks," he said.

"Yeah, well I guess as long as Little Dick is willing to pay the fiddler, he'll get to enjoy the dance."

"Glad it's him and not me," Jake said.

"You sure changed your mind in a hurry," I said.

"I've had time to consider it. I'd just as soon not be seen with a hatbox dangling from my saddle."

"Or anything else for that matter, is that it?" His grin grew larger.

We stepped back inside Roy Bean's. Jake traded his hat and coat with Jonas Fly, only Jonas's hat and coat were too small for him.

"Why do I have to trade you my hat and coat, Mr. True?" Jonas asked looking out from under the brim of Jake's hat which set low on his head because of its too large size.

Jake explained how he wanted Elijah Hook to think we were riding out of Paint Town together. "Hook's got good eyes," Jake said. "I want him to think you're me. Wearing my hat and coat will add to the ruse. Even with his good eyes, he can't see that good to tell it ain't me wearing them duds of mine."

Jonas sighed heavily and tried to push the hat out of his eyes as he put on Jake's greatcoat.

Roy Bean made one more offer to Cleo in order to get her to change her mind about leaving: "I'll bump up your cut to sixty-five percent," Roy Bean said. "And I'll even cut the price on your room and board if you'll stay."

"You can bump it up to a hundred percent, Roy Bean and feed me fried chicken on a blue plate and I'd still be leaving. A few more years of hanging around this place and I'll be as useless as Homer's dog."

Roy Bean rested his chin in the palm of his hand, his gaze full of dejection.

"I'll probably go to Texas and be murdered by John Wesley Hardin," he said. "It will be on your conscience if I am, Cleo."

"Nobody said you have to go to Texas, Roy Bean," Cleo said. "You could go to California or Ohio if you wanted to. What is the big attraction about Texas?"

"I think there is more opportunity in Texas," Roy Bean said. "That's where I'll go, unless you change your mind. I guess if John Hardin does kill me, it will be because of you leaving."

Cleo rolled her eyes and gave him a kiss on the cheek and

said, "If I was you, Roy, I'd go somewhere where there ain't any killers as mean as John Wesley Hardin. I'll write you a letter when I get to Cheyenne."

"Good luck in getting your man, Jake," Little Dick said, offering Jake his hand. "I hope there is no hard feelings about me winning Cleo away from you."

Jake shook Little Dick's hand.

"No there ain't," Jake said. "Sometimes things have a way of working out for the best."

"Well, I never expected to go after a killer and come back with a sweetheart," Little Dick said out of the hearing of Cleo who had gone into the back room for something. "I guess I'm as surprised as anybody."

"Most men would be," Jake said. "All the times I've hunted for desperados, I never once came back with a sweetheart instead."

Cleo appeared carrying a yellow parasol and a pair of high-button shoes.

"You think there is room enough on the back of your horse for these?" Cleo asked Little Dick. "I hate to leave them behind?" Little Dick rolled his eyes and said, "Is that about the last of it?" Cleo offered him a pout, then a peck on the cheek.

"I just want to look my best when I walk the streets of Cheyenne," Cleo said. "Wearing high-button shoes and having a parasol to keep the sun off is what real ladies do."

"It's just a lot of extra things to carry is all," Little Dick said half-heartedly. Cleo gave him a look that wilted the rest of his resistance.

"Make sure and make a good show of it," Jake said to me as I got ready to leave with the others. "I want that black scoundrel to believe that we've all left and are not coming back. I want him to think he can waltz in here and get a full belly and a peaceful night's rest without having to worry about one single thing. Then, I intend on stepping up behind him with this big Smith & Wesson of mine and surprising him."

"Don't misjudge his ability," I said.

Jake offered me that knowing look of a man who has spent his lifetime hunting down hardcases and desperados.

"Like I said, Mac, it ain't necessary you doubling back."

"I'll be back," I said. "You can count on it."

Jake remained inside while the four of us mounted up, looking for all the world like we were quitting the town and quitting the chase. And in a way, we were. I told Little Dick to lead the way, followed by Cleo then Jonas. I brought up the rear. I wanted us strung out so that if Hook was watching, he could easily count our number. Like Jake, I wanted him to feel completely confident the town was his.

"The weather is very pleasant," Jonas commented as soon as we had cleared the town. "I find it hard to believe that just a few days ago I nearly froze to death in the deep snow."

"That's the way this country is," Little Dick said. "One minute everything is hunky dory, and the next you are froze stiff as a board in some snowbank. You are a very lucky man, Jonas."

The sky was so bright and blue it hurt to look at it. I had a feeling crawling up my spine that we were being watched. I could almost feel him watching us through the scope mounted on his Sharps.

I didn't look back or act in anyway concerned even though I knew it was likely he had his sights trained on my back.

We arrived at a creek by midmorning and rested there. Cleo said she was getting chaffed from riding and went off into the bushes with a tin of salve to rub on her thighs.

"She's more delicate than you might imagine," Little Dick said, staring off toward the bushes.

We hunkered long enough to give the horses a blow, and I smoked a cigarette and kept thinking I should be back in Paint Town with Jake. The fact that Jake had been bested by Hook once already, kept nagging my thoughts. That, and the fact that Jake had a tendency to drink heavily gave me the urge to climb aboard the bird and ride back to the town.

The only reason I didn't ride back right then and there was the fact we hadn't been gone long enough, and a man with a scope in open country could spot a jackrabbit if he was watching. I'd have to wait long enough for Hook to drop his guard, then hope like hell I could make it back before it was too late.

When we remounted, I spurred the speckled bird alongside a dusty bay Jonas was riding, one we'd purchased from Roy Bean.

"Tell me what you think, Jonas," I said.

He looked at me from under Jake's big hat.

"About what, Mr. McCannon?"

"About Elijah Hook," I said. "Tell me what you think about him."

"As I told Mr. True," Jonas said with a shrug of his slight shoulders. "Mr. Hook seemed a pleasant enough fellow and treated me well."

"That's plenty strange," I said.

"How so?"

"It doesn't fit with what I've heard about him. The man is accused of a lot of bad killings. Why would he let you just walk away? Doesn't make sense."

"I've thought about that too," Jonas said. "In light of what you and Mr. True have told me. In point of fact, he could have killed me easily. In fact, he was big and strong enough to have snapped my neck with his bare hands. But he never even once threatened me."

"He had a higher purpose for you," I said.

"Yes, I agree" Jonas said. "To carry the note proclaiming his innocence."

"I don't put much stock in that, Jonas. Every man in a state prison claims to be innocent. I've never known a man to admit his guilt yet."

"He was very compassionate and kind to the girl as well," Jonas said. "She seemed to dote on him."

"Sugar Brown."

"There's no doubt she's as in love with Mr. Hook as much as Little Dick is with Cleopatra."

"I guess, as they say, Jonas, love *is* blind."

"I can only guess that it is," Jonas said. "I've never had the experience of being in love myself. Though, Miss Cleo is quite attractive, don't you think?"

He looked dopey under that big hat of Jake's; dopey and forlorn and out of place in this hard country. But he had pluck and was willing; I had to give him that much.

We rode along across the wide sweep of valley that was still white in places, brown in others from the melt off. In the far distance a range of blue mountains rose against the pale edges of sky and a hawk caught the warm air rising up from the ground and rode it on stiff outstretched wings as it scouted for a winter hare or field mouse.

We camped at noon by a stand of cottonwoods, the limbs and trunks darkly wet.

Little Dick made a meal out of some smoked beef packed in tin cans that he had purchased off Roy Bean before we left. Smoked beef and crackers and peaches.

"I figured we'd at least eat well on the trip home," Little Dick said. Cleo sat next to him on a blanket and said, "This reminds me of a picnic I once went on when I was married."

Little Dick said, "I didn't know you were married, hon."

"I was once," Cleo said. "But you don't have to worry, my husband was killed in a train wreck."

"Train wreck!"

"He was a engineer on the Rock Island railroad back in Illinois and his train went off a bridge and killed him."

"That's a sad story," Little Dick said.

"It left me a widow and me not yet twenty," Cleo said. "I guess after it happened, I just sort of lost my way for a time. That's how I ended up in the *life.*"

Little Dick cleared his throat; plainly he was uncomfortable with Cleo's public revelations about her past.

"Well, you'll just have to tell me all about it sometime when there is just the two of us," he said.

"It's damn hard for a gal to make a living and be on her own in this country," Cleo continued, undeterred by Little Dick's suggestion she refrain from further details of her life.

"When Eldon died in that train wreck, all he left me was seventy dollars and a house with rent due on it. Why what was I to do? I didn't know no skills such as sewing or cooking or teaching. I was young and pretty, those were my skills."

"Yes, well . . . ummm," Little Dick said.

"I'm surprised that an attractive woman such as yourself didn't remarry," Jonas said with avid interest in Cleo's tale of woe.

Ever since we had carried him in from the cold that day back at Roy Bean's and Cleo had spoon-fed him soup, Jonas had a difficult time keeping his eyes off her. He took every opportunity to speak with her and share her company; though, Little Dick made sure he never left Cleo alone for very long in Jonas's presence.

"Why yes, darlin', I had plenty of marriage proposals," Cleo said, perking up a bit now that she had two men showing a great deal of interest in her.

"But the more I thought about marrying again," she continued, working her words around a slice of peach, "the more I realized that there wasn't a thing in the world to keep the next man I might marry from plunging off a railroad bridge with a thousand tons of steel on top of him just like the first one— or something equally disastrous! I'd just be putting my fate back into the hands of undependable and unreliable men if I was to marry again without anymore skills than what I had— being young and pretty. I have since learned that men are weak creatures and can be killed in any number of ways. I have been a widow once and do not recommend it."

Little Dick was squirming on the blanket as Cleo related her views on marriage and men.

"Maybe this conversation is better suited for another time, sweets," Little Dick muttered.

But Cleo paid no heed to Little Dick's suggestions. Instead she leaned a little closer to Jonas and said, "It ain't that I don't like men you understand. I do. I like 'em about as well as a woman can like anything. But marriage! No sir, I'd just as soon pass on that subject."

"I suppose I can easily see your point, Miss Cleo," Jonas said.

"Of course you can!" Cleo declared, patting Jonas on the knee. He nearly swooned from her touch and Little Dick gritted his teeth at the gesture.

"Maybe we should stretch our legs for a bit before we get back on our horses," Little Dick suggested to Cleo.

"Naw, you go on ahead, hon. I think I'll just sit here and rest. My thighs are chaffed from riding. I don't feel much like walking—it'd just chaff me more was I to."

"Well, then maybe I'll just sit here as well," Little Dick said, plopping back down beside her on the blanket.

I saw the hope that Little Dick would take a walk by himself and leave Cleo unattended, quickly fade from Jonas's expectant eyes.

Cleo was enjoying the attention and the peaches equally.

It caused me to think briefly of Etta Landrow and Tom Feathers and the way I'd felt about them sharing company and I realized that Little Dick and Jonas Fly weren't the only men in this world who knew the bitter taste of jealousy.

I walked over to the speckled bird and stroked her neck and checked her feet just for something to do. Then I jerked the Creedmore from its boot and checked its loads before seating it again.

I rolled myself a fresh cigarette, watched as my little party sat around eating peaches and vying for one another's attention.

I was a long way from home, wherever that was, and wasn't getting any closer. I was tired of being outfoxed and sleeping in cold lonely places, and missing the company of a good woman. I wanted to put Ben's death to rest and bring his killer to justice.

"This is where I turn around."

They looked up.

"You want me to go back to Paint Town with you?" Little Dick asked.

He was a good man, but his heart was no longer in the chase. One of the reasons it wasn't, was sitting beside him on the blanket. I couldn't really blame him for wanting what any man wanted.

"No, you three go on to Cheyenne. Jake and me can handle this now that we know where Hook is."

"I hate to quit on you like this," Little Dick said.

"You're not quitting on me," I told him. "Go on back to Cheyenne."

"Yeah, well . . ."

We shook hands. Jonas lifted Jake's big hat from his head and said, "Here. Take this back to him and tell him it's too big for me. He probably misses not having his hat."

"I'll see that he gets it, Jonas."

"I wish I had a bottle of my patent medicine to send along too," Jonas said. "Mr. True seemed to be very fond of my patent medicine."

"Maybe next time we meet, you'll be back in business," I said. "Then Jake can buy a bottle or two from you."

He hunched his shoulders.

"Maybe."

Cleo said, "If you see Roy Bean, tell him I am truly sorry that he feels like he has to go to Texas on account of me, and that I hope John Wesley Hardin don't kill him."

I told Cleo I'd pass along her message as I swung up on the bird and turned her head west once more. I'm not exactly sure what if anything a horse thinks about, but it wouldn't have surprised me if the bird was thinking she'd seen that same country before.

I figured to make Paint Town just after dark.

28

I put the bird into an easy lope back to Paint Town. I wanted to make sure I arrived under cover of darkness. Evening came on early that time of year, the setting sun turned the sky from blue silver to crimson. From a slight rise in the land, I could see the town's lights spread out in the distance twinkling in the deepening dusk like flecks of gold glittering in the bottom of a miner's pan.

A chill wind blew out of the northwest, down from the far blue mountains and a coyote barked from somewhere off to my left.

I crooked a leg over my saddle horn and rolled myself a shuck waiting for full night to descend before riding the rest of the way into Paint Town. My fingers were stiff from the increasing cold and the wind picked at the tobacco I curled inside the cigarette paper before I could twist the ends closed. I struck a lucifer off my belt buckle and cupped the flame between my hands to shield it from watchful eyes.

The smoke felt good as I drew it deep into my lungs and tasted its heat. Sitting on the bird like that, smoking a shuck, reminded me of my trail-herding days when I would ride night-hawk and spend my time between looking up at the stars and waiting for the herd to jump off its bed into a full-out stampede. Longhorns were the spookiest most unpredictable creatures God ever put on this earth. Between them and the wild Mexican cattle, it gave a man pause and tested the nerves. I was just as glad some of that time was behind me now.

There was a lot of bad things about herding a thousand head of beef up a trail for three months at a time: Stampedes and too little sleep were some of the worst. Throw in river crossings, thieves, bad grub and too little pay and you just about described the entire experience. Hell, it was almost all bad; but there was some good.

The good came from making friends of men you could rely on to save your sorry hide the minute your horse got pulled under by a wild river or was gored by some rank longhorn steer. It was having the company of someone to drink with and whore with and sit around the fire with. Men you knew well enough to swap stories and lies and memories of women you loved and women you lost and the ones you hadn't yet met but hoped someday you would. It was listening to some old waddie play his mouth harp at night or listening to the wind or the call of a hoot owl that made you understand the Big Lonely and why men became drovers.

It wasn't the cattle or the horses you rode or the trails you went up or back down again that made cowboying the memory it was; it was the men you rode with and fought with and buried along the way. Men like Little Dick Johnson and Jake True and Ben Beadle. The kind of men they weren't hardly making any more of.

The speckled bird shifted her weight and I stripped down the smoke and let it scatter in the wind, then uncorked my leg and touched spurs to her and walked her down the slope toward Paint Town.

Halfway there, I pulled the Creedmore and rested it across the pommel of my saddle; I felt the press of the Remington self-cocker against my left hip, and the slight weighty tug of the Colt Lightning .41 I carried in a shoulder rig under my coat. The Lightning was a backup that I'd bought several years ago down in the Settlements where I worked a short time as a

deputy U.S. marshal. It had once belonged to a Cherokee policeman whose wife had used it to kill him with in a fit of jealousy
over another woman; then, she'd pawned the pistol in a hard-
ware store to pay her man's funeral expenses. "Ain't love
grand," said the clerk who sold me the gun. It had pearl handles
and good balance and I paid twenty-five dollars for it knowing
the price was too much for a bird's-eye handled Colt, but some
things you can't put a price on.

The main street was deserted, quiet as church on Monday.
The soft plop of the bird's hooves in the half frozen mud was
the only sound I heard beside that of my own breathing and
the creak of cold saddle leather.

I neared Roy Bean's establishment with as much caution as
I could manage. It didn't seem likely there would be trouble
waiting, but that's when it always comes—when it doesn't
seem likely.

I checked the reins and sat there a minute in front of the
store trying to see through the panes of frosted glass. All I
could make out was yellow light coming from inside. I walked
the bird around to the back of the building, dismounted, propped
the Creedmore against the rear wall and pulled both my pistols.
If I was going to do close-up work, I wanted to do it with my
revolvers.

I touched the smooth porcelain knob on the door, gave it a
turn and pushed the door open just enough to slip inside.

Up the short hall and to my right was Cleo's room; it still
had a woman's scent about it. The door was partly ajar and I
checked to make sure no one was inside. It was cold and empty
and dark. *Business closed!*

Up ahead, at the end of the hallway a curtain separated the
back part of the building from the main room. A light shone
on the other side and along the bottom where the curtain didn't
quite reach the floor.

I took a deep breath, thumbed back the hammers of both
pistols and stepped to within a few inches of the curtain. Using
the barrel of the Lightning, I moved the curtain far enough to
see into the main room.

Roy Bean was sitting on a chair holding his head.

I stepped out into the room and said, "Roy Bean, where's Jake?"

Roy Bean looked up. His eyes were red and miserable, his face flushed red. He mumbled something.

"Were you injured? Did someone come and crack your skull?"

He shook his head, a pained expression etched his features.

"Nnnnnnuh . . ."

"Jake," I said. "Where's Jake?"

Roy Bean weakly pointed toward the front door.

"Neerrr . . ."

"Speak up, make some sense!" I ordered.

"He . . . gone," Roy Bean muttered.

"Was it Hook?" I said. "Did Hook come here and take him?"

He said something I couldn't understand.

"Damnit Bean! Tell me what happened here!"

"Maah tooth!" he moaned. "It's maah tooth. Infected."

"To hell with your tooth! Where's Jake?"

Roy Bean reached down at his feet and lifted a pair of pliers and held them out to me. "Gotta . . . pull . . . it!" He touched his fingers to his swollen jaw and gave a yelp. "Owwww!"

A single tear leaked from his right eye.

"You tell me about Jake," I said. "Where is he?"

"Went . . . after . . . the col . . . red. *Oh sweef Jesus!"*

Now tears leaked from both eyes; Roy Bean was in plenty of misery. Too much misery to tell me what I needed to know about Jake's disappearance.

The man, Homer, the one with the dog that trailed him everywhere, came in the store just then.

"What's wrong with you, Bean? Somebody sock you in the jaw?"

Roy Bean looked in too much pain to explain it.

"Take up those pliers and pull his tooth!" I said.

"What?"

"Pull his tooth!"

Homer looked uncertain, looked at his little spotted dog.

"I ain't no dentist! I'm a bachelor."

I pointed at the pliers with the barrel of the self-cocker, then brought it down hard across Roy Bean's skull. He tumbled to the floor like a sack of potatoes.

"You broke his skull!" Homer said. His little dog yipped and pranced around on its paws.

"Just cold-cocked him so you could pull his tooth, now get on with it."

I rolled a shuck and smoked it as Homer proceeded to pull Roy Bean's tooth. He cranked and pried and finally pulled it out; a bloody piece of bone that he dropped in a beer glass. Homer was sweating hard.

"He might want to keep it for a souvineer," he said, watching the tooth sink to the bottom of the beer glass. I walked outside and busted ice from the top of a rain barrel and filled a bucket with the cold water then doused Roy Bean with it.

He came to with a start, sat up sputtering and waving his arms.

"Holy Mother of God!"

"Now tell me where I can find Jake True," I said.

He blinked several times, felt his jaw, winced, worked his tongue inside his cheek and said, "You pulled it out!"

"It was me," Homer said.

"Oh," Roy Bean said. "I didn't know you knew how to pull teeth."

"This fellow here had to cold-cock you," Homer said. "You would never have stood the pain."

Roy Bean felt the back of his head, winced again, spat a bloody flume and said, "Now I hurt in two places."

"You'll hurt in more than two places if you don't tell me about Jake," I said.

He pulled himself off the floor and staggered behind the bar.

"The black fellow come," Roy Bean said, pulling the beer tap until his glass flowed over with foam and dark brown beer. "You want one?"

I waved him off. Homer said he'd have a beer and so would his dog. Roy Bean poured them each one

Roy Bean took a sip of the beer, spat again, wiped a sleeve across his grizzled mouth, then took a long swallow.

"Only he didn't come alone," Roy Bean continued, filling his glass again. "He had a little *nigra* girl with him. She's the one that actually came in. Jake was sitting over there. Drinking beers as fast as I could pour them. I guess he was a little off his game when that nigra girl came in."

"Go on."

Roy Bean took another swallow of his beer, made a face. "Feels better, that rotted tooth not being there. Homer, maybe you *are* a dentist. Maybe that is your true life's calling."

Homer shrugged his shoulders and patted the top of his little dog's head.

"Maybe so, Bean. Maybe I could start charging everybody that wanted their teeth pulled."

"What do you think, Mr. McCannon?" Roy Bean said.

When he saw I wasn't in the mood to discuss his dental problems he offered me a sober stare.

"Like I said, that little gal came in, looked around, and when she saw Jake, she walked right over to him. Said, 'How do,' and tried to sit on his lap." Bean hacked, coughed up more blood, then swallowed the last of the beer.

"Finish telling me about the girl," I said.

"Jake asked her where her sweetheart was hiding and why didn't he come in with her. She said he had left her, dropped her off right outside the town limits. Jake said he didn't buy it—a fellow like Hook leaving his sweetheart behind." Bean wiped at the corners of his mouth, inspected the watery blood.

"The nigra gal said Jake could believe what he wanted to, but it was the God's truth! Jake said, 'Where is that sonbitch, I've come to arrest him and take him back to Ft. Smith so's he can dance at the end of a short rope!' But the girl stuck to her story of being abandoned." Roy Bean paused and looked around nervously.

"Then suddenly, there he was! Came in the back same way you did! Had a big buffalo gun trained on Jake, said if Jake even thought about moving or going for his piece, his name would be in tomorrow's newspaper in the obituary column. I guess that black buck didn't know we ain't got a newspaper in this town."

"Get on with it!"

"I think if Jake hadn't drank as many beers as he had, there might have been one damn bloody fight and I'd be mopping up brains! But Jake knew he'd been bagged—least he acted like it. It was smart of the black to send in that nigra gal first and throw Jake off like he did."

"Cut to it!" I said; Roy Bean was a long-winded cuss; the kind that could do well as a Justice of the Peace the way he enjoyed hearing his own voice.

"The black said he was an innocent man and didn't understand why Jake kept chasing him all over half the country. Said he was tired of running from the law and bounty hunters like Jake. Then Jake said, 'If you ain't guilty of anything, why are you running?' And the black said, 'I'm running because you keep chasing me. But I'm warning you here and now—I ain't running no more!' "

Roy Bean had to pause long enough to draw himself another beer and taste it before continuing.

"Then it happened!"

"What did?"

Jake tried to pull his piece only the girl grabbed hold of his arm, scratching and clawing like a wild cat and both men's guns went off only Jake's missed the mark and the darkie didn't."

"Jake's dead?"

"Dead as anyone can get," Roy Bean said, shaking his head. "He's out in back in that little shack you boys slept in the other night. I had Ab and Lum come and carry him over there."

It was a piece of news I hadn't wanted to hear.

"Hook and the girl," I said. "What about them?"

"They left," Roy Bean said. "Fellow kept saying how Jake had brought it on himself, the killing. That he never meant to kill Jake, just talk him out of chasing him. Said he was sorry about the trouble, asked me if I would sell him some grub to take with them. That and an extra coat for the gal because of how cold it was."

Roy Bean hunched his shoulders.

"What could I do?" Then he spat a bloody gob into the

spittoon near his feet and looked at Homer's spotted dog and wagged his head as though he and the dog knew something the rest of us didn't.

I took a lantern out to the little shack in the back. Lying on a cot, his arms folded across his chest, was Jake True, one of the last good men I knew. His head was cocked slightly to the side, his features gray as stone. His moustaches and unshaven whiskers were black against his bloodless flesh; his lips were slightly parted so that a little of his teeth showed. He could have been a man simply taking a rest from the world. Only this time, the rest would last forever.

I took a blanket from one of the bunks and drew it over him; I noticed the red flowered stain across the front of his shirt and my fingers brushed against his cold skin.

I wondered why he had done it, tried to pull his pistol with a loaded rifle pointed at him? He had to have known what the results would be. I pulled a chair up next to the cot and sat there with him for a while and smoked a cigarette.

The thought crossed my mind that maybe Jake felt he'd simply run out of options, that if he didn't try and take Hook while he could, that he was never going to take him. Maybe Elijah Hook wasn't the only one tired of the chase. Sometimes a man gets so tired and worn out, he will go for something that's not there and it ends up costing him.

I said good-bye to my old friend one last time then walked back into Roy Bean's store.

Roy Bean pushed a cigar box across the counter.

"I collected his personal effects," he said. "Thought you'd want to have them."

I opened the lid of the box. It contained eighty dollars in script, ten dollars silver, a dented pocket watch, a straight razor with a yellow bone-handle, a note pad and stub pencil.

"Here's his pistol, and saddle bags too." Roy Bean said, laying the gun and bags next to the cigar box. The rosewood grips of the big pistol were worn and smooth. Some of the bluing was worn from the cylinder. The saddlebags were soft, heavy. They contained an extra shirt, two boxes of cartridges and a set of wrist irons with the key still in the lock.

I peeled off some of the script and gave it to Roy Bean along with the pistol and said, "See he gets a decent burial." Roy Bean nodded.

"Now tell me," I said. "Which direction did Hook and the girl go when they left?"

29

I was forced to wait until daybreak before starting after Hook and Sugar Brown. Chasing after them at night would have been futile. Even though Roy Bean indicated they were heading west when they left his place, they could have veered off in any of a hundred directions along the way. First light, I'd be able to track them easily enough across the thawing muddy ground.

Roy Bean fell asleep atop his counter and Homer and his dog eventually left once the beer barrel was tapped dry. I slept as much as I could in a chair most of the night and thought about the last several weeks of my life ever since I'd received Ben's letter down in Del Rio. One minute I'd been a lawman in that dusty little border town, and the next, I was on my way to Cheyenne to work for my old friend in a small detective agency he'd begun.

Detective! It seemed about as strange a notion to me as being a stage actor.

Funny where life leads us, I thought as I sat there with my eyes half closed listening to the wind creep along the eaves of the store and Roy Bean's snoring.

My life in that sleepy little Texas border town had been fairly simple; an easy way for man to earn a living. The winds were warm, the women pretty, and the mescal free flowing. Then, as they are wont to do, things changed. A Mexican bandit named Pancho Vega—a man I'd become friends and drinking companions with—grew jealous over a sloe-eyed señorita we both had taken an interest in. I should have known better. Whiskey and women shared between friends never have a happy ending. Pancho Vega ended up pulling his pistol on me and I shot him. It didn't sit well with the mayor or town council or the many cousins Pancho had just across the river. I left for Cheyenne the same day Ben's letter asked me to come join him.

Hell, what did I have to lose but my life.

Then after I arrived, Ben asked me to go to Deadwood and that's where I met a woman named, Alexandra Dupage, and she and the murdering mob there nearly became my undoing. By the time I arrived back in Cheyenne, I was ready to look for a new line of work. But Ben's murder changed all that.

So here I was, sitting in a chair, listening to the creeping wind and the snores of a man named Roy Bean and waiting for another cold sunrise. It left a metallic taste in my mouth and a throbbing pain behind my eyes. Between fits of sleep, I counted the dead and missing of my past: My late wife, Mary Lee McCannon, my son Samuel, Ben Beadle, Pancho Vega, and Jake True. Alexandra Dupage, May Smith, Etta Landrow, Billy Cody—they were among the missing. And, there were others as well.

The world I had long been familiar with was changing a lot faster than I wanted it to with each passing year. I told myself that once I caught Elijah Hook and delivered him to Ft. Smith, I would go and find my own peace. A place where the wind didn't howl so much and a man didn't have to walk around with two pistols on his person; a place with a porch where a man could sit and have his morning coffee and watch the world go by. A woman like Etta Landrow sitting there on the porch didn't hurt the image any. I'd had enough of the hard life; there had to be better ways of living than tracking down killers and hard cases.

Daylight broke and a rooster crowed and Roy Bean sat up and stretched his arms and back.

"I guess you'll be leaving now that it's light enough to see," he said, testing his jawbone.

"I'd like to stay around and see that Jake gets a proper burying," I said. "But maybe now that Hook thinks he's not being followed anymore, he won't have his guard up."

"I'll see your friend is treated properly," Roy Bean said. "Then I think I'm going to pack up and head for Texas." He looked around. "Without Cleo here to entertain the cowboys on payday, I'll go bust in two, three months."

"Good luck to you down in Texas," I said and shook his hand.

"How are the señoritas down that way?" he asked. "Pretty, I hope?"

"Be careful of the pretty ones, Roy Bean. Find yourself a plain-looking woman and you'll be okay."

"I'll keep that in mind, McCannon."

He stepped out on the porch and watched as I saddled the bird then mounted up.

"That is an unusual color for a horse," Roy Bean said. "I'll give you fifty dollars for her and even throw in that long-necked bay out yonder in the corral."

"No thanks, Mr. Bean," I said. "I think I'll stick with what brought me here."

He grinned.

"At's good advice, whether it's horses or women," he said.

"I agree."

The tracks were fresh; dark clots of mud thrown against the patchwork of snow following the road westward toward the blue mountains. Tracking Hook and the girl would be easy.

I followed the tracks all that day, they stopped once by a little stand of pines and had a lunch of sardines and crackers judging by the empty tins lying around. I stayed long enough to chew a strip of jerky and have a smoke before continuing after them.

As the day drew to a close and the light turned blue silver in the east and smoky rose to the west, I topped a rise and saw a single light flaring up out of the growing dusk down below me. I knew it was their camp.

I dismounted and waited. There wasn't anything to do but wait.

I waited a long time. Then, when I figured they were settled into their blankets for the night, I decided it was time to take them down. I jerked the Creedmore from its boot, took Jake's set of wrist irons I had been carrying in my saddle bags, and ground reined the bird before starting the long walk down the hill toward the camp.

I took my time, bending low so that I wouldn't stand out against the skyline. It took me close to half an hour to reach the outer edge of their camp.

I squatted and listened. I was hoping to hear the heavy breathing of the sleeping. Only that's not what I heard.

I stepped into the ring of fire light and said, "That'll have to wait!"

Hook jerked bolt upright, Sugar Brown was beneath him; her naked breasts small, exposed to the dancing light of the fire.

"If you go for your weapon," I said to Hook whose eyes shifted toward the Sharps leaning against a saddle, "I'll kill you here and now."

Sugar Brown pushed herself to a sitting position, bringing the blankets up to cover her nakedness.

"It's him," she said to Hook. "That's one of the mens was with Jake True!"

"McCannon," I said. "In case you forgot, Sugar, the name's McCannon."

"What you got to do with all this?" Hook said. "You after reward money, that it?"

He was a big man, muscular. The light danced off his black taut skin; his eyes glittered like wet coals.

"Jake True was a friend," I said. "So was Ben Beadle, the man you shot and burned back in Cheyenne."

"Whoa up!" Hook said. "I ain't never shot and burned no man. Cheyenne or no place else!"

"Yeah, well I guess you can plead your case in front of Judge Parker in Ft. Smith. I don't care to hear it."

There was a long drawn-out instant when I thought he might reach for the Sharps and try me, just as Jake had tried him back at Roy Bean's. Right at that moment, it didn't make that much difference to me if he did; I was tired and I could still see the stone cold face of Jake True lying on that little cot back at Roy Bean's place. If Hook was foolish enough to force me to take his life, then I was more than willing to oblige him.

"Please don't shoot my man!" Sugar Brown pleaded "He ain't never hurt nobody!"

She clung to him, her small thin arms gathered around his thick shoulders. I saw the heavy look of defeat in his eyes, the fear in hers.

"What's it going to be, Hook? You want to do this the hard way or the easy way?"

"You let her go," he said, "and I'll go back peaceful."

"She can go where she wants," I said. "I've got no business with her."

"Go'n, Sugar," he said. "Scat on outta here. Take one of them hosses and the money it's in my pants and go'n."

"Ain't leavin' you, Elijah."

His eyes jerked in his head, twisted to the side to look at her.

"Gal, do what I tell you—this ain't nothin' but trouble, this here is!"

She shook her head.

"Ain't goin', can't make me!"

His stare slowly came round to me again.

"I ain't killed nobody mister. This is all been a bad mistake. What you're doin', is makin' it worse."

"You killed some friends of mine," I said. "Tell me you didn't."

"It was his doin', not mine. All I did was ask him to leave off on me. He jerked his piece, I did what I had to do!"

"He's dead, Hook. That's what I know."

He slowly shook his head, his eyes lowered.

"Ain't nobody understands anything," he said. " 'Specially no white man, I guess."

I picked up his Sharps, kicked over the blankets, saw no other weapons. I took the buffalo gun by the barrel and brought the stock down hard against a large rock and flung the pieces off into the dark. Then I tossed the wrist irons to him and they landed near his feet.

"Put them on. One around your wrist, the other around your ankle."

He picked them up slowly, cautiously. I saw something painful come into his eyes as he looked at the manacles.

"Been chained a'fore," he said.

"Price you pay for your crimes," I said.

He swallowed hard, blinked.

"Like I told you, mister, I ain't committed no crimes."

"That's for Judge Parker to decide, unless you want me to," I said. "Put them on."

"White men," he said. "That's all that's in them courts— that's all what them judges are—white men!"

"Save the lecture. I can take you back or bury you here. You chose which white man you want to deal with. Me or the judge."

He locked the irons onto his right wrist and ankle, stared at them, then lifted his gaze to me once more.

"You doin' a wrong thing here, mister."

"I don't think so, Hook. Two of my friends are dead because of you. I've had lots of time to think about that."

"He didn't do nothin'!" Sugar Brown cried.

"You ought to put some clothes on," I said.

I gathered their horses and started back up the hill to where I'd left the bird.

"You just leaving Elijah an' me here?" Sugar Brown said. "Him all chained up like dog—you jus' leavin' us here?"

"Going to get my animal and a little rest. I suggest you do the same. I'll be back down in the morning."

She started to protest but Hook told her to, "Hush. Go'n do what the man says, Sugar."

I looked at him; his stare was unflinching.

"It's a long way back to Ft. Smith, mister," he said.

"Yeah," I said. "Plenty of time for a man to talk himself into trying something dumb."

I walked their horses back up to where the bird was reined and tied them off before spreading my blankets on the ground. I could see the dwindling campfire down below. I wasn't worried about Hook and Sugar Brown going anywhere the way I'd had him cuff himself.

I made myself a cigarette and smoked it and wondered why I wasn't feeling very victorious at having captured them. Maybe it was because it was like Hook said: there was still a long way to go until we reached Ft. Smith. It flashed through my mind as brief as dry lightning, that there was maybe one chance in a thousand, Hook was telling the truth about his being innocent; but I told myself, to hell with that notion.

Still, the way he looked at me when I told him to put the chains on. That was a hard thing to do, look in a man's eyes who had been chained before.

I told myself I was tired, worn out from the chase; that was why I was letting things creep into my mind that had no right being there.

The most dangerous man in the world is the one who can make a lie seem like the truth.

I drew both pistols and slept with them at the ready that night. I'd come too far to make a mistake. And when I finally stubbed out my smoke and closed my eyes, I closed out all thoughts of any possibility that the black man was innocent.

30

I saw the bloody scrape marks around his wrist and ankle where he had tried to pull free from the irons.

"That's cold steel," I said. I reached into my saddlebags and found a tin of salve and tossed it to Sugar Brown along with the key to the irons.

"Unlock him and rub some of that salve on his wounds," I said. "Then when you're finished with that, make some breakfast unless you want to travel on an empty stomach."

I sat and smoked a cigarette with the Creedmore across my knees while Sugar Brown tended to Hook's wounds.

She was delicate in her treatment of him even though he tried to get her to forgo the efforts.

"Don't need treatin'," he muttered as she dipped her fingers into the salve and smeared it across the cuts.

"Does too, Elijah. Those cuts'll get all infected, poison your blood."

"So what if they do? You think that white man gonna care if I suffer a little bit?"

She glanced around at me, her fox brown eyes filled with hurt.

"Elijah tell it true what he say about white men bein' so hateful against a black man."

"Finish up little sister, we've got a long ride ahead of us," I said.

I had no interest in engaging in a conversation with either of them about what white men and black men thought of one another. I'd fought for the North during the war. And there were plenty of good brave black troopers who fought and died with the rest of us Union boys. And when a man is hugging the ground under the withering fire of lead shot and chain, it doesn't matter much what color his skin is, because the color of his blood is exactly the same, and so is his fear.

As though he read my thoughts, Hook looked directly at me and said, "You fought in the war, didn't you?"

It was spooky.

"What does that have to do with anything?" I said.

"Johnny Reb," he said. "You fought for ol' marse Lee."

"No, I was on the other side, one of Grant's boys."

His gaze shifted slightly.

"You sayin' that 'cause they lost, or 'cause its true?"

"Like I said, what difference does it make?"

"What outfit was you with?"

I glanced at the rising sun.

"It's getting late," I said.

"You want to fix that breakfast or travel hungry?" I asked Sugar Brown again.

She finished applying the salve then handed me back the tin before digging around in a gunny sack next to their saddles. I watched her take out a thick slab of salt pork and a can of beans along with a small bag of Arbuckle coffee and a blackened pot.

I rolled myself another cigarette and smoked it; Hook never took his eyes from me.

"I was with the Tenth," he said.

"That where you learn to shoot that long-range gun?" I said. "With the Tenth?"

He half smiled, but it was more from bitterness than amusement.

"Learned a lot of things in that war. Killin' was jus' one of them."

"Killing white Southern boys," I said. "That give you pleasure did it?"

His gaze shifted from me to Sugar Brown who was bent over the fry pan, the sound of the bacon beginning to sizzle.

"I did what I had to," he said. "What they ordered me to do, I did."

"Judging by the way you killed those renegades the other day, I'd say you were good at it."

"I can shoot if that's what you mean."

"Why'd you shoot those renegades?" I asked, my curiosity renewed. "Why didn't you just let them take us on back at that run-down cabin? You could have ridden away. Fact is, you could have ridden away plenty of times—why didn't you?"

"Tired of runnin', mister," he said. "Tired of bein' chased."

"Still doesn't explain why you did those renegades."

He took a long deep breath, let it out.

"Wanted to prove I was innocent case it came to that."

"I don't get it," I said. "How does shooting those braves prove anything?"

"I figure you and those other men catch up to me, I explain it—why I kilt 'em. Then you see I ain't guilty of no murders of no white men."

"You lost me, friend."

"Those bucks killed a white woman and her man over near Bridger two weeks back. Slit her throat after they used her. Cut the man's eyelids off so's he'd have to watch, then drove a stick down his throat. They weren't just a pack of starvin' red trash."

"You hear that, about them killing the woman and her man?"

He shifted his look again to Sugar Brown, who had paused to look at two of us.

"Didn't hear it," he said. "Saw it. Come up on it less than an hour after it happened. The bodies still warm."

"How do you know the ones that attacked us at the cabin was the same ones that killed the white couple?" I asked.

"Mister, I fought Indians all over the plains with the Tenth after the war. They called us Buffalo Soldiers. They hated us and fought us—but they feared us, too. I learned to tell sign of the different tribes. I learned to track too. It was them.''

"So you figured to do a good turn for the white man?"

He shook his head.

"Don't understand nothin'."

"Explain to me what I don't understand, Hook."

"I had a chance to end the misery they were spreadin', and I took it. Then I think to myself, was you and those other men to catch me, I'd explain it so you'd see I ain't no cold-blooded killer. I'm just me. Just a man been accused of doin' wrong. I figure maybe if I show you and the others the truth—you see I ain't guilty of nothin'. Maybe you let me alone—let me go on. I guess I was a damn fool for thinkin' it."

"It's a hell of a story, I'll give you that."

He lowered his gaze.

"Don't matter no more," he said. "Might just as well hang as to keep on runnin' like a damn ol' rabbit bein' chased by a pack a hounds."

Sugar Brown sat down beside him while the bacon fried and the coffee boiled. She put her slender arms around his neck and said, "Don't worry Elij, honey. I ain't gonna let him take you back to Ft. Smith."

I looked at her.

"A man appreciates a woman's strong love for him," I said. "But don't test me,child."

Then I saw it—the same look in each of their eyes; a look that let me know I couldn't possibly understand what they were feeling toward each other or toward me, or white folks in general. I picked up my plate and forked out a few strips of bacon from the pan and then poured myself a cup of coffee and sat back down again.

"Eat while you have the chance," I said. "We won't be stopping again until noon and then only briefly."

It was a somber meal under a somber sky. Gray clouds were bunched together like one large rumpled blanket and it threatened to snow again before the day was through.

I told myself not to let the fact that Hook was an ex-Union

soldier who had fought for the same side I did, get in the way of my judgment. Everything pointed toward his guilt, and that guilt included the killing of two of my friends. Not to mention all the others he was accused of murdering.

I guessed Hook to have been a good man at one time, just as we all had been. But war has a way of changing a man, and maybe it changed him from whatever he once was into a killer. I knew plenty of men who had come away from that war with a taste for blood, the same way they had a taste for opium or whiskey or women.

There never was much good found in any war, but it does teach you one thing: Survival. And so that is what a lot of us did after the war—we survived the best way we knew how. For some, it was robbing trains and banks. For others, it was wearing a badge or hiring out as stock detectives. For the more independent-minded, it was bounty hunting, or cattle rustling. Just about anything we could do to earn a living with the gun skills we'd learned. And it didn't hurt any if the line of chosen work had a little spice to it, for a lot of what happened after the war seemed mighty damn boring at times.

I could only guess the ways the war had changed a man like Elijah Hook. The black man had it harder than most the rest of us after the war. No glory, no return.

We finished our meager breakfast and scraped out the tin plates and tossed them back in the gunny sack along with the pot and the Arbuckle.

"It don't mean nothin' to you?" he said, "that I shot those renegades, maybe kept you and your friends from a slaughter? Don't mean nothin' that I sat here and told you the Lord's truth about I ain't never killed no white men like they say?"

"You killed Jake," I said.

"He pulled his gun! He was goin' to kill me!"

"He had reason to."

"No. He didn't."

"Get on your horse," I said.

He looked at the wrist irons lying on the ground.

"You goin' to chain me again?"

I looked at them too.

"No. You ride ahead of me, don't try to run."

He helped Sugar Brown gain her seat in the saddle, then put himself on the back of his horse while I mounted the bird.

"Lead out, that way," I said, pointing to the east.

"Why that way?" he said. "The Nations and Ft. Smith are south of here."

"We're going to Cheyenne. Take the train from there," I said. "Easier than riding the whole way back."

"Faster too," he said. "That way, you'll get to see me hung a whole lot quicker—ain't that it?"

"That's not what I was thinking. But if that's what you choose to believe, feel free."

His skin looked blue black under the sunless sky; I noticed the soles of his shoes were peeling away and the cuffs of his pants were frayed. The coat he wore was too small for his large frame. Whatever his crimes had been, they sure hadn't paid well.

I gave a nod for him to lead off. He looked at me a moment longer, then turned his face away and tapped his heels to the ribs of his bay. Sugar Brown was riding the smaller sorrel and she clicked her tongue and slapped its withers with the ends of her reins until it trotted alongside Hook's horse. I fell in behind them.

I didn't care if they talked to each other while we rode. I wasn't worried about them plotting an escape even though Sugar had sworn she wasn't going to let me take Hook back to Ft. Smith. I didn't figure there was much I needed to fear from a ninety-pound lovesick girl. And Hook already knew what the options were.

She looked small riding next to him, like a child. And now and again, she would tap her reins over the withers of the little sorrel forcing it to keep up with the long stride of the bay.

The wind swept sand and tumbleweeds across the open land. I could feel the bite of it, like the sting of a scorpion against my ears and face and the back of my hands.

I thought of the warm winds of south Texas, how a man could close his eyes and be caressed by them in way that was nearly as comforting as a woman's touch.

The taste of tequila and mescal floated into my thoughts. So too, did the sounds of a lively mariachi band and the clicking heels of dancing señoritas whose dark flashing eyes dared you to imagine the pleasures they possessed.

I shifted the collar of my coat up around the back of my neck with cold stiff fingers, trying to cut the wind. Del Rio and those warm nights seemed a lot longer away from the Wyoming Territory than they actually were.

A red-tail hawk flapped mightily against the buffeting wind, its body and wings dark against the ashen sky as it sought the refuge of a distant stand of pines, or perhaps some winter prey against the patches of snow and frozen sage.

I thought if I were you old hawk, I'd be flying away to Texas to sit in the warm sand and wait for spring to come again.

The hawk gave a single shrill cry that sounded like pain, and the sound shivered through me as neatly as did the icy wind.

Ahead of me rode a small slight girl who knew only life's indecencies and the unrelenting love for the big black man next to her.

I remembered an old pistolero named Bat Belgraves who I'd met down in a New Mexico gambling den. He liked to drink shot glasses of whiskey in his beer and brag that he killed thirty-one men and swore an oath that: "If they take me back to Texas, they won't take me back alive!" A one-armed deputy marshal ended up shooting Belgraves through the lungs over a two-dollar debt. Belgraves died a slow and pitifully painful death. But, they never did take him back to Texas.

I wondered if Elijah Hook had similar thoughts about going back to Ft. Smith. And if he did, which one of us might end up like Bat Belgraves—bleeding and suffering our last hours away on some lonesome and faraway spit of land?

I tried not to let myself think of the answer as I watched the hawk suddenly dive and disappear behind a ridge. A rabbit or a mouse no doubt on the other side, cowering amid the sage, unaware that death was coming on this cold gray day that was bleak and without hope.

Then, without warning, Sugar Brown turned her little sorrel

around, trotted back to where I was riding the speckled bird, and when she came to within five or six feet of me, she brought her right hand out from inside her coat. Something small and silver flashed in her hand. It took me a second to realize it was a derringer.

Then she pulled the trigger and something white hot flashed inside my skull.

31

The little gun popped like a whip crack. The slug punched into my ribs carrying me from the saddle.

There was an instant of free fall, then the ground came up and slammed me hard and I felt the rush of air from my lungs.

"What you gone an' done, girl!" Hook's voice sounded far away.

"Couldn't jus' let him take you back to Ft. Smith, Elijah!" I heard Sugar say, her voice as plaintive as the hawk's cry.

I felt myself sliding down a long dark tunnel, the voices of Hook and Sugar Brown growing rapidly more distant.

I tried rolling over to get to my hands and knees, but I was having a hell of a time just trying to breathe. I tasted bile in the back of my throat. If I was lung shot, I was going to die the same painful prolonged way Bat Belgraves had died. I fought as hard as I could not to die, but I was falling faster and faster down that dark tunnel.

And then a distant howling brought me gradually to the light: a yellow flame of light that danced up from the ground.

"You ain't kilt him, Sugar."

It took a moment for my eyes to fully focus on the dancing

flames of the campfire and in the distance I heard the mournful call of a coyote in the surrounding darkness.

The blue black face of Elijah Hook hovered above me, the edges of his eyes egg white, his teeth smooth and slightly rounded, gleaming like sea shells behind his parted lips.

"I thought maybe Sugar kilt you sure," he said.

My throat was so dry I could barely swallow. He put a canteen to my lips, said, "Drink it slow." Some of the water trickled down the sides of my mouth as I tried to get my throat to work.

A dull ache crawled up through my core and when I tried shifting my weight it felt like someone was twisting a knife blade against my ribs. The pain turned suddenly sharp and snatched my breath away.

"You lost some blood," he said. "I did the best I could to stop it."

I tested the wound with my fingertips. A cold wet bandage covered the area.

"Tore up a pair of Sugar's clean drawers," Hook said. "It was all we had to make a bandage with."

I pulled my fingers away, saw the smear of blood on them.

"The bullet's still in you," he said.

"Why didn't you take off when you had the chance?" I said.

"Sugar wanted to. She thought for sure she kilt you." He looked down at the bloody bandage, then back at me.

"I ain't guilty," he said. "And I ain't gonna start being guilty of anything now. If you die, then so be it. But it ain't gonna be because I just left you out here to bleed to death."

I noticed the butt of my self-cocker sticking from the waist band of his pants.

"That's my pistol," I said.

He looked down at it.

"I'm holdin' it for you."

"That's mighty kind of you."

"There's been enough gunplay," he said. "You up to eatin'?"

Sugar Brown appeared with a plate in one hand, a fork in the other. She knelt down beside me, stared at me, said, "Brought you some beans, a biscuit. Ain't much, but it's gonna have to do."

I tried taking the plate from her, but the effort was more than I could stand. Just the movement alone sent a wall of flame through me.

"Better let me," she said. I opened and closed my mouth around the forkful of beans she fed me. In spite of the pain, I felt half-starved, half-sick.

"I couldn't let you take Elijah to Ft. Smith," she said. Her gaze was defiant. "I dint want to shoot you."

"Then why did you?"

I saw her shift her gaze to Hook.

"He's my man, you dint give me no choice."

I ate a few more forkfuls of beans before the retching started. Whatever had gone in, came back up. My skin felt hot and damp like the air over a southern swamp. I could feel a fever growing in my blood. Maybe the bullet hadn't killed me outright, but if the wound became infected, there was still a better than even chance I would die. It was another lesson the war had taught me—the bullet didn't always kill you outright.

Hook came back over and squatted next to me.

"Either finish me off, or get me to a doctor," I said. He saw the beaded sweat covering my face; he knew the same thing I knew.

"I'll ride off to the north," he said. "There's pines up on that far slope. I'll cut some poles, make a travois. Go soon's it's light."

"Whiskey," I said. "You got any whiskey?"

"Mash. Got a little bit a mash."

He left, his boots crunching on the frozen ground, returned in a few seconds with the bottle.

"Try this," he said.

I drank what I could trying to put a fire in my belly to fight the one in my brain. I thought of Bat Belgraves, the way he'd died, the time it had taken. I didn't want to die like that, slow, a minute at a time. I wanted it to be quick, not eaten up by a fever-fueled blood infection.

"Go on, drink the rest, you want to," Hook said, as I tried to hand him back the bottle. "You need it a whole lot more'n me."

Sugar Brown's wide-staring eyes softened from the defiance they had held earlier. She looked like she wanted to say something to me, but realized there were no words that would change anything. Her face recessed into the shadows.

"She's feelin' bad about what she done," Hook said. "You want me to make you a cigarette?"

He didn't wait for my answer, but reached inside his pocket and pulled out paper and tobacco and began rolling a shuck. He twisted off the ends and handed it to me then struck a match off the heel of his boot and then held the flame to the tip. I drew in a lung full of smoke and it felt good. A small comfort from the pain. I watched as he rolled himself one.

"Learned lots of bad habits in the army," he said. "The use of tobacco was one. Liquor was another." Then he looked over his shoulder, into the deep shadows where Sugar Brown was sitting.

"Loneliness," he said. "At's another thing a man learns about in the army. Learns to crave a woman just as much as he craves whiskey and tobacco once he's gotten himself a taste for 'em."

He struck a second match to light his own cigarette and the flame flared against his coal black features. Twin flames danced in his dark eyes for a moment before he snapped out the match.

Half my brain was buzzing with the low hum of the fever slipping through my bloodstream. Hook's deep resonate voice rode the edges of my consciousness and I tried to stay with what he was saying.

"Guess the whiskey and tobacco and women ain't so bad, though," I heard him say. His face was tilted toward the stars and I wasn't sure if he was talking to me or to himself.

"That was all the army ever taught me, I'd be a happy man." He looked down at me, his face a black moon, his eyes glittering wet.

"I know you probably like most white men, thinking wan't nothin' better for a black man than to be able to shoot them rebel white boys and get away with it." His eyes became fixed on me, like he was trying to see inside my skull.

He shook his head slowly.

"I never took no pleasure from it, seein' a boy get shot in the face, have his legs and arms blown off, hear him screamin' for his mama and the Lord Almighty. Ain't nobody human can take pleasure from somethin' like that."

It felt like demons were crawling over my skin. I closed my eyes. Hook was saying something about being forced to hide in trees and about a Rebel officer who had a long wiry beard and played the fiddle. None of it was making much sense to me because the buzz in my blood had grown as loud as a hundred cicadas and it felt like my veins were stretched taut as piano wire. The ground beneath me began a slow spin that grew faster and faster until I felt my fingers digging into the cold earth trying to hold on. And I knew with all certainty, that I was going back down into that dark tunnel again only this time I wasn't sure I would be coming back up.

Something bright pressed against my eye lids and I opened them just enough to see slits of blue sky overhead. Sugar Brown came into view.

"I made coffee, you able to sit up and drink some?"

Sometime during the night the fever had raged and brought me murderous dreams and a sick feeling that rotated in my belly.

I nodded and she put a tin cup of coffee in my hands. They shook so bad the coffee sloshed over the edges and she had to take the cup from me.

"Elijah's off cutting some poles to make a travois," she said. I saw her staring toward the distance. "Gone up to where them trees is at. Told him watch out some big ol' bear don't get him. He laugh and say Sugar don't fret all the time. But I do."

Then she turned her head just enough to look at me out of the corner of her eye.

"So much trouble," she said, then turned back again to watch the distance.

I slipped in and out of consciousness several times. At one point, I felt myself being lifted and placed on a blanket. I opened my eyes and saw Hook's face high above me.

"That should do," he said. "Leastwise we can travel with him till we find someone to heal him or bury him."

Every inch of my skin was on fire, and every jolt over a rock or rut in the landscape brought me untold misery. I began to pray for death. It seemed ludicrous that such a small gun had brought me so much misery. I slept in fits, woke in starts, bit the inside of my cheeks until I could taste blood. I kept thinking about Bat Belgraves and knew I was dying in the same way he had. It all seemed so unreal: that I would die at the hand of a slight, brown-skinned girl whose only two possessions were her fierce loyalty and a hidden derringer.

I cussed myself for having allowed it to happen. Then, I thought of Ben. He had probably never suspected he would die the way he had either, alone and unsuspecting. He was as healthy and vital a man as there was. He had fought hostile Indians, drunken cowboys, armed and dangerous men of every ilk and had lived to tell about it. Then one day, someone just walked in and killed him. I had asked myself a thousand times how a thing like that could happen. Now I knew the answer.

As I rocked and bounced along on the travois, I felt like death was following along behind us, like some lean and hungry wolf just waiting for the right opportunity. I felt like laughing. If dying would end the yellow heat gnawing through my guts and bones, then the old wolf was welcome to me.

I wondered what Ben's thoughts had been in those final seconds of his life. Did he even have time for final thoughts, like I was having now? I closed my eyes and prayed that when it was time, I would face the old wolf honorably and without fear.

The sky turned sullen, the sun lost behind a blanket of gray smudge. I felt the sting of hard snow against my face and eyelids. I opened my mouth and let the snow touch my tongue. I thought it an omen, that it was snowing, that the sun had gone out.

I watched the fading landscape, sought the old wolf.

32

Droplets of wet snow like cold tears slid down my cheeks and collected in my moustaches and tasted cool against my tongue. The gentle sway of the travois, the scraping sounds it made as the ends of the poles cut lines into the frozen ground. The swish of the horse's tails. These were sounds and events I remembered as I drifted in and out of consciousness.

Then finally, our journey came to a halt.

I heard Hook's deep voice call out:

" 'Lo there in the cabin!" followed by the rusty sound of hinges.

"Got a wounded man here!"

Then for a long time there was nothing said.

"How'd he get that way?" I heard a woman's voice say.

"My gal shot him."

"Why'd she shoot him?"

"He was taking me to jail. She didn't want him to take me to jail. That's why she shot him."

"Maybe you better keep moving, then," the woman said.

"Can't. We do, he'll die. He's almost dead as it is. What with this snow and cold and the hole in him. He don't die one way, he'll probably die another. Freeze to death, maybe bleed out.''

More silence.

"What was he taking you to jail for?" the woman said.

"Murder. He thinks I killed some men."

"Did you?"

"None that mattered to him."

"I let you in, maybe you might kill me too."

"Don't it stand to reason," Hook said. "That was I a killer, I wouldn't be haulin' him around, goin' to all this trouble, him tryin' to take me to jail?"

I heard steps in the snow, then a shadow came into view. She was holding a twin-barrel shotgun; it looked too heavy for her. She was plain and tall. What I could see of her features through the oval of a wool scarf tied about her head and face, were her ruddy cheekbones and light green eyes. She had a wide thin mouth and pale colorless lips. She was bundled in a mackinaw and wool trousers that were stuffed inside stovepipe boots.

"You're right," she said. "He is near dead. Better take him inside."

Somehow, between them, I was lifted from the travois and half-dragged, half-carried inside a low-slung cabin with ice cicles hanging from the eaves.

"Put him over there on that cot," I heard the woman say. The cot was near a stone fireplace and the heat from its fire felt immense after all day in the cold. I felt the ice particles in my moustache melt and drip onto my lips and chin.

The best thing about being in the cold was it had partially frozen the pain in my side. Sugar tugged off my boots and Hook removed me from my coat and the woman handed them a blanket to cover me with.

I heard her say, "He might not last till evening."

I could feel the heat of the fire against the side of my face, then felt it begin to melt the stiffness in my joints. Then, it released the frozen pain in my side as well. But it was the sort of comforting heat that made me drowsy, made me long to close my eyes and drift to another place. I wondered as I felt myself slipping away, if dying would be as bad as I'd imagined.

I didn't remember dreaming.

I awakened to a room that was dark except for the dancing flames of the fireplace. I saw the blanket-covered shapes of Hook and Sugar Brown on the floor not far away, the glow of fire on their passive faces. I wondered where the woman was. I tried to move, the pain stitched in my side. I sensed someone step from the shadows, cross in front of the fireplace, then pause next to the cot.

"You've not passed on," she said,

"No. I guess this is going to take longer than I thought," surprised that my voice was barely above a whisper.

"I guess you can thank me for that," she said. "I cleaned out that mess of a wound. Lanced out the sickness, put some ointment on it. But that bullet is still in you somewhere. I imagine it broke some of your ribs is what it done."

As tall as she was, her face was receded in the shadows, but her hands hung at her sides. They were large hands, red at the knuckles.

"I could stand a drink," I said, trying to speak around the dryness in my tongue; it felt like it might snap off.

She slipped away, I heard the soft pad of her feet on the puncheon floor, then she returned with a dipper that had droplets of water falling from it.

I forced myself to a sitting position and she held the dipper while I drank, my own hands were still unsteady. The water was sweet and cool and I asked for more. I cupped my hands over hers as she held the dipper for me.

"You still got a fever," she said. "I can feel it through your hands."

I leaned back, felt the rough logs behind me.

"I'll probably die here in your house," I said. "I'm sorry you had to be the one."

"Folks's have died in this house before, I reckon" she said. "You won't be the first."

"I've got some makings in one of my coat pockets," I said. "A shuck would taste good."

She found my tobacco and papers and made me a cigarette without saying anything until she'd finished. She rolled the smoke like she'd had practice at it. Then she handed it to me and scraped a match over one of the fireplace stones.

"First time I made a cigarette in two years," she said. "I hope it's to your liking."

"It's fine," I said, as she touched the match to the end and I drew in some smoke and let it back out again. She brought the match close to her face and blew out the flame. I saw in that brief moment, that her hair was undone, hanging loose in a long pigtail as thick as a rope. Her hair was the color of winter brown.

"She really the one that shot you?" she asked. "That young gal?"

"She did."

"You don't look like a man that would let a bitty girl shoot you," she said. "Fact is, you don't look the sort of man that'd let anyone get close enough to shoot you."

"I wasn't expecting it," I said. "But, how can you tell just by lookin at me?"

"By the way you dress," she said. "That backward-turned holster on your left hip. That shoulder rig you're wearing. You're not just some puncher off one of the ranges."

"You're right," I said. "I'm not."

"So how did it come to pass that you let that little gal put a bullet it you . . . a man of your profession?"

"I made a mistake," I said.

"What sort of mistake?"

"I trusted that she wouldn't shoot me. I was wrong."

"I guess you'd know that better than me," she said.

"My name's McCannon," I said. "Quint McCannon."

She didn't say anything, but I could tell she was staring at me from the shadows.

"Mattie," she said. She didn't offer a second name.

"Mr. Hook said you was taking him to Ft. Smith."

"Cheyenne, then Ft. Smith. That is correct."

"He says he never killed anybody, except that he had to. That he is an innocent man."

"What would you expect him to say?"

"Don't act like any killer I ever met," she said.

"You met many?"

"A few," she said. "Better get some sleep, it's late."

A few.

I tossed the last of the shuck into the fireplace and for that brief act, it felt like a hatchet was buried in my ribs. I sank down on the bunk and stared at the flames. Maybe there was a time when I thought dying was the worst thing that could happen to me. Now, I wasn't so sure it wasn't living with a bullet between my ribs.

The fever flared from the center of my being, then began to crawl through my blood like a hundred hot snakes and the rest of that night I fell from one twisted dream to the next.

I heard sounds of muted conversation, movement through the thick fog in my head. I heard the sounds of boots knocking against the floor, then the opening and closing of a door accompanied a rush of cold air.

When I was finally able to open my eyes, I saw the woman, Mattie, sitting alone at a table at the far end of the room. Pewter light coming through a window above her, lighting the edges of her face. It was a strong face.

She must have known I was watching her, for she slowly turned her head toward me and set down the tin cup she'd been holding between her hands.

"You up to some breakfast?" she said.

"I don't think so. Where's Hook and the girl?"

"Gone," she said. "I sent them for what passes as a doctor in this country. Doc Kettle, lives up near Beaver Valley. He mostly doctors animals when he feels up to it and isn't drunk. I don't know he can do you much good, but if you ain't passed over by the time he comes, I figure he can't do you much harm either."

Her clothes rustled when she stood up and came over to the cot.

"You best try and eat something," she said.

"No appetite for it," I said.

"Coffee and sugar," she said. "Dip some bread into it, it's easy on the belly. Least try."

She helped me to sit up then brought me the coffee and a chunk of bread to dip into it. I managed a few bites; it could have been a fancy sit-down meal at Delmonico's as hungry as I felt.

"You still look peaked," she said, then laid her left hand across my forehead. "Still carrying that fever, too."

"I don't know what's keeping me alive," I said. "It's not for trying." Her hand felt cool and smooth as marble against my skin.

"Best thing for a fever is a cold bath," she said.

I offered a weak smile.

"You're hotter than a stove," she said.

"That's okay if I am." The thought of a cold bath caused parts of me to draw into a clench.

"No. It would be less than Christian of me not to do what I know works."

"No," I said. "Maybe another smoke would help just the same."

"Foolish man," she said and stood up.

I watched as she pulled a large wooden tub from behind a curtain and set it in front of the fireplace. Then she put on her mackinaw and began carrying in buckets of water from outside to fill the tub with.

"Creek runs right past the house," she said, when she saw the look on my face. Every time she went out and came in again, snow fell off her boots and a swoop of cold air came in with her.

I was too weak to do anything but watch. And when she judged that she had filled the tub adequately, she came over and said, "You want help getting undressed."

"I'd as soon die of the fever as sit in a tub of cold water," I said.

She began undoing the buttons of my clothes. I tried to stop her. She said, "Don't make this any harder than it has to be," and brushed aside my hands.

The room was beginning to slip out from under me as she peeled off the last layer of my clothing and helped me to my feet.

"I can't do this," I said.

"It won't be as bad as you think. Just get in and sit down all at once. That's the best way."

I had no strength to resist or argue. I let her help me step into the tub. The water felt like fire, she lowered me into it. I gasped, my heart felt like it would lurch out of my chest, and my knuckles turned white gripping the sides of the tub.

"Stay with it," she said.

I shivered and shook and my teeth chattered uncontrollably. She dipped some of the water up over my head and shoulders and I thought I would come clear out of my skin. And then after a time, the torture seemed to ease and I felt my fever beginning to shatter inside like glass hit with a rock.

She took a bar of harsh yellow soap and said, "I might as well wash your hair as long as you're already wet and willing," and commenced scrubbing my skull.

Her fingers were strong, but gentle as she worked at my scalp and it felt good to the point I closed my eyes. Then she kneaded the muscles of my neck and shoulders and I felt a release of old pain that had been knotted there for years dissipate under her knowing hands.

"You 'bout ready to get out now?" she said after she had finished rubbing my muscles. My skin felt warm and glowing where her hands had been.

"I'm not sure."

She helped me to stand, then dried me with a scratchy towel, rubbing it over my skin until it reddened, then wrapped the towel around my middle and helped me back to the cot. She combed my hair straight back and put a fresh bandage over my wound then drew a blanket over me.

"How do you feel now?" she asked.

"Better," I said. She laid the palm of her hand once more on my forehead.

"Fever feels like it's broke some," she said. I asked her to help me with a smoke and she did and I sipped a little more of the sugar sweetened coffee with it and felt halfway normal for the first time since I'd been shot.

Then suddenly, I began to shiver. She brought me more blankets but nothing seemed to help. It felt like I was being held in the jaws of some large invisible beast that was trying to shake the life out of me.

The room started spinning out of control, my bones felt like they were shattering at the same time my flesh was being peeled away. I heard sounds coming from my mouth, but not words; the sounds were guttural, like an animal makes that's trying to survive.

My only coherent thoughts were that death had finally decided to come and was trying to shake me loose from my earthly bonds. Then in the midst of everything, I had a fleeting vision of wife and son waiting across a wide river, their arms outstretched toward me. I wanted to go to them, but something was holding me back, clawing at my soul.

Then it felt like I was being wrapped in the arms of grace and a slow comforting heat began to penetrate through the icy tomb I was encased in. Slowly, ever so slowly, I was pulled back from the nether world of lost souls and found myself once more in the room of the cabin.

And when at last my limbs ceased to shake and the last traces of cold crept away, I slept in a silken shroud of sleep, the stillness in me complete, the rest undisturbed by dreams or ghosts or gnawing death.

When I awakened, Mattie was sitting there at her table, a tin cup held between her large hands, her sea green eyes fixed upon me.

"You're better now," she said.

"Yes, I think so."

"Nearly lost you."

I nodded.

"It felt like all hell was breaking loose," I said.

She tilted her head, the tail of hair lying over her right shoulder a soft brown against the linsey-woolsey shirt she wore.

"It was a strange ride," I said. "I've never been so cold. It was like my bones were breaking from the inside."

"You talked crazy talk," she said. "Jibberish."

"I was freezing and then I felt a warmth," I said. "A strange and wonderful warmth."

"Fever, that's all," she said. "It does you like that. One minute you're freezing, the next you're burning up."

"No, it wasn't like that. This was different."

"You want me to make you a cigarette?" she said.

"No."

"Don't know why Doc Kettle hasn't come yet. Maybe Mr Hook and that girl got lost."

"Maybe they just kept on riding," I said. "Maybe a doctor isn't what they went to find."

She blinked.

"Mr. Hook didn't strike me as the type to leave you high and dry. Think if he was going to do that, he'd done it before he brought you all the way here."

"Maybe it wasn't his idea," I said.

"You mean the girl talked him out of it?"

"She loved him enough to shoot me," I said.

"Well, if he hasn't come by this evening," she said, looking toward the window with its failing light. "I'll go for Doc myself come morning."

"I think maybe you did a good thing," I said.

She turned to look at me again, the cup still between her hands, the steam lifting against her face.

"What do you mean?"

"Getting into bed with me," I said. "Sharing your warmth, taking my cold into your own body."

She didn't say anything.

"I better get supper started, case they come. Maybe you could stand to eat something." She stood, her back toward me.

"Mattie."

"The fever makes a body crazy," she said.

"I know what I know."

"I better get supper ready."

I'd only realized what she had done midway through our

conversation. A flash of it came to me, the warmth of her bare flesh pressed against me, her plain face there before mine, inches away, the soft sweet breath of her mouth against my eyes. At first I'd thought it a dream risen out of the stark cold of my nightmare. But now that I recognized the reality of what had happened, I recalled time and time again awakening and feeling her arms around me, her legs entwined in mine, wrapping me with her body until the aching cold was replaced with the warmth of summer winds.

I wondered why she would deny it. Then I realized there could be a thousand reasons and not one of them was any of my business if she didn't want me to know.

She had saved me.

"What's your name?" I said.

Keeping her back to me as she fed kindling into the stove, she said, "Mattie. I thought I told you. Did you forget?"

"No. I remember it was Mattie," I said. "I'd like to know your full name."

"Mattie Blaylock," she said.

"You have a man, Mattie Blaylock?" I asked.

She hesitated in her feeding of the stove.

"A sometimes man," she said.

"What does that mean exactly?"

"Mean's he comes and he goes. Right now, he's gone."

"When's he coming back?"

She picked up another piece of kindling, shoved it into the stove, the hungry flames.

"I don't know if he *is* coming back," she said. "You'd need to ask him." Then she turned and looked at me, the wide-set light green eyes filled with something akin to old sorrows.

"Trouble with men," she said, "is you can never count on them. "They're always finding ways to leave you."

"How many ways are there?" I said.

"Enough to fill a woman's heart with regret and her soul with broken promises," she said.

"He just ride off, your man?"

"This time, and a half dozen times before," she said.

"But he always comes back."

"No, not always. Some times I go and find him. If he don't come back by spring, I reckon I'll probably go and find him again. Like I did the last time he didn't come back."

"Maybe this time he'll come back," I said.

"Maybe he will," she said. She seemed to grow smaller as she talked, like the weight of talking about him was shrinking her.

I watched her touch the back of her wrist to her cheek.

"Getting warm in here," she said.

"It's the warmth I remember," I said.

She gave me a narrow look.

"One man gone and one half dead," she said. "Some gals just don't have any luck at all."

"Thank you for what you did."

She looked out the window and said, "They don't come soon, they'll miss supper."

"This man you're going to find in the spring if he don't come back before then," I said. "What's his name?"

"What difference would that make to you?"

"I just thought if I ever ran across him, I'd tell him what a damn fool he's been."

She turned her head just enough to show me her profile, a slight bittersweet smile played on her lips.

"Earp," she said. "Wyatt Earp. Buffalo Hunter, prospector, gambler and sometimes politician. I suspect you live long enough, you'll have heard of him, probably even run into him. He's a man that don't stay in one place too long at a time. Really itchy feet, that man."

I was already familiar with the man's name, but I did not let her know that I was. Once or twice in the last cattle drives Ben and I had taken north out of Texas into Kansas, the name Wyatt Earp had been spoken around the rail heads of Wichita, Kansas.

What I'd heard of the man hadn't been flattering.

I promised myself that if I ever did run into him, I *would* tell him what a damn fool he was for leaving a woman like Mattie Blaylock.

I owed her at least that much.

She stared out the window at the dying light, then turned again to look at me and I saw the same dying light in her eyes.

33

Just as evening light turned to an almost dusty rose, I saw Mattie look up from her coffee cup. She went to the window, looked out and said, "They're coming."

I didn't say anything; in a way, I was sorry for the extra company.

I heard foot-stomping on the porch, then the latch of the door lifted and they came in: Hook and Sugar Brown and a short, heavy-set man wearing a stovepipe hat with a bent crown.

"Mattie," said the man.

"Doc."

"That him?"

She nodded. He looked my direction.

"Shot you in the brisket, eh?"

"Close," I said. "More like the short-ribs."

"Damn," he said. "That must've hurt like hell."

"It did. Still does."

"I'll bet."

He set leather bag down atop the table.

"You got more of that coffee, dear?"

"Plenty," she said. "You know me and coffee."

"Good, I'll have a cup to warm my innards, it's damnable cold out there."

"How about you, Mr. Hook?" Mattie said. "You and the girl want some coffee, something to eat?"

"Yes'm. Coffee and victuals would do just the trick," Hook said, glancing my way.

Sugar Brown kept her gaze lowered, avoiding mine.

"You look a sight better," Hook said, noticing that I was sitting on the side of the cot, maybe noticing my hair was combed and washed.

"You were expecting maybe I'd be dead," I said.

He glanced toward Sugar, then said, "Didn't know."

Doc Kettle removed his coat and hung it over the back of a chair. He was wearing a patchwork vest over a collarless shirt. His black trousers were shiny from use. He went over and stood in front of the fire and rubbed his hands together. The fire seemed to glow red in his chubby cheeks.

Mattie gave him a cup of coffee, but before he drank any of it, he went to his leather bag that was on the table and took out a silver flask of whiskey and poured some into his cup.

"How 'bout you, Mr. Hook, you want a taste of this?"

Hook nodded, held out his cup, his lips parted slightly as he watched Kettle pour the coffee in.

"Mattie?" Kettle asked, holding forth the flask, the firelight glinting against the metal.

"No, Doc. I've seen what a thief whiskey can be. I won't allow it to steal my mind."

Doc grinned, showing a double row of gapped teeth.

"Good for you 'ol girl! It's the worst insult a man can do to himself—get drunk as a pole-axed mule and go about showing the world what a fool the devil sauce has made him!"

Then Doc took a long sip of the coffee and licked his lips.

Mattie set the table with a meager meal of fried pork, biscuits she'd prepared in a dutch oven, pinto beans and some turnips she'd taken from a burlap sack next to the stove and cooked in pot of water.

She fixed me a plate and brought it over.

"Can you do this on your own, or do you require my help?"

"Let me try it on my own," I said, glancing at the others who had seated themselves around the table. "You've done enough already. Sit down and eat your meal."

She looked at me for a moment longer than was necessary, then joined the others at the table.

I still didn't have much of an appetite. The bullet lodged in my side had wounded my desire to eat as much as it had my flesh. But I tasted some of what was on my plate, taking small bites and holding them in my mouth a time before swallowing.

I watched the man, Doc Kettle, eat. He went at his food with dogged determination: his forefinger pressed on the back of his knife as he cut into his pork, his jaw moving in a steady rhythm as he chewed, his eyes never leaving what was on his plate. And when he'd finished the last scrap, he took one more biscuit and swiped it back and forth across the drippings and ate that as well. Finally, he lifted his whiskey-laced cup of coffee and washed everything down with it before wiping the tips of his fingers across his vest.

"Damn wonderful meal, Mattie. Worth the ride out here."

"Glad you enjoyed it, Doc."

"Wyatt ain't back yet?" Doc asked.

"Not yet."

Doc shook his head; his hair stuck out from his skull like wild patches of sage frozen in a hard wind.

He snorted.

"You're too fine a woman to waste your prime on a man like that," he said. "You know any time you want, you can come out and stay at my place. I ain't got but one bed but it's big enough for two."

He had the look of a wanting man, but Mattie's gaze was unyielding.

"Please Doc, I didn't call you out here to discuss my choice in men or how big a bed you got."

Doc fumbled around in the pockets of his vest and shirt fronts and finally found what he'd been searching for: a small black cheroot which he promptly fired up then blew a ring of gray smoke that lifted and broke against the ceiling.

Hook and Sugar Brown were still working on their meals,

as was Mattie, but she seemed less interested in food than did the others.

"You figure on getting around to looking at the patient sometime this evening, Doc?" Mattie said. "Or did you just ride all this way for a taste of fried pork and talk about what a big bed you got?"

"Oh, I ain't forgot," he said. "Just that I got plum famished on such a long ride. And a meal ain't really a meal until you've had a good *seegar* to go with it."

"And maybe another cup of that whiskey coffee?" she said.

"Point taken, madam," he said, and stood from the table. Taking up his leather bag, he walked over to the cot I was sitting on.

"Pull back your shirt son, let me see that bung hole at young gal put in you." I could smell his sour breath.

"Mattie tells me you do most of your doctoring on animals," I said.

"Animals, cowboys, and shot-in-the-brisket gunfighters," he said. "Whatever comes along and needs doctoring. In this case that'd be you. Now pull back your shirt and let me look."

I did as he ordered, figuring that it didn't really matter what sort of doctor he was, or wasn't. Someone had to try and take the chunk of lead out of me. He looked about as willing as anyone in the cabin.

He brought one of the lamps in close and examined the wound with the tips of his fingers after he'd peeled away Mattie's bandage. Then he opened his bag, took out a long metal probe, the kind I'd seen surgeons use in hospital tents on the battlefields at Shiloh and Lookout Mountain and a lot of other bad places.

"You might want to lean back and think about something else," Doc Kettle said.

I stared at the ceiling and clamped my jaws shut until my teeth ached while he poked and prodded with the probe.

"Think I feel it," he said at last. I was sweating, my hands were damp and cramped from making fists with them.

"That or a piece of bone," he added, straightening and

blowing out a stream of blue smoke whose smell caused me to want a cigarette.

I watched as he took out a metal pan, laid the probe in it, then took out a long slender instrument that looked like thin pliers and placed it in the pan next to the probe. Then he removed a bottle of rubbing alcohol and poured it over both instruments, the blood from the probe swirled pink in the pan as it mixed with the alcohol.

He waited a few seconds then took up the thin pliers.

"This is gonna be a little uncomfortable, better take a drink of ol' tosc," he said, handing me his whiskey flask.

"I'll wait for a drink until after you take the bullet out," I said, declining his offer. "I suspect it will taste better then."

"Suit yourself, son. You don't mind I have one, do you?"

"Go ahead."

I watched the lump of his throat in the loose sack of his unshaven neck as he took a swallow from the flask, then screwed the cap back on and slipped it back into the same side pocket of his jacket he'd taken it from.

"Here goes. I'll try to make it quick, if not painless."

Surprisingly, it didn't hurt much more than the probe. Until he caught hold of the bullet and began to retract it. That's when it felt like someone was driving a railroad spike into me. It took Hook and Mattie to hold me still long enough for Doc to bring out the object he'd grabbed onto.

"Bullet!" he declared, dropping the small partially flattened piece of lead into the pan. It clattered around like penny.

"Now this is gonna burn," Doc said, as he poured some of the alcohol directly into the wound. He was right. It burned enough to make my eyes water and sting. He asked Mattie if she'd mind dressing the wound since she'd done such a fine job of it before.

"You ready for that drink now, son?"

I took a swallow, then a second before handing it back to him.

"Lucky it was a small caliber," he said, eyeing the slug of lead in the bottom of the pan. "A .44-40 might have blowed out your insides. Liver, intestines, all that good stuff. I think

what happened was, that round bounced off a couple of your
ribs and just run out of power to do you much damage. I once
had a man got himself shot in the skull but all the bullet did
was bounce off. Knocked him cold as a pickle, but didn't kill
him. Course, such things is rare.''

"Well I guess we were both lucky," I said.

He grinned his picket-fence grin.

"I guess maybe so."

"Thanks," I said.

He shifted the cigar from one side of his mouth to the other.

"Hadn't been them two friends of yours come and got me,
you would've ended up dead of lead poisoning," he said. "It's
been known to happen."

I looked across the space of the room to Hook, his gaze
came up from his plate and met mine.

"Yeah, I guess I owe them a debt of thanks as well," I said.

"You going to stay the night, Doc?" Mattie asked.

"No. Marfina Goodlaw is expecting twins anytime. Got to
get back and see how she's holding up. I know sure as anything
I'm down here, she'll have them twins way cross the valley.
Best get going. Thanks for the supper."

"How much do I owe you for the call?" I said.

"Ten dollars ought to cover it."

"Would you take a good Creedmore rifle instead?" I said.

"Another busted hand," he said. "Ain't never met a drifter
yet had a nickel to his name."

"I'll pay for his care," Mattie said.

"No Mattie, I'll count the supper and your company as
payment," Doc Kettle said. "Just keep in mind that offer,
huh?"

"You come out for a chicken supper some Sunday," she
said. "But find yourself another party for that big bed of yours,
Doc."

He nodded.

"Some Sunday for sure, Mattie." He set his hat on his head
and gave us all a final look before closing the door behind him.

Mattie watched him from the window even though it had
grown dark outside then set to bandaging my wound.

Sugar Brown stretched her arms and said she was tired then took a blanket and curled up on the floor in front of the fireplace.

I asked Hook to make us a cigarette and by the time he finished, Mattie had finished with the dressing. She began clearing the table as Hook handed me one of the shucks he'd rolled.

"Tell me the details on Jake," I said.

He looked through the haze of blue smoke from his cigarette.

"I thought I already did."

"There wasn't any other way than that you shoot him?" I said.

He shook his head.

"No sir, there wan't any I could see. I didn't ever think he'd try pullin' his piece with my Sharps on him, but he did. Whole thing happened so fast, wan't nothin' could be done about it. Man had to know one of us was going to end up dying."

"What about the man in Cheyenne?" I said.

"What about what man in Cheyenne?" he said.

"You shot and burned a man in Cheyenne," I said. "He was another friend of mine."

Hook's eyes lifted slowly.

"Didn't kill no man in Cheyenne," he said.

"You were there."

His head bobbed.

"I was there. Stopped long enough to get some things to keep goin' on—some flour and sugar and bacon."

"A woman I know says she saw a black man running away from where my friend's office was just before it started burning. I reckon that'd have to be you."

I could see Mattie standing there, the dirty dishes in her hands, waiting, listening.

Hook took the shuck from his mouth, held it between his fingers, the smoke curling up around them.

"I was going down back of that alley, when I heard something," he said. "Something like glass breaking. I was trying to keep to myself account a I know Mr. True be trailing me. I heard the glass breaking. I look inside one of them buildings where it come from. I see a man done busted a kerosene lamp on the floor.'' A sheen of sweat glistened on Hook's broad forehead.

"Seen another man, down on the floor, look like he dead. Face in a ring of blood. Then I seen the yellow-hair man strike a match and toss it down into that kerosene from the busted lamp. I ran, mister, 'cause I know it's trouble what I seen.''

"Yellow-hair man?'' I said.

"That's what I seen,'' Hook said. "Tall skinny man, well-armed.''

I knew only one man that fit Hook's description of the killer. Long Bill Longly! It took me a full minute to adjust to the news. Somehow, knowing it was Longly, made it even harder to accept. Longly wasn't worth half a spit compared to a man like Ben Beadle. I felt my anger grow white hot.

Hook squatted there on his heels, staring at me.

"Jake told me about another man he said you killed then burned,'' I said.

He shook his head.

"No. I told you already, I ain't killed no innocent folks. Got me mixed up with a freed negro named Kimbo Luke. I know Kimbo Luke. Fact is, I was chasing him until I found out Mr. True was on my trail. I had to break it off and deal with Mr. True. I ever find Kimbo Luke, I'll kill him myself. Kimbo Luke and me from the same section of the Settlements. Only Kimbo Luke is low-down and low-life. That's the man what done the killings of all them folks—not me.''

"Then how come you're the one caught the blame?'' I said.

"To most of them white lawmen, us colored all the same.''

"More to it than that.''

"No. No there ain't.''

It wasn't just his words that convinced me Hook was telling the truth, it was his eyes.

"I'll take my weapons back now,'' I said.

He looked at me a long time.

"You and the girl are free to go,'' I said.

He turned his head to look at Sugar Brown lying asleep on the floor.

"You giving up on taking me back to Ft. Smith?'' he said.

"That's what I'm saying."

"What about her? What about that she shot you?"

"She did what she thought needed doing," I said. "I won't hold that against her."

He looked at his burned down shuck then tossed it into the fireplace before handing me back my self-cocker and the Colt's hideout pistol.

"I guess me and Sugar get goin' first light," he said. "Still ain't too late to find Kimbo Luke an' kill him."

"You want my advice, Mr. Hook?"

He looked at me.

"Let someone else take care of Kimbo Luke. Sooner or later, someone will kill him. Take the girl and go to Texas. Lots of pleasant places down along the border where the weather is warm and a man and a woman could grow a garden and raise a brood of kids. There are worse things in life."

All the tension seemed to go out of his dark face at once.

"Maybe so," he said. "Maybe so."

Everyone settled in and the light of the fire danced around the room and up the walls and for the first time since I'd been shot, I wasn't having to fight the rages of the fever. I felt weak and my mouth was dry, but I knew I wasn't going to die, at least not just yet, and in a few days, I'd be up to riding again.

New losses, old pain. That part was never going to change. But I felt a sense of renewal and grateful to be alive. As much as it worked around the edges of my mind, I didn't let myself think about vengeance or Bill Longly. Not for the last few hours of the evening. There would be plenty of time for that come morning. I lay there in the darkening silence.

I saw her shadow pass in front of the firelight.

"Mattie."

She sat on the edge of my bed.

"How are you feeling?"

Her hand rested atop one of mine.

"Like I might live," I said.

"I reckon soon's you're up to riding, you'll be leaving."

"That's what I'm thinking," I said.

"I heard what you told Mr. Hook, about taking Sugar and

going down to Texas—down along the border. About the garden and raising a brood of kids.''

"I can think of worse things."

"Sounds like a man who's wanting," she said.

"I won't deny it."

"Maybe once Wyatt gets back, I'll see if maybe he'd be interested in going to Texas," she said.

"That sounds like a good idea, Mattie."

Her fingers squeezed my hand. It was warm now, her hand. Warm and large and gentle.

"Wasn't for Wyatt . . ." she started to say.

I put my arm around her.

"You're a good woman, Mattie. Wyatt's a fool. He knows anything at all, he knows that much."

She leaned her head against my shoulder.

"Sometimes I get so lonely waiting for him to come back," she said. "Sometimes I think maybe I shouldn't wait, I should go on and find me someone who cares enough about me not to leave."

"You can't help what you feel," I said. "None of us can."

I felt the wetness of her cheek against my neck as she lifted her head.

"Sometimes I think I have to be strong just because of the way we live, Wyatt and me," she said. "But I don't always feel so strong."

"Mattie, you want to cry, go ahead."

The sobs were like small, fluttering birds trying to leave her chest as I felt the dampness of her tears through my shirt. I didn't mind holding her while she cried out her pain.

A few moments later she dabbed at her eyes with the back of her wrists.

"I'm sorry," she said.

"Don't be."

"I should have met someone like you before I met Wyatt," she said. "Someone that wouldn't steal my heart and run away with it."

"Maybe I would have done the same thing, Mattie. How do you know I wouldn't?"

She straightened, patted my hand.

"A woman knows," she said. "Which man will end up hurting her, and which won't."

I kissed her damp cheek.

"Thank you, Mattie. Thank you for everything you've done."

I saw her shadow cross in front of the fireplace again, then felt the empty place next to me where she'd sat.

I lay back on the cot and closed my eyes and thought that tomorrow would be a new day for all of us. And maybe a better one.

34

The next morning, I stood on the front porch of the cabin and watched as Hook saddled his and Sugar Brown's horses. The weather was cold, but clear. The sky was like blue silver and the sunlight sparkled along the surface of snow.

"I sorry I shot you, mister," Sugar Brown said as she came out of the cabin and stood next to me.

"No more sorry than I am, little sister."

"I glad you lettin' Elijah go. He says we goin' to Texas where it's warm."

I nodded. Her gaze flicked away, off toward the corral.

"You think any more white mens be comin' after him?" Sugar asked.

"I'll send word back to Ft. Smith that he's dead," I said.

Her eyes grew wide.

"Dead?"

"Do you think they'd believe me if I told them the real story?"

Then her face softened with understanding.

"I guess they wouldn't."

"Maybe later, when all the dust has settled and someone

kills Kimbo Luke, the truth will get told. For now, being considered dead might be the best thing.''

"Yessir."

"Sugar."

"What?"

"He's a good man."

Her face brightened.

"I know he is."

Hook finished saddling the horses and came striding toward the cabin. He had a wide smile and his teeth showed white against his blue-black face.

The two things happened almost at the same time: the sound, like rolling thunder that shook the air, and Hook being lifted off his feet—his arms flung wide—the easy smile replaced with a twisted mask of pain and surprise. His large body slammed to the ground, a flower of blood turning the snow beneath him crimson.

Sugar screamed and ran from the porch. Mattie threw open the door of the cabin, her wrists and hands dusted with flour.

"What is it! What's wrong?"

"Get back inside and get down!" I shouted and went for Hook. The wound in my side made it seem like I was dragging an anvil as I crossed the open stretch of ground. But I managed to reach Hook and when I did, I saw the same look in his eyes I'd seen in the eyes of other men who had taken a killshot.

His hands were twitching and his mouth was gasping for air causing his chest to rise and fall like a bellows.

I was about to try and get him to his feet when the thunder of the big-bore gun shattered the air again; an explosion of snow stung my face and eyes.

"Get back to the cabin!" I yelled at the girl.

But she wasn't listening; she was lost somewhere in her own shock and grief.

I bent and lifted Hook under the shoulders. I didn't have enough strength to carry him, but maybe I could drag him. But when I lifted his body up, his eyes sprung wide and he mouthed a single plea: "No!"

A bloody plume of foam spilled from the corner of his mouth.

His gaze shifted from me to Sugar.

Then he said his final words:

"Kimbo Luke."

Before she could protest or scream or cling to him for another second, I had her by the waist half carrying, half dragging her toward the cabin while the hole in my side burned like a hot coal.

Twice more the air was shattered by the big gun and snow kicked up around us, but I didn't stop or slow down until we reached the cabin.

Then we were inside, lying on the floor, Sugar Brown next to me, my breath coming hard, sweat soaking through my shirt, the stitch in my side tearing at my nerve endings.

Mattie was crouched behind a wall.

"What is it, Quint? Who's out there?"

"Kimbo Luke," I said.

She looked at Sugar; the girl's expression was frozen into a mask of disbelief, her hands glazed with the blood of her man.

"Watch her," I said, and crawled to the corner where my Creedmore was propped near the foot of my cot. The heavy *splat* of rifle slugs slamming into the outer walls of the cabin sounded like metal rain.

"Mr. Hook?" Mattie said, as she put her arms around Sugar. "He's . . ."

I shook my head. She put her right hand up to her mouth, then reached down and stroked Sugar Brown's wet face.

I took up a position at the window, checked the lay of cover out beyond the cabin. There was a stand of pines maybe a hundred yards distance. That's where he had to be.

I flipped up the tang rear sight on the Creedmore and peered through it and sighted down the long blued barrel and brought the front sight in line.

I scanned the tree line hoping to catch a glimpse of movement, a flutter of shadow in among the narrow shafts of sunlight dancing through the trees—anything that would give me a target. He was smart enough to know that even a puff of smoke would be detected, and so had ceased firing at the cabin. Now it would turn into a waiting game. At least until one of us got tired of the waiting.

"Can you see him?" Mattie asked.

"No."

She took a deep breath, let it out.

"How did he know?"

"There is only one way," I said. "He's been trailing us."

I saw the look of confusion on her face.

"Maybe because Mr. Hook was after him," I said. "Maybe he decided to turn the tables."

Sugar began to rock back and forth in Mattie's grasp. A soft moaning sound keened from her throat like a low wind that comes before a winter storm. I turned my attention to her for a moment. I'd been there myself—lost in the head—when Mary Lee and our son had died. I knew her need to run, to escape the reality, to cry and curse everyone including God for the pain that you couldn't describe if you had a thousand years to try.

A sudden explosion blew out the window near my face just as I started to turn my head again.

Shards of glass sliced my cheek, and one drove a splinter just above my right eye. A trickle of warm sticky blood clouded my vision for an instant until I wiped it away with my sleeve.

Mattie was holding her breath, staring at me, at the tiny cuts that razored my face.

"Stay where you are," I said.

"He'll come, won't he?" Mattie said. "When it gets dark, he'll come and burn the cabin with us in it."

"He'll try."

I could see the next question form itself in her eyes.

"I'll need to kill him before it gets dark," I said. I pulled off my bandanna and dabbed at my face and pulled out the sliver of glass sticking like a needle in my eyebrow.

"Damn him!" Mattie said.

"Damn him to hell!" I said.

"No, not Kimbo Luke," she said. "Damn Wyatt for leaving me here alone!"

I brought the Creedmore back up, rested the barrel on the

remains of the shattered casing. Judging by the destruction, Kimbo Luke was using a Big Fifty maybe, like the one Hook had carried. He probably had it fitted with a brass scope as well.

Again, I scanned the tree line searching for something, anything that would give him away. I had to get him before nightfall. Mattie was right. Kimbo Luke would come after it got dark and burn the cabin. And with just the one door, those of us that didn't burn, he would shoot as we came out.

I held my breath and drew the front sight of the Creedmore in a line even with the front row of the pines. I picked a spot, then squeezed off a round then cleared the window just in case.

"Did you see him?" Mattie called. "Is that why you shot?"

"No. I just wanted him to know I was looking for him."

She let her breath out, offered me a disappointed look.

"We don't stand a chance, do we?" she said.

Sugar Brown had a vacant stare; she was staring into a world that lay somewhere beyond the keening of her grief. She sat on the floor next to Mattie, her arms locked around her drawn up knees.

Another round hit the cabin.

The stress was taking its toll on Mattie. Every time one of the rounds slammed into the outer wall, she flinched like she had been slapped.

I noticed blood was leaking through my bandage; the side of my shirt was sticky from it. But a leaky wound was the least of my problems.

I picked sections, ten, twenty feet apart, and fired rounds into the tree line. If nothing else, maybe I'd get lucky just once in my life and kill the son of a bitch by accident. In between shots back and forth, there were long silences, then the roar of the big gun and another slug slammed into the outer walls. But I was never quick enough or lucky enough to even catch a glimpse of the smoke from his rifle.

The rest of the day we sat and watched the sunlight that angled through the shattered window cross from one side of the room to the other. I went through the options over and over again in my mind. There were damn few.

Finally, I knew what I had to do. It was less than an hour until the sun would set beyond the blue mountains.

"There's just one way," I said.

"What?" Mattie said.

I pulled the Colt *Lightning* from my shoulder rig and handed it to her.

"What's this for?" she asked.

"In case I don't make it back," I said. She blinked, uncertain.

"For you and her," I said, nodding toward Sugar Brown. "If he makes the cabin and starts it afire. Better this than being burned alive."

She swallowed.

"I'm going to try and make the horses. If I can make the horses, maybe I can make the tree line."

She looked at the pistol I'd placed in her hand.

"I don't know if I can," she said.

"You might not have to," I tried to assure her.

I moved to the door, the Creedmore in my right hand, crouched there for a moment, then lifted the latch. With the pain throbbing through my side, I wasn't going to be able to move fast, but if I stayed low and kept moving, I might make one of the saddle horses.

I gave it a silent count of three, then ducked out the door. It would take two or three seconds for Kimbo Luke to try and put a sight on me; I figured he'd have to be damn lucky, or I'd have to be damn unlucky for him to hit me with the first shot.

I'd just cleared the porch when the roar reached my ears and a spray of snow kicked up in front of me. I quick changed direction, heard the thunder of the second shot, didn't see it hit anything, but heard a slapping sound behind me. The horses were nervously prancing inside the corral. Maybe thirty more paces.

Boom!

Sugar's little sorrel reared, tossed sideways and went down. *Kimbo Luke had read the plan.*

I kept moving, hoping I could reach Hook's mount before Kimbo Luke could put a sight on it. My boots sloshed through the soft icy snow. My breath came hard in short bursts of vapor that clouded in front of my face. I was within a few feet of the horse when the thunder rolled again buckling the forelegs of Hook's mount. It went down, its muzzle digging into the wet snow, its eyes rolled white, then the rest of its body toppled over, the shod hooves flailing the air.

I heard myself cuss as I turned toward the speckled bird, who stood unsaddled inside the corral, her ears pricked. Then the roar of the big gun, and I went down, flinging aside the Creedmore as I toppled. I was down to one last possible— that of faking my death. Kimbo Luke was too damn good a shot to continue to miss. I had to make him think he was a tad better than he was.

For a long time I lay there on the cold snow-covered ground under the unyielding silence. The icy wetness soaked through my coat and shirt and I wasn't sure how long I could lie there without moving. I'd made sure to pull the self-cocker as I was falling and lay with it under my body, holding it in my right hand.

I lay with my face turned to the side. Through slitted eyes, I could see the red sun touching the tips of the blue mountains; the sky was the color of brass. I waited for Kimbo Luke to come and burn the women inside the cabin.

More time passed before I heard the sounds of footsteps crushing the wet snow, coming closer. I had to make sure my timing was right, that he would get to within pistol range before I made my move. Anything less and he would burn the women.

At one point, I heard the steps pause. I listened, then figured he had stopped to inspect his work on Hook. I heard the sound of his breathing, like a whistle of air through his teeth and nose. I tried to hold my own breath.

He took his time. I guessed him to be going through Hook's pockets. Then I heard him grunt and the crush of boots on wet snow again. They came close, then stopped.

"White man," he said, almost as a grunt. "I'll take you and put you in the cabin along with that darkie yonder and them two women, and burn you all up. Fust, let's see what you got in them pockets!"

I felt his hands going through my jacket pockets, pulling out my Ingersoll watch, my tobacco and papers, the book Alexandra Dupage had given me, the one about Don Quixote, the one I hadn't finished reading and maybe never would.

His breath was hot against the back of my head.

"What's this!" he snorted. I could hear him turning the pages of the book.

Then I could feel his breath again as his hands gripped my shoulders and turned me over.

"Big mistake!" I said, then fired.

The first shot knocked him backward, I came up and fired again. The second shot spun him around and put him to one knee. He had the look of a man who'd just lost everything he had in a single hand of poker. In a way, he had.

He fumbled with the Sharps and I saw my third shot shatter the top button of his coat.

The pages of the book fluttered near his outstretched hand along with my nickel-plated watch and makings. I picked them up and put them back in my pocket along with the book about an old man in search of his life.

I noticed, looking at him, Kimbo Luke was a lot shorter and thinner man than was Eljiah Hook. His color was lighter, too. It made me wonder why the law down in the Settlements had mistaken one man for the other. Then I remembered what Hook had said about white lawmen and white man's justice, and I understood why the mistake, if that is what it was to begin with—a mistake.

I picked up the Sharps lying nearby, brushed the snow from the brass scope and from around the trigger guard. It was a hell of a hunk of iron. Then I gathered up my Creedmore and walked back to the cabin to let Mattie know she wouldn't have to use my other handgun after all. Kimbo Luke would do no more burning, except maybe in hell.

35

It snowed that night. There was a white ring around the moon. I sat at the table across from Mattie; we drank coffee and listened to the broken sobs of Sugar Brown as she slept a fitful sleep on Mattie's bed. Mattie had some laudanum in a blue bottle which she gave Sugar to help her sleep. Mattie said Wyatt had bought her the laudanum in Colorado Springs when they were there because of her nerves had been acting up.

"It wasn't my nerves," Mattie said. "It was the way me and Wyatt were getting along. In between the good times, there were a lot of bad. Doc recommended Wyatt buy the laudanum and give it to me."

"Doc?" I said. "You mean Doc Kettle?"

"No," she said. "Doc Holliday."

I remembered the stony-eyed man I'd met in Deadwood. It was a small world.

Mattie went on to say how the laudanum had put her mind in a fog whenever she took it.

"Things'd get rough between Wyatt and me and I find myself in that fog just wandering around, feeling all loose in my joints, like I want to float off the earth. After a time, it got to where I wanted to be in the fog more than I wanted to be with Wyatt.

It didn't help matters between us, so I finally put the bottle up in the cupboard and left it there. For a time after, I had cramps because of it.''

"The things we do to each other," I said.

She smiled sadly.

"Yes. I wonder sometimes if a man and woman were meant to live together. Don't know many that have ever done it well.''

I thought of Mary Lee and wanted to tell Mattie that there were people who could live together and love each other. But the woman who sat across from me had her mind full of her own troubles, so I kept the thought to myself.

Earlier, Mattie had helped me wrap the two dead men in blankets and carry them to the lean-to.

She had looked at me and said, "They will freeze stiff left out here, we should bury them.''

"The ground's frozen," I told her. "The burying will have to wait until spring.''

She looked horrified.

"What about wolves?" she said. "Won't the wolves come and get at them?''

"Tomorrow, I'll take a rope and pull them up on the roof of the cabin.''

"Dead men on my roof!" she exclaimed.

"Unless you want them in the house.''

"There's no other way?''

"It's a sorry place to have to die," I said, "Wyoming in the winter.''

"It seems improper," she said, "dead men on the roof.''

"There's no other way, given the situation," I said.

"Maybe a cowboy will come by with a wagon and you can have them taken into the nearest town and they can be put in storage until spring," I suggested. "If you had a wagon, I'd take them with me to Cheyenne.''

"I suppose I should be grateful instead of complaining," she said. "We could have all been burned up by Kimbo Luke.''

She looked tired, her eyes weary over the rim of her cup.

"That was a brave thing you did to save us all," she said.

"It was a necessary thing," I said. "There was little that was brave about it."

She rubbed the upper parts of her arms as though she'd suddenly chilled.

"If you hadn't been here . . ." She didn't finish the thought.

"If I hadn't been here, then most likely, neither would Kimbo Luke," I said. "You can look at it either way."

"We can only guess," she said. "He might have come along sooner or later and burned us anyway."

"If you want, you and the girl can go with me to Cheyenne," I said.

She stared at me for a moment, her green eyes dark as jade in the low light.

"No. Wyatt might come while I'm gone. I better wait for him case he decides to come back . . ."

"I'll ask the girl in the morning if she wants to ride back to Cheyenne with me," I said.

"She can stay here with me if she wants."

"That's kind of you, Mattie."

"Not so kind as you might think," she said, "It would beat staying here alone with dead men on my roof."

"I suppose it probably would."

"She might want to stay at least until spring when we can give Mr. Hook a decent burial," Mattie said.

"Well, we can ask her what she chooses to do first thing in the morning," I said. "I think I'll spread my blanket on the floor. You take the other bed."

"You know," she said. "I'm not suggesting anything, but if you wouldn't mind so much, maybe we could both share the bed . . ."

Then pausing for a moment, she added, "I just feel worn out and empty and could use a man's arms around me. Does that make any sense to you?"

I waited for her to change into her nightgown and slip under the blankets with me. The light dancing in the fireplace, shadows climbing up the wall and dancing against the beamed ceiling, made the fact that Mattie's lank warmth next to me seem a natural condition. It all felt so sheltering from the snowstorm outside the cabin. She lay with her back to me, and I put an arm around her.

"It's been a long time since I had a man in my bed," she said, "and it feels good."

"It feels good to me too, Mattie."

In a few minutes, I could hear the steady breathing of her sleep, feel the warm blow of her breath against my wrist. It truly did feel good to have the comfort of a woman's body next to mine on that cold wintery night. I fell into a sweet, peaceful, undisturbed sleep.

The next few days, we rode out the winter storm that had piled snow up to the bottoms of the windows. Mattie mended my shirt and I brought in buckets of snow to melt into water for washing and drinking. Sugar Brown talked to herself, talked to her dead lover through the ceiling like he was up there on the roof listening to her.

I cleaned and oiled my weapons, fed the speckled bird and the lone jack mule Wyatt had left Mattie—I suppose for the purpose of riding into town if she got tired of waiting for him to return.

I read portions of *Don Quixote* to them at Mattie's insistence and she found it to her liking, and even Sugar would stop talking to Hook long enough to listen to the tale of old Don and his man-servant Sancho Panza's misadventures.

It was a good way to pass time and let my wound heal, reading about the noble old warrior who thought sheep were armies and windmills were the foe.

Mattie enjoyed listening with her eyes closed.

"That true, about that fellow?" Sugar asked at one point. "He really crazy like that?"

I didn't want to tell her it was a work of fiction, that Don Quixote and Sancho Panza were not real people. I guess partly, because if they weren't real, they should have been.

"They're as real as any of us," I said. "And I'm not so sure the old man is as crazy as he seems."

She smiled.

"Them two sound like me and Elijah, traveling all over."

Mattie's gaze met mine.

"I've got a man does the same thing," Mattie said. "Always getting ideas in his head and chasing after them. I guess men are just born with itchy feet and crazy notions floating around inside their heads."

Sugar laughed, and Mattie laughed with her.

On the fourth day, the sun came out and began to melt the glassy ice cicles hanging from the eaves.

I felt up to riding. Being in the company of women, made me think more than once, of another woman—one I'd left up in Nebraska. The sooner I finished what I'd begun—finding Ben's killer—the sooner I could try and get my life back around to normal. Maybe that meant returning to Ogallala and seeing if Etta Landrow was still interested in a man who'd gotten tired of riding the Big Lonely.

"I'm pulling up stakes," I announced at breakfast. The eyes of the two women were on me.

"You must feel perky," Mattie said.

"Perky enough to ride to Cheyenne and finish some business," I said.

"You gonna leave?" Sugar said. "You gonna jus' go off an leave us?"

"I want you to have this, Sugar," I said, handing her the book.

"But I don't know how to read much," she said.

"Maybe Mattie can help you with it."

Mattie patted the girl's arm.

"Sure. You and me will read the covers plum off that book. And when we're finished, spring will have arrived."

"Tell you what," I said. "Soon as I've taken care of my business in Cheyenne, I'll ride back this way and check in on you. And if you're still here, we'll have a picnic."

She seemed uncertain, so did Mattie.

"I'll swing by and tell Doc Kettle to check in on you in the meantime," I said.

"Tell him to bring a chicken and we'll have that supper I promised him," Mattie said. "You like fried chicken don't you, Sugar?"

I gathered my gear, my Creedmore and saddlebags. Mattie

handed me the Colt pistol I'd given her the day I'd shot Kimbo
Luke.

"You keep it," I said.

"No, I'm no shootist," she said. "Sides, Wyatt left me an
old double buck I keep under the bed. I guess if I was to have
to depend on hitting anything, I'd most likely hit it with that
double buck than this little pistola. You take it, I've a feeling
the business you're going to Cheyenne for will require you to
be well-heeled."

"You are wise beyond your years," I said. "Are you sure
you won't keep it?"

"I'm sure."

I put on my coat and hat, and stepped out into the brilliant
sunlight that was made even more brilliant the way it glared
off the snow.

I saw the bird prick up her ears as I approached the corral.
She knew we were leaving. The muscles under her hide rippled
with anticipation.

"Don't bite me and don't buck me off just because I haven't
ridden you in a week," I said as I laid the blanket on her back,
then set the saddle down atop it.

She snorted through wet black nostrils and tossed her head.
I stroked my hand along her neck and spoke a little Spanish
to her as I reached under her belly and grabbed the cinch strap.

She pawed the snowy ground as impatient as a saint in a
saloon waiting to get going.

I put the bit between her teeth and adjusted the bridle, then
led her out of the corral. Mattie came from the cabin, I could
see Sugar standing in the doorway.

"I put some chuck together for your ride," she said, handing
me a burlap sack. "I don't reckon there are many restaurants
between here and Cheyenne."

I tied the sack to the horn of my saddle.

"You and the girl going to be all right?" I asked.

"We'll make out until Wyatt gets back," she said.

"I'll ask Doc Kettle if there is someone who can come with
a wagon and get those corpses off your roof and take them to
town to be stored."

"It'd make me rest easier," she said, "knowing I don't have dead men on my roof."

"Mattie."

"What?"

"Wyatt doesn't deserve you."

"Hell, I know that. But what's it got to do with the way I love him?"

"I finish up my work in Cheyenne, I'll swing back by."

"You do that," she said. "And if we're not here, you'll know Wyatt came back and got us."

"I hope he does."

"So do I."

"Would you mind so much I gave you a kiss on the cheek?" I said.

"On the lips would be better," she said. "The only way a man should kiss a woman is on the lips. Kissing on the cheek is for women to do."

I kissed her on the lips. It was a dry, light kiss that sealed our friendship and respect for each other.

I put a foot in the stirrup, then found myself in the saddle for the first time in more than a week. It felt odd, like I was ten feet up in the air.

I heeled the bird over to the porch.

"I'm counting on you to help Mattie out here," I said. Sugar was holding the book in her hands.

"You learn to read, everything else will be easier for you. Go with Mattie if her man comes to get her. Things have a way of working themselves out, Sugar. You'll see."

She blinked and her lower lip quivered.

"Bye," she said. "Thank you for the book."

"You're welcome."

I reined the bird's head around and spurred her into an easy trot. She didn't seem to mind the snow and took to it like she'd been born in a barn on Christmas day.

I didn't look back. I didn't have to. I knew both women would be all right without me there, that life would catch them up and carry them on to whatever destinies awaited them. As it would us all.

36

The weather remained remarkably good, with only an occasional spitting of snow mixed with alternating sunshine and clouds.

I stopped by Doc Kettle's yellow clapboard house in a little settlement halfway up a valley surrounded by craggy snow-covered slopes. Doc's was the only house that wasn't built of logs and the yellow paint you could spot from a half mile off. Mattie had given me directions, told me about Doc's penchant for the unusual when it came to paint.

The air over the valley was smudged with wood smoke drifting out of blue metal stovepipes poking through the shake roofs. Except for the occasional bark of a hound to lazy or cold to show itself, the valley was as peaceful as a graveyard.

I knocked on the door of Doc Kettle's place and stamped the snow off my boots while I waited for someone to answer. In a few seconds the door opened and there was Doc, his walrus moustaches hiding most of his mouth, his eyes rimmed red. I could smell the liquor on his breath; it came out warm and sour when he spoke.

"I know you from somewhere?" He squinted at me as though he was trying to see me through the bottom of a whiskey glass.

"You dug a bullet out of my side back at Mattie Blaylock's," I said.

Then the knots of uncertainty fell out of his lumpy face and his big shaggy moustaches lifted in a lippy grin.

"Oh yeah," he said, "at's right. Looks like you lived in spite of my operation." I could hear the phlegm rattle around in his throat as he laughed at his own sense of humor.

"So far I'm still walking around as you can see," I said. "You mind if I step in for a minute."

"No, come right ahead. Mattie come with you?"

"No. Matter of fact, that's the reason I stopped. I'd like you to check on her in a few days."

"She ailing?"

"No. She's fine. Just that I'm on my way to Cheyenne and she and the girl are out there alone."

"You mean that little tan child?"

"Yes."

"Where's the big colored fellow, at friend of hers?"

"He's laid out on Mattie's roof."

"Roof! What's he doing up on the roof?"

"He was shot and killed," I said.

"How'd at happen? You shoot him, did you?"

"No, a man named Kimbo Luke shot him."

"Seemed like an alright fellow to me. Why'd this Luke shoot him?"

"It's a long story, one I don't have time or inclination to go into."

"I still don't understand him being on the roof."

"Only way we could make sure the bodies didn't get molested by wolves," I said.

"Bodies? There's more than one?"

"Kimbo Luke's laid out on the roof, too."

"Sounds like I left from out there just in time," Kettle said. "Who knows, if I had stayed the night, I might be on the roof along with them other fellows."

"So, you'll make it a point to go out and check on Mattie and the girl in a few days?"

He nodded.

"One more thing," I said. "If there's someone around here who has a wagon, maybe they could go out and bring in the bodies. Mattie doesn't much care for having dead men on her roof."

"Don't blame her. At's an awful thing to have on your roof, corpses is."

"Thanks for everything, Doc. I promised Mattie I'd stop back this way. I'll bring you the ten dollars I owe you for the care."

He looked skeptical but offered me his hand and said I ought to keep an eye on the wound in case it got infected again.

I camped that night by a little stream whose waters shimmered with blackness against its snowy banks. I boiled water and threw in a pinch of coffee from the sack of chuck Mattie had fixed me and cut a slice of dried beef and put it between some crackers.

Afterwards, I smoked a shuck and drank the rest of the coffee as I sat cross-legged on my soogins and listened to the deep silence. The night was black with stars and the moon still had a circle around it. Then from nowhere, I heard the long mournful call of a gray wolf just as I tossed out the dregs of my coffee and stubbed my smoke. He sounded as lonely as I felt.

I figured to make Cheyenne in two or three days of steady riding. I wished then, that Mattie would have thought to slip a pint of mash whiskey in the gunny to help ward off the cold and silence. But wishing didn't make it so. I didn't much miss liquor, but there were times when I did. Wind swept down from the blue mountains and I didn't get a lot sleep that night with thinking of the coming days. I kept my head on my saddle and my feet toward the fire and managed as best I could.

The next day dawned bright and clear and I rose early. My back and legs felt stiff enough to break if I moved too quick. I didn't bother with breakfast.

Late that afternoon, I came to a settlement of sorts; it was just a few homesteads, four or five little log structures.

A man was chopping wood out front of one of homesteads. He looked up as I checked the reins of the bird.

He was solidly built with a face full of burnished whiskers.

"There a place here I could get a meal?" I said.

"Depends," he said. He had the heavy drawl of a southerner.

"Depends on what?" I asked.

He looked at me, the bird, our trappings. Then his gaze drifted to the stock of the Creedmore and back up to me.

"You a lawman?"

"Would it make a difference if I was?" I said. "About getting a meal?"

His tongue came out and licked at his lips, the moisture freezing on the tips of his wiry beard.

"Step on down," he said.

I followed him inside the log hut. A woman sat nursing a baby in one corner of the room. She looked up when we entered but made no attempt at covering her breast. The baby had a pale head with veins as blue as ink. The infant made a sucking sound, then sighed, then started nursing again.

"Maylou, man here lookin' fer a meal."

She was as pale as the infant, like neither of them had ever seen sunshine. She had a thin face, high cheekbones and hollow eyes, like the infant had sucked most the life out of her.

"There's beans," she said. "That's it. Just that pot of beans. Got a little sow belly in it."

"Look," I said. "I don't have any money, but I have a good watch I'll give you. Maybe it would fetch three or four dollars from someone that needs a good watch." I reached in my pocket and took out the Ingersoll and laid it on the table. I'd bought the watch in Laredo from a man with a club foot who was selling them on a street corner one summer afternoon. It kept better time than half the railroads.

Neither one of them said anything; the man took a plate down from a plank shelf and ladled out some beans from the kettle hanging in the fireplace. He set the plate down next to the watch. Then he picked up the watch and examined it.

"Say it keeps good time does it?"

I nodded. The beans had little taste, but they were hot and warmed my belly and that's about all I could ask for.

I didn't encourage conversation, concentrating instead on the plate of beans, figuring to eat and get on my way.

The man said, "That a Colt pistol you're wearin'?"

"Remington," I said. "Forty-four, forty. Self-cocker."

"Had me a good pistol once. Big Navy. Thirty-six caliber. Had pearl grips."

"You in the war?" I said. "That where you come by the Navy?"

"Rode under Mosby," he said. "Some of us had Navies. Cap and ball models. I ended up having to trade mine after the war for a mule to plow my ground with. The mule died before I could plant. Every thing went plum to hell the day that war ended. I wish now I'd never traded my pistol for that mule."

"It was a hard war in lots of ways," I said.

"You don't sound like you fought for the Gray," he said. "The way you talk, I mean."

"I didn't."

Something bitter and hurtful flashed in his eyes like he had suddenly opened up a drawer filled with tintypes of dead loved ones. Then he snorted and said, "I shot a lot of you Yankees in that war with that Navy of mine. I'd still be shootin' Yanks if Marse Lee hadn't turned over his sword to that little hide-tanner, Grant."

"Yeah, well," I said. "I guess that war's been over a long time."

He grunted.

"Some of us is still havin' to live with it," he said. I knew what he meant.

"You want another plate of beans?"

I nodded. My belly had been scraping my backbone all day.

The woman was watching me. Her hair was the color of dusty wheat, long and stringy and uncombed.

"At pistol," the man said, setting the plate of beans in front of me. "You be willin' to trade it?"

"No."

"You ain't heard what it is I got to trade fer it," he said.

"I have need of my gun, mister. It's not for trade."

He swallowed. I could see the fever of excitement burning in his gaze.

"Trade you a turn with Maylou for at pistol," he said, his voice hoarse. He wiped a knuckle under the tip of his nose.

"Like I said, the pistol's not for trade."

He jerked his head around, glanced at the woman. She simply stared back.

"How 'bout whiskey then?" he said. "You got a jug in your saddle pockets? I'd trade you a turn with her for a jug."

"No whiskey," I said, feeling a knot well in my gut. "You make it a habit of trading your wife to strangers for pistols and whiskey?"

"She ain't my wife," he said. "Sister-in-law. Least she was till my brother, Bill, died. Hit hisself in the leg with a ax choppin' firewood. Gangrene set in. Died from it. Left her with a belly full of kid. Took her in is what I done. She needs to earn her keep same as the rest of us. Hard fact, but that's the way things is out here."

"That war must have done something to you it didn't do to the rest of us," I said.

His brows knitted.

"You was a Yank," he said. "How'd you know what that war did to us who lost?"

"I wouldn't," I said. "But don't insult me again."

"You ain't invited here no more!" he said.

I laid the fork down and stood up. The woman continued to stare. The infant at her breast had fallen asleep, its head tilted to the side, the small lips pursed; a pearl of milk lay in the corner of its mouth. It didn't look like it would survive the winter. Maybe in that way, it was lucky.

I still had two days riding ahead of me before I reached Cheyenne. There wasn't much I could say or do to a man who had lost everything in the war including his soul. The woman would have to figure it out at some point and make her own decision. The Rebel had been right about that part: It was a hard life.

I mounted the bird, the saddle leather creaked from the cold. The man said, "Don't come back round here, mister!"

I touched my spurs to the bird. The sooner I got to Cheyenne and finished my business with Bill Longly, the better.

37

Little Dick was sitting at a table with Cleopatra and Jonas Fly when I came in. It was an hour past sunset and except for the three of them, the only other person in the diner was Persimmon Bill. He was eating a bowl of mush with lick poured over it.

"Mr. McCannon!" Jonas said. He was the only one unoccupied at the time. Little Dick and Cleo were busy counting the day's receipts, and Persimmon Bill was staring into his bowl of mush like it was a crystal ball that held the future of the human race.

As soon as Jonas announced my name, the others looked up.

Little Dick squinted through the curl of gray smoke coming off his cigarette. Cleo had her hands full of loose change.

"Goddamn!" Bill declared, bits of wet mush clinging to his moustaches. "Look what the cat drug in!"

It'd been a long ride, I must have looked like hell and death warmed over. That's about the way I felt.

Little Dick stood up and hobbled over and extended his hand.

"Glad to see you made it back, Quint, what the hell took you so long?"

"For steak and a cold beer, I'd be happy to tell you," I said.

"Where's Jake, outside tying up the horses?"

"Jake didn't make it," I said.

"Hook?" he said. "Was it Hook at killed him?"

"Yeah. But it's not what you think."

Little Dick's forehead knurled into fleshy ridges.

"Hell, I don't see how that could be!" Then he looked toward the window. "I don't see Hook, neither—you kill him?"

"I didn't, someone else did."

"Well I guess it don't matter who killed who as long as Hook got his. Leastwise he won't be doing any more slaughtering and burning."

"He wasn't guilty," I said. I could hear Eljiah Hook's words echoing in my head.

"Say what?"

"We chased down the wrong man. Hook turned out to be innocent."

"Shit, Quint. You got me more confused than a Chinaman at a baseball game."

"Jonas," I said. "I'd consider it a favor if you would take my horse down to the livery and see she gets put up."

"Sure, sure," he said, putting on his coat. I noticed he was wearing an apron.

"Just a little something to tide me over till I can save for another mule and a wagon," he said, almost apologetically.

"He needed work, I had work," Dick explained. "I seen better at waiting tables, but he's steady. Now you want to tell me how it is Hook ended up killing Jake but ain't guilty of anything?"

I sat down at the table across from Cleo. Persimmon Bill picked up his bowl of mush—carried it like it was the last gold out of the Black Hills—and joined us. Little Dick threw a steak the size of a dinner plate on the fire and drew me a beer.

I explained what had happened, how Jake had made a fatal mistake and how I'd tracked down Hook and Sugar Brown and the part about her shooting me. I told them about Kimbo Luke and the rest of it. When I finished, Little Dick leaned back and his chair and said, "I'm a sonbitch! Then it was Long Bill that killed Ben?"

"It looks that way."

"I ain't surprised." Persimmon Bill said. "But why'd he do it?

"That's what I came back to find out," I said.

"He was in here eating supper an hour ago," Little Dick said. "Him and Dave Beltrain. Eating and belching up their food like a pair of shoats."

I started to reach for my watch to check the time, then remembered I had traded it for a plate of beans to a man who was willing to swap his woman for a Colt pistol or a bottle of mash.

"They're probably over to the Blue Star," Little Dick said. "Beltrain runs him a faro game and Long Bill sorta hangs around lapping up Beltrain's crumbs."

"You take on one," Persimmon Bill said, a spoonful of mush gripped in his left hand, "you'll have to take on both of 'em."

"I've thought of that," I said. "Maybe it doesn't have to come to that. Maybe Beltrain is smart enough to stay clear of a fight that's not his."

"I'll go over with you when you're ready," Little Dick said.

"No. I appreciate the offer, Dick."

We both knew that Dick wasn't a gunfighter. And even though he lacked fear, he was no match for men like Dave Beltrain and Long Bill Longly.

"You want me to," Persimmon Bill said. "I'll go find me a goddamn shotgun and assassinate the sons a bitches while you palaver with 'em. I'll sneak up behind 'em and blow out their backbones."

"Tell you what, Bill. Why don't I borrow a dollar from Little Dick and instead of you going to find a shotgun, you go get us a bottle so when I get back, we can do a little serious drinking?"

"Shit," Bill said. "If that's what you want."

"I smell that steak burning, Dick."

"Did Roy Bean go to Texas?" Cleo asked. "Or did he find himself another whore?"

"He was still trying to decide whether he should go or not when I left," I said. "But he didn't find himself another whore. That's all I know for certain."

"He's too far out in the toolies to do much business anyway," Cleo said. "Even if he had him a hundred whores. Ain't but one or two cow outfits out there." She was stacking the loose change in front of her into little silver towers.

"Roy Bean's an enterprising soul," she added. "He just gets dopey-eyed sometimes. Dreams of someday meeting an actress and becoming famous his ownself. Man sure can dream big."

"He talked of practicing the law," I said.

"Whatever gave him that idea?" Cleo said.

"He thought maybe he would be good at it."

"Hump!" Cleo snorted. "Knowing that man, he'll probably go practice the law someplace there ain't nothing but rattlesnakes and scorpions and outlaws and end up running some little rum joint in the middle of bejezzus!"

"He sounds like my sort of man," Persimmon Bill said. "I don't care much for towns neither. Maybe I'll get to Texas sometime and look him up. You say his last name is Bean?"

"You ain't never going to Texas, Bill," Little Dick said.

"Why ain't I?"

"Because it's too damn far to walk and you're too poor to buy a horse. And even if you did buy a horse, you're too old to ride it. You might just as well stay here and forget about going to Texas."

"You know, this mush could use a little more lick," Bill said. "Pass me that maple syrup would you."

I ate the steak with a hunger long ignored and washed it down with the glass of beer Dick had drawn me. Then I made myself a shuck and smoked it.

"That chuck looks like it's brought all the life back into you," Little Dick said. "You walked in, I thought you was a ghost. You want another steak?"

"No, that one was plenty."

We sat there in silence for a time while I smoked the cigarette. It got quiet enough you could hear the paper burn and Little Dick's regulator clock ticking above the door.

"Time I pay a visit to Long Bill," I said when I finished the smoke.

"You sure you don't want us to go with you?" Dick said.

"Yeah, you sure?" Persimmon Bill said. "I can get us that bottle of whiskey after I assassinate them sons a bitches!"

"No. It's better I go alone."

Jonas Fly came in knocking snow dust from his hat and shoulders.

"Starting to snow again," he said. "It's pretty, but awful cold. Do you think spring will ever come to these parts again?"

I checked the loads in my pistols, then stepped out into the night air. It was time to finished my business.

I walked down to the Blue Star. The lights from its windows lay on the snow in yellow squares. I opened the door and went in.

The place was doing a good business. On a snowy night, there isn't much for men to do except drink and gamble and proposition working girls. Judging by the crowd, they were mostly cowboys, one or two of them could have been bull whackers or prospectors waiting out the winter so they could go back up into the Black Hills come spring.

I worked my way through the crowd looking for Long Bill. The sawdust floor was puddled with melted snow from wet boots and a blue smoke haze floated in the air. There was the loud mixture of voices, of men talking to one another on various subjects such as the weather and cattle and horses, and of course, women.

The cowboys were mostly young, pink-cheeked boys with little or no hair on their faces. But there were a few old punchers among the bunch. Men whose gazes were fixed on their own images in the big mirror of the back bar. Men who'd long ago run out of idle conversation. Men who saw in their own reflection the grizzled faces and tired eyes that held a string of bittersweet memories of lost opportunities, squandered wages, and a lifetime of drifting. And somewhere inside those memo-

ries too, were the sweethearts they'd left behind, and the ones
they were still hoping to find. Those eyes knew more than they
were telling. They knew of long winters that were getting longer
each new season, and a trail that was soon coming to an end.
They knew lots of things they weren't telling. Thoughts that
weren't given to idle conversation.

I saw Dave Beltrain dealing faro amid a heavy haze of smoke
from the players ringing his rig. A chubby young woman stood
next to him with her hand resting on his shoulder. I could see
the silver-plated Policeman's model pistol lying on the table
next to his right hand. The badge pinned to his vest was the
size of a liberty dollar. It looked out of place on a man like
him.

But it wasn't Beltrain I'd come for.

I continued to look through the crowd, but didn't see Long
Bill. I gave half a thought that he might be out making rounds
then discarded the possibility. Long Bill wasn't the sort of man
to do any honest work.

I went to the bar and ordered a beer, figuring I'd give it a
few minutes to see if he came in.

I kept watch by looking at the mirror in back of the bar.
And in a single reflective moment, I thought to myself that I
wasn't much different than the old hands who stood alone,
their bellies pressed up against the bar while they sipped their
beer and thought of lost sweethearts and trails they could have
taken but didn't.

Something caught my eye. I turned in time to see Long Bill
coming down the stairway still buckling his belt. I looked along
the upper hall, saw the prostitute, Shady Sue, leaning against
the jamb in an open doorway. Her eye was nearly swollen shut.

I stepped away from the bar, pushing my way through the
crowd, taking the self-cocker out of my hip holster and dangling
along my leg as I moved to the foot of the stairs.

"You're under arrest, Longly!" I said loud enough for him
to hear me above the din. He looked up, his hands still fumbling
with his belt buckle; he stopped three steps from the landing.

"What the hell you talking about, McCannon?"

His hair was lank and stringy, his face shone with sweat. I noticed the knuckles on his right hand were red.

"The murder of Ben Beadle," I said.

He raised the hand with the red knuckles to his mouth and swept his shaggy moustache with his thumb and forefinger.

"Well now, you got some proof of that, do you?"

"An eyewitness," I said.

"Eyewitness my ass! You better let go of something you're not up to. I could kill you in a heartbeat."

"If you were armed, maybe you could," I said. "Trouble is, the only weapon you got is what you're tucking into your pants. Let's go!"

I still hadn't lifted the self-cocker, but I'd thumbed the hammer back. I could see his gaze drift downward to the blue metal barrel.

"This is horse shit!" he said.

"I didn't come here for a discussion. Let's go!"

The room had gotten quiet; I heard someone cough, the sound of a chair scraping across the floor. It was like everyone was holding their breath waiting to see if I was going to shoot Bill Longly and give them something to talk about for the next ten years.

"Put your piece away, McCannon!"

The voice was Dave Beltrain's somewhere behind me.

"Don't get into this, Dave," I said without turning around.

"Why not? It's my town, Longly's my man. You come in starting trouble, what'm I supposed to do, just stand around with my thumb up my butt?"

"You'd be better off if you did, Dave," I said.

"No, you're wrong, McCannon. You see to take me on would mean you'd have to turn around and raise that iron you've got hanging at your leg. Me, all I got to do is pull the trigger on this Police Colt. You figure out what the results would be."

"One more chance to back away, Dave. That's what you've got."

"Fuck you!"

I spun around, bringing up the self-cocker. Our two shots

sounded like one. I felt his bullet rip through the sleeve of my coat. Mine took him mid-chest and carried him across a table where there was a pile of loose coin that fell on him like silver rain as he crashed to the floor.

Long Bill jumped on my back and began pummeling me with his bony fists knocking the pistol from my hand as his weight pushed me to the floor with him atop me swinging those long arms. I felt the pain in my side flare up like fire as I could feel the old wound tearing apart.

Longly's right fist crashed into the side of my head and his left glanced off my cheek. His eyes were glassed over and his teeth were bared behind the shaggy moustache. Then his hands went around my throat and clamped down like a vise shutting off my air. My left arm was pinned beneath me, beneath his weight atop me and I tried separating his hands from my throat with my free hand.

His wrists were knobs of hard bone and sinew and he put all his weight behind the strangling grip trying to squeeze the life out of me. My free hand gave up trying to tear his hands away from my throat as I fumbled to pull the backup from my shoulder rig. But one of his knees bore down against the pistol and I couldn't reach in and jerk it free.

The strength in his hands flowed out of his arms and shoulders and came to a choking confluence at my windpipe. I could feel my own strength starting to lag as my lungs screamed for air.

"I told you you ain't up to me! I told you I'd kill you in a heartbeat!" Longly's shouted threat came in a spray of sour breath as the beads of sweat from his forehead dripped onto my face.

He worked his hands harder still and I could feel myself starting to slide down a dark tunnel that held no light at the end. The fleeting thought that he was going to kill me flashed through my mind.

The strange thing was, I wasn't scared—I was mad!

Longly had killed Ben, and now he was going to kill me and get away with both murders! Something terrible went through me in a flash of hatred and anger like I'd never felt before. Like a bolt of raw lightning! I swung my free hand with everything I had and crashed it into the center of his face, feeling the bone and cartilage of his nose shatter into a spray of blood.

His hands released their grip and went to his face. I pulled the backup pistol from my shoulder rig and pressed it to his guts, thumbing back the hammer as I did.

"You want to finish it?" I said.

The blood leaked through his fingers as his eyes nearly crossed looking down at the cocked revolver.

He rolled off, onto his knees as I pushed myself to my feet and stood over him. "Let's go!" I said.

"Where?"

"Where do you think?"

He staggered to his feet and I marched him outside, my head still throbbing from his blows.

"You taking me to jail?"

"Not before you tell me why you did it?"

"To hell with that!"

I shoved him into an alley, pressed the barrel of the pistol to a point just below his left eye.

"I don't have any reason to save you for the hangman," I said. "You want, I'll shoot you in the face!"

He swallowed behind the mask of blood.

"He got a wire on me. Beadle did."

"Wire?"

"Some work I did up in Montana."

"What sort of work?"

His muddy eyes shifted in their sockets.

"What sort of work?"

"Killed a kid—a rancher's kid. Man name, Jensen. He put out a ten-thousand-dollar reward on me!"

"You've done other work," I said. "Similar."

His head darted side to side.

"Not like this. The kid was ten years old."

"You shot a ten-year-old boy!"

"It was a long way off," he said, flecks of blood sputtering from his mouth. "Shot him from a quarter mile off. I was up there doing stock detective work. I thought the kid was a rustler.''

"So Ben got a wire on you and was going to arrest you and take you back for the reward."

He nodded his head.

"I wasn't going back to Montana, let that man hang me. It was a goddamn accident I shot his boy! I wasn't going to let him hang me over no goddamn accident!"

"Why didn't you just get the hell out of town instead of killing Ben?"

A dull look compressed itself behind his eyes.

"I dint think to."

"Beltrain know about the wire?"

"He knew. Shit, he dint care."

I brought the barrel down hard across his collarbone and stepped back as he slumped to his knees.

"Jaysus!" he yelped, the tears welling in his eyes.

"It's going to feel worse than that when you're standing on the trap waiting to hit the end of the rope," I said. "Another thing. After they hang you, I'm going to send a wire to Jensen up in Montana and let him know."

38

Long Bill was hanged on the fifteenth of December under a wintery sky with most of the town turned out for the event. A circuit judge named Figgs, sentenced Longly and when he heard the judgment, he looked at Figgs and said, "This is one hell of a Christmas present you've gave me. I hope you know that!"

Figgs hammered his gavel down hard and said, "If I could hang you twice, I would."

I didn't go to the hanging. I went to Little Dick's cafe instead and had a cup of coffee and smoked a shuck.

"See you didn't go?" Little Dick said. "Me neither."

"It's not something I would take any pleasure in, seeing a man hang," I said. "Even if it is Long Bill's hanging."

"I guess they'll drop him through the trap whether me and you are there or not," he said. "I think Persimmon Bill went."

"Where's Cleo?" I asked.

"Buying herself another dress," he said. "Woman sure has a thing for dresses."

"You thinking of getting married?" I said.

"You think she'd have me?"

"She could do worse."

He squinted through the smoke of his cigarette.

"Hell, I reckon she could," he grinned.

"I hear tell the town committee is considering hiring Jonas as the new chief of police," I said.

"At's another thing," Little Dick said. "I think he'd do all right, but I sure do hate to lose a good waiter like him. Man's conscientious."

"Life goes on," I said.

"Sure does. What about you? What're your plans?"

"Thinking of going up to Nebraska, see Etta."

"Huh!" he grunted. "I ain't surprised. "But I thought you told me there was some local joker up there looking to horn in?"

"Who knows?" I said. "Maybe she's married by now. Thought I'd just go and see what's up."

"You thinking of coming back this way?"

"It could happen," I said. "But with Ben dead, there's not much here for me."

"Friends," he said. "You got friends here. Me and Cleo and Jonas to name a few. Friends is an important thing to have."

Persimmon Bill came through the door stomping the snow off his boots.

"Well, he's gone to perdition," Bill said. "Long Bill is probably dancing with the devil in hell right now. Good hanging, you boys should've been there."

"Do you want some coffee?" Little Dick asked.

"Could you lace it with a little sour mash?"

Dick spilled some whiskey into Bill's coffee and pushed it across the counter to him. Persimmon Bill tasted it, smacked his lips and said, "At's good. Where's Cleo?"

"Buying a dress."

Bill's face screwed itself up.

"At's too bad, I like lookin' at her when I come in."

"Don't look too hard," Little Dick said. "Say, you ever waiter before?"

I shook hands with Little Dick and Bill and went to the room I kept at Kung Chow's. I was gathering my things for the trip to Nebraska when Kung came in.

"You leave, Mistah Quint?"

"This time, maybe for good, Kung."

"Oh that's too bad. I sorry to see you go. You funny man, I gonna miss you. Maybe I keep your room for you case you come back."

I shook hands with Kung, he was a warm friendly man with a gentle spirit and the right outlook on life; such men were rare. I'd miss his company.

I walked down to the livery. Slaughter, the liveryman was repairing a bridle.

"Come for that off-color horse, did you?" he said.

"Came to see if you were interested in buying her," I said.

"Hmmm. How much you want?"

"Eighty dollars," I said, "and I'll throw in my Dunn Brothers saddle."

"Eighty's a lot," he said.

"Take it or leave it."

"Done," he said, and pulled a roll of scrip out of his pocket.

"I'd rather it was in gold," I said. "Double eagles."

"I'll have to go up to the bank if you want double eagles."

"I'll wait. My train doesn't leave for an hour."

He left, I went to the stall where the bird had a mouthful of hay.

"This is where we part company," I said. Her ears pricked up and her big dark eyes came round to look at me.

"You sure turned out to be a hell of a horse." She tossed her head as though she half understood what I was saying. I spoke a little Spanish to her and reached in my pocket for some lumps of sugar I'd taken from the cafe. I held them in the palm of my hand while she sniffed them for a second, then the soft muzzle dipped down and lapped them up.

"I guess you've given up trying to bite the hand that feeds you," I said. "It's a lesson a lot of us hardcases should learn to appreciate."

I took a brush and a curry comb and worked it over her hide. Slaughter came back with the gold coins in his hand.

"Here's your double eagles," he said. "Eighty dollars, four double eagles, just like you wanted."

"I've changed my mind," I said.

"What? You trying to hold me up for more money?"

"No. I've decided not to sell."

He looked sorely disappointed.

"The saddle neither?"

"No, I'll need the saddle if I keep the horse."

"Well, I guess it's your horse and saddle to do with what you want," he said.

"Sorry for the inconvenience," I said.

We shook hands and I threw a lead rope over the bird and hefted the Dunn Brothers in my free hand and walked down to the train station.

"You don't know how bad I could have used that eighty dollars," I said to the bird. She walked along behind me like she was worth a thousand.

I told the station master to put her in a box car along with the saddle. He said it'd cost me an extra twenty dollars to ship her. I told him to go ahead, and walked back up to the cafe. I didn't want to, but I was broke and had to ask Little Dick for a loan, even if it meant I had to swallow my pride.

I was halfway there when Jonas Fly came running up the street calling after me. He had a piece of yellow paper in his hand.

"Mr. McCannon. I've a wire just came for you," he said, nearly out of breath.

He handed me the telegram.

"Pretty nice, huh?" Jonas grinned.

"Damn right it's pretty nice."

"Heck, you earned, I'd say."

The telegram was from Montana Territory. It said simply: "Justice has been done, my boy can rest in peace now. Have sent the ten-thousand-dollar reward money to the bank in Cheyenne to be deposited in your name. Thank you for letting me know that Aaron's murderer has been captured and will be hanged. Respectfully, Ethan Jensen."

Hell, Nebraska was looking better by the minute.